MEMENTO MORI

Medicus
Terra Incognita
Persona Non Grata
Caveat Emptor
Semper Fidelis
Tabula Rasa
Vita Brevis

MEMENTO MORI

A Crime Novel of the Roman Empire

RUTH DOWNIE

BLOOMSBURY PUBLISHING

NEW YORK · LONDON · OXFORD · NEW DELHI · SYDNEY

BLOOMSBURY PUBLISHING
Bloomsbury Publishing Inc.
1385 Broadway, New York, NY 10018, USA

BLOOMSBURY, BLOOMSBURY PUBLISHING, and the Diana logo are
trademarks of Bloomsbury Publishing Plc

First published in the United States 2018

Bloomsbury Publishing Plc does not have any control over, or responsibility for,
any third-party websites referred to or in this book. All Internet addresses given
in this book were correct at the time of going to press. The author and publisher
regret any inconvenience caused if addresses have changed or sites have ceased to
exist, but can accept no responsibility for any such changes.

ISBN: HB: 978-1-62040-961-9
           eBook: 978-1-62040-962-6

LIBRARY OF CONGRESS CATALOGING-IN-PUBLICATION DATA
Names: Downie, Ruth, 1955- author.
Title: Memento mori: a crime novel of the Roman empire / Ruth Downie.
Description: New York: Bloomsbury, 2018.
Identifiers: LCCN 2017034339 | ISBN 9781620409619 (hardcover) |
ISBN 9781620409626 (ebook)
Subjects: LCSH: Romans—Great Britain—Fiction. | Murder—Investigation—
Fiction. | Great Britain—History—Roman period,
55 B.C.-449 A.D.—Fiction. | GSAFD: Historical fiction. | Mystery fiction.
Classification: LCC PR6104.O94 M46 2018 | DDC 823/.92—dc23 LC record
available at https://lccn.loc.gov/2017034339

2 4 6 8 10 9 7 5 3 1

Typeset by Westchester Publishing Services
Printed and bound in the U.S.A. by Berryville Graphics Inc., Berryville, Virginia

To find out more about our authors and books visit www.bloomsbury.com and
sign up for our newsletters.

Bloomsbury books may be purchased for business or promotional use.
For information on bulk purchases please contact Macmillan Corporate and
Premium Sales Department at specialmarkets@macmillan.com.

For Lynda Hammond, Jean Reid, and Jennie Bewick.
One day we'll find a walk where all the hills go downward.

Britannia hodieque eam adtonita celebrat tantis caerimoniis
ut dedisse Persis videri possit.

*Britain today performs the rites [of magic] in such an awestruck manner
and with such grand ceremonies that you would think it was they who had
given it to the Persians.*

Pliny the Elder, Natural History

Tot aquarum tam multis necessariis molibus pyramidas videlicet otiosas
compares aut cetera inertia sed fama celebrata opera Graecorum.

*With such an array of vital structures carrying so many waters, compare, if you
will, the idle Pyramids, or the useless—though famous—works of the Greeks!*

Frontinus, On the Aqueducts of Rome

MEMENTO MORI

A NOVEL

IN WHICH our hero, Gaius Petreius Ruso, will be . . .

Accompanied by
> Tilla, his wife
> Mara, their adopted daughter
> Narina/Neena, a British slave bought in Rome
> Esico, another British slave bought in Rome

Informed by
> Conn, Tilla's half brother
> Albanus, his former clerk
> Virana, now wife of Albanus and the birth mother of Mara
> Catus, chief engineer at the baths

Exasperated by
> Valens, an old friend and former colleague
> Justus, a slave with an undesirable job

Saddened by
> Serena, Valens's wife (deceased)

Attacked by
> Pertinax, Serena's father and brother of Catus. A retired chief
> centurion
> An unknown assailant

Surprised by
    Gleva, a woman with designs on Pertinax

Confused by
    Twin boys, the sons of Valens and Serena
    Brecc, brother of Gleva, otherwise known as *that bloody native*

Puzzled by
    Terentius, Catus's young assistant and lover of Serena

Warned by
    Memor, a haruspex, interpreter of the will of the gods
    Dorios, a worried chief priest

Impressed by
    An old soldier and his elderly slave woman

Assisted by
    Latinus, a bathhouse manager
    Gnaeus, a retired dispatch rider
    Kunaris, a landlord with aspirations

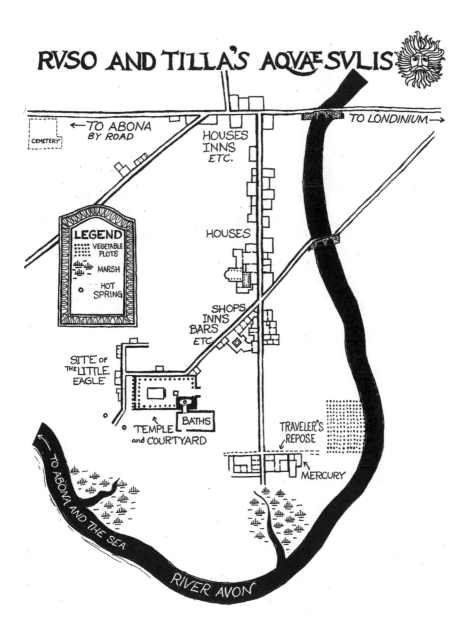

RVSO AND TILLA'S AQVÆ SVLIS

← TO ABONA BY ROAD

CEMETERY

TO LONDINIUM →

HOUSES INNS ETC.

HOUSES

LEGEND

VEGETABLE PLOTS

MARSH

HOT SPRING

SHOPS INNS BARS ETC

SITE OF THE LITTLE EAGLE

BATHS

TEMPLE and COURTYARD

TRAVELER'S REPOSE

MERCURY

TO ABONA AND THE SEA

RIVER AVON

MEMENTO MORI

1

IT WAS BARELY light when the man leaned his elbows on the stone window ledge, stared out at the steam drifting above Sulis Minerva's miraculous hot waters, and wondered how best to frame last night's disaster.

The roar and the heat of the blaze had been frightening. Worse were the screams that still echoed in his memory, cutting across the frantic shouts of the rescuers who were slapping at the flames with useless beaters and flinging buckets of water that had no effect at all.

The fire had been terrible, but that was not the reason Latinus was here to consult the goddess in the chill before the sun awoke. The problem was that two of the three people who had perished in it were visitors.

Of course, the deaths were nothing to do with his baths. Nor with the sacred spring in front of him, nor the temple beyond it. But as the news spread, no one would remember the hundred paces that separated the smoking ruins of the lodging house from his own safe and comfortable bathing establishment. No one would care that the visitors who had died, soldiers on leave, had been carousing all evening and were said to be so drunk that even if they had heard the shouts of warning they would not have understood them. No: The only word that would get around was that Aquae Sulis, the greatest healing shrine in Britannia, was a dangerous place. The gods were angry. The sick—who tended to be nervous types anyway—would think twice about coming here. They would take their ailments and their devotion and their money to other shrines: sacred places where the water might be drearily cold but at least the guests wouldn't be burned in their beds.

"What should I do, holy mistress?" he asked the steam, very quietly, because the sound of a stifled cough out in the temple courtyard told him Catus hadn't been able to sleep, either.

The goddess did not reply.

Raising his voice, Latinus called out "Hello?" It was something he had taken to doing ever since he had so startled one of Sulis Minerva's priests that the man tripped on his robe, stumbled over the railings, and nearly baptized himself in her waters.

The tall figure of the chief engineer strode into view.

"Morning."

Catus grunted, which was only to be expected from a man with no manners. Still, having started a conversation, Latinus felt he was owed a reply. "Did you find your niece?"

"Not yet."

Since Catus's niece was currently having a fling with a man who wasn't her husband, it was unlikely she wanted to be found, especially by her male relatives. Still, they had persisted in searching for her last night long after the fire was under control.

Having expressed his polite and insincere concern, Latinus moved on to the subject any normal person would be eager to discuss. "Terrible business last night."

But all he got was "Uh" and then "If you see the lad, tell him I've started the rounds."

"I will." Although since the lad was the one who had likely spent the night cavorting with Catus's niece in some secret love nest, the chances of him turning up at this hour were slim.

Latinus heard the jingle of keys and then the service door slammed: Catus presumably heading into the bath suite to check the furnace and then around to admire the smooth flow of the eternal spring waters as they ran into the Great Bath, around the system, and then out and away down the drains. With luck, he would be long gone by the time the visitors flocked in to bathe. The last thing anyone needed today was to be greeted by a bad-tempered water engineer.

Latinus gazed into the gently rising steam. Behind him he could hear the sound of scrubbing and the scrape of cold ash being raked out of the furnace, and Catus's voice issuing orders to the slaves. As if Catus owned the place. As if any of this would last for long without the visitors. And as if the visitors would be here without Latinus, the manager who made his living—and that of most other people around here—by bringing them in, keeping them happy, and keeping them spending. Latinus had once tried to point this out, but the chief engineer tartly reminded him that without someone to control the waters, the place would still be a weed-infested bog with a few hairy natives peering at each other through the mist.

Today, though, it would fall upon Latinus to protect Sulis Minerva—and, coincidentally, his own business—from the fears that would send her worshippers elsewhere. No doubt the council of magistrates, the priests, and all the various associations would meet and argue over how to mitigate the damage. Meanwhile, Latinus had to get on with it.

He would have to call his staff together before opening time. He would tell them—as if they might not know already—about the terrible events of last night and warn them that the visitors might be a little nervous today and in need of gentle handling. If asked about the fire, the staff were to stress the number of lives saved. The alertness of the terrier that had sounded the alarm. The demolition of the workshop next door to the stricken inn: a bold act that had created a firebreak. The quick thinking and bravery of the local residents, especially the Veterans' Association, who had been meeting nearby and had been determined to protect the town's honored guests at all costs. Perhaps—

He frowned, distracted by something on the surface of the water. The bubbling of the spring made many strange patterns, but he had never seen one like that. He leaned farther out into the poor light, craning his neck and trying to squint through the shifting vapor. Possibly some prankster with no respect had thrown something unsuitable into the pool. He would have to tell the priests. The temple slaves would fetch the net and fish it out.

For a moment he thought it might be a sudden rush of the black sand that the goddess sometimes sent up from the depths with her sacred water, but it was more tangible than that. Something was drifting about in there. It was as though the figure of the goddess herself were rising up from the depths! It was . . .

The steam shifted sideways, moved by an unseen current of air.

"Oh, holy Minerva!" he whispered. And, before he could stop himself: "This is a disaster!"

"What is?"

Catus must have finished with the furnace and was passing through the hall on his way to inspect the main bath.

Slowly, Latinus extended one finger toward the gently bubbling surface of the pool. He was aware of Catus clambering up beside him, leaning out to get a better look. The engineer gave a stifled cry and drew back from the window. Latinus heard the door crash against the wall and Catus reappeared outside. For a moment the engineer bent across the railings, staring into the pool. Then he stepped over the barrier and sat at the water's edge. Finally, ignoring the dangers, he took a deep breath, slid in, and began to swim.

Latinus made no effort to help, or to interfere. He was transfixed by the sight of the dead woman floating facedown in the steaming water.

Catus had found his niece.

2

"SOMEBODY ASKING FOR you at the gate."

Gaius Petreius Ruso, who had been butchering a slaughtered sheep with unnecessary precision, looked up to see his wild-haired brother-in-law standing over him. A large axe dangled from the brother-in-law's hand, the sharpened blade glinting in the afternoon sun.

Conn sniffed. "You here or not?"

The sniff was deliberately annoying. On the other hand, Conn's offer to protect him from unwanted visitors was a kind of favor. Doubtless leaving the new arrival waiting at the gate had the added advantage, from Conn's point of view, of making them feel uncomfortable. That was how Ruso deduced that the visitor must be a Roman. "Did he give a name?"

"He was at your wedding. The skinny one."

Ruso frowned. An alarmingly large number of people had turned up to help him and Tilla celebrate their marriage anew in the way of her tribe, and almost a year later it was hard to remember any of them. The only especially skinny Roman he could call to mind was now living three hundred miles away.

Conn said, "He's in a bit of a state."

Ruso cleaned the scalpel, placed it back in his medical case, and wiped his hands on his leather apron before flinging a cloth across the carcass and heading for the front gate.

"Albanus," offered Conn, when it was clear Ruso wasn't going to beg for the name.

Albanus? He quickened his pace. He could think of no reason why Albanus would turn up at a native farm on the northern border of civilization unless it was bad news. He glanced around the cobbled yard to reassure himself that his wife had not returned unexpectedly from market. What if his friend had come to ask for the baby back?

It was hard to determine exactly what Albanus had come to do, because he was indeed in a bit of a state. The thinning black hair was plastered to his skull with sweat, his tunic was filthy, and he was clinging to the giant oak tree by the gate as though he might collapse without it. Nevertheless he managed to inject some pleasure as well as relief into the cry of "Sir!"

Ruso pulled the gate open and Albanus mustered the energy to stand up straight and salute. Ruso flung off the apron, stepped forward, and clapped his exhausted and smelly friend in a warm embrace. For a moment Albanus held onto him like a man afraid of drowning, then let go and said, "I'm so terribly sorry, sir."

Only Albanus could turn up unexpectedly after so long and begin with an apology. Ruso said, "It's good to see you."

Albanus eyed the discarded apron and the bloodstained hands. "I do apologize, sir. Are you in the middle of operating?"

"Not exactly." Ruso reached for the traveling bag that was lying in the grass by the gate and led his former clerk to a bench in the sun beside the nearest of the round houses that squatted in the yard under their heavy cones of thatch.

Albanus, who seemed to be having some difficulty walking, lowered himself gingerly onto the bench and leaned back very slowly until he was resting against the wall.

"Something to drink?"

"In a moment, please, sir. I should tell you the news first. You may remember that earlier this year Doctor Valens offered me the post of tutor to his boys in Aquae Sulis."

"You wrote and told me. Has something gone wrong?"

"Sir, I'm sorry to have to tell you that Doctor Valens's wife"—Albanus's throat convulsed as he swallowed—"Doctor Valens's wife is dead, sir."

Ruso sat down faster than he'd intended. "Serena?" As if he were hoping his old colleague might have some other, unknown wife whose passing he need not mourn.

"I'm afraid so, sir."

"What was it?"

Albanus shook his head. "Doctor Valens is very distressed, sir."

"Of course he is. This is terrible news. How are the boys?"

"Very distressed also, sir. Although they're being shielded from the worst of the details." Albanus paused until one of Ruso's other relatives by marriage had crossed the yard carrying a bucket of milk and disappeared under the porch of the main house. "I'm afraid there was some unhappiness between Doctor Valens and Mistress Serena, sir."

"Well, we all knew that. But he was always fond of her in his own way."

Albanus's "Yes, sir" sounded more dutiful than heartfelt. "Unfortunately Centurion Pertinax is . . ." The long pause suggested that he had run out of words.

"I can imagine," Ruso said. There had always been a shortage of words to describe Serena's father.

"Centurion Pertinax is accusing Doctor Valens of murdering her."

"What?" Ruso stared at him. "That's ridiculous!"

"Quite, sir. But the centurion is talking of hiring a prosecutor. He plans to demand a trial when the governor comes to celebrate the Feast of Sulis Minerva in twelve days' time."

"How could he possibly think Valens would do a thing like that?"

Before Albanus could reply, the brother-in-law strolled into view, still clutching the axe, and inquired in British, "Everything all right?"

"I've had some bad news," Ruso told him in the same tongue. "I have to go to Aquae Sulis straightaway."

"Oh," said Conn. Then, with just the right balance of sarcasm and solicitude, he added, "There's a shame."

★ ★ ★

Refreshed by several cups of water—he had turned down an offer of the local beer—Albanus was now finding other things to apologize for, including disturbing Ruso's stay with the in-laws.

"Not at all," Ruso assured him. "You did the right thing in coming here." He glanced around to check that Tilla had still not returned and then added, "To be honest, it's a bit of a challenge living with the wife's family."

Albanus tucked his feet under the bench, away from the beak of an inquisitive chicken, and glanced around at the huddle of native houses. A goat wandered into the yard and stood on its hind legs to snatch a mouthful from the haystack.

"Get off!" Ruso strode across to chase it away. A barefoot boy appeared from behind the house, hauled the goat down, and waved cheerily to them both. Ruso returned to the bench. "Bloody thing. You wouldn't believe the amount of work that went into making that stack. Scything all that grass, turning it over and over to dry, lugging it in . . ." He stopped. "Sorry."

"It must be very different to what you're used to, sir."

"Hm. My former employers in the military want to know why I've gone native. The natives still can't understand why the military are building Hadrian's bloody great wall across their farm. Some of Tilla's relatives seem to think I'm personally responsible for it. And both sides think I must be a spy."

"It must be very difficult, sir."

From anyone else, that might have been a rebuke. From Albanus, it was genuine sympathy. Still, it was a reminder that his own problems were nothing compared to what was happening down in Aquae Sulis.

"Tell me what happened to Serena."

"Doctor Valens found that she'd been stabbed in the heart, sir."

Ruso imagined the horror of having to do a postmortem examination on one's own wife. He closed his eyes and tried to chase the thought away by picturing Serena in life: the broad shoulders inherited from her father; the shining dark hair swept back in a no-nonsense bun; the occasional baffled expression that betrayed the naïveté behind the stern exterior. *Stabbed in the heart*. What a cruel waste of a vibrant young woman.

"It was, ah . . . there were other complications, sir."

Albanus had had many days on the road to rehearse his account of the death, but it seemed he was still going to need prompting. "What sort of complications?"

"She was"—Albanus paused to cough—"she was found floating in Sulis Minerva's sacred spring, sir."

Ruso had never been to Aquae Sulis, but he could imagine the shock that the discovery of Serena's body must have caused. Not only a violation of life but a desecration of the most famous shrine in the province.

It was only when Albanus added "She seems to have been there for several hours, sir" that he remembered what he had heard about the temperature of the water. "Oh, dear gods."

"The business about the spring is confidential, sir."

"Of course." The priests would have taken hasty steps to purify the site and to keep the dreadful news quiet.

"And as if that wasn't bad enough, sir, on the same night two visitors and a local died in a fire and another man went missing."

"What?" It was enough to drive a man to a belief in the anger of the gods.

"The authorities are trying to deal with it all quietly so as not to spread further panic among the rest of the visitors, sir."

"Well," said Ruso, seizing on the only aspect of this chain of disasters that seemed at all susceptible to logic, "gods or no, Serena's death was obviously nothing to do with Valens. If a man wants to get rid of his wife, he divorces her."

"Centurion Pertinax is of the opinion that he didn't want to get rid of her, sir."

"Really?" It was not often that Ruso found himself sharing an opinion with Serena's father. "So why is he blaming Valens?"

Albanus cleared his throat. "My own wife is of the view that all those curses people have thrown into the sacred spring over the years have finally come to fruition, sir."

"I see," said Ruso, not adding that if a reasoned and sensible view were required, Albanus's wife was the last person in the empire whom he would consult. "Tell me."

"Well, sir, Aquae Sulis isn't just a healing shrine. People with grudges inscribe terrible curses on thin sheets of lead and fold them up and throw them—"

"I know what curses are. I meant tell me about the night."

"Sorry, sir."

Ruso listened while Albanus explained about the death of two off-duty legionaries and their landlord in a lodging house fire, assuming that sooner or later the reason for accusing Valens of stabbing Serena might become clear. "And when I left," Albanus continued, "the chief engineer was still trying to find his assistant. The young man vanished on the same night and hasn't been seen since."

"That looks very suspicious."

"Yes, sir."

"Did this assistant have any reason to harm Serena?"

"No, sir. Quite the opposite, in fact. She was, ah . . . they appeared to be very good friends."

" 'Very good friends'?"

"Very good friends indeed, sir, if you see what I mean. Doctor Valens was understandably upset about it when he found out."

"I see." At last, a motive for a husband to turn violent.

"He came all the way across from his new posting in Isca to see Mistress Serena and they had an argument. Mistress Serena left the house after sunset, and that was the last anyone saw of her alive. Or the young man."

Ruso sighed. If he had not known one of the married couple for even longer than they had known each other, he might have begun to think Pertinax had a point. "Perhaps," he said, "Serena went to tell this assistant engineer chap it was all over, and he attacked her in a fit of jealousy and then fled."

"Let's hope so, sir . . . I mean, of course we all wish such a terrible thing had never happened at all, but—"

"I know what you mean," Ruso assured him. "It'll be a further disaster if Valens is convicted of the murder. Especially for their boys." He got to his feet. "You didn't bring a vehicle or a horse, I suppose."

Albanus shifted position on the bench. "I never want to sit on a horse again, sir. Unreliable, uncooperative, and uncomfortable. I was very glad to hand the last one back at the staging post. After that, I walked."

It was oddly comforting to know that some things hadn't changed. "Sit here and rest while I go and pack," Ruso told him. "We'll sort out the transport later."

Instead of resting, Albanus adopted an expression of intense concentration. He reached his arms out, leaned forward, raised his backside into the air with his knees still bent, and slowly eased himself upright. "I'll come and help, sir."

Anything, Ruso supposed, was better than being abandoned in the middle of a native farmyard where goats, chickens, and wild-haired barbarians clutching axes might approach you at any moment, and one of them might address you in a tongue you didn't understand.

"Sir, I'm afraid I completely forgot to ask after your— Ah!"

Ruso followed his gaze and saw that a cart had drawn up under the oak tree in the lane. A slave leapt down to open the gate and gave the mule a friendly rub on the nose as Tilla took the reins. Tilla drove into the yard, spotted Albanus, and almost forgot to pull the mule up before it too helped itself to the haystack. That was when it dawned on Ruso that his announcement of an immediate and lone trip to Aquae Sulis was not going to be well received.

3

THE AVERAGE NATIVE house was nowhere near as ghastly as most Romans were led to expect, but in one respect Ruso felt British homes were deeply inferior to proper buildings: The living areas were separated from the bedrooms only by flimsy wicker screens and bright woven hangings. His own small family shared a house with another, and there was nowhere to be sure of holding a private conversation. If you wanted to keep something quiet, there were two choices: talk outdoors, or risk suffocation in the stench of the cow house.

Fortune was kind today, and the British sun god was still in one of his unreliable good moods. Ruso and his wife left the exhausted Albanus asleep on their bed and their daughter with the baby-minder, and began to pick their way through the rough grass to where the land behind the farmstead dropped down toward the stream.

Even then, escape was not easy. A couple of the innumerable grubby children, who were related to Tilla in some way, hurried over to ask where they were going. When Tilla said, "For a walk," the older one announced, "We'll come with you."

"Not this time."

"It's all right," insisted the smaller one, "we're allowed near the soldiers if there's grown-ups."

Tilla took Ruso by the arm. "My husband and I want some time on our own."

"Ha!" squealed the older girl, who must have been seven or eight. "We know what you're going to do!" They both giggled.

"Then you will leave us to do it in peace, or I will see to it that your mother beats you," said Tilla calmly. This set them both running back toward the houses, evidently delighted to have something to shriek about.

As they walked, Ruso could hear the musical *tink-tink* of hammer on chisel from farther up the valley. This time last year he had been a legionary medic and responsible for the health of those quarrymen. When disaster struck, it was his duty to scramble up the landslide and try to release Pertinax from beneath a tumbled boulder.

Tilla said, "You are very quiet."

One of the very few points of similarity between Tilla and Ruso's first wife was that *You are very quiet* was always a prelude to *What are you thinking?* "I'm thinking about Serena's father," he told her, preempting the question.

"I am sad for him."

"The day he was injured in the landslide."

"And you were late for supper, and I did not know where you were, and I was cross."

He could still picture Pertinax now, trapped halfway up an unstable heap of mud and broken rock. "He didn't expect to get out alive. He was asking for someone to get a knife up to him so he could go quickly rather than slowly."

"He is a brave man. Even if he is always very rude."

Ruso cleared his throat. "I had to find some way to keep him going while I got ready to amputate the leg," he said. "So I told him that if he didn't live, Serena and the boys would be dependent on Valens. And he said, 'The man's an idiot,' and I agreed with him."

"Are you wishing now you had not said it?"

"Not really. I don't think anything else would have worked. But it's sad when you can use your best friend as a threat."

Tilla sniffed. "Your best friend should have treated his wife better and he would not be in this mess now that we have to go and sort out for him."

He let the *we* pass.

"Why do we have to go? Does Valens not have important friends who can speak for him?"

"They've gone back to Rome. Hadrian put new men in charge when he came to visit."

They made their way on down the hill, past grazing sheep that barely bothered to look up. The sound of workmen in the quarry was louder now. Somewhere way above them all, a late skylark was trilling. Suddenly Tilla said, "Oh, dear."

"Mm?"

"Nothing," she said. "It is the way with bad news. You forget for a moment because it is too hard to believe. And then you think, *Why am I sad?* And then it jumps out and knocks you down again. Serena, of all people!"

He nodded. He had had a little longer to get used to the shock, and there came a point when you no longer wanted to say how terrible something was all the time. You just wanted to be numb and silent and get on with the things that needed doing. And the thing that needed doing was for him to pack and leave at first light tomorrow for Aquae Sulis, because his oldest and best friend was in trouble.

"I do not think any of what Albanus told you can be true," she said. "About Serena being in the next world, yes. That must be true or he would not be here. But the rest makes no sense. She would never leave Valens. Not as long as your law says the father keeps the children. Serena would never give up her boys."

Ruso had concluded long before now that Valens would never completely leave Serena, either, because he would lose any access to her father's substantial savings. But in the circumstances that was not a helpful observation, so instead he said, "Serena does have a history of rash decisions. She pursued Valens halfway across the province."

"One rash decision," Tilla corrected him.

"If he hadn't done the decent thing and married her, her reputation would have been ruined."

"For choosing the man she thought she loved?"

Sometimes he wondered whether the British mind was really as alien as his wife's conversation implied, or whether she only said these things to bait him. "You know it would."

She said, "Have you ever thought how odd that is?"

"No."

"A Roman man chases a woman and everyone thinks it is normal. Or even how clever he is. A woman chases a man for the same thing and you all pretend to be shocked."

"That's different."

"Is it not good for a woman to want a man?"

"Well, of course, but . . ." He was glad nobody else was listening. "It's good for a woman to want her husband."

"But before he is her husband, she is not supposed to want him?"

"You know what I mean."

"I know it makes no sense," she told him.

He left her to have the last word. Any further explanation on his part would only sink him deeper into the mire. Besides, he didn't want to be drawn into an irrelevant argument about men and women before he had to break the news that he needed to travel fast, and that meant without the encumbrance of a wife, a baby, and two slaves.

He was aware that she was speaking but he was not paying much attention until—"What did you just say?"

"I said, if Valens wanted to murder anybody—"

"He wouldn't," he said. "He never laid a hand on her."

"I said if. If he did want to, it would be Serena's father. Valens could make the death look like old age, or an illness, because he is a doctor. Then she would inherit all her father's money and he could help her spend it."

"Sometimes, wife, I worry about what goes on in your mind."

"But Pertinax is not the one who is dead," she continued. "So it was not Valens."

"Of course it wasn't. He wouldn't do a thing like that. Besides, he was fond of Serena." He wondered how many times he was going to have to repeat those words in Aquae Sulis. He would have to sound more convincing than he did now. Was Valens fond of Serena? On reflection, he couldn't ever remember him saying so. But then, had Ruso ever discussed his own feelings about Tilla with anyone else? Of course not. And most certainly not with Valens. What went on between a man and his wife was none of anyone else's business. "Pertinax will probably think better of the accusation when he's had a chance to calm down," he said. "The grief must be affecting his reason."

Tilla said, "Valens was fond of Serena as long as she was a long way away."

"He was fond of her in the way that you'd be fond of"—Ruso paused to scratch one ear with his forefinger—"a spirited but difficult horse."

"A *horse*?"

He skirted a clump of nettles growing out of a dip. "To be honest," he said, "once the initial attraction wore off, I think he was secretly terrified of her. He avoided her by being busy working."

"That is not a difficult thing for a doctor to do."

Ignoring the acidity of his wife's tone, he said, "And it didn't help when Pertinax chose to interfere."

"You cannot blame a father for trying to protect his daughter. Will you not do the same for Mara one day?"

He pushed aside the frightening prospect of their chubby, newly crawling daughter growing into a young woman who fancied herself in love with some unsuitable oaf.

"And before you tell me again that she should never have chased him, Valens should have known better than to flirt with a girl that age. She thought he meant what he said."

He did not reply. He was recalling a long-ago conversation with Valens in the chaotic bachelor quarters they had shared when Ruso first joined the Twentieth Legion. Much had faded from his memory, but not the moment when Valens had observed that Serena was the only child of a successful man who must surely have plenty of money.

"Poor Serena," Tilla said. "I think she could never understand what she had done wrong. So, when do we set out for Aquae Sulis?"

"I thought you might want to stay here with the family," he said, as innocently as he could manage. "We've only been back a few weeks and I know how you hate the constant moving about."

A shadow passed over her face. "I am glad to be home," she agreed. "But now when I say anything about where we have been, somebody says, 'Oh, in *Rome* . . .' as if I am trying to annoy them."

This was a revelation, but it had not come at a helpful moment. "I need to get there quickly, Tilla," he confessed. "I can't be delayed by—"

"I have thought of this," she told him. "And I talked to Albanus, and he says we can get a fast carriage to the coast and go by ship. And why did you not tell me he is to be a father?"

"Ship?" he repeated, desperately groping for a reason why this was not a sensible idea.

"It is the quickest way," she assured him. "And we can all travel together! Isn't that good?"

4

THE SAIL BILLOWED out, the ship creaked and tilted to starboard, and the blessed shelter of the riverbanks was sliding away again. As they headed out into the restless waters of the Sabrina estuary, the deck bucked and swayed beneath Ruso's feet. He thanked the gods that the journey was almost over. Tilla was right: The trip had been fast, but that was the only thing that could be said in favor of traveling by sea when you didn't have to.

He found a vacant patch of sunny deck and lay back with his eyes closed, pretending to be asleep. He was never a good sailor, but there was definitely something malevolent about the way this little ship wallowed and rolled.

He must order his thoughts, because these next few hours would be the last chance for him to piece together Albanus's version of events before he arrived in the middle of what was bound to be a deeply unhappy situation. Albanus had done his best to tell him all the details of the disaster—several times—but it was very difficult to care about anything anyone said to you when you were feeling seasick. Especially when you suffered the added embarrassment of finding that none of the remedies you recommended for your patients seemed to help. But now, after a few blessed hours of relief while the ship took them upriver to the fortress of Isca, he was feeling much better. He must pull his thoughts together before his stomach took over again.

As far as he had been able to grasp, the trouble had started when Valens turned up unexpectedly at the house that Serena shared with her father and uncle in Aquae Sulis. The men were out at some meeting for military veterans. The only other adults at home were the domestic staff and Albanus, who'd been in the children's room supervising writing practice when the sound of Valens and Serena quarreling carried down the corridor. It was impossible to make out most of the words but they must surely have been arguing about Serena's lover. He abandoned the alphabet and took the boys out to look for the heron that could sometimes be seen fishing by the river toward the end of the day.

That was the full extent of Albanus's direct knowledge, and it wasn't much help. Of course he had a version of what had happened afterward—doubtless everyone did—but it was based on no more than hearsay and speculation. When Serena left the house on her own just after sunset—something the staff had confirmed—she might indeed have been going to meet her lover, but it was too late to ask either of them now.

As far as Albanus knew, Pertinax had been unaware of the trouble at home because the veterans' meeting was interrupted by a cata-strophic fire at the Little Eagle inn almost next door. In the days that followed there were rumors that the fire had been started delib-erately, but at the time they were too busy fighting it to ask those sorts of questions. Their efforts had limited success. The landlord succumbed to the smoke, and all attempts to save two guests trapped in their room upstairs were beaten back by the savagery of the flames.

The old centurion and his brother Catus had arrived home weary and soot stained in the late hours of the night, only to find a worried housekeeper who explained that Serena had not yet returned. Nobody seemed to know for certain where she had gone.

Pertinax, his brother, and the houseboy (who had been a boy for many decades) had gone straight back out to look for her. Natu-rally, their fears had centered on the fire, although they could think

of no reason why she might have been near it. They also went to
the lodgings of Serena's "very good friend" Terentius, but she had
not been seen there and neither had he. When they found Valens
in the bathhouse helping the temple medics to tend the injured, he
denied all knowledge of his wife's whereabouts.

Serena had finally turned up at first light, when the bath manager
and her own uncle Catus had found her . . . "well, you know where,
sir."

Albanus was not one to repeat secrets where they might be overheard. Now here he was again, disturbing Ruso's meditations.
"Sir?"

Ruso lay deliberately still on the deck and tried to breathe
naturally.

"Sir?" There was a hand shaking his shoulder now.

"Go away."

"Yes, sir. In a moment, sir. But it really is best if you get up and
walk around."

"I'm not sick," he insisted, but the very mention of the word
brought on the first ominous stirrings.

"Only a couple of hours now, sir. That's it. Up you get!"

"You're a heartless bastard, Albanus."

"Breathe deeply and look at the horizon, sir."

"I've never felt as bad as this before."

"Yes, sir."

Ruso clutched the rail and groped for the question that had been
forming in his mind earlier. "Did anyone see Valens leave the
house?"

"I don't believe so, sir. Centurion Pertinax was extremely cross
about that."

Ruso would have felt more sympathy for Pertinax's staff had he
not been fighting the sensation that everything behind his ribs was
preparing to crawl up into his throat.

"Can I get you some water, sir?"

Ruso shook his head.

"Not far to go now, sir." Albanus leaned on the rail beside him
and pointed. "Look, you can make out the coast over there."

Ruso squinted at the blur on the horizon and wondered vaguely
if it was too far to swim. Except he didn't much feel like swimming,

either. From somewhere farther along the deck his wife's voice called, "Is he sick already?"

"This is the worst bloody ship I've ever sailed on."

"It must be very difficult, sir," Albanus agreed.

"You're humoring me, Albanus."

"Yes, sir."

5

WHEN THE SHIP finally docked at Abona, Ruso staggered away to make the obligatory, if scarcely deserved, offering of thanks to Neptune. Then he found a quiet street and forced himself to walk up and down it, taking deep breaths until he regained the will to live. Meanwhile one of the household slaves managed to wander away and get lost, and they were still looking for him when the afternoon boat upriver set off without them. It was not a good start, but at least it gave Ruso an excuse to travel the rest of the way on dry land. He left Tilla and Albanus to find the lad and bring the luggage tomorrow while he went to bargain for the hire of a decent horse.

Twenty miles later, the nausea was a distant nightmare.

Ruso had never had reason to visit Aquae Sulis before, but now— seeing the setting sun bathing the surrounding hills in light, glinting on the ripples of the river, and gilding the pale stone of a temple that soared above the surrounding buildings—he felt like a hero from one of the old stories: a man finally reaching home after years of troubled wandering. He slackened his grip on the reins and let the sweating horse relax at last. It hung its head as it ambled the last few hundred paces down the long hill into town.

The stable was just past the first crossroads, exactly as Albanus had told him. He had to wait in line to hand the beast in. There seemed to be plenty of people arriving in town this evening and he was glad he wouldn't have to seek a bed from strangers. But when he reached the Traveler's Repose and asked for Doctor Valens, he was dismayed to find that this part of Albanus's information was out of date: Doctor Valens had left several days ago and said nothing of where he was going. Just as in all the best stories, Ruso's arrival at his destination meant that a new set of trials was about to begin.

Despite its name, the Traveler's Repose was not especially restful. It was in what was plainly a tourist area that had been built as close to the temple complex as decency permitted, and both the dining area at street level and the snack bar across the road were crowded with customers. As he entered, several men hunched around the nearest table glanced up, decided he was nothing to worry about, and carried on with their illegal gambling.

The gray-bearded landlord, who introduced himself as Kunaris, ushered him up the stairs and assured him in fluent Latin with a native accent that he was being shown the best room in the house. That was the good news. The bad news was apparent from the amount of unidentified luggage strewn about: Several other travelers were also planning to repose in the same bed.

"I'll take it," he said, wishing he had brought the fleabane that was back in the medicines box with Tilla. Still, the day was fading and there was scant chance of finding anything better in the dark. He would sleep on the floor in his cloak and find something more suitable tomorrow before the family arrived. With luck, he would find Valens too.

The landlord was saying something about them having a fine dry evening for the parade.

"Parade?" Seeing the man's surprise at his ignorance, Ruso added, "I've been living up on the border."

There was a definite hint of sympathy in "Ah, I see," and Ruso was glad that Tilla was not there to take offense at this insult from a Southern tribesman.

The landlord assured him he had picked the best possible time to visit. "The usual parade tonight and then we've got the governor coming for the Feast of Sulis Minerva in three days."

This cheerful announcement had the unintended effect of reminding Ruso that the potential date of Valens's murder trial was growing ever closer.

As if sensing some reluctance, the landlord said, "You're all right to leave your bag, sir: We keep the door locked."

Ruso pushed aside the question of how that would stop the guests stealing from each other. He would achieve nothing by staying in the room. Nor did he want to sit alone in the bar. He ordered some water for a hasty wash, put on his other tunic, ran his fingers through his hair, and went out into the cool of the September evening to see what all the fuss was about.

The streets were surprisingly busy, with people waiting for the parade already lining the sides of the road and others flocking toward the blare of horns and trumpets. Shops and stalls were still open. The soft lamplight that displayed astrologers and scribes and jewelers and a late-opening shoe mender was attracting customers and moths. The smell of roasting meat reminded him that he had not eaten properly for days. As he drew closer he could hear the wailing of pipes above the tinny irritation of a metal rattle. Spurning a cheery offer from a brothel keeper, he joined the crush under the archway and emerged into the temple courtyard, where there was torchlight and louder music.

To a man who had recently walked the streets of Rome itself, the temple looming above them was nothing remarkable. The painted stone Gorgon staring wide-eyed from a triangular pediment that rested on a mere four columns looked more worried than terrifying. But by the standards of Britannia, this was a grand affair. There was certainly nothing like it where Tilla came from, which was what allowed the gray-bearded landlord his sense of superiority. The chattering crowd spilling into the courtyard around him seemed excited, as if they knew they were part of something special.

He moved forward through the flow of people. Small children were being carried on their fathers' shoulders while bigger ones raced about, ignoring warnings from their parents about getting lost and not climbing on the altars. Prostitutes and peddlers were strolling amongst the crowds in search of customers, the former offering glimpses of flesh and surreptitious caresses, the latter with trays bearing strings of glass beads and fancy hairpins and little pottery altars and models of creatures meant to represent gods.

Food stalls had been set up under the torchlit colonnade, and there were queues. He avoided the shellfish: The memory of sharing lodgings with Valens after he had eaten a bad oyster was still vivid. Instead he joined one of the longer lines on the assumption that there would be something worth waiting for at the end of it, and the satisfied customers pushing past him brought a smell of fried chicken that made his mouth water. Stuck in the line, he nodded politely to the trio of girls immediately in front of him. They ignored him in favor of a couple of youths who were lolling against the wall of the colonnade. The girls could hardly have given Ruso a clearer message if they had spoken it aloud: *You are an old man.*

As the queue inched forward, the girls huddled together, whispering and giggling and glancing over their shoulders. One of the youths shouted something. The tallest girl tossed her head and shouted back before linking arms with her friends to drag them away. Instantly the youths detached themselves from the wall and swaggered across the pavement in pursuit. The girls, turning to make sure they were following, shouted at them to clear off.

Ruso wondered if the girls' parents knew where they were. Did they not know a young woman had been murdered here less than a month ago? If this was how things were in Aquae Sulis, had the lax attitudes gone to Serena's head? It was a sharp reminder that no matter how Roman that temple might look, this was Britannia. The rules here were different, as his wife was often at pains to point out.

They weren't going to be different for Mara, though, whatever Tilla might think. Mara was going to be the best-protected young woman in the province. He would see to it.

A man with a military haircut wandered past, poking at something steaming in his hand and grumbling loudly that it was still pink in the middle.

"Where did you get it?"

The man gestured over his shoulder to the front of the queue.

"You should complain."

"I am, mate. Didn't you hear?" The man carried on past. Ruso was not the only one who stepped out of the line and moved on.

It struck him that if this gathering were taking place up on the border it would be a security nightmare. Even here, where everyone seemed to be good-natured, there were a lot of older men with a military bearing, and he wondered if they were all genuine veterans or if some were serving soldiers in plain clothes. Most of the temple slaves in their red-bordered tunics also looked as if they were built for war rather than for worship. Yet so far, both Roman and native appeared to be enjoying themselves.

Serena's killer could be walking amongst them at this moment, but her murder, the disappearance of her lover, and the deaths in the fire less than a month before did not seem to have dampened the visitors' spirits. Aquae Sulis knew how to throw a party—and therein lay a problem. Many of the people here must have come in search of holidays or healing. They wouldn't know each other. Any useful gossip would be restricted to the locals. Worse, any visitors who had been in town on the night of the murder could well have gone home, taking vital information with them.

There was a shriek and then cheers as flaming torches arced upward from somewhere over near the altar. Others rose and fell in swift succession. Just as the crowd had grown used to the juggling, one of the performers scrambled onto another's shoulders. The cheers turned to gasps as he lowered one of the lit torches toward his upturned face and finally right into his mouth. When he lifted it out, the light had died—but then he blew on it and the flame sprang back into life. While the crowd shouted its approval, more than one mother nearby warned her young not to even think about trying that when they got home.

The entertainment was cut short by a pay-attention! blast on the trumpets. Men were shouting, "Stand back! Clear the way to the steps!" The burly temple slaves formed a cordon to hold the crowd back. All around Ruso there was pushing and shoving as people tried to shuffle out of the way while still getting a good view. Finally a corridor was opened up between the archway and the temple. Ruso could just about make out a high stone altar in the middle of the cleared space, and a couple of priests tending a fire basket beside it.

The trumpets fell silent. A sound of chanting rose from somewhere outside the courtyard and grew louder. Ruso, now as desperate to eat as he had been desperate not to on board ship, hoped this wasn't going to take too long.

A short, wide priest appeared through the archway. He limped up and down in front of the crowd, using one hand to clutch a

combination of toga and walking stick, and the other to banish evil
by shaking a metal rattle.

The chatter died away, but then came a disturbance that proved
the security wasn't as tight as it would have been farther north.
While the crowd waited for the priests' assistants—why could
civilian processions never all move at the same speed?—a tall woman
in swirling green robes wandered in through the archway. She was
swaying on her feet in some kind of dance and seemed to be talking
to herself. Her wild red hair was bare to the evening sky and as she
saw the crowd watching she raised both braceleted arms skyward
and howled like a wolf.

The security staff were holding back, evidently unsure of themselves and waiting for an order.

Ruso was wondering how soon somebody would take charge,
when the man in front of him shifted and he caught a glimpse of a
gleaming gold torc around the woman's neck. That was when it
struck him that the meandering, muttering creature might not be
a drunk who had infiltrated the parade but was actually a part of it.

The unfortunate sacrifice, a white goat, was led in next. It was
followed by an angular brown man wearing a white hat with a point
on the top that was shaped—perhaps unintentionally—like a hopeful
penis. Ruso was still digesting this as a group of choristers appeared,
performing a hymn whose only distinguishable words were, predictably, "Sulis Minerva." They were followed by men carrying bright
banners and accompanied by a chorus of coughing as the incense
wafted into the crowd.

After another pause a collection of togas and native cloaks
marched in and joined the rest of the procession as it wound its way
around the courtyard. "Here she comes!" announced a voice somewhere near Ruso, and indeed a golden statue of a larger-than-life-
sized woman now lurched out from under the archway with only
inches between the top of her helmet and the stonework. The statue
edged forward on the shoulders of more men in white robes.

"Hail, Sulis Minerva!" cried the rotund priest and the red-haired
woman in unison, raising their hands toward the statue.

"Hail, Sulis Minerva!" yelled the crowd, surging forward. The
temple slaves, clearly well used to this, had linked arms to hold them
back lest the flower-festooned goddess be knocked off her bier and

crush her worshippers. Ruso braced himself and resisted the pressure behind him.

"Ow!" squealed a young woman somewhere close by. "It's no good pushing, I can't move. There's all these people in the way."

Ruso twisted around as far as he could manage. "Virana!" He plunged backward into the crush, causing more complaint.

In the poor light he heard a delighted cry of "Doctor!"

A hand grabbed his own and pulled. Finally they escaped from the press and into a shadowy space beneath the colonnade. Warm arms were flung around his neck, a pregnant belly was pressed up against him, and his nostrils were filled with a smell of rosewater and something more earthy. He was dimly aware of the crowd falling silent and of someone making a speech too far away to be clearly heard.

"I knew you would come!" Virana told him. "Isn't it sad about Mistress Serena?"

Someone nearby hissed, "Sh!"

Virana gave a "Hmph!" of disgust and dropped her voice to a stage whisper in Ruso's ear. "They found her just near where you were standing, on the temple steps. She must have been trying to get to the goddess for help, don't you think?"

Ruso opened his mouth to answer, but she had not finished.

"And now poor Doctor Valens is in trouble! I don't care what they—"

A third figure joined them, leaning in very close with a smell of stale sweat and a whisper of "If you two don't shut up, they'll hear you at the front. And then they'll want to start all over again."

Ruso murmured an apology, but Virana was unrepentant. Dragging him to the back of the colonnade, she pressed him against the wall next to the statue of some military hero and mouthed into his ear, "I don't care what they say about him, he did love her. You should have seen how upset he was when she wanted to divorce him! Is my husband with you? I told him, you must go and fetch Doctor Ruso and Tilla and they will sort it all out, and here you are!"

"It all sounds terrible," he whispered, attempting to disentangle himself. Virana was just as unsettlingly attractive as before, and just as pregnant as when he and Tilla had first met her. At least this time she knew who the father was. Or, rather, he hoped she did. "Albanus will be back tomorrow," he told her. Albanus had refused to get onto another horse until the memory and the bruises had faded. "He's bringing the others up from Abona by boat. I was hoping to meet Valens tonight, but I can't find him."

"You've missed him," she told him. "He's over in the fort at Isca. He came to the shop to say good-bye a few days ago. He had to go back to his hospital."

A timely blare of trumpets covered Ruso's expletive. While he had been enjoying the temporary relief of the ship's docking at Isca, it had never occurred to him to step ashore and ask if Valens had returned to work.

"You could send him a letter," Virana suggested.

Someone else was making a speech now. They were at the annoying distance where the sounds of the words could be heard but their meanings could not. He whispered, "Who's looking after his boys?"

Virana sniffed. "The boys are with Officer Pertinax. I said I would help because they know me but he said no. He said he is their grandfather and he will manage. But really Gleva is looking after them, because she wants to look good in front of him."

He frowned, trying to remember who Gleva was.

"Did my husband not tell you? She is the one who wants to marry Officer Pertinax."

"She must be a brave woman."

Out in the courtyard, the speech came to an end. There was the sort of pause that suggested something was going on—probably the sacrifice of the goat—but the rising mutterings amongst the crowd as the pause continued said that most people couldn't see what it was and were getting bored. Finally the choir burst into another chant and Virana said, "Am I allowed to ask about . . . ?"

Perhaps she did not know how to begin, either. He should have raised the subject before, but he had been wondering how to start the sentence. *The baby?* Your *baby? The baby you gave us?*

Mara. Albanus must surely have read her the letters giving news of her child.

"Mara's doing very well," he said. Better, in fact, than her adoptive mother. Tilla had spent much of the voyage worrying that Virana would take one look at her beautiful healthy daughter and demand to have her back. "You'll be able to see for yourself tomorrow."

"She is coming here?"

Was that just Virana's old habit of pushing her hair out of her eyes and repinning it, or was she—for once—lost for words? Finally she offered, "I am glad she is doing well," and patted her belly. "See? If the gods preserve me through the birth, I am keeping this one. Albanus is very proud of me."

He grinned. "He did mention it once or twice."

"Only once or twice?"

He had forgotten her tendency to believe everything she was told. "Once or twice every hour," he told her. "I am glad to see you so well."

Whatever she said next was drowned by a triumphant fanfare from the trumpets and wild cheering from the holiday crowd. When they could hear each other again, he found out that the words she had been shouting in his ear were exactly what a man in his situation wanted to hear. "Have you eaten?"

"Not yet."

She hooked one arm around his. "You can take me to the Traveler's Repose," she told him. "Their food is good and the wine is cheap. But on the way—" She broke off to squeeze his arm and huddle against him. "You must come with me. I have something very special to show you."

Ruso hoped his apprehension didn't show.

6

THAT LAST BURST of cheering seemed to have signaled the end of the parade. As Virana steered him across the courtyard the crowds were drifting away. Too late, he realized where she must be taking him. Moments later he found himself staring across a large oval pool surrounded by low railings.

"The sacred spring!" She flung out one bare arm to present the pool to him, proud of her surprise.

Ruso swallowed. Virana, of course, had no idea of the significance of what she was showing him. Albanus had managed to keep the details of Serena's fate secret even from his own wife.

Below them, steam rose gently in the light of the flickering torches. Out in the center of the pool, several paces away, the surface twitched as small bubbles rose from the depths.

"It comes up from inside the ground and it is already hot!" she announced. "See the steam?"

Other visitors were admiring the pool, chatting and pointing out the disturbance in the water, all under the watchful eye of a muscular slave in a temple tunic. There was a small splash as someone tossed in a coin, and circles of glinting ripples chased each other to the edges.

"Don't you like it?" Virana sounded disappointed. "I thought you would be interested. They say the water can cure all sorts of things."

"I don't know what to say." *Poor Serena, drifting all alone in that heat . . .* "It's . . . it's remarkable."

Virana said, "You should throw in a coin and make a prayer for Doctor Valens."

He handed her two coppers. "You do it."

Her childish delight reminded him that she must still be only, what, sixteen? Seventeen? She closed her eyes and murmured something before flinging first one coin and then the other high in the air, making as much splash as possible. He supposed there must have been very few times in Virana's life when she had had money to throw away.

The lighter mood vanished almost as quickly as his cash. Watching the ripples fade, she whispered, "People throw curses in there too."

"So I hear."

"People who live here used to say it was a joke, but they don't say that now. Not after Mistress Serena died and those poor soldiers were burned in their beds. And did you know her friend has disappeared?"

"I heard. Have you any idea where he went?"

Ruso felt warm breath against his ear. "They're telling people he's gone on a trip," she whispered, "and lots of people think he murdered Serena and ran away, but I think they are all wrong. I think something very bad has happened to him because he was a friend of Serena. And I think it was Gleva who made it happen."

"The woman who wants to marry Pertinax?"

"She is a woman who is used to having her own way. Everyone says that she thought Mistress Serena was trying to stop her from marrying Pertinax."

"And was she?"

"Oh, yes!" She moved away from him. "I think," she said, loudly enough to be overheard, "that down under that water there is a very bad curse with Mistress Serena's name on it. And I think it was put there by Gleva, and she is the reason all the bad things happened, and I do not care who hears me say it."

The chatter around the spring faded, and several people turned to stare at them.

Ruso reached out and took Virana by the arm. "I think we ought to go and eat now."

The gray-bearded landlord noticed Ruso across the crowded bar of the Traveler's Repose and came over to the table to bid him good evening and introduce his wife, a straggle-haired woman with a worried expression. Ruso put his spoon back into his beef-and-vegetable stew. He had already declined Virana's well-meant but impractical invitation for his entire household to share the one room she and Albanus rented over a shop that sold bathing supplies. "Can you suggest anywhere I could get a family room tomorrow? The rest of my people are arriving in the morning."

Kunaris suggested the Mercury inn, conveniently next door and so comfortable that the governor himself would be taking it over shortly for his stay. The wife, he explained as if to excuse the way she had just hurried off, was working herself to the bone getting everything ready. But for a couple of nights a family room might be found.

It might have been the unwatered wine she had poured herself, or perhaps the excitement at the thought of Mara's imminent arrival, that inspired Virana to offer more information. "My husband is bringing his wife here," she announced, "and I shall see my baby!"

"Very nice," murmured the landlord.

Meanwhile, Virana took another gulp of wine and decided that her explanation needed clarifying. "This man is not my husband," she said, indicating Ruso. "He is married to somebody else and so am I."

Ruso was aware of the two elderly women at the next table falling silent to listen. Even the gamblers in the corner seemed to have gone quiet. He could think of nothing to say that would make the truth sound any less scandalous, and Virana plowed on. "My husband is traveling with his wife, and she looks after my baby, and they are all coming here tomorrow."

"Very good." The landlord glanced at Ruso as if he was wondering whether this was how they all went on in the North. "I hope you all enjoy your stay."

Not half as much, Ruso supposed, as the rest of the bar would enjoy speculating about it.

7

WHEN THEY HAD eaten, Ruso escorted Virana home to the shuttered shop and waited outside, savoring the heady scents of the perfumed bathing oils inside until he heard the rattle of the lock being secured from within. Then he strode back through the dark streets to the Traveler's Repose.

When he arrived, the landlord bent down behind the bar and produced the bag that should have been safely stowed away in the room above. For a moment Ruso wondered if he was being evicted for dining with somebody else's wife, but the man proceeded to usher him toward the stairs. "I've moved you to another room, sir," he said. "Sorry about the mistake earlier. I didn't know who you were."

Ruso felt his spirits lift. Albanus had mentioned the Veterans' Association, and he had already guessed that this healing shrine must attract plenty of retired soldiers with old injuries to nurse. Maybe a legionary from the Twentieth had remembered him with gratitude.

The man pushed open the door. "Here we are, sir."

A stench of cheap wine, unwashed body, and stale urine wafted out from the darkness. Ruso stepped back. It seemed whoever had remembered him wasn't grateful. "I'm not sleeping in there!"

"I'll leave you a light, sir." The landlord used his own lamp to light one in a bracket on the wall, and as the flame swelled Ruso could just make out another guest's bag lying on the floorboards beside a cheap gray jug. The jumble of blankets beyond appeared to contain a body. The worst of the stench must be coming from the pot in the opposite corner. It was unlikely to clear, because the only window was high up on the opposite wall and about eight inches square.

He said, "I'll stay where I was."

"That room's full now, sir."

"You promised it to me!"

The only response was a fading series of creaks as the landlord descended the stairs.

Ruso crossed the corridor and rattled the door of the first room, which had blossomed into luxury in his memory. It was locked. Someone farther along shouted, "Keep the noise down!"

Alone in the hallway, he pondered the likelihood of finding better lodgings at this time of night, and dismissed it as hopeless. Besides, this was where Albanus had told him to go. Perhaps someone would bring a message from Valens.

He peered back into the new room. Whatever was in the pile of blankets seemed to be asleep already. There was plenty of space on the floorboards. It was only one night. He would lie near the door, and make sure his knife was within reach.

The moment he closed the door, the blankets shifted. A creature lurched to its feet and staggered toward him, crying out something unintelligible.

Ruso yelled at him and sprang back, pulling out the knife. He fumbled for the door latch with his free hand, but the creature wasn't approaching now. Instead, it was backing away with its hands held out to fend him off.

"Steady on, Ruso," it said. "It's me."

"Jupiter's bollocks!" He could still feel his heart thumping as he slid the knife back into the sheath. "Why didn't you say so? I could have killed you."

Valens—for the creature had Valens's voice, although it took a moment to recognize the haggard features in the lamplight—gave a wild giggle. "After you'd come all this way to see me? That would be ironic. Like something out of one of those miserable Greek plays."

"They told me you weren't here."

Valens leaned back against the wall and scratched at an itch on his scalp. "Good," he said. "I'm paying them a lot of money to say that. Sorry about pouncing on you. I've been going insane stuck in here on my own. I was afraid you might not come."

"You look terrible." And then, because the words had to be spoken even though they wouldn't help, he said, "I'm very sorry about Serena."

"Thanks."

In the silence that followed, Ruso heard a burst of laughter from the bar below. There were over-jolly shouts of "Good night!" and footsteps clumping up the stairs. Someone paused on the landing to fart before going into the room that had once been partially Ruso's. Finally, since Valens did not seem to want to talk about his wife, he tried, "How are the boys?"

"No bloody idea. I daren't go out. I assume Pertinax is still looking after them. If he finds me, I'm a dead man."

"I heard. He's not thinking straight."

"None of us is thinking straight. Somebody's murdered my wife."

Ruso began to unstrap his traveling bag. "How long have you been hiding in here in the dark?"

"Three days. I think. I've lost count. After the funeral I went back over the water to Isca, but it turns out Pertinax is an old friend of their legate. Wrote and told him I was a desperate criminal and ought to be locked up on sight."

"But you're their medic! Surely they know you well enough—"

"I only transferred down there a couple of months ago," Valens reminded him. "To be nearer the family, I might add, but nobody seems to remember that. Anyway, the legate and Pertinax go back decades. Luckily one of his clerks owed me a favor, so I managed to get away before they came for me. So technically I haven't disobeyed an order. I'm just absent without leave."

It was a fine distinction that Ruso doubted the legate would bother to acknowledge when it came to punishment. "And you came back to Aquae Sulis?" It did not make a great deal of sense.

"I'd already told Albanus I'd wait for you here. The landlord seemed like a sensible chap when I stayed here before—in a much better room, I might add. Besides, it's the last place they'll look for me."

"What if somebody talks?"

"They haven't so far. Most of the staff just think I'm a stray drunk." He looked around at the shabby room and rubbed his unshaven chin. "I think I may be turning into one. I started off doing exercises but now I can't be bothered. It's easier to sleep."

Ruso put his hand on his friend's shoulder and was alarmed at how the bones protruded. "When did you last eat?"

"I'm not hungry."

"You should—"

"I'm not a bloody patient, you don't have to—" Valens stopped. "Sorry."

"I'm trying to help."

"I know. You've come a long way, and I'm grateful to you. And to Albanus. I'm amazed he made it, to be honest. Is he here too?"

"He's following with the baggage train."

Valens looked puzzled. "What have you brought?"

"People. Tilla and Mara. With the housemaid and our other slave."

Valens's eyes widened. "The whole household?"

"Tilla wanted to pay her respects at Serena's graveside, and she thought Virana would like to see the baby."

The truth was that he was the one who had raised the subject of Mara, in the hope that this would dissuade his wife from traveling, but Tilla had replied that Mara liked traveling by sea. *Besides, I cannot go there and say to Virana, "I have left your precious baby miles away in the care of somebody else."* Once Mara was coming, they had to bring the baby-minder, and young Esico might as well come too, because why leave a slave behind as free farm labor for a family who constantly teased him about his funny southern accent? Assuming he'd been found by now, Esico would also be on his way upriver on tomorrow's tide.

"To be honest," he said, "I'm hoping the whole crowd will keep each other busy so you and I can get on with sorting this mess out." Holding his breath, he stepped across to pick up the pot. "If you're paying this discreet landlord good money, he should at least get this emptied. While I'm down there I'll find you something to eat. And I'll organize some clean water and a towel. You smell like a camel."

★   ★   ★

It was not until later, when they were wrapped in their cloaks like twin chrysalises, that Valens said into the darkness, "Who'd have thought we'd end up like this, eh? You, a family man dragging a vast retinue around with you, and me, alone in a stinky cell on the run from a murder charge."

"You won't be in here for long."

"No. I could go outside and be caught and have my head chopped off."

Ruso rolled over and adjusted the position of the traveling bag he was using as a pillow. His efforts left it just as uncomfortable as before, but in a new way. "You need to tell me exactly what happened."

"I know" was followed by a long silence. Then: "It seems ridiculous now, but it never occurred to me that we might not sort things out one day."

Ruso said nothing.

"You know how it is. Women have these ideas, and expectations, and . . . anyway, I assumed we'd just go on the way we were. Then, when her father was out of the way and I'd finished in the legions, we would just totter into old age together, watching our boys have boys of their own. She could enjoy telling me to get my feet off the table and I could develop an interest in—oh, I don't know. Learning to play the lyre. Collecting rare butterflies."

It seemed that despite his outrageous neglect of his wife while she was alive, Valens had still harbored dreams of the happy home he had done little to create. Ruso said, "Tomorrow I'll see what I can find out about the boys."

"I never wanted anyone else, you know." Then, perhaps sensing his friend's incredulity, Valens added, "Not seriously."

Ruso hoped his "Mm" did not sound too skeptical. This was not a time for recriminations.

"I never imagined—well, I suppose I should have guessed. Apparently he looks deceivingly pink-cheeked and innocent. And underneath, he was worming his way in, playing with my boys, trying to steal my wife while I was away serving the emperor."

"And Pertinax didn't notice?" There were times when Ruso's throat still constricted at the memory of Pertinax's hands around it after the centurion supposed—wrongly—that Ruso was trying to seduce the sixteen-year-old Serena.

"Pertinax? He thought the sun shone out of the sneaky little bastard's backside."

"So he didn't know what was going on?" Pertinax must be losing his edge in his retirement.

"Oh, he knew. Lover boy was a friend of the family."

Ruso tried to imagine Pertinax having any friends who were not heavy-fisted centurions, and failed.

"Pertinax's brother is the chief engineer here. Chap called Catus. Keeps the place running, makes sure the hot rooms stay hot and the water only goes where it's supposed to. Pertinax came to visit him and liked the place so much he decided to retire here. Then he persuaded Serena to come south and look after them both in their dotage. Apparently I can look after myself."

Since a man who worked in a legionary hospital had his accommodation provided, often slept on the job, and was in a position to raid the kitchens, Ruso felt Pertinax might have had a point.

"I was never keen on her coming here. You know what spa towns are like."

"Not really," Ruso admitted. "Only by reputation."

"Well, if it's anything like Baiae, things can get a bit wild. But then I thought, *Serena? Seriously?*"

Ruso could remember a time when Serena and Valens had been a bit wild too. "And then this other man—"

"Terentius," said Valens. "You don't have to avoid saying his name. Terentius is Catus's protégé. Assistant engineer. Deputy drain clearer. Golden boy in charge of the bath plug."

"And he vanished on the same night Serena died?"

"Exactly. That's why I had to get you here. I can't go after him with Pertinax on my tail. You have to find him for me."

"You think he's the one who—"

"Of course he is! Who else would it be?"

"I don't know," Ruso told him. "I don't know what's been going on here. That's why I need you to tell me exactly what happened."

8

B Y T H E T I M E Ruso woke, morning had already forced its way through the small window of Valens's room and was illuminating the scuff marks of long-departed furniture on the far wall. There was no sound from Valens. Hearing voices and the clatter of crockery downstairs, Ruso fetched some bread and cheese and much-watered wine for breakfast.

"So," said a voice from the floor on his return, "what's the plan?"

Ruso placed the tray far enough away to force his friend to get out of bed. The immediate priority was to arrange some accommodation for his own family, but it seemed tactless to say so. "Who can I talk to who'd know where this Terentius chap might have gone?"

"Not a clue," Valens admitted, eyeing the food and apparently deciding it wasn't worth the bother of moving. "I don't know much more about this town than you do. The one who knew him best would be Pertinax's brother, but I doubt you'll get much help there, especially since the brother's bound to realize who you are as soon as you start asking questions. What about young Virana? She's full of hot gossip."

Ruso shook his head. "She doesn't know where he is. She thinks it's all to do with curses anyway. Albanus hasn't told her anything. He says we need to be discreet."

"Hmph."

"It won't hurt to start with," Ruso pointed out. "There's no sense in upsetting people who might be able to help. Who knows the truth about where Serena was found?"

But Valens did not know that, either. "It was the brother who found her. Somebody must have helped him get her out of the water, but I couldn't tell you who. It was all done by the time Pertinax came to the Repose and woke me up to tell me what had happened."

Ruso tore off a chunk of bread. "I'll have to start with Pertinax, then."

"There must be some other way."

Ruso, who could not think of one, took refuge in the fact that the bread was very chewy.

"Don't tell him where I am."

"I haven't seen you," Ruso told him. "I've come hundreds of miles to find you and now I've no idea where you are."

"I've probably wandered off into some woods and done away with myself."

Ruso turned to him in alarm. "You aren't planning to, are you?"

"Of course not. Not now you've turned up. You're surprisingly good at this kind of thing. You'll help me sort this out, we'll see the bastard who killed Serena nailed up, I'll get my boys back, and you'll have the satisfaction of knowing I'm hugely in your debt."

"Right," said Ruso, not sure whether to be flattered or alarmed by his friend's confidence.

"Well, you don't want to have come all this way for nothing, do you?"

"No." He reached for a last swig of watered wine and got to his feet. "I'd better get on with it, then. What are you going to do?"

Valens shrugged. "Any suggestions?"

"You could do with a shave."

"No mirror. Are you offering to do it?"

"No." Ruso looked around the room. There wasn't even anything in here to tidy up.

"Read?" he suggested vaguely. "Write something? Take up—I don't know."

Valens leaned back with his hands behind his head. "There were a couple of wood-lice in the corner yesterday. If they come back, maybe I'll train them to race."

He left Valens staring at the stains of old leaks on the rafters and went to book a room at the inn next door. At least he knew how to do that.

The outside of the Mercury gleamed with fresh limewash and cheerful paintings of gods around the door. It was certainly of a higher class than the adjoining Repose and probably quieter too. Within a few paces, the paved street on which they both sat gave way to a narrow lane leading past a stable to a few vegetable plots. Beyond them, Ruso could see white drifts of morning mist still hanging over the river.

Inside, his boots clicked across the smart tiles of the bar area. Beyond the bar was a large private dining room, its walls painted with frescoes of elegant gardens. Perhaps this relative tranquillity was why Kunaris—who turned out to manage both this and the Traveler's Repose—could name the price while still keeping a straight face. When Ruso tried to haggle, the landlord assured him he was lucky to get two connecting rooms at short notice in the busiest week of the year, and so close to the temple—especially as they were getting ready for the governor's visit. But if sir wanted the name of somewhere farther out for travelers on a budget . . . ?

No, sir did not. From the Mercury, although sir did not say so, he could slip next door to visit Valens whenever he wanted. Besides, he was deliberately avoiding the main residential streets that clustered around the wharf. That was where Pertinax lived.

He told himself he was not putting off his visit out of cowardice; it simply made sense to wait until Albanus arrived. Albanus, as the children's tutor, had a valid reason to go to the house. That didn't make the prospect of meeting Pertinax any less alarming, but at least Ruso might get past the front door. Then, out of courtesy, he would have to warn Pertinax that he was going to be talking to people about Serena's death. He wasn't looking forward to that.

In fact, the more he had found out about this whole dreadful business, the less he was looking forward to getting involved, especially now that Terentius's trail had had three weeks to go cold. But he had to concede that Valens was right: If he didn't sort things out, who else would? And if he failed to find the real killer and Pertinax

somehow managed to secure a murder conviction, even if Valens
were to escape, his boys would be left without a father.

So he wasn't going to fail. But at the moment it wasn't at all clear
how he was going to succeed. He needed some time to think, away
from the pressure of his friend's presence. He made his way down
the lane from the Mercury, past the stable to where the paths that
meandered across the vegetable plots had baked dry in the recent
good weather. Ahead of him, the morning sun was chasing away the
last wisps of mist to reveal the river, lying low and distant between
broad banks of mud.

Even after, what? Six years in Britannia? Ruso still found it
extraordinary that rivers tens of miles from the sea should rise and
fall so dramatically twice a day, and in a manner that rarely bore
any relation to the rainfall higher up their courses. Sometimes, as
he had once assured his brother in the distant south of Gaul, you
could even see it happening in front of you as you stood and watched.
He suspected his brother had classed it as one of those travelers' tales.
The sort that claimed there were places in India where no shadows
fell, and tribes whose men lived to a hundred and thirty without
growing old. People liked to believe the outlandish. Like Virana's
idea that the killing of Serena had been brought about by a few
words scrawled on a lead sheet and thrown into water.

He supposed it was quite possible that Pertinax's would-be girlfriend had made some sort of offering to Sulis Minerva to smooth
the path of her courtship. But making an offering, or even forming
a curse, was a far cry from seizing a knife and plunging it into
another human being. Far more likely that the guilty party was, as
Valens had assumed, the vanished Terentius. The former golden boy
in charge of the bath plug.

As he drew closer to the river, the sound of rushing water was
accompanied by a whiff of latrines. He turned aside for a breath of
clean air before resting on the sand-colored stone and leaning over
to see water gushing from a drain and flowing out down the mud
bank to join the river. Holding out one hand above the outlet, he
was fairly certain he could detect warmth. So this was where Pertinax's brother Catus finally disposed of Sulis Minerva's watery
offering after it had washed through the bathhouse and cleansed
the latrines. And that was why nobody had built on this prime

riverside location, leaving the land and the smell for carrots and cabbages and an old woman who was stooped over to pick beans.

He strolled up to the wharf, but it was clear nobody was expecting any boats. The warehouses along the waterfront were shut and the only people around were a couple of old men mending ropes in the sunshine. He could see why: Although a heavy timber walkway had been built out from the riverbank, it barely reached the water, which was noticeably lower than it had been earlier. Below it a collection of small boats lay on their sides in the mud, waiting for the river to come back.

One of the old men told him that if his family were coming up on the next tide, they would not arrive until well past noon. At least, Ruso was fairly sure that was what he said. The combination of the British tongue, the local accent, and the absence of teeth made it hard to tell. Ruso's attempt to clarify how they knew about the tides also left him little wiser than before. He thanked them both and walked away, wondering whether the man really had said, "Neptune rises to greet the goddess of the moon," and if he had, whether it was a genuine attempt to help or a mocking reply to a foreigner asking a silly question.

Whatever the exact schedule of today's tide, it was obvious no decent-sized boat could tie up at the landing stage for some hours. There was no point in hanging around there. He would go back and take a proper look at the place where Serena had been found. This time without Virana spilling nonsense into his ear about curses.

9

THE COURTYARD LOOKED less awe-inspiring this morning than it had at night. A slave was standing on a box so he could reach to scrub the top of the carved stone altar. Beyond him, the swish of brooms was accompanied by the tinkle of broken crockery tumbling across stone. Last night's stalls had disappeared, leaving only bare tables and awning poles stacked away in a corner. Pigeons burbled and strutted about, pausing to stab at the last scraps of fallen food. At the top of the temple steps, more slaves were busy setting out a display of Sulis Minerva's treasures and relics on tables under the porch. Higher still, the painted relief of the Gorgon on the pediment looked more benevolently concerned and less worried than it had last night, which was perhaps appropriate for the deity of a healing shrine. If the patients who came here seeking healing were anything like the ones Ruso usually met, they were frightened enough without needing further discouragement from the artwork. Although since all the Gorgons in the old tales were women, it was a mystery why the sculptor had chosen to give this one a man's face with a sweeping British moustache.

Whatever its strangeness, this was the only face that had definitely looked down upon Serena on the night of her death. Maybe if Ruso tried hard enough he could convince himself that Sulis Minerva might be willing to help. He turned right, deliberately avoiding the pool of the sacred spring, and began to make his way around the courtyard.

A burly slave sweeping up nearby bent to retrieve an abandoned sandal from a scatter of faded petals, then walked over to the colonnade and propped it against one of the pillars.

Ruso said, "How can anybody lose just one sandal?"

The man stood with his large fists wrapped around the broom handle and his eyes respectfully lowered. Ruso had put him in an awkward position: If *How can anybody lose just one sandal?* was a genuine question, he would be rude to remain silent. If it was merely rhetorical, he would be rude to speak. Ruso said, "I suppose it was too late to look for it. Can you get in here at night?"

"The temple court is always open, sir."

"Perhaps you can help me," he said, stepping closer. "I was hoping to meet someone who works here while I'm in town, but he's gone away. An engineer called Terentius. You don't know where he lodges, do you?"

The slave shifted awkwardly. "You'd have to talk to the bathhouse manager, sir."

"I'll do that."

Ruso moved away to let the man get on with his duties. The excited barking of dogs drew his attention to the temple. Two men were making their way down the steps, one carrying garlands of flowers and the other accompanied by three small hounds on leads.

The slave with the flowers began to drape them around the freshly scrubbed altar. His companion was towed out under the archway by the sacred dogs. Ruso carried on with his circuit of the courtyard. There was a service entrance at the back, behind the temple, but the door was locked. Presumably it was locked at night too. The temple itself, high up on its podium, could only be entered through the massive doors at the front. So anyone lurking behind the temple at night—a lover, a murderer—would be well hidden.

He must find out how dark it had been on the night Serena died. He had already established that there had been no parade. As far as Valens was aware, the temple was being put to its normal use: to allow patients to sleep in the healing presence of Sulis Minerva and the sacred dogs. It seemed no one had noticed anything unusual until someone raised the alarm about the fire at the Little Eagle.

Had Serena come here voluntarily to meet Terentius? He was the golden boy in charge of the bath plug: This was his place of work. If he had a key to the bathhouse, the couple could have met there in privacy, enjoying the fading warmth of the under-floor heating. Or had Serena gone somewhere else entirely that night, for reasons that he was unable to guess, and been brought here against her will? What if Terentius hadn't been involved at all? What if his disappearance was just a remarkable coincidence?

Where the hell was he supposed to start?

10

THE GODDESS'S GIFT of gently bubbling hot water conferred no blessing on this visitor. Ruso stood above the pool and pictured Serena drifting there alone in the darkness, unaware of the curses and the coins lying in the depths below her. Unaware too of how her unwilling presence would be seen as a shocking desecration of a holy spring.

He tightened his grip on the railing and forced himself to think practically. Serena had inherited her father's solid build, and if she had been a dead weight, it would have taken a strong man—or someone with help—to move her far. So it was likely that she had been stabbed close by. Had there been bloodstains? He needed to ask someone, but not until he had found out who was already privy to the truth about where she was found. Until then, he was just another visitor.

He was leaning forward, wondering how easy it would be to topple over the low railings if you were struggling with an attacker—surely the most likely scenario—when a voice called, "Careful, sir!"

Ruso looked up to see a pink head with a fringe of lank hair above narrow shoulders, all framed in the central window of the bathhouse. The man's features were brightened by a smile that didn't quite reach his eyes, followed by "Good morning, sir. Can I help?"

Ruso straightened up. "Sorry. I was just wondering. What happens if you fall in?"

The smile faltered. "I'm afraid the holy spring isn't suitable for bathing, sir. But the baths will be open just after midday."

"So late?"

In what was evidently a practiced speech, the man explained that the bathhouse was reserved for ladies only in the mornings, in line with the emperor's ban on mixed bathing. "But we open to all on selected evenings for festivals and private parties. Perhaps you would like to visit the temple instead, sir? We have some fine works of art and treasures on display. Most of our visitors are very impressed with it."

Ruso thanked him for the advice, although he had no intention of following it. In other circumstances he would have been happy to visit the temple of a healing god, but he was here to inquire about a murder, not about miracles, and he certainly wasn't going to waste a morning gazing at statues.

Before he could retreat, another voice, so close that he was startled, said, "Let me show you around, sir." Then, addressing the pink head in the window, it said, "You carry on, Latinus. I'll make our guest welcome."

The head vanished. Noting the name of Latinus as someone he probably needed to speak to later, Ruso found himself standing beside a short, wide figure whose thinning curls matched the gray bags under his eyes. The face and the shape and the walking stick looked familiar, but it was a moment before his memory added the toga, the rattle, and the cries of *Hail, Sulis Minerva!*

"You're the priest."

The man, now wearing a smart cream linen tunic with three stripes over the shoulder, inclined his head. "Dorios. Honored to be the chief priest of Sulis Minerva. Also chief magistrate."

No wonder the man looked weary under the weight of all that responsibility.

"And you are?"

"Ruso."

"Ruso!" repeated the man, as if he had been looking forward to meeting him all week. "Welcome to Aquae Sulis!"

Ruso wondered why such an important official was bothering to offer a guided tour to a stranger, especially a stranger who had expressed no desire at all to see the temple. Was he intercepting any visitor who showed an unhealthy interest in falling into the spring? Or was he just a generous host, keen to welcome visitors and show them what Aquae Sulis had to offer?

Dorios steered him in the direction of the temple steps. The polite question about Ruso's journey led to a surprised "All the way from the border?" and progressed through the obligatory inquiry after the progress of the emperor's Great Wall to "And are you a soldier yourself?"

"Not these days." Too late, Ruso realized that he should have invented a cover story. He did not want to admit any connection with Serena straightaway. But a town full of sick people and their healers was not the place to admit to being a doctor, either, so he said, "I've been in Rome," and quickly changed the subject, leaving the man to imagine something far more mysterious and glamorous than the reality. "I've got a letter to deliver while I'm here. I need to find a chap called Terentius. I'm told he's an engineer at the bathhouse."

But sadly it seemed Terentius had moved away the previous month. The building project he was working on had run into difficulties and been abandoned, and Dorios did not know where he had gone.

"Is there anybody I could leave it with?"

The priest was full of regret that there was not, which was just as well, because Ruso hadn't written it yet. Indeed, only the other day the chief engineer had been lamenting the lack of a forwarding address. "We'll just have to wait until he makes contact. But you know what young men are like." The sagging features lifted into a conspiratorial smile. "I expect he's busy."

Since he was probably busy running away, it would be a long wait.

"I hope you haven't had a wasted trip."

"Not at all," Ruso assured him, adding with sudden inspiration that he was there on behalf of a friend with some money to invest.

"Ah, I see!"

Ruso hoped he did, because his own imagination was struggling to fill in the details of the wealthy friend. "But if you could keep it quiet . . ."

"Of course, sir."

With luck, the man wouldn't keep his promise and Ruso would become someone whom people wanted to meet.

"In fact, sir, you've just witnessed the need for a project that might interest your friend."

"Really?" Ruso noted that now he had a rich friend, he had become "sir" again.

"The emperor himself suggested an expansion of the temple area when he came to visit. And as part of it we'll be building a second bathhouse so everyone can have access all day." Dorios raised a stubby forefinger in the direction of the sacred spring. "At the far end of our present bath building."

"So that wasn't the project that was abandoned?"

"Oh, no, sir. That was something else."

"So what was that?"

Dorios shook his head sadly. "It was a wild venture, sir. An attempt to tame one of the other outlets of the goddess's waters. Frankly, it was ill-considered from the start and the omens were never good. Whereas the East Baths project has been carefully planned over several years, and our own haruspex has declared the omens to be very promising."

Ruso said, "I see," because he had no idea what a man who was keen to invest in expanding bathhouses might say.

Dorios seemed to take his cool response as an invitation to be more forthcoming. He raised one hand as if he were asking for a moment to think something over, then said "Yes" to some argument that had apparently been going on inside his head. "Yes, I think we could see a little of the bathhouse if you wish. I'm sure Latinus—he's our manager—won't mind." He gestured toward the door beside the spring. "Shall we?"

Ruso followed the priest through a side door and hoped the imaginary friend wasn't going to be more trouble than he was worth.

"We'll have a corridor through here for privacy," explained Dorios, indicating a space marked off by a row of movable wooden screens that meant all Ruso could see of the echoing changing hall was a pod of painted dolphins leaping across the ceiling. A sudden shriek drew his attention to the pale flesh of a young woman retreating through a gap farther along the screens. Evidently she had not expected to find two men standing there.

While Dorios explained the merits of the building alterations, Ruso gazed up at the dolphins and wondered whether Terentius and Serena had met beneath them on the night of the murder. He was now standing where the manager had been when he called out, *Careful, sir!* Behind him were the glassless windows that opened directly onto the pool where Serena's body had been found. He considered a new possibility. What if Serena had been attacked in here? Anyone wishing to heave a body out through the window would have had a struggle, but what if she had used the last of her strength to scramble over one of the sills herself? If Terentius could unlock the door after hours to let her in, he could lock it again to trap her. She could have tumbled into the water while trying to escape from him.

Meanwhile the priest was busy telling him about—what was it? The emperor's interest in architecture, the redecoration plan, the hope that Ruso would enjoy the facilities in the hot and cold rooms later in the day . . .

Aware that the man had stopped talking and was looking at him as if expecting a response, Ruso said, "Mm."

"Excellent!" The smile reappeared. "Because if he could get here in time, I'm sure we could arrange a space for him at the governor's dinner."

Another reminder, as if one were needed, that the wretched visit of the governor was drawing closer with every hour that passed. The imaginary friend, though, must be looking forward to it. He now had an invitation to the best dinner in town. "I'll let him know."

Ruso turned and rested his elbows on the sill of the central window, wondering if a woman who had been stabbed through the heart could possibly muster the strength to—

"It's a fine sight, sir, don't you think?"

The priest had joined him, gazing beyond the pool to where the morning sun was gilding the steps and columns of the temple. Ruso agreed.

"People talk about Londinium and Camulodunum," Dorios continued, "but those of us who have the pleasure of living here know that these are the most important buildings in the province."

Ruso raised his eyebrows and waited to find out what was so special about Aquae Sulis apart from the cheap hot water supply.

"You'll be aware of the trouble with the natives in the past, sir."

"I was up on the border for the last lot," Ruso told him, narrowly stopping himself from adding that he had treated many of the Roman casualties. While everyone called it "trouble," *disaster* would have been a better word.

"And you'll have heard the old tales of the mad queen's rising in the East."

Mad if you were a Roman. Heroic if you were Tilla. "Boudica."

"Exactly. We're very glad we still have military men like yourself to keep us safe, sir. But here at Aquae Sulis we like to think we're showing the natives a new way forward. Coming together in joint worship. Their Sulis, our Minerva. Their traditional shrine, our stunning architecture."

Their moustache, our plumbing. Victory by water engineering. Ruso tried to sound suitably impressed, then could not resist adding, "I saw you have a native priestess."

If the priest saw the unsettling resemblance between Boudica and the flaming red hair of the native priestess, he chose not to acknowledge it. "The natives have a, ah . . . a rather different understanding of priesthood from us, sir."

A rather different understanding of priesthood was a diplomatic understatement. While Boudica had been busy burning her nearest Roman city to the ground and massacring its residents, the Roman governor of the province had been on the far side of the island wiping out most of the Britons' religious leaders. Coming together in joint worship must require a deliberate act of amnesia.

"But," Dorios continued, "we are making progress. The shrine is increasingly popular with both groups. The extra bathing suite and the temple expansion are only the first steps. Ideally we would like accommodation for the patients separate from the temple, a better roof over the main pool, and perhaps a small building to protect the spring from the weather."

It seemed there were investment opportunities to match all purses. Ruso said "Ah" in what he hoped was a suitably enigmatic fashion. No doubt Dorios was looking forward to introducing the imaginary investor to his fellow magistrates. And no doubt all the grand plans for expansion would be knocked sideways if a whisper got around that the temple staff had been so slack as to allow the body of a woman who had been murdered—sadly, these things happened—to pollute Sulis Minerva's sacred spring. It was the sort of desecration that could bring about disaster, and so it had proved for Aquae Sulis: That very night, the goddess had sent a terrible fire and burned innocent men in their beds.

The fact that the one hadn't necessarily led to the other wouldn't matter. People didn't listen to logic when they were choosing their holiday destinations. Or their healing shrines.

Ruso ran one hand through his hair. "Listen, I know I'm probably asking the wrong person, but does the goddess really answer the patients' prayers?" He had never understood how remedies dreamed up while spending a night in the presence of the god, often accompanied by sacred dogs or snakes, could succeed where conventional treatment had failed. What was it Cicero had said about dreams? That dreams didn't teach reading and writing, so why would they teach medicine?

Dorios, however, had no such doubts. "Oh, yes. Absolutely. You must go into the temple and read the testimonies on the wall. Some of them are quite remarkable."

"I will," he promised, pushing aside a sudden and irrational stab of professional jealousy. He needed to hurry this tour along. He had urgent inquiries to make, and hanging around in the bathhouse was not going to answer them. "The baths are smaller than I thought."

"Ah, but there's more!" Dorios announced. "This way, sir." He led his guest along past the screens and hauled open a massive door.

This was more like the scene Ruso had been expecting. The two men stepped into the fug of a vast hall that enclosed one steaming bath the size of a sixty-foot swimming pool, with a smaller one beyond it. Green light filtered down into it from the high glass windows, and the delicate song of a pair of pipes hung in air that was thick with the scent of oil and hot bodies and the minerals of Sulis Minerva's water. Between the heavy columns that held up the roof beams, the steps around the bath were adorned with several pale figures and a couple of brown ones in various stages of submersion. Children were splashing about in the arms of their maids. Or their mothers. Without the distinction of clothes, it was hard to tell. A naked woman with her eyes closed was performing a leisurely backstroke from one end of the pool to the other.

"This is the place to bathe in the sacred waters, sir," Dorios informed him, apparently oblivious to the heat and the naked woman. "I'm afraid we can't linger."

Ruso wiped his forehead with the back of his hand and thought of basking seals, and sirens, and then, looking again at the clientele draped over the steps, of beached jellyfish. He realized one of the jellyfish was glaring at him and averted his gaze. This was, after all, the ladies' bathing session, despite the presence of the old boy on his knees scrubbing the paving, and the inky-fingered man sitting behind a scribe's desk, chatting to the girl selling pastries and drinks, and another fellow beside a painted board whose snake-on-a-stick motif pronounced him to be a healer.

He followed Dorios back to the entrance and to decency, declined a cup of Sulis Minerva's wondrous water—it would be a long time before he wanted to drink from that spring—and excused himself from a guided tour of the temple by saying he had to meet his family.

"Do come back and bathe later on, sir. I can vouch for the water myself. Marvelous for all manner of aches and pains. We have highly skilled doctors and masseurs on-site throughout the day. And of course there are plenty of good places to eat and drink. Any of the staff will be pleased to direct you. Whatever you need, don't be afraid to ask!"

"I won't," Ruso assured him. But he was confident that neither *I need to get my friend out of that terrible room* nor *I need to catch the man who murdered Serena and dumped her in your sacred spring* would be needs that any of the staff wanted to discuss.

11

TILLA PAUSED TO lift the blanket and check that the braid harness around Mara's chubby form was firmly tied to her minder's wrist. Baby and slave were both asleep in the sunshine, but there was no telling which of them would wake first. Satisfied that Mara could not crawl unheeded around the stacked amphorae and drop over the side into the river, Tilla stepped past Albanus. He barely looked up from the new scroll he had bought yesterday from a dealer in the port. She threaded her way between the sweating rowers to the prow of the boat. A cool breeze ruffled her hair while the gray-green waters slid past below her, almost close enough to lean down and touch.

The river was narrower here. Earlier they had passed under spectacular gray cliffs. Now the water lapped against dark woods on either side of them, and the bends in its course made it impossible to see very far ahead. They had passed other craft but at the moment there were no boats in sight. Only a little landing stage with its scatter of huts set well above the waterline marked the presence of humans.

Tilla glanced back at Esico. The gangling slave was leaning over the side and trailing one hand in the water. She called to him to join her and said in his own tongue, "I thought we had lost you yesterday, Esico."

"Me, mistress?" The innocent tone was belied by the pink flush spreading up his neck and across his cheeks.

Esico's tendency to dawdle over jobs that did not interest him often meant he was gone longer than expected, but yesterday's disappearance into the backstreets of Abona had been unusual even by his standards. Tilla, who had a fair idea of why, had decided to wait until they were alone to tackle him about it. "Is it true that if we had sailed along the coast toward the sunset, instead of turning up this river, we would have reached the lands of your people, where the coast is rocky and the tides are high?"

"The Dumnonii are not my people now, mistress."

"Even so." She could only imagine how a family might long for news of a lost son. "That is where your father is a warrior and an elder?"

Esico mumbled something about not knowing where to find his father. She assumed the lad had gone to ask about him in Abona. Seaports were fine places for picking up news. It seemed there had been nothing, which was why he had come back, claiming to have got lost—a poor excuse in a town by the sea where you spoke the local language. Still, Tilla knew how lonely it was to be a slave in someone else's tribe.

"Somebody among your people will know, surely? What is the name of your home? We must send a message to say you are safe and well."

"My father is not an elder now," Esico admitted. "There was trouble. Now other people are in charge."

"Was that how you ended up as a slave?"

"Yes, mistress."

So. Rival leaders had deposed the father and sold the son. It was an old story. Nobody wanted the warrior children of ousted leaders hanging around, causing trouble, and he was lucky he had not been murdered. Certainly he could not go home. "Do you have brothers and sisters? A mother?"

"All dead, mistress. Perhaps my father too."

"We can try to find out while we're down here if you like."

But Esico did not seem especially interested. Perhaps he would rather imagine his father to be alive than know for certain that he was not.

"You can go and sit down now," she told him. "Do not wander off again when we get to Aquae Sulis or I shall have you brought back and beaten. We need you for unloading."

Farther back, the baby and her minder had not moved. The minder—the slave they had actually gone out to buy when Tilla had taken pity on Esico as well—had never shown any sign of wanting to go home. There was nothing Neena missed about her own tribe: Even there she had always been a slave.

"Not far now, miss," said the captain, who must have supposed she was getting impatient. "Got to catch the tide right to go up, see? You time it wrong, you'd be stuck in the middle with mud on either side."

It struck her how often men made conversation by telling you things they thought you ought to know. Which was sometimes useful, except they rarely stopped to find out how much you knew already and sometimes they expected you to listen with wonder to total nonsense. Like *Women only have babies in the eighth or the tenth month of pregnancy* or *Not many people know that women have fewer teeth than men.* Still, the captain's words were kindly meant, and today she felt reassured to know they were in experienced hands in this wild landscape where Serena had died and where Mara's real mother might even now be planning to ask for her back.

"I have never been to Aquae Sulis," she told him. "Is the sacred spring as strange as they say?"

"You won't be disappointed," he promised her.

"My husband has gone ahead to find somewhere to stay. I hope there will be rooms. I heard there was a fire."

"The Little Eagle," he agreed. "Tragic business. Burned down last month. Guests roasted in their beds."

"Really? That is terrible!"

"It was," he agreed. "But don't you worry, it won't happen again."

She glanced back at her family. "How can anyone be sure of that? Are the houses there badly built?"

"From what I heard, the fire was deliberately set."

"That is even worse! Who would do a thing like that?"

The boatman leaned in closer. "They're saying it was a jealous husband, miss."

"A jealous husband?" Tilla was running out of ways to say *How terrible!*

"Course, the family tried to cover it up. The feller this woman was playing around with must have run off, and the family had her body away before anybody could see, but you know how people talk. It's looking like the husband got wind of where they were meeting and set the place alight."

"With other people still inside?"

"Twenty-two, I heard. Guests and staff. I heard the landlord was lost trying to get the last ones out."

"How dreadful!" So this was how the pollution of the sacred spring had been covered up. Serena's body must have been swiftly removed and hidden away, and someone had sent out a juicy rumor to compete with the truth. Now both Serena and Valens were besmirched by it. "So her husband set a fire to kill them both and her lover ran away and left her to die?"

"That's what they reckon," the man told her. "Least, the boyfriend's not been seen since and they never found his body. And now the husband's cleared off too."

"Nonsense!" put in a woman's voice from behind them.

Tilla turned to see a middle-aged woman who had sat quietly spinning a brown fleece for most of the morning.

"You're getting two things mixed up," continued the woman. "The wife wasn't killed in the fire. That was two soldiers and the landlord. She was murdered by the lover on the steps of the temple, and then he ran off."

"That's not what I heard," offered a third voice. "I heard the husband did away with both of them and threw the lover's body in the river."

"Whatever it was, it wouldn't have happened if she'd behaved like a decent woman."

The opinions were coming so fast now that Tilla could barely keep up with who was speaking.

"I heard her and the lover both killed themselves."

"What happened to his body, then?"

"No, her father killed them both. He could do that, you know. If he caught them together under his roof. My cousin works for the governor's office in Londinium and he says you can't prosecute a man for keeping his daughter honest."

"Then why's the father blaming the husband?" demanded the boatman. "I heard there's a reward for bringing him in."

Nobody had an answer for that. Tilla hoped the news of the reward was not true. Otherwise it would only be a matter of time before Valens was caught.

As the boat rounded another bend in the river, they emerged into sunlight and sparkling water. A bridge appeared ahead of them and she wondered whether the whole of Aquae Sulis was still debating the murder like this. It seemed the authorities' attempts to prevent panic amongst the visitors had gone awry. Starved of real information, people were not panicking. They were excited.

12

THE RUTTED TRACK that led to the site of the fatal fire was the sort of street every town had, no matter how smart its public face might be. The one where the skinny barefoot children and mangy dogs stopped chasing each other to stare at you as you passed. The one where the paint was peeling and where bright patches of fresh reed betrayed doomed attempts to plug leaks in the thatch. It was the sort of place where an off-duty legionary without much money might rent a cheap room to retire to at night because he was planning to spend most of his waking hours enjoying himself in the expensive part of town.

Glancing down to where the track petered out into lush meadow with a glimpse of the meandering river beyond, it occurred to Ruso that the ill-fated Little Eagle might have boasted some pleasant views. It was impossible to know, because all that was left of it now was the stark black wasteland at his feet. He could still feel the faint catch of the burning at the back of his throat when he inhaled.

A large area set back from the road had been fenced off, much of it with fresh timber. The burned ground crunched under his feet as he strolled across to take a look. The words DANGER—KEEP OUT had been scrawled across the timbers in several places with charcoal.

As he approached he could hear the soft gurgle of water, but the gaps in the fence had been filled with panels of woven hazel and a chain kept the gate clamped tight against its post. He followed the perimeter and, finding what he was looking for, crouched to dabble his fingers in the warm stream flowing out from under the fence. A few hardy weeds were beginning to reestablish themselves where the soil had been disturbed. This, he supposed, must be the failed building project. He had not realized it was next door to the fire.

Glancing downstream, he saw that the flow of water joined with another. To his surprise, the second one had steam rising from it too. Wondering what the goddess's bounty had looked like before Rome arrived to tidy it up, he began to pick his way through the weeds toward the source of this other water. Perhaps a few moments alone with nature would help him order his thoughts.

He never found out because of the body.

Thin, naked, motionless, facedown in the pool with faded ginger hair floating around its head like a curtain.

Another one. A second dead body in the sacred waters.

Not if he could help it.

He plunged forward, his feet slipping in the wet. Shouting for help, he straddled the body and seized it under the arms. Then, bracing himself against the weight, he staggered backward, hauling it up out of the water.

It came to life in his arms. It yelled at him and fought its way out of his grip, knocking him back so he sat down heavily in the warm mud. Then it spun round and tried to punch him.

Ruso grabbed the freckled arm in mid-flail. The man dropped to his knees in the water.

"Sorry," Ruso told his unintended victim. "I thought you were drowning."

The man raised his other hand to push dripping hair off his face. He glared at Ruso with eyes that were blue in the middle and pink everywhere else. He said in British, "Can't a man speak with his gods in peace without you lot trying to interfere?"

Ruso repeated his apology, this time in his wife's tongue, and released the arm.

"Uh." The man sat back on his heels. "I thought you were one of them."

"I *am* one of them," Ruso told him, easing himself up from the mud just as a wiry figure in a work tunic appeared and demanded in Latin, "Someone wanting help?"

"My mistake," Ruso explained. "Sorry. Thanks for coming over."

The new arrival eyed the native and said to Ruso, "If he's bothering you, just say so."

"I think I was the one bothering him," Ruso admitted.

The newcomer watched the native splash a few paces across the shallow pool and sit down in the water at the far side. Then he said to Ruso, "Don't put up with any nonsense from him, mate," before tramping off in the direction of the street.

When he had gone the native said, "At my age I might have died of shock."

"You might," Ruso agreed, wondering if this was the prelude to a demand for compensation.

But instead the native busied himself rubbing a graze on his elbow and observed, "A Roman with the voice of a Brigante, eh? We don't get a lot like you around here."

"Nor anywhere else," Ruso told him. "Sorry about dragging you out." He nodded toward the water, which was now swirling with mud. "Is it good?"

"Your lot haven't ruined this one yet, but give them time."

"What's going on with the one behind the fence?"

The man's face creased into a grin. "They were told not to interfere with that spring. I told them, my sister told them, their own people told them, but they knew better. Till Sulis gave them a bloody nose."

"What happened?"

"You can't disrespect our goddess and get away with it."

"What did Sulis Minerva do, exactly?"

"Sulis," the man corrected him, sliding down into the pool. "The Minerva bit is yours. Your gold statue, your stone temple, your problem. Coming in or not? Don't go in the middle, you'll get stuck."

Ruso hesitated for a moment, then pulled off his tunic and slid in to lie beside the native in the heat. It wasn't unpleasant, as long as you didn't wonder what the swirling mud was hiding, or imagine what you might smell like afterward, or compare it to lying in the clear waters off the southern coast of Gaul with the sun on your face and the sand shifting beneath you as the warm waves lapped over your skin.

"So, what are you, then?" said the native. "A spy?"

"A doctor," said Ruso, suddenly tired of subterfuge. "My wife is Brigante. Corionotatae tribe."

"Never heard of them. You learned her tongue?"

"I wanted to know what her family were saying about me."

"You should get on all right with Sulis Minerva, then. You the Roman with the Brigante voice. What do they call you?"

"Ruso. What do they call you?"

"Your lot mostly call me *that bloody native*. Or *that priestess's brother.*"

Ruso said, "Ah," seeing the resemblance in the fading red hair.

"At home I'm Brecc to my face and *the awkward old sod* behind my back."

"Where's home?"

The man jerked a thumb over his shoulder. "Up over the hill, well clear of your lot."

Ruso said, "I'm trying to find the man who was in charge of whatever's locked up behind that fence."

"You won't find him around here. Murdered his woman and buggered off is what I heard. Driven mad by our goddess as punishment for attacking her spring."

"And did Sulis burn the Little Eagle down too?"

The man slid down so only his face was showing above the water. "You ask a lot of questions."

"It was my friend's wife who was murdered."

"Hm." The man sank away under the water. Only a stream of bubbles rising through the murk marked out the place where he was lying. When he came back up, Ruso was holding his own breath, waiting for the result of the awkward old sod's consultation with the goddess. "What do you think?"

"I think," said the man, wiping the water out of his eyes, "that all this asking questions is going to get you into trouble with your own people."

"Where do you think the engineer might have gone?"

The man shook his head, scattering drops onto the rippling surface of the water. "There are things that only Sulis knows," he said. "And she's not telling."

13

THE RIVER WAS icy after the warm pool, and dipping into it washed away any doubts Ruso might have had about the need for a second bathhouse. Still, it left him clean, and if he looked odd walking back toward the site of the fire in squelchy sandals with his tunic sticking to his wet skin, at least he didn't smell of the hot spring.

Now he looked more closely, he could make out the stone rectangles of wall foundations in the blackened ground. A few scorched red floor tiles were still in place, open to the sky. Some of them were supporting the foot of one of the massive props that had been installed at an angle to shore up the wall of a snack shop that was still open for business. It must have had a narrow escape: There were black burn marks in the thatch. He ran his hands through his wet hair, straightened his tunic, and chose a bench outside in the sun to dry off.

The brisk young woman who appeared did not seem to notice anything unusual about him, announcing in Latin, "It's a beautiful morning, sir!" Before he could reply, she turned aside to address two small children who had followed her out. "You two, go and find your pa. You know you aren't supposed to go bothering the customers."

The children began to shuffle toward the back of the bar, turning to look at Ruso over their shoulders. Too late, he realized he should have said they weren't bothering him.

"So, what can I get you, sir? We have wines from Gaul and Italia and the new vineyards in the East, local beer, or our famous healing water hot from our very own spring."

Ruso glanced at the fenced-off area. "The one that says DANGER—KEEP OUT?"

"Oh, that's just to stop anyone falling in, sir. The water's perfect."

"What does it taste like?"

"I'll ask my husband to fetch you some. Fresh and hot as the goddess intended. Nothing added, nothing taken away. Just the thing to see you through the day."

None of this answered his question about the taste.

"It'll do wonders for your digestion."

If Ruso had purchased all the concoctions and extractions he had been assured would do wonders for his digestion over the years, he would be bankrupt by now. And if this one was so good, why was he the only customer? Still, Aquae Sulis's waters were unique, and this source was a safe distance from the spring where Serena's body had been found. "I'll try it."

The husband, who turned out to be the man who had answered Ruso's call for help earlier, was dispatched to fetch the water. The wife retreated to the kitchen, and, left to his own company, Ruso shifted round on the bench to get a better look at the jauntily painted walls of the bar. They were adorned with pictures of birds in trees, fish apparently swimming in midair, and goddesses pouring water from golden vessels. One of the goddesses, he noted, had a face remarkably like the small girl who was now peering at him from behind the counter. It was all designed to offer good cheer. It was a shame that, even on a bright morning with the town full of visitors, the only person here to be cheered was himself.

The husband returned clutching a dripping jug, but instead of pouring he bent down, peered at Ruso, and declared, "It is you, sir, isn't it?"

"We met just now."

"No, sir, before that. Don't I know you?"

"Possibly," Ruso agreed, groping in his memory for an earlier recollection of the face now inches from his own. "Who do you think I am?"

"You're that doctor, um—"

"Ruso?"

"Ruso! That was it. The eyesight's not what it was, but I never forget a name. Good to see you again, sir!"

Ruso grasped the proffered hand and wished that he could say he, too, never forgot a name. Or a face. "I'm sorry, er—"

"Gnaeus, sir. You wouldn't remember me. Never ill. I was a dispatch rider at Deva."

"Ah!" said Ruso, feeling it was only polite to feign some sort of recognition. "Gnaeus! How are you?"

The man sat down across the table and lifted the jug to pour. "These are trying times, sir. Trying times. But we keep going. Me and the wife. Drink up, sir, it'll do you good."

Moments later Ruso was wondering what had possessed him to ask for the water. It was not as bad as he had expected from the smell: It was worse. And instead of being hot as promised, it was lukewarm, which made him think seriously of vomiting. "That's horrible."

Gnaeus grinned. "That's how you can tell it's cleaning your system out, sir."

Ruso hoped it was doing nothing of the sort. "So," he said, setting the cup aside.

"Trying times?"

"We started out all right here, sir. But now look." The veteran held a hand out to indicate the deserted bar. "Setting up here took most of my discharge grant. Still, like the wife says, at least we've got somewhere to live."

Ruso tried to think of something helpful to say, but it was hard to know how to encourage anyone who thought that a business serving ghastly water in an unappealing backstreet was a good investment. "Losing the inn must have been a blow," he suggested.

"Terrible, sir, terrible. Two lads from the Second Augusta burned in their beds, and the landlord killed trying to get them out. But it's not the Little Eagle going that's finished us. It's losing the baths."

"The baths?" They had seemed perfectly intact earlier this morning.

"The Veterans' Association were building new baths over our spring. In fact, they were in here having a meeting about it the very evening the fire broke out."

"And we were lucky they were," put in the wife.

"Right enough," said Gnaeus. "If they hadn't gone straight out and pulled down the workshop next door, we'd have gone up in smoke too."

The wife nudged her husband. "Show the doctor your hands," she urged.

The man shifted uncomfortably on his seat. "It's nothing, woman."

"It's not nothing," she declared, reaching for the nearest arm and pulling it forward. "See?"

Ruso saw the pink shine of freshly healed burns.

"He went into that fire and pulled people out with his own hands," she announced proudly.

"Couldn't get all of them, though," muttered the husband.

"You did very well to get any," she told him, putting a hand on his shoulder.

Ruso nodded agreement. "I heard it was bad."

"Never seen anything like it," Gnaeus agreed. "You wouldn't believe the heat. We stopped it spreading, but we just had to let it burn itself out. So now here we are, all held up with props and nobody to serve, instead of being just down the road from a big new suite of baths and one of those fancy lodging houses like they have in Rome."

Ruso, who had lived in one of the lodging houses they had in Rome, was perhaps less grieved than the man had intended. "Can't they start again?"

Gnaeus shook his head. "That haruspex feller came and had a look and he said the fire was an omen and the goddess wanted them to stop what they were doing right away."

The wife retreated behind the bar and returned with a jug of wine, two more cups, and a plate of bread and olives. Ruso nodded his thanks and helped himself to an olive. "Lots of people must be disappointed now the project's been abandoned." These two would not be the only people who were facing a serious loss: There must have been investors who were funding the costs of building, and Terentius had lost his job.

"You can't argue with the gods, sir. It wasn't just the fire. That same night, the leader of the veterans lost his—ah, you might remember him, sir. Centurion Pertinax."

"His daughter," said Ruso. "She was married to a friend of mine."

The man's eyes widened. "Not that doctor, the one who—"

"Valens," Ruso reminded him. "You probably met him at Deva too. And, no, he didn't."

Gnaeus shrugged. "If you say so, sir. I have to say he did a nice job with these."

He held out both hands for inspection, flexing his fingers.

"He's a good doctor," said Ruso, glad of the opportunity to say something positive about his friend.

"He took charge of that bathhouse, sir, just like it was the hospital back at Deva."

"You were treated in the bathhouse?"

"In the changing hall, sir. I did think afterwards that he was a bit calm for a man who'd just murdered his wife. Maybe you're right. Maybe the other one did it after all."

Ruso, tearing his thoughts away from the fact that Serena could not have been attacked in the changing hall if it was full of injured firefighters, said, " 'The other one'?"

Gnaeus turned to his own wife. "Tell the doctor what you saw."

The wife shook her head. "Oh, that poor lady!"

Ruso tried not to look too eager.

"They think I might be the last person who saw her alive. Apart from the one who killed her, that is."

"Really?" He had made a good decision in coming here.

"It makes me feel a bit ill just remembering it," she said. "We were so busy dragging everything out in case the fire spread. And I had to watch the children. If I'd said to her, 'Come in and sit down'—"

"But she wasn't looking for somewhere to sit down," pointed out her husband. "She was with that Terentius."

"I know," conceded the wife. "But now I know what happened to her, I can't help thinking, *If I'd done something different . . .*"

"I'm sure everyone feels that way," Ruso assured her, thinking of Valens trapped in his dingy room with his regrets. "When did you see them?"

"I keep telling her," put in the husband, "you couldn't do nothing. No more than I could get those lads out of the fire. It's fate."

"It's fate," she agreed, reaching out for the girl who was tugging at her skirts and lifting her onto her lap.

Ruso said, "Did you see them before or after your husband was treated by Valens?" but neither of them could remember.

"Everything happened so fast," the wife explained, cuddling the girl close as if to protect her.

"I heared all the shouting," put in the girl. "There was mans up on the roof throwing water."

The mother glanced at her husband and rested her head against the child's. "But we're all safe now. Aren't we?"

The girl nodded solemnly. "All safe now."

"Anyway," said the husband, "after that, it was all over for the new baths. Not that it would have taken much."

"Really?" Ruso prompted again, deliberately taking a mouthful of bread to allow Gnaeus plenty of time for the tale of woe he was clearly eager to share.

"They had problems from the start," Gnaeus explained, lifting the boy and sitting him on a hairy knee so the child could reach the bread. "The architect fell ill and went back to Rome. The engineer they wanted wouldn't touch it, even though he was in the Veterans' Association himself, so they put the youngster in charge. The builders kept telling him it would be all right. They were supposed to have the piles hammered down by midsummer, but they couldn't get down to anything solid. They were still crashing away over there right up to a few days before the Little Eagle went up in flames. Then the fire took the toolshed and the fence and all the struts for the crane with it."

"All that banging went right through you," put in the wife. "Some days it made the cups dance across the table. And the water was always muddy. We had to let it settle and go cold before anyone would touch it."

"We kept asking what was happening," put in her husband, "but all they said was 'These things take time.' And then all the builders cleared off because the investors wouldn't give them any more money till they saw some progress, and now it's not happening at all. Tell you the truth, I can't help wondering if the builders led that young lad on a bit of a dance."

"I'm sorry," Ruso said, wishing he could say something more comforting. His own father had been practically bankrupted and driven to an early grave by the delays and escalating costs of building a temple for their hometown. "Have you thought what you'll do now?"

The veteran helped himself to an olive and paused to spit out the stone. "I've thought," he said, "but I haven't come up with any answers."

The wife smoothed the daughter's hair. "It's early days yet," she urged, picking at a tangle. "We'll find somewhere to go. You'll think of something."

"Right," said Gnaeus, not sounding convinced but clearly taking the hint that no more anxiety was to be expressed in front of the children.

Ruso reached for the cup and took another gulp of the water. "Remarkable," he said, putting the cup down and wondering whether or not to inflict the rest of it upon himself just because he was paying for it.

"Yes, sir," the wife agreed. "That's what a lot of people say."

"You don't have to finish it, sir," Gnaeus offered. "But could you do us a big favor? I'll refill the wine and you just sit there for a bit and make it look as though we've got a customer."

14

A S T H E B O A T rounded the last bend, Tilla tied a bow of white braid in Mara's hair: a decoration she had only just taken to adding now that there was enough hair to comb up into a topknot. Then she pulled the little blue socks out of her bag and put them over Mara's feet while the baby-minder held each chubby leg still in turn. The tunic, mercifully, was still clean and the cloths were dry. "There's a smart girl!" Tilla announced in British, leaning back into the cramped space by the sun-warmed amphorae to admire the full effect. Mara, pleased, gave a big grin that displayed her latest new teeth.

Tilla lifted her daughter up so she could see the top of a building looming above the trees. "We are going to Aquae Sulis," she told her. "See? There is the temple. And look, who can you see waiting for us? I told you he would be there! There is your—" She stopped.

Beside her the baby-minder said softly, "Is everything all right, mistress?"

Tilla swallowed. "It is fine, Neena," she said, using the abbreviation that the family had coined for Narina's name. "Just someone I have not seen for a long time."

Someone who was returning Albanus's cheery wave, but instead
of looking at him she was craning to get a better view of the baby
in Tilla's arms. The baby, meanwhile, was bouncing up and down
with such excitement that Tilla had to tighten her grip.

"Clever girl!" cried Neena.

"What?" Tilla turned to her.

"She said *Papa*, mistress!"

Tilla blinked. For a moment she thought the slave was talking
about Virana, who was waving and bouncing in very much the same
way as her daughter. "Did she?" She pressed her face close to Mara's
soft pink cheek. "Did you say *Papa*? Clever girl! There he is, look!"

The captain called for the passengers to sit down while they
docked, then shouted at the gaggle of small boys who were jostling
for position on the landing stage to get out of the way. The boat
glided in and bumped so gently against the massive timbers that
Tilla was on her feet again almost straightaway, waving to her
husband and assuring the eager boys that, no, her family did not
need lodgings, even in a very clean respectable house that was run
by their widowed mother, or grandmother, and was the cheapest
in town. No, they did not need help with the bags, either.

Somehow, just in those few moments, Mara managed to pull the
ribbon awry, lose one sock, and dribble down her clean tunic.

By the time the sock had been rescued and the boys had retreated,
Virana was crouched on the very edge of the landing stage, her
knees wide apart to make space for her belly. Tilla felt the baby tense
in her arms as Virana leaned so far out, she seemed about to topple
into the boat.

"Oh, look at you!" Virana cried, reaching out one hand to stroke
the baby's cheek. "Hello, little one!"

Mara tried to burrow into the crook of Tilla's neck. Guessing
what was about to happen, Tilla cuddled her closer and tried to gain
her attention. "Look, Mara! This is Virana. We like Virana!"

Virana did not read the signs. "Mara, it is me!"

Mara wailed in fright and fought to get away.

Virana's eager smile crumpled and died. She withdrew her hand
and used it to push her hair out of her eyes.

"Sorry!" Tilla called over the crying as she cuddled the baby close
and tried to console her. "She is just shy. Mara, stop now! Sh!" She

still could not bring herself to use the word *mother*, so she said again, "This is Virana. She is our friend!"

Virana struggled to her feet. Her face was pink. "I thought she would . . ." She pushed her hair back again. "Silly me."

Tilla passed the baby to Neena. Ignoring the ladder farther along, she swung one knee up onto the planking and reached out. "Pull me up."

Virana helped her onto the landing stage. Albanus abandoned the luggage and stood wringing his hands and asking his wife if she was all right, which plainly she was not, and then looking at Tilla as if he was hoping she would tell him what to do.

Tilla forced a smile and indicated Virana's bulging belly. "I am happy for you both. You will make very good parents."

Virana was not so easily distracted. "She doesn't like me!"

"She doesn't *know* you," Tilla explained. "She is like that with everybody new at the moment. It is the way babies are."

Virana sniffed. "But I am not new!" Albanus handed her a cloth. She wiped her eyes and nose on it and handed it back. "She saw me and cried."

"She will forget about this before you know it," Tilla promised, stifling a shameful sense of relief that the baby had not recognized the mother of her birth.

Back in the boat, Mara's complaints were fading as Neena sang her the song about the three little wolf cubs.

"I want her to like me."

"She *will* like you, just as we do." Tilla caught sight of her husband, who had retreated to supervise the unloading of luggage. He knew how little sense Virana had; did he not think to warn her to go slowly? Of course not. It would not have crossed his mind even at the best of times, and he had other things to worry about now. She said, "Have you seen Valens? How is he?"

Virana blinked the tears from her eyes. "Has nobody told you? I am glad to see you, but you have come all this way to help him, and he is gone!"

Nobody paid much attention to them as they lugged the baggage through the streets to the lodgings, and it occurred to Tilla that they looked just like all the other visitors who came to a place like this: a couple of ordinary families arriving hot and tired from the journey at the start of a shared holiday. Two comrades who had served in the legions—you could always tell; was it something about the walk?—and who had settled with local women. One pair were expecting their first baby; the other, wealthy enough to afford two slaves, already had a child: a girl with one sock on, a crooked braid in her hair, and a blotchy pink face. Tilla had her propped on one hip now, because Neena needed both hands to carry the surprising number of bags needed for such a very small person. Behind them, Esico and her husband were hauling a trunk between them that had boxes of medical kit strapped on top.

Suddenly, Virana said, "Do you not think she looks like Marcus? Around the eyes?"

Tilla glanced over her shoulder and was relieved to see that Albanus was busy chatting to her husband while struggling manfully with a cumbersome bag that left him walking lopsided. "I don't remember him."

"You know, the big handsome one?" Virana hurried ahead of them to get a better view of the baby. Once Mara realized she was being looked at, she turned away and buried her face in Tilla's shoulder, but Virana was unabashed. "She does look like him, I am sure of it! I was so hoping she would be Marcus's! Do you think I should send him a message?"

"A message?" Tilla tried not to sound too appalled. Virana was fragile enough already.

"To tell him he is a father. Do you not think he would be proud?"

"I do not care what he would be. And neither must you now."

Virana shrugged and dropped back to walk alongside. "Oh, well. She might not be his anyway."

Looking for a distraction, Tilla eyed the big white building with the high roof that filled the view at the end of the street. "Is that the famous hot bath? You must show me around."

She felt the girl's hand on her arm. "We must talk first," Virana murmured. "You must be very careful. You don't want to end up like poor Mistress Serena."

Tilla said, "Why? What did she do? No, wait." They were approaching a busy snack bar with tables on the street. "Tell me when we are alone," she added, just as her husband called from farther back, "Turn right!"

A few more paces down the narrow street, Virana announced, "This is the Mercury."

On one side of the open doorway was a bright painting of a god clutching a cockerel. On the other side, gazing at the god adoringly, stood a buxom goddess with a scepter in one hand and a ladle in the other.

"I have never been in the Mercury," Virana confided, craning her neck to see what she had been missing. "It is very expensive."

Tilla took the hint. "You must come inside and talk to me."

Virana and Mara exchanged wary glances as they passed from the sunlit street into the dark of the bar. The woman behind the counter looked up from serving a customer and nodded a greeting. While they waited for the others to catch up with them, Virana gazed around her, clearly impressed. "See those tiled shelves!" she urged. "So much easier to keep clean. And look: The cups and bowls match! And see, through there is a real dining room with couches! Do you think it is as nice upstairs?"

The fine dining room was unusual, but to Tilla the rest of the Mercury looked much like any other inn, although it had a better smell than most. In addition, the furniture was intact, the walls were not scrawled upon, and there was no drunk asleep in the corner. Her husband had chosen well.

The men arrived, and as they clumped up the stairs to find their room, Virana said, "I am so pleased about Marcus. I have been thinking about all of them and he was the nicest of the lot."

15

VIRANA SURVEYED THE room with an air of disappointment. "I thought a suite in the Mercury would be grander than
this."

"It is very quiet and peaceful," put in Albanus from the doorway,
perhaps worried that Tilla would be insulted.

Tilla flung back the brightly striped bed cover and the blankets
to check the sheets. "It looks clean," she said. "And there are glass
windows that open." The main room was also bigger than she had
expected, and the walls of both this and the little side room that
made this a "suite" gleamed white with fresh limewash. A green
curtain on a length of twine could be pulled across one end of the
main room to hide the bed, and there were a couple of rolled-up
mattresses in the other room for children or slaves to sleep on. But
she could understand why Virana felt let down: Like many people
brought up on a ramshackle native farm, the girl had never quite
been able to shake the idea that the words *Roman* and *wealthy* always
went together. She had been expecting the kind of luxury furnish-
ings she had seen in paintings. Instead there was a bed with a pot
underneath it, two mattresses, two rugs, one cupboard, and a couple

of lamp brackets nailed to the wall. The only other items in here were those they had brought themselves.

"I have stayed in many rooms," she told Virana, smoothing the bedding back into place, "and this is a good one."

The men went back downstairs. To Tilla's surprise, her husband had announced that, since there was no farm work for Esico to do now, the lad would be working at the Traveler's Repose next door. It seemed odd, but it saved the bother of finding him things to do all the time and making sure he did them. Esico had been very quiet since he had wandered off in Abona, as if being so close to his old home had brought back unhappy memories. Perhaps, if there was time, she would make some inquiries of her own about his father.

She closed the door so that the baby could not escape and tumble down the stairs. Then she and Neena began to unpack while Virana insisted that somebody needed to do something about Gleva.

Tilla knelt to place a stack of clean baby cloths on the shelf in the cupboard. "Who?"

"The one who wants to marry Officer Pertinax," Virana told her. "How is she getting on with the pot?"

"The pot?" Tilla glanced up and realized Virana had shifted her attention to the baby. "As you see," she said, admiring both the speed of Mara's escape from the pot and Neena's deft grab to put her back in place. "She is not as interested as we are."

"I really wish I could tell Marcus."

Tilla closed the cupboard. "And what do you think would happen even if you could find him? You will be upset if he does not care. Your husband will be upset if he does. And so will mine." She unstrapped his rolled-up cloak from the outside of a traveling bag. "Hang that on the peg behind the door and tell me about this Gleva."

Virana glanced at the baby-minder, who was crouching beside Mara at pot level to encourage her.

"You can speak in front of Neena."

Virana hooked the cloak on the door, pulled out the worst of the creases, and said, "Gleva is chasing Officer Pertinax because he is the leader of the veterans and she wants to use him to get power and to annoy the chief priest."

"I don't suppose she told you this herself?"

"Mistress Serena told my husband. Gleva says she had a message in a dream that she would meet a soldier, but Mistress Serena thought she made it all up."

It felt strange to be hearing Serena's opinions from beyond the grave, spoken by the wife of someone whom she must have seen as a hired hand. "Why did Serena tell Albanus a thing like that?"

"She said she wanted him to help her talk some sense into her father."

"*Albanus?*" It was not that Albanus had no sense but that Pertinax would brush him aside like a fly. "I can see what this Gleva wants," she said, "but why would Pertinax be interested in a woman like that?"

"That is what everyone wonders," Virana agreed. "And when you see her, you will wonder too. But she uses a love potion. She is driving Officer Pertinax wild with lust."

If that was true, no wonder Serena had been worried. Tilla had always felt that Romans made an unnecessary fuss about what they called witchcraft and superstition, but everyone knew that for a love potion to be effective, it must weaken its victim. Pertinax was already old and crippled. Weakening him further could finish him off.

"Serena found out and told her to stop, but Gleva just laughed and said 'Don't be silly.' Can I sit on your bed? I need to put my feet up."

"Go ahead."

Virana flopped onto the bed and lay on her back with her legs in the air like a stranded beetle while she pulled off her sandals. "So then Serena went to her father and warned him about the love potion. Ah, that's better . . ." She dropped the second sandal onto the floor and stretched out on the striped cover. "But he just got cross and he told her not to be silly, that he wasn't ever going to marry Gleva anyway. And Gleva heard him say it, so she went to the sacred spring and put a curse on Serena, and now see what has happened!"

Tilla shoved an empty bag under the bed alongside the box of medical supplies and the case that held her husband's surgical instruments. It seemed this Gleva had cause to be angry with both Serena and Pertinax. She sat on the trunk at the end of the bed and said, "I need to know exactly what happened."

"Did Albanus not tell you anything at all on the whole of the journey?"

"I need to hear it from you." She needed to know, also, how much of the truth Virana had been told. "You may remember something Albanus has forgotten. Something that will help us to save Valens."

"Poor Doctor Valens! He was so handsome. Well, he still is, I expect. I could see why Mistress Serena ran away to marry him. And he looked so upset when he came to see her. I felt sorry for him."

"You saw him when he visited?"

"Oh, yes. He was walking past the shop and I called to him and he came in to say hello. Of course, I knew all about her and Terentius—everybody did—but I didn't say anything. I thought he must know because of how he looked, but I couldn't be sure. And that would be awful, wouldn't it, if he didn't know and then I said something about it?"

"It would." It seemed Virana was learning some tact at last.

"But then after he was gone I thought perhaps I should have made sure he knew."

"I would say not."

"Oh, good. But it didn't matter because he found out anyway. When he went to the house they had a huge argument."

"Valens and Serena?"

"Albanus heard the start of it. Then he took the boys out for a walk, because he could see the shouting was upsetting them. And they never saw Mistress Serena alive again." The bed creaked as Virana wriggled to get comfortable. "Can I use this pillow?"

"Yes. What happened to Serena?"

"Such a terrible thing!" Virana lifted her head and shoved the pillow underneath.

Tilla waited, biting back the temptation to cry, *Yes, but what was it?*

"Then afterwards—well, it was like Doctor Valens had turned hollow, poor man. And everyone is blaming Terentius, but Officer Pertinax always said it was him."

"Said it was Valens?"

"Officer Pertinax wouldn't let the boys stand next to Doctor Valens at the funeral." Virana heaved her belly sideways and propped herself up onto one elbow. "And now Gleva has moved into the house to help look after them, and—" She stopped, and then scrabbled up the bed and grasped Tilla by the arm. "Of course! I know what she is planning!"

"You do?"

"She is going to marry Officer Pertinax and have a son of her own and then she is going to poison them!"

"She is going to *what*?"

"Poison them. Doctor Valens's boys. So her own son will inherit all the centurion's money."

Tilla blinked. "Did Serena tell your husband that too?"

"No. I have only just thought of it. But it is the sort of thing they do in Rome. Albanus told me all about it."

"Albanus told you women in Rome poison their stepchildren?"

Virana pursed her lips. "Not all of them," she admitted. "But it's true, I swear. You ask him."

Tilla had never come across any cases of poisoned stepchildren in Rome, but she had only spent a few weeks there. Who was to say what went on in such a crowded city? And was it so very different to what happened here? As soon as Esico's father had lost power over the tribe by the rocky shore, Esico had been sold to a slave trader.

"We have some time yet," she assured Virana. "Pertinax and Gleva are not even married, let alone parents. And if he's said he won't marry her—"

"But now he has lost Serena, he might change his mind. And Gleva might already be pregnant, even though she is old. She is using magic."

"Mm." Tilla frowned. Albanus had said very little about this Gleva on the journey, and had certainly never suggested that she might be Serena's murderer. Perhaps he had not taken the business of love potions and the curses as seriously as he should. What if Gleva had prayed for the help of Sulis Minerva to seduce Pertinax? What if she had lured Serena to the spring, stabbed her, and tipped her in as an offering to the goddess?

Tilla bent her head and pressed her forefingers into the inner corners of her eyes. She was getting even more excitable than Virana. She must try to think clearly.

"Are you all right?"

"Just a bit tired after the journey." She got to her feet. It was no good trying to reason while Virana was still talking, and now Mara was wailing because Neena was putting her cloths back on and she preferred to crawl around with a bare bottom.

"I know all the scribes who work around the baths," Virana was saying. "Gleva is not clever at reading and writing like you and Mistress Serena. She would have had to pay one of them to write the curse for her, so I will find out which one, and he can tell us what she wrote. And I can try to find out where she bought the love potion." She shifted her weight on the mattress. "This bed is too hard. I'm glad I haven't got to sleep on it."

At the sound of male voices approaching up the stairs, she clambered to her feet. "I'd better go to work. The boss at the shop is a proper old misery. She'll complain to Albanus again, and Albanus will get all worried."

"Are you supposed to be working now?"

"Oh, she's so fussy. I always make up the time later. So, shall I find the scribe? Then we can put a curse back on Gleva."

Tilla was about to say they would do no such thing, when it occurred to her that speaking to a curse writer might not be such a bad idea after all. She put her finger to her lips and Virana nodded. This was between the two of them. The men would not understand. Rather than let them worry about it, they would not be told.

16

THE SPRAWLING TOWN house where Pertinax was now
living had been built to make the most of an east-facing rise.
Ruso closed the heavy gate on the bustle of the street and then
he and Tilla—who had insisted on coming to pay her respects—
followed Albanus up the steps through a steep garden. Above them
was a terrace with a fine view over smaller properties toward the
river—which had now filled its channel and glistened in the afternoon sun—and out to the hazy hills beyond.

The slave who answered the door seemed surprised to see
Albanus. The hesitant tone of his assurance that the master was at
home suggested they might not be about to receive a warm welcome.

They were barely inside the cool shade of the house when two
identical dark-eyed boys with Valens's curls and Serena's olive skin
came rushing into the entrance hall from the courtyard garden
beyond, shouting, "Albanus!" Both boys grabbed at his tunic, talking
over each other in their desperation for attention. "Albanus, if an
elephant had a fight with a Cyclops, who would win?"

"I've lost a tooth, Albanus, look!"

"It would be the Cyclops, wouldn't it?"

Albanus said, "Does the Cyclops have weapons?"

"Grandpa said he would put a thread around it and pull it out but I did it all by myself."

"He ran away from Grandpa," put in the other twin, abandoning the Cyclops problem to score a point against his brother.

"You might not remember Doctor Ruso and Tilla," Albanus told them, placing a hand on each boy's shoulder and turning them to face his companions. "They are friends of your father."

Both boys looked up at their visitors with mild curiosity. It was clear from their faces that they didn't remember either of them. The problem was mutual: While Ruso recognized them as a pair, he had never been able to tell Valens's sons apart. Rather than cause offense, he had always addressed them as a joint entity. "Good afternoon, boys." It was a deception he was sure they saw through even at the age of four.

"When will Pa come to see us?"

"As soon as he can," Ruso assured them, wishing he had more to offer. "I'm sure he misses you."

"Our ma died."

Tilla crouched down to their level. "We are very sorry," she said. "You must miss her very much."

The boy who had lost the tooth nodded. "She's not coming back ever." To Ruso's alarm, the child began to cry. He wished he had not agreed to bring Tilla. Why did she have to encourage this sort of thing?

The boy's brother moved to put an arm around him and looked up at Ruso. "He keeps on crying. I tell him to stop, but he wants Ma."

Tilla produced a cloth from somewhere and helped the boy to wipe his eyes. The brother said, "Thank you, miss," and Ruso heard an echo of their mother. Serena had always been strict about manners. *Say thank you to the lady!*

It was not at all appropriate for a man to scoop a friend's child up in his arms and promise to bring his father back soon. Nor would it be fair. He had no power to change anything here. So instead he stood awkwardly while Tilla dealt kindly with the tears, and he was relieved to hear uneven footsteps approaching: the soft scuff of leather on tile alternating with a dull thump.

A square-shaped, square-shouldered man with iron-gray hair and an impressive nose lurched into view. Even though he walked on one real leg and one wooden stump, and he looked thinner and older than Ruso remembered, Pertinax still had the kind of presence that seemed to suck all the air out of a room as soon as he entered it. He was followed by two men of about the same age. They were wearing civilian clothes, but they looked as though they would reach for invisible swords as soon as Pertinax gave the order.

The centurion glanced at his sniffling grandson, scowled at Ruso, and ignored Tilla completely, turning his glare to Albanus. "You're back, then."

Albanus gulped. "Yes, sir."

"Well then, lads." Pertinax reached down to usher the twins toward a side door. "Time for lessons."

As Albanus was following the boys out, Pertinax said, "You."

Albanus snapped to attention.

"Come and see me afterwards."

Albanus managed, "Yes, sir," scuttled out, and was reminded of what to do next by a roar of "Shut the bloody door!"

The door clamped shut. Pertinax beckoned with one finger, and Ruso followed into a sparsely furnished study that took him straight back to their days in the Twentieth Legion. Pertinax's full armor and crested helmet were displayed on the same wooden stand in the same position they had occupied in his office up in the fortress at Deva. There was still a folding desk that was too small for him and even a couple of notices hung on the walls. It all spoke of a man who was not settled into retirement.

Pertinax sank down into his own chair and left Ruso to stand before him and worry about what would happen next: another reminder of life in the legion. Ruso was aware that Tilla had slipped in and was standing beside him. He hoped she wasn't about to say something tactless. Or indeed anything at all. There had not been much time to bring her up-to-date on the walk across here.

As if the silence were Ruso's fault, Pertinax demanded, "Well?"

He said, "I'm very sorry about the loss of your daughter, sir."

Pertinax grunted something that might have been thanks. "Not as sorry as I am. Not nearly as sorry as those boys will be for the rest of their lives."

"No, sir."

"You didn't come all this way just to say that."

Before he could reply, Tilla spoke up. "We would like to pay our respects at your daughter's tomb, sir."

There was a silence, during which Ruso willed his wife not to say anything else and Pertinax doubtless expected her to realize that she had spoken out of turn in a meeting between two men. Finally he addressed his response to Ruso. "Up on the hill behind the house. Just beyond the main road. The one that's not finished."

Ruso put in, "Thank you, sir," before Tilla could intervene further.

"I didn't expect to need it yet." The chair creaked as Pertinax leaned back. "And now we've got that over, you can tell me where he is."

There was no point in pretending he didn't know who Pertinax was talking about. "I can't, sir. He left town before I got here."

"Can't or won't?"

Ruso realized he was standing to attention. He made a deliberate effort to relax. Neither of them was a soldier now.

Pertinax said, "You're like all the rest of them. You think I'm some kind of irrational grief-struck fool."

Ruso's "Not at all, sir" hopefully drowned out his wife's "I think—"

"Your pal, the layabout you're covering up for as usual, seduced my girl when she wasn't old enough to know better. Then he made a great song and dance about doing the honorable thing and marrying her. As if he were doing us both a favor. Since then he's neglected her. He's taken her for granted. What's worse, he's neglected his children. Then, when she finally finds herself a decent young man, your friend stabs her in the heart rather than let her go to someone else."

Even Tilla had no reply for this. It was not the time to point out that Valens was a gifted and occasionally hardworking doctor, and that he was entertaining company. None of that made up for his longstanding lack of enthusiasm as a husband and father. Still, he was not a murderer. Ruso said, "Sir, I really don't think—"

"What you think doesn't matter. I won't keep quiet. When the governor comes, I'll get justice for my daughter. He's a good man. I served with him back in Upper Germania. He'll run a fair trial."

"Valens didn't kill your daughter, sir."

"You'll find out."

"For the sake of the boys, sir—"

"You dare—" The chair scraped back as Pertinax sprang up. He grabbed the desk for balance and almost tipped over with it. One of the veterans stepped forward to help and Pertinax snapped at him to get back. Finally upright, he roared with a voice that would carry across a windswept parade ground, "You dare to come to my house and tell me what's good for my boys?"

Ruso stepped in front of his wife, afraid the man was going to heave the desk into the air and fling it at them. He could feel his own heart thumping, and the remains of the unwisely heavy late lunch lay like a stone in his stomach. Behind him, a floorboard creaked as one of the veterans shifted position.

Pertinax sank down again, and Ruso let out a long, slow breath. This was civilian Aquae Sulis, not the legion. He could not be punished for insubordination. On the other hand, it was never wise to poke an angry lion with a stick, even for the good of its grandchildren.

"Well?"

At least he hadn't ordered them to get out. Maybe even Pertinax was mellowing in his old age. "My wife and I had the greatest respect for your daughter, sir." Even if Serena had taken some years to realize that Tilla was not a servant.

"Then let her family grieve in peace."

Tilla stepped out from behind him to face their host. "Doctor Valens is grieving too, sir."

Pertinax turned his gaze on her for the first time. "So you do know where he is."

Ruso swallowed. Tilla wisely followed his cue and remained silent.

"Talk or don't talk, it doesn't matter," Pertinax continued. "I can have you followed." He bent and retrieved the inkpot that had rolled under his chair. "Clear off, the pair of you. And stay out of my family business."

"I intend to find out the truth, sir," Ruso told him, determined not to leave before he had made the situation clear. "I'll be making inquiries and I'd appreciate your understanding, if not your cooperation."

"Out!"

Ruso grabbed his wife and shoved her out of harm's way again. The inkpot flew past his ear and exploded against the wall, narrowly missing one of the veteran guards.

Maybe Pertinax wasn't mellowing after all.

17

THEY MADE THEIR way out to the late-afternoon warmth
without speaking. As Ruso crossed the terrace to the garden
steps he mused that the view from Pertinax's house didn't seem so
fine now. The sparkling river was inappropriately cheerful and the
sparrows squabbling in the hedge seemed to be mocking him. What
sort of insensitive fool hoped to persuade a bereaved father to see
reason?

Tilla paused to pluck a dead rose from the rambler that had been
trained along the wooden terrace railings. "There are weeds in the
flower beds," she observed. Now he looked, he saw that the little
ornamental hedges between the beds were straggly and in need of
a trim. He supposed the gardens had been Serena's domain: once a
joy, now another reminder and a burden.

Tilla said, "I am sorry about telling him—"

"It doesn't matter," he told her. "He'd already guessed that we
know where Valens is."

"But if he has us followed—"

"He won't have the resources to follow me, you, and Albanus."
At least, he hoped not.

The gate in the wall below them creaked open and a stranger began to make his way up the steps. The man was breathing heavily and his face had an unhealthy pallor. He was taller and balder than Pertinax, but that nose was unmistakable. They waited on the terrace to let him pass, and his nod of greeting turned into the involuntary jolt of a cough. He struggled to draw breath as the coughing fit threatened to overwhelm him. Finally he turned aside to spit into a cloth.

Ruso said, "Gaius Petreius Ruso, sir. Are you Serena's uncle Catus?"

The man grunted. "My brother said you would turn up." He made them sound about as welcome as a fly laying eggs on his dinner.

"I served under your brother in the Twentieth, sir. My wife and I knew Serena well. We grieve for her."

Catus nodded and lifted an unsteady hand to wipe his brow. "A terrible loss," he said. "I doubt my brother will ever recover." His voice trailed away into silence and he swayed alarmingly. His face was like chalk.

Ruso and Tilla grabbed an arm each. "Sir, I think you need to sit down." They led him to a wooden bench scattered with rose petals. "Just sit down and try to breathe normally. Any pain in the chest at all?" There was not, but the man was alarmingly thin and Ruso was fairly certain he had glimpsed a spatter of red on the cloth. "It's a warm day to be hurrying up steps."

The man had to fight a fresh fit of coughing before he could say, "Don't patronize me, son. I was your age once. Walked the—length of the Augusta—aqueduct in an afternoon." A pause for a tentative breath. "Can't get up my own garden now."

There were footsteps behind them, accompanied by a jingle of metal. A tall red-haired woman had come out of the house. The blue plaid tunic suggested she was a native; the keys at her belt said she held authority. She seated herself beside the engineer, put a hand on his shoulder, and said in Latin that leaned toward the local accent, "You look weary, Catus. Is there anything I can do?"

Ruso felt Tilla's boot pressing onto his toes and realized he was staring. Surely this woman could not be the notorious Gleva?

"He needs water," he told her.

She said, "Who are you?"

Ruso gave her his name. Adding the words *I'm a doctor* did not work its usual magic.

"I hope you're not the one who's been upsetting Pertinax."

If she really was Gleva, then Tilla must surely be amazed too. He had wondered vaguely what sort of woman might want to take on Pertinax, but nowhere in his imaginings had he considered the flame-haired dancing priestess from last night's parade.

Tilla said, "We have not come to upset anyone. We are here to grieve and to help."

"I'm a doctor," he repeated, hoping his shock had not been too obvious. "This man needs some fresh water."

The bald head lifted slightly. "I'll be all right. You can all stop fussing."

The hand resting on Catus's shoulder was almost as big as Ruso's own. "Of course you are all right," the woman agreed. "Are these people bothering you?"

Catus said, "Not as much as you are."

The priestess got to her feet. "These are very difficult days," she observed to no one in particular. "I will tell the staff to bring water. Try not to upset him."

When she had gone, Catus said, "Wretched woman. Everyone's gone mad." A pink petal drifted down and landed on his arm. He stared at it as if he were too tired to brush it away. "A terrible loss," he repeated. "Two young lives ruined."

Ruso said, "I'm told the missing man was your assistant."

"Terentius. Fine lad. Good engineer." The man paused as if he could feel another cough rising, then carried on. "Only had to tell him something once," he said. "I suppose you're here to defend the husband."

"I'm trying to find out what happened, sir. Anything you can tell me would be helpful."

A murmur of "Sir?" heralded the arrival of Pertinax's aged houseboy with the water. Catus took a long draft and sat cradling the cup with both hands, staring at the weeds peeping between the flagstones of the terrace. His breathing had steadied now. "She was a sensible girl, Serena. Thought almost like a man. Not silly like some of them."

Ruso said, "It must have been very upsetting to find her, sir."

"You're wasting your time, Doctor."

Not wanting to push further, Ruso waited.

"It's no good you trying to stir it all up again. My brother's taking it to the governor. If you want to do something useful, hand over that murdering husband of hers for trial."

"But—"

"I suppose he thinks I didn't see him there that night."

Ruso said, "Valens?"

"Prowling around the courtyard. I saw the knife in his hand."

"*Valens?*"

Catus paused to clear his throat. "I would have said something," he said. "But it was dark, and I thought I was alone there with him. He'd just had an argument with my niece. I didn't want trouble."

"You saw Valens in the temple courtyard with a knife? The night Serena died?"

"Did I not make myself clear?"

"Did you see Serena or Terentius there too?"

"I told you, I thought I was alone with him. Not much sense asking questions if you don't listen to the answers."

"What made you think it was Valens, sir?"

But the man's interest had drifted to his niece. "I won't say she wasn't headstrong. Took after her father. He should have been firmer with her. He should never have let her marry that idiot. What sort of father marries his daughter off to a doctor? Might as well take her to the theater and offer her to the actors."

Ruso, who had witnessed the courtship, said, "I don't think your brother had much say in it, sir."

"If I'd said something to him, they might both still be alive."

If only . . . Ruso suspected he would be hearing a lot of that over the next few days.

Tilla said, "He was unlucky you were there at that very moment to see him, sir."

Catus grunted assent. "Only went across to make sure the sandbags were doing their job around the drain."

Tilla said, "What do you put sandbags round the drain for?" as if she was genuinely interested.

"High tide after heavy rain," he explained. "You get the river flooding back up the drain into the bath and you've got a terrible mess."

"It must be a lot of work," Tilla sounded impressed.

Catus grunted again. "Nobody notices what engineers do till it goes wrong."

Now that Tilla had neatly established what Catus himself was doing in the courtyard at night, Ruso said, "I don't understand how you knew it was him in the dark, sir."

"It was him. That bath oil. Smelled it on him at the house."

Tilla said, "Bath oil?"

"Terentius wouldn't have stood a chance," Catus continued. "Good lad, but never had weapons training. No good for the legions. Deaf in one ear."

The man was right: Ruso had sat on many recruitment panels as medical assessor and none would have passed Terentius as fit for training unless someone higher up had overruled them. A legionary needed to be able to hear orders from all directions. So an attacker who knew which side to approach him from would have had the advantage of surprise. But the idea of Valens prowling about in the dark with a knife was ridiculous. Besides, if Terentius had been a victim, where was his body? It was much more likely that he was a killer on the run. And this man might be able to help track him down. "Sir, Terentius could be safe somewhere. We could help you look for him."

"Utter waste. All that time I spent teaching him. All that work he did. All the plans. And now he's gone, and they want to blame him for murdering my niece."

" 'They'?" Ruso had not realized he might have allies in seeking to accuse Terentius.

"Bad for business to make a fuss. Blame the lad who can't be found." He leaned sideways and spat on the ground. "Cowards."

"Who's blaming him, sir?"

"Cowards, every one of them. His whole life was here. He could have had a future."

Not if he were caught and convicted of murdering Serena. And then there was that business of the veterans' failed building project over behind the temple complex—the one Terentius had been involved in. The one that had allegedly upset the gods and must have cost the investors dearly. No wonder the young man was nowhere to be found.

"Sir, the building work at the other spring . . ."

"All wrong, right from the start. I told them they'd have trouble with that land, but nobody wanted to listen. They should have hired another architect, not left it all to the youngster."

"Did Terentius get the blame?"

"I told him, 'Never mind, my lad, you'll learn from it. You can still step into my shoes when I retire.' Course, he had a lot of daft ideas of his own about water levels and draining the silt out of the spring. I told him, 'That'll never work,' but who knows? He might have been right."

Tilla said, "You must miss him terribly, sir."

Catus was shaking his head slowly from side to side. "I won't find another lad like that to follow me on. It's too late now."

Ruso said, "Where do you think he is, sir?"

"They're sending me a replacement from Londinium. Have to start all over again with some feller nobody's ever heard of."

Tilla said, "Maybe Terentius saw the knife too, sir, and decided to keep away from it." She seemed to realize that she had inadvertently conceded that Valens might have been armed, and hastened to add, "Perhaps the person who killed Serena is someone else that none of us knows about."

"Hmph."

She said, "We will gladly help you to look for Terentius."

"You won't find him now. He's long gone."

"He could tell us exactly what happened."

Catus put the cup down, lowered his head, and grunted with the effort of pushing himself up from the bench. "The last thing Serena's boys ever need to know," he said, "is exactly what happened to their mother."

Ruso stood beside him. "Sir," he said, "if your brother insists on bringing an accusation against Valens, the lawyers will tear the whole story apart in front of everyone. Word will get around. If we can find Terentius, he can talk to the governor in private and we might be able to spare the boys from the worst of the trial." Even as he said it, he was shocked to realize how easily he had abandoned one of the basic principles of civilized society: that trials should be held in public.

"None of it will bring my niece back."

"What do you think would be best for her children, sir?"

Catus shook his head. "It's my brother's decision, not mine. He's hiring the lawyer."

"But he is wrong!" put in Tilla before Ruso could ask who the lawyer was.

"My brother respects the law." Catus paused to grab the cup and drain the last of the water. "Your friend will be accused in public in front of the governor. I shall say what I saw. The boys . . ." He paused. "The boys will have to live with what their father did."

Somehow, despite making a totally misguided accusation, Pertinax had ended up on the moral high ground here. Ruso said, "Sir, if you could—"

"A lesser man than my brother would take vengeance into his own hands."

Before Ruso could reply, there was a crash behind them as the door was flung back against the wall, and Pertinax roared, "I told you to get out of my house and out of my family's business!"

For a moment Ruso froze. Then he looked more carefully at the aging grandfather with one leg missing who was tottering toward them, calling for his staff to "throw that pair off our property!" and for his brother not to say another word, and realized that what he felt was more pity than fear.

If only Valens could say the same.

18

WELL!" SAID TILLA, hauling open the gate that was there to stop stray animals from wandering up the path to the cemetery. "Gleva was not what I was expecting."

Her husband, cradling the jug of wine they had just bought, lifted the gate back into place with his free hand and dropped the rope over the post. "Perhaps that woman's not Gleva. Perhaps she's just . . ."

"Just what?"

"I don't know," he confessed.

"Are you sure she was the same person you saw in the parade?"

He said, "How many six-foot redheads do you think there are in a town this size?"

"She might be a sister, or a cousin."

"It was her."

From Virana's description she had thought this Gleva must be a person of no importance who was seeking to raise herself, but what was it Virana had said about her wanting to annoy the high priest? The idea of a priestess attaching herself to the leader of the veterans made some sort of sense. A powerful woman seeking influence might well knock aside someone like Serena who stood in her path, and who better than a priestess to understand the power of a curse?

"The question is," he said, "why does Pertinax fall for it? She's not unattractive, but you'd think he would go for a woman who knows her place and won't embarrass him."

"Virana says she is using a love potion."

The snort told her what he thought of that.

"What, then? You are the one who cannot understand a man wanting a woman who does not know her place."

"I didn't mean—"

"If not a love potion, then what?"

He said, "You think I know what's in the mind of Pertinax?"

"He is a man," she pointed out. "So are you."

He thought about it for a moment. "I imagine she fusses over him," he said. "She makes him feel important."

"Oh. And does he not wonder why?"

"Why would he care? She's probably sensational in bed."

She wondered if he could tell how Gleva was in bed from looking at her, or if it was just a guess. There was no point in asking: He would just say whatever he thought would cause the least trouble.

If only a woman could, just for one day, look out at the world through the eyes of a man.

He said suddenly, "I wish I'd known who she was when I was talking to her brother."

Only when she said "Her brother?" did he tell her about the man who had invited him to bathe in one of the sacred springs.

How could anyone forget a thing like that? With some unease she asked, "You did go in, yes?" and was relieved to hear that he had. To refuse the invitation would have been a great insult.

She paused to pick some white bindweed flowers from the hedge beside the path. "What is his name and his people?"

"Brecc. I never found out much about the people."

That was the first thing a Briton would have asked. Then, no matter how far apart their homelands, they would have tried to find something or someone in common. Perhaps a well-traveled horse trader, famous for spotting winners with his one eye. Perhaps a local man who had once visited the borderlands and brought back a wife, or a fresh scar, or a bad joke. But this Roman from Gaul, no matter what tongue he spoke, could not offer any of the sort of connections that would make him truly accepted amongst the local tribes. Which made being invited into the pool even more of an honor than he could ever understand.

"This must be it," he said.

The grass around the tomb had been trampled by recent visitors. Pausing to stand beside him, Tilla gazed at the square little house built of the local honey-colored stone. Its tiled roof was barely higher than her own shoulder. The studded oak door was just big enough to admit a funeral urn. Above the door was a blank space, waiting for a carving or a slab that would speak everlasting words to honor the dead.

The sun was low now, and her feet were chilly in the shadow of the tomb. Almost without thinking, she stepped back. "We should look at the others. Just to make sure."

They walked along the row of tombs that lined the road, serenaded by the warble of an evening blackbird. There were three more little houses, two with low walls around them as if the dead had their own gardens. There were tall square pillars, and simple stones set in the ground, and several wooden posts, and many more mounds with no other marker. All the letters on the memorials spoke unfamiliar names.

"I have been thinking," said Tilla. "What if Serena took her own life? Is that not the sort of thing honorable Roman wives are supposed to do when they are in trouble over a man?"

He stared at her. "Unless somebody saw her do it, we'll never know."

"Perhaps there is a knife lying under the water with all the coins and the curses."

"Perhaps there is," he agreed. "But I can't see anyone dredging the pool to find it. And besides, it could have been thrown in by the murderer."

"Or it could be a gift from someone asking help from Sulis Minerva."

"A knife?"

"Our people leave precious gifts underwater for the gods to find," she assured him. "If you really want to honor a god, why give rubbish like brass coins and lumps of lead with writing on them?"

"If you really want to honor a god," he said, "why not spend your money on a temple everyone can see, instead of throwing your valuables into a bog?"

He was clearly so pleased with this answer that she decided not to argue.

A string of pack ponies was ambling along the road toward them, and the native boy sitting on the lead pony nodded a greeting. "We are looking for the tomb of our friend," Tilla told him in his own tongue. "She was called Serena."

"Sorry." The boy shrugged. "I can't read either. You'd have to ask somebody from town."

The stone of the final memorial glowed golden in the last rays of the sun. Tilla mouthed the letters to herself, making out,

To the spirits of the dead
L VALERIUS FORTUNATUS,
who lived fifty-three years
Centurion in the II Augusta
This memorial was placed by his freedmen.

She supposed Fortunatus had no family here to remember him. The older soldiers would have left their relatives behind across the sea, and not all of them made new families here. Not all of them would have met someone like herself or Virana, or been powerful enough to tempt a Gleva, and there were still many tribes where few people would mourn a lost soldier.

"It's not that one," said her husband, who sometimes forgot that she could read for herself now.

"It must be the little house with no name," she agreed.

Serena had an unfinished tomb but she did at least share the glorious view down over the valley to the river and the hills beyond. It was not, perhaps, such a bad place for your ashes to rest. Although Tilla did not know why, once you were safely in the next world, you would care very much where your ashes lay.

There had been a time when she would have been sure of what happened to lost friends. She would have known how to honor them. But instead of becoming clearer as she grew older, her understanding of the next world had become less certain. Especially since she had begun mixing with foreigners.

Now she knelt on the crushed grass in front of the little house, laying down the bindweed bells she had picked on the way up the hill, and felt lost and helpless. Her husband wandered around the tomb with the wine jug, peering at the roof. "I can't see anywhere to pour it, can you?"

Since neither of them could see a special opening, he knelt beside her on the grass with the jug still full.

She said, "You should say something."

"Me?"

"This is your people's custom, not mine."

He cleared his throat and seemed to be trying to remember the words. After much thought, he said, "We have traveled many miles over land and sea to bring you these small offerings, Serena. You were cruelly taken from us, and we grieve for you. Hail and farewell."

She waited for more, but instead he ran a thin stream of wine into the grass outside the oak door and then walked around, encircling the house with the offering. When all the wine had soaked away, he joined her again and sat back on his heels. She expected him to say something else, but he seemed to have finished. It did not seem very much to mark a whole life that had been snatched away.

She said, "May the gods grant you a safe journey and a happy life in the next world, Serena." Then she sat back beside her husband in the shadow of the tomb.

The sun was nearing the end of his day's journey now, and a breeze shivered through the grass. Tilla wondered what it was like to live in the next world, and whether you knew what was happening in this one or whether you needed to be told. If you did not know, it would be very annoying to have visitors who only came to say good-bye and then sat around looking respectfully miserable. "Your boys are well, sister," she said. "We saw them this afternoon. Their grandfather is looking after them and Albanus has come back to teach them, and they are very pleased to see him. While we were there I took some of the dead heads off your roses. I think everyone is too busy to look after them." She paused, wondering what to say next. She was not going to worry Serena by talking about the redheaded woman who now carried the keys of Pertinax's house. "Virana's new baby is not in this world yet," she said, "but Mara is crawling now and she is starting to learn to speak."

Casting around for more news, it struck her that there was something any murdered person would want to hear. "Your father

wants justice for you, and so do we. We are trying to find out what
happened. If there is any way you can tell us who did this to you,
we are listening."

They waited in silence for a word, or a sign. But if Serena spoke,
it was in the warble of the blackbird, and in the cold wind moving
through the grass. Tongues that mortals could not interpret.

She felt her husband's hand on her arm. "We have to go now,"
she told Serena, "but we will come back and see you."

She sat for a moment longer in case there was a reply. Then they
both got to their feet and, without consulting each other, stepped
backward, still facing the silent tomb with the white bells of bindweed outside the door. Without water, the flowers would be brown
and dead by morning.

On the way down the hill, Tilla picked at the grass seeds that
had caught in the fine wool of her wrap and said, "I feel sorrow for
Serena's father."

"The whole thing is a mess."

"He has lost his child and he is in the clutches of that Gleva, who
cannot be trusted. And now we have come to trouble him."

"As he said, we're just like all the rest of them."

"But we are not," she said. "Because Valens and Serena are our
friends."

She heard a growing rumble and squeak of wheels and the clop
of hooves on the hillside above them. They paused to watch an official carriage speed past, swaying with the bumps in the road. She
said, "How long before the governor gets here?"

He said, "With luck, Pertinax won't get an audience with him
until after the feast of Sulis Minerva. That's happening the day after
tomorrow."

It was not long enough. She said, "The man Serena's uncle saw
with the knife. He could be somebody else who used the same bath
oil as Valens."

"He may not have existed at all. But we can't prove that."

"It was a strange thing to make up. I will ask Virana. She was in
the oil shop when Valens came to town."

"The trouble is, with both of them having served in the same
legion, Pertinax will have plenty of dirt for his lawyer to sling at
Valens in his speech."

"It is not a crime to be a neglectful husband and to flirt with lots of other women," she pointed out. "What the lawyer needs to show to your governor is that Valens is the person who killed Serena."

"From what I hear of court cases, that's not how it works."

She frowned. "How else can it work?"

"The art, as I understand it, is to give a speech making Valens sound like such a monster that everyone believes he's guilty of killing Serena and probably half a dozen other people as well."

Tilla shook her head. Romans were sadly muddled in their thinking. No wonder they had to write down all their laws and then pay men to argue over them. "If Valens does not go to the trial," she said, "will this man still make his horrible speech?"

"If Valens doesn't turn up for the trial, I imagine the governor will assume that he's guilty and he's exiled himself. He'll never get the boys back."

As they made slow progress down the path that threaded between the houses to the main street, she said, "Do you think Serena's father really believes Valens did it? Or is he saying that so he can keep the boys?"

"As long as I've known Pertinax, he's always said exactly what he meant. It's a wonder he got promoted as high as he did."

They turned right into the street and headed back toward the temple and the baths. Her husband glanced behind him a couple of times and then pulled her into an alleyway and made her wait with him, listening. After a few moments he was satisfied that Pertinax had not yet sent anyone to follow them.

She said, "Gleva is big and strong. She could have killed Serena to get her out of the way."

He paused to consider it, and then said, "If she did, what happened to the boyfriend?"

"I know," Tilla agreed. "Gleva should be the one, but if she was, the rest of it makes no sense."

19

BACK AT THE courtyard the sound of chanting was drifting out through the archway. Ruso glanced in to see five or six barefoot figures dressed in white being escorted up the temple steps. Tonight's complement of sick and injured, he supposed, preparing to sleep in the presence of the goddess, her attendants, and her holy dogs, and hoping for a miracle.

When they reached the Mercury, Tilla went straight upstairs to make sure Mara and Neena were settling in. Ruso slipped into the Traveler's Repose next door under the cover of the dusk and ran up the stairs to see Valens and Esico.

Safely in the room of the still-unshaven Valens, Ruso sent Esico next door to borrow a mirror from Tilla and instructed him to pick up food from the bar on the way back.

As soon as the door was shut, Valens said, "Do I really have to have him? It's bad enough being stuck in here without having an audience."

"You do," Ruso told him. "I can't be in and out of here all the time. Pertinax is threatening to have me followed to find you. Esico can bring you whatever you need and he can take messages."

"It would help if he had more Latin. I have to say everything three times and even then he looks clueless."

"You can teach each other." It always surprised Ruso how many years his comrades could spend in Britannia without picking up the language. Still, he supposed, if you had a Roman wife instead of one who came with a host of stubbornly monolingual relatives, and who insisted on speaking to your daughter in her native tongue unless you were there . . . He opened the door to make sure there was no one listening outside, then held it shut. "Now, quickly, while he's out: Tell me exactly what happened with Serena."

"Again?"

"Start from earlier. Tilla's got some ideas about this woman who's moved in with Pertinax. Is it true she and Serena were enemies?"

"Gleva." Valens sighed. "I knew nothing about her till Serena wrote to say her pa was entranced by some mad native priestess who was after his money. Serena couldn't get any sense into him so she wanted me to come and talk to him. But I'd only just wangled the posting to Isca and I couldn't get the leave. Besides, I'm the last person he'd listen to."

"So you didn't come."

"You sound just like—" Valens stopped and took a long breath. "I didn't simply ignore her," he said. "I wrote and explained why I wasn't coming and told her not to worry, it was probably just a passing affair and he'd get over it. I mean, can you imagine Pertinax turning up at a centurions' dinner with some wild dancing barbarian on his arm?"

Ruso could not. Serena, on the other hand, must have been able to picture it clearly enough to beg for help. "What did she say when you told her you weren't coming?"

"There wasn't much she *could* say, was there? She suggested I should write him a letter."

"And did you?"

Valens shifted uncomfortably. "I gave it quite a lot of thought. But do you seriously believe anything I said would make the slightest difference to Pertinax?"

It might have made a difference to Serena, but no doubt Valens had worked that out for himself by now.

"Anyway, I didn't hear another thing until I got this one." He groped under the mattress and produced a thin slice of wood folded in two.

Ruso carried the letter across to the lamp and peered at the neat script.

Serena to Valens

Husband, I had hoped to see you in person but as you are unable to take leave I have to tell you in a letter that I wish to discuss divorce. Our marriage has been a disappointment to us both and as we rarely spend time together I do not expect that its ending will be a matter of great sorrow to you, nor even of great surprise. As you are not in a suitable situation to look after the boys I suggest you allow them to carry on living with me as before. I am sure we can make arrangements for you to visit them so little will change.

I wish you the best of health.

Underneath, squashed into the remaining space, was the sentence *My father will be writing to you about return of the dowry.*

Ruso said, "So then you came to see her."

"I managed to get three days. Came straight across as soon as I could get a boat."

Valens's ship had docked at Abona, and, like Ruso, he had hired a horse as the quickest means of reaching Aquae Sulis. He had arrived late in the afternoon, snatched a quick cleanup at the baths, and hurried to Pertinax's house. Pertinax, to his relief, was out at a Veterans' Association meeting.

"So, what happened?"

"Well, I spent some time with the boys, of course. Then Albanus took them off for lessons. After that, I think they went out for a walk."

That confirmed what Albanus had already said.

"I've only seen them once since then," Valens continued. "At the funeral, with Pertinax standing over them like a guard dog."

"Was anyone else there at the house? That night, I mean."

Valens thought about it for a moment. "The other staff, I suppose. I'm not sure who they have at the moment. Oh, and her uncle was around, but he didn't stay. He lives there too."

"Tell me about the argument you had with Serena."

"Do I have to? It's not really relevant."

"Do you want an argument with me as well?"

Valens lay back on the mattress and put his hands behind his head. "I thought there was a chance to get her to see some sense," he said, "till I found out that the reason she wanted the divorce wasn't my fault at all." His head lifted. "While I was off on the emperor's service—"

"You don't have to make the speech to me. I'm not the governor."

The head went back down. "I want you to make it clear we were only living apart because I was doing my duty."

"Me?"

"Well, you'll be defending me, won't you?"

It had not occurred to Ruso that Valens was expecting him to be an advocate as well as an investigator. "Who's Pertinax's lawyer?"

"Some silver-tongued crocodile from Londinium, apparently. I've no idea what the name is."

This did not sound good.

"Pertinax told me about him after the funeral. I think he was hoping to frighten me into confessing. He said admitting my guilt would save the boys from all the upset of a long trial."

Each side was threatening the other with how terrible the effect of a legal battle might be upon the boys, but neither was willing to back down in order to spare them.

"Don't look so worried, Ruso. You'll have this all sorted out by the time he gets here, I'm sure."

Ruso cleared his throat, and decided not to think about the consequences if the sorting-out didn't go as well as Valens seemed to expect. "Go back to the argument."

"What I was going to say," Valens continued, "was that this chap had promised Serena that if she were single he would marry her. So I said, 'But you aren't single,' and she said she might as well be, and . . . oh, you know how these things go."

Ruso, whose first marriage had been even less of a success than that of Valens and Serena, had a fair idea.

"Apparently I'd failed some sort of test by not supporting her over the business of her father and the madwoman. To be honest, I thought that was a bit rich, under the circumstances. Of course now I regret saying what I said. But at the time—well, wouldn't you be annoyed? Whatever you think of this Gleva, at least Pertinax is a single man. He's free to canoodle with whoever he likes."

They both paused as a board creaked in the corridor outside. Then they heard a door click shut. Ruso checked outside again, then sat on the floor with his back against the doorjamb. "Then what happened?"

"Is all this really relevant?"

"I don't know."

Valens lifted one leg and crossed it over the other. "I can't really remember what order it was all in," he said. "I know we talked about the boys. She wanted to keep them with her and I said no, and she said that my wanting to take them showed how little I really cared about them." He looked up. "We would have worked something out, obviously. *No* was just the sort of thing anyone would say in the heat of the moment."

"I know."

"I think that was when she said she was going out." His voice thickened. "I asked if she was meeting this Terentius and she told me to mind my own business. So I told her she shouldn't go out alone just as it was getting dark, and she said—" He paused, pulled himself up to sit against the wall, and continued. "She said she was always alone, and it was too late to start running around after her now."

It was true, but the words must have been painful to hear and even worse to recall.

"I wanted to go with her," Valens said. "I wanted to meet him man-to-man. But she begged me to stay out of it and not make a scene." He paused to pull the blanket straight. "I knew where he worked, of course. So I decided I'd think about it overnight and confront him in the morning, without her around."

"She went out on her own? None of the staff went with her?"

"Apparently not."

Ruso said, "And after she'd gone, what did you do?"

"Obviously I couldn't stay in the house. I came here to the Repose and I sat in the bar downstairs. Just me and a large jug of fairly indifferent Rhodian. And then someone came running in, shouting about a fire, so I thought I'd abandon the wine and go and see if I could help."

Ruso said, "And you didn't see Serena after she left the house?"

Valens fingered a stain on the corner of the blanket. "The next time I saw my wife," he said, "was when they called me in to do a postmortem examination."

"They asked you? Or you told them you would do it?"

"Does it matter?"

"It might."

Valens put the blanket down. "To be honest, I can't recall. I can remember not wanting to do it. But then I couldn't bear the thought of anyone else doing it, either."

There were no words that would help. Ruso didn't even try.

"It was obvious they weren't going to let me get involved with planning the funeral, so it was the last thing I could do for her."

A final, sad token of respect. A major tactical mistake. Ruso said, "Tell me what you found."

"A single knife wound. Not much to see on the surface but it was something long and thin that penetrated the heart. Judging from the angle, it was done by somebody right-handed. As Terentius was, I'm told."

So were most people, and military training added to their numbers. You couldn't have men in formation wielding swords in whichever hand they chose. "Anything else?"

"There was nothing else suspicious that I could see." Valens cleared his throat. "No sign of self-defense, no cuts or bruising to the hands or forearms, that sort of thing. But she'd been in that water for some time. You can imagine."

Ruso, who didn't want to imagine, said nothing.

"My wife was stabbed"—the voice was flat—"and she must have seen the man who did it; but as far as I could tell, she didn't resist. So either he took her by surprise, or she knew him."

The strains of a popular song floated up the stairs. Down in the bar, people were enjoying a jolly evening.

Ruso said, "Perhaps whoever it was—"

"Terentius. Who else?"

"But why?"

"I've been thinking about that a lot," said Valens, leaning back against the wall. "I think she must have changed her mind when I said she couldn't keep the boys. She didn't tell me because she was too angry, but I think she went to tell him that it was over. And I left her to deal with it on her own."

Ruso was reminded of his conversation with Serena's uncle: *I would have said something . . . I didn't want trouble . . .* And with the young woman at the bar by the vanished Little Eagle: *If I'd done something different . . .* "You couldn't have known what would happen."

Valens said, "There are rare moments when I find that a useful thought."

Ruso adjusted his position and decided that when Esico reappeared he would send him around any unlocked rooms to scavenge some furniture. This sitting on the floor was ridiculous. "I'm stiff," he observed, easing his shoulders. "Dragging all that luggage about. I'll go for a massage tomorrow. Is there anyone you'd recommend?"

But there was not: Valens did not live here and had only nipped over to the baths for a quick cleanup before the day of his visit turned into a disaster.

"Yes, I heard you smelled of bath oil when you arrived at Serena's."

"Who told you that?"

"I've been making inquiries, as you asked me to."

"It smelled all right in the bottle," Valens observed. "Young Virana was very excited about it. Hot off the delivery boat and the latest thing. Which it probably is if you're her age. What's the matter?"

Ruso lifted his head from his hands and eyed his friend for a moment in the lamplight. "I've traveled hundreds of miles to get here," he said. "Albanus has done the journey twice. My family took the risk of being drowned at sea, and we all did it willingly because you said you needed help."

"I'm more than grateful to you. I'm hugely indebted. I wish I could offer you a decent place to stay, but you see how it is."

Ruso was aware of footsteps on the stairs. "That's the problem," he said. "I *don't* see how it is."

The footsteps stopped, and someone with exquisitely bad timing knocked on the door. Ruso called, "Just a moment!" and turned back to Valens. "I thought I saw," he said, "but now I don't know what to believe."

Before Valens could answer, there was another knock at the door and Esico's voice called, "It is food and . . . the other thing, sir!"

When the lad entered, Valens helped himself to the mirror—for which Esico had forgotten the Latin already—and scowled at his beard. Ruso peered at the contents of the two bowls on the tray. "What is it?"

The bony shoulders rose toward the large ears. "I wait in a line. I ask for food. This is what they give."

Esico had forgotten to fetch anything to drink, which was a good reason to send him back down the stairs immediately for wine and a water jug.

When he was gone, Valens sat up straight. "So. What don't you understand?"

"After the argument, you came here and sat drinking mediocre Rhodian."

"Yes."

"And you don't know where Serena went."

"I assume she went to the temple courtyard."

"What makes you think that?"

"Well, that's where they found her, isn't it? It's right next to Terentius's workplace." He paused. "It would be a good place to meet him after dark."

"Was there anyone else there?"

"No, only—" Valens stopped. Then, very softly, he said, "You bastard."

For a moment neither of them spoke. Then he said, "I didn't do it, Ruso."

"So you said."

"I thought you were my friend."

Ruso said, "You thought I would believe everything you told me."

"I swear, on the lives of my children, I never touched her!"

"You followed her, didn't you? You followed her to see where she went and who she met."

"I followed her to make sure she was safe!"

"Then why—" Ruso scrambled up and stood over his friend. "Why wasn't she safe? What else haven't you told me?"

"Nothing!" Valens was up now, standing eye to eye with him. "She went into the temple courtyard. She hung about under the portico near the spring. That evil bastard turned up. I watched them for a bit and then—"

"And then what?"

"And then, to my eternal regret, I went away."

"You *went away*?"

"Yes!" Valens lowered his voice. "She was always complaining that I never did what she asked. This time I thought I should try."

"I see." Ruso wished he could believe it. "Was Terentius armed?"

"I don't know. It was dark under the portico."

"What about you?"

"Me?" Valens put a hand on his own chest as if he needed to clarify who Ruso was talking about. "We're wasting time here, Ruso. You need to be going after Terentius."

"Were you armed?"

"Talk to the people who know him. Find out if there's anywhere he would go. Ask if any of the temple staff know anything. Come on, man. You've done this sort of thing before. You know what to do much better than I do."

"So when you followed her you didn't take a weapon with you?"

The dark eyes met Ruso's own, offering an expression of outraged innocence. Ruso grabbed his friend by the shoulders, yanked him forward, and crashed his head back into the wall plaster. "Just tell me the truth!"

Valens rested against the wall, staring at him in apparent amazement. Blood was oozing from a bitten lower lip. Ruso stepped back, breathing heavily. "Well?"

Valens wiped his mouth with his fist and examined the smear of blood. "I told you the truth," he said. "I saw them and I walked away. That's it."

"Other people might believe that." Ruso kept his voice as steady as he could. He had the feeling that if he once lost control, he would not know where to stop. "I've known you too long. You were seen in the courtyard with a drawn knife. You're not the sort of man to walk around with weaponry on display just in case somebody shouts 'Boo' from the shadows."

"Who told you I was armed?"

"Never mind."

"Bloody Catus. He'd say anything to back up his brother. The veterans were meeting in a bar, you know. Find out how much he'd had to drink."

Ruso deliberately unclenched his fists. He took a step backward. "That's it," he said softly. "I came to help. I thought you deserved it. I thought Serena deserved it. But I think her father's managing pretty well on his own." Under his hand the door latch snapped up like the crack of a whip.

"All right!" Valens called him back. "I'm sorry. I haven't been thinking clearly. Please, Ruso, don't—"

"Show me the knife."

Valens sank into a crouch and ferreted under the mattress again. This time he handed over a full-sized military dagger with a decorated scabbard and heavy hilt. "Do you know I could legally have killed Terentius if I'd caught him in my house?"

"He wasn't in your house."

"But I bet he'd been in Pertinax's."

Ruso slid the dagger out of its sheath and turned the blade so it glinted in the lamplight. It was long enough to run a man through from front to back.

"Legally speaking," Valens continued, "if Pertinax caught them together in his house, he could have put them both to death. His married daughter and her seducer."

Ruso stared at him. "You're not suggesting that's what happened?"

"Of course not. But it wasn't me, either. Look at that blade. Any wound from that would be twice the size of the one I found."

Ruso put the knife away and handed it back to Valens. "Who else saw Serena's injuries?"

Valens swallowed. "Her family laid her out. But I didn't lie."

"You know you should never have done the postmortem. What were you thinking?"

"I *wasn't* thinking! Would you be thinking if something like that happened to Tilla?"

Ruso conceded that he would not.

"You need to go after the boyfriend."

"I will. But I need to know exactly what I'm up against."

Valens pressed the back of his fist against his lower lip again and glanced down to check that the bleeding had stopped. "I had the knife out because I was afraid if he saw me, he'd go for me," he confessed. "But they were too busy kissing to notice anybody else. And then I heard footsteps, and I thought, *This is madness.*" He lifted the dagger. "So I put this away and hid until whoever it was had gone. And I went to get drunk instead. That's the truth."

"You didn't approach Serena or Terentius?"

"I swear, they never knew I was there."

Ruso said, "Why didn't you say that in the first place?"

Valens shoved the knife back under the mattress. "Because I knew even you wouldn't believe me."

20

RUSO SAT WITH his elbows propped on his knees and his feet dangling from the bench. He could feel his head sagging lower and lower but could not summon the energy to raise it. His dry lips tasted of salt. He was vaguely aware of the sweat trickling down his forehead and dripping from the end of his nose. He wished somebody would bring him a drink, but asking would mean lifting his head and taking a deep breath of scalding air, and he could not be bothered.

The wooden bath sandal slid off his left foot and hit the tiles with an irritating clatter. It had landed sideways and he stared at it, considering the angle at which he would have to bend his foot in order to get the sandal back on without burning himself on the hot floor. Perhaps he should stretch his foot out now and try to flip the sandal upright. But perhaps instead of flipping over as he intended, it would slide across the floor, out of reach. Then he would have to hop across on the other sandal to pick it up. Best to do nothing. Leave it for later.

He knew he should get up and clear his head in the cold plunge, but it was all too much effort.

Besides, if he got up, it would be the first step to going back to the room at the Mercury, and Tilla would be there, and there would be questions. She would be full of ideas and expect him to comment on them. She would be trying to work out who had really killed Serena, and he didn't want to have to tell her that it might be better not to know.

He had come into the hot room for some solitude, in order to think. But other late bathers had insisted on clumping in and out and talking just for the sake of making noise, and when they weren't talking they were grunting and complaining about the heat, and sitting next to him, and saying hello. As if he looked like someone who wanted to engage in conversation.

Three of them—or it might have been more; he didn't look beyond the feet within his line of vision—had lumbered in and sat comparing ailments. Each seemed determined to prove that he had a more serious and intractable complaint than the man before. None of them had a good word to say about the expensive doctors who had failed to cure them. Each was now enjoying the benefits of a detailed personal prescription from the goddess herself.

How, exactly, did the goddess communicate the words *figs in goats' fat*? Or *boil together pepper, wax pitch, and olive oil*? Ruso was on the verge of asking when her patients left and some off-duty legionaries arrived and sat bemoaning the loss of their comrades. They were convinced the natives had set the fire at the inn. One of them declared that the natives' choice of a woman for a priest was downright provocation, and someone else pointed out that they'd deliberately picked one that reminded everybody of Boudica, and they all agreed that it shouldn't be allowed. Somebody ought to do something about it before that lot took over again and had everyone living in mud huts and murdering each other. When some bold soul in the corner piped up that Aquae Sulis was a place of peace and reconciliation, one of the soldiers agreed that nobody wanted trouble, "but if they keep starting it, they'll have to take what's coming."

Ordinarily Ruso might have felt obliged to slip some challenging question into the conversation, but at the moment he was no longer sure what he thought about anything.

And now there was a voice saying, "Sir?"

He ignored it, but instead of going away it said more loudly, "Sir?" and when he didn't respond, its owner had the nerve to tap him on the shoulder. "Sir?"

"I'm busy."

"Sir, are you feeling all right?"

"I'm fine."

"You look a bit warm, sir. Let me help you to the other room."

Ruso pushed away the proffered arm. "I'm fine. I'm thinking."

To his relief the attendant said, "Very good, sir. Just call if you need us," and retreated.

Ruso lifted a corner of the towel he was sitting on, dabbed at the drip on the end of his nose, and discovered to his annoyance that the towel would not stretch far enough to wipe his forehead even though he sagged forward to the point of overbalancing. He considered lifting his backside off the bench to release more towel, but that was too much bother. He let the linen drop and wiped his forehead with one sticky arm.

One sandal on.

Valens had murdered his wife. He, Ruso, the man sitting in the bathhouse, staring at his feet, was a gullible fool.

One sandal off.

Valens hadn't murdered his wife. He, Ruso, the man sitting in the luxury of the bathhouse while Valens was trapped in a dingy room apart from his family and in fear for his life, was a traitor.

Valens had definitely lied to him, though. He had lied about following Serena, and he had tried to lie about carrying a knife. There was no way of avoiding it. All you could do was speculate on the reasons. And the trouble was, Tilla would want to speculate. At length. Whereas he himself . . .

He licked his lips again, savoring the salt. He didn't want to have to think about it, let alone talk.

"Sir, the baths are closing in a moment."

He wanted to sit here all night, staring at his feet and pretending Serena wasn't dead: just somewhere else. In a world where none of it had happened.

"Sir, are you feeling all right?"

"No," he said, stretching out one foot to retrieve the sandal. "No, I'm not."

21

Ruso crouched down behind the stack of crates in the backyard of the Traveler's Repose and thanked the gods that Kunaris relied on the heavy bar across his gate and not on a guard dog. The landlord probably didn't expect intruders to stand on an empty barrel in the yard of the Mercury next door and scramble over the wall. But then, when Ruso had decided on this plan just before dinner, it hadn't occurred to him that the back door of the Repose would be left open on a fine night. Now he just had to trust that the vision of anyone glancing out into the yard would not have adjusted to the dark.

From where he was hiding, he was close enough to hear the clatter of crockery and the hiss of hot fat from the kitchen. A silhouette appeared in the doorway. Ruso peered through a gap between the crates, hoping to see either Valens or the gangling form of Esico. Instead it was something far more solid, which swiftly resolved itself into a burly bar slave with an amphora resting on one shoulder. The slave walked straight past him. There was a loud crack and a clatter at the far end of the yard. He must have dumped the empty container on the pile by the gate.

The crates only hid Ruso from people standing at the kitchen end of the yard, not from anyone approaching from the alleyway. But there was no time to climb back over the wall, so he stayed motionless, hood pulled down and cloaked arm up to cover the pallor of his face. The footsteps came back toward him. The man stopped. He was almost within touching distance. He smelled of fried onions. From beneath the hood Ruso could see only half the figure, and it was hard to tell which direction he was looking in.

Fortune was kind: The night was not as clear as it had been earlier, and thin clouds had veiled the moon. Ruso heard a faint scuffle close by and forced himself to stay still as something—a mouse? a rat?—ran over his foot and scuttled away. It was just as well Tilla wasn't here.

The man grunted, appeared to stretch, then paused to scratch his crotch before going on his way. Ruso let his breath escape at last and eased himself into a more comfortable position before straining again to hear what was going on indoors. They were taking longer than he had expected, but he heard nothing that would suggest a wanted man had been apprehended while making his way from the stairs to the back door.

Valens couldn't have mistaken the message, because—rather than trust Esico's Latin—Ruso had scrawled it on a wax tablet.

I think the Mercury is being watched. Will be waiting for you in the yard of the Repose at the start of the third hour of the night. Use the back door and cover yourself up. We're going for a walk.

There was nothing to do but wait and hope that if Pertinax had someone stationed in the alleyway at the back of the Mercury, he—or she—was no better than the very obvious spy he had placed at the front. Admittedly Pertinax was not known for his guile, but he could surely have done better than that scruffy native pretending to be asleep over his tankard of beer while glancing up every time someone came or went. There was something familiar about him too: Ruso was almost certain he'd seen the man before, even though he couldn't remember where. The old centurion really was losing his touch. Unless, of course, the native was a decoy and the real spy was someone else . . .

No. Pertinax was never that subtle.

More movement at the door. Ruso put one eye up to the gap between the crates and was relieved to see two familiar shapes emerge into the yard. The pallor above Valens's cloak suggested he had shaved off the beard. Esico was carrying a traveling bag. When they drew closer Ruso pulled both his companions back against the wall, out of sight of the open door, and hissed to Esico, "What have you got there?"

Valens answered: "My things."

Ruso was baffled. "We're not going on holiday."

"I'm not leaving them behind!"

"You'll be back in half an hour."

"What?"

Ruso rammed an elbow into his friend's ribs. "Keep your voice down."

Valens lowered his voice but was still indignant. "I thought you were getting me out!"

"I *said*," Ruso hissed in his ear, "we were going for a walk."

"I thought you meant—"

"We'll have to dump the bag by the gate."

"I'm not dumping my things for someone to—"

"Nobody's going to check the rubbish heap in the dark. Now, shut up and let's go."

"Where?"

"Out. Esico, leave everything there."

Moments later they had lifted the bar on the gate and were striding three abreast toward the temple courtyard. Ruso's reasoning proved correct: The few people who were out in the street to witness their approach were more concerned with keeping out of their way than with getting close enough to identify any of them. Just in case, he led his companions past the arch, round a few unnecessary corners, and in and out of shadows. Only the one main entrance to the courtyard would be open and he wasn't going to use it until he was certain they wouldn't be followed and trapped.

Safely inside and under the colonnade, he led them into a dark corner where they could hide and watch for anyone else moving about. The perpetual trickle of Sulis Minerva's hot water overflowing from the sacred spring sounded louder than it had in daylight. Out in the open, he could make out the pale rectangle that must be the main altar, and above it the silhouette of the temple looming against the sky. One bright gold streak marked a gap between the doors. Beyond them, the goddess's eternally burning lamp must be illuminating the hopeful sleepers and their attendants. He thought he detected a whiff of incense.

Thicker clouds drifted across the moon, and the pale shape of the altar faded into its surroundings.

Finally confident they were alone, he said softly, "Right. Esico, keep a lookout. If you see anyone at all, just say *Good evening, sir* loud enough for us to hear. Got that?"

"No, master."

If there was one thing Ruso had successfully managed to teach his superfluous slave, it was that while there were many failings that could be forgiven, pretending you understood instructions when you didn't was not one of them. He translated the order into British. "Got it now?"

"Yes, master."

He drew Valens aside. "I want you to walk me through exactly what happened."

"I don't see how that's going to help. I didn't see anything."

Ruso didn't see how it was going to help, either, but he had no better ideas. "You followed Serena from Pertinax's house," he prompted. "What was she wearing?"

He could hear Valens scratching his head. "Some sort of thin blue drape. It was a warm evening."

"And was she still dressed the same way when they found her?"

"Yes. Is that significant?"

"Too early to say," said Ruso, who didn't know himself. "How light was it?"

"Just the stars," Valens said. "But I didn't need much light. Her sandals had nailed soles. I could hear them clack on the paving. I followed the sound."

"Right," said Ruso. "Good." Like her father, Serena had never been one for subterfuge. "What about your own shoes? Would she have known you were there?"

"I was careful."

"And she walked down the main street?"

"Straight down here from the house and through the arch."

"Alone?"

"Yes."

"And you followed her."

"Yes."

"With the dagger drawn?"

"Of course not. That's illegal."

"Show me exactly where she went."

Valens led him across the open courtyard, past the altar and the pool, and back under the colonnade not far from the side door that led to the baths. He counted off the row of identical stone pillars, each of them broad enough for an average-sized person to hide behind. "It was somewhere here," he murmured, placing one hand on the stone and peering into the shadows. "Near that seat." Ruso thought he could make out a low rectangle near the back wall of the colonnade to his right.

Serena had stood motionless behind a pillar, apparently unaware that her husband was standing three pillars farther along. "Downwind," Valens added. "I knew if she got a whiff of that bloody bath oil, she'd realize I was here."

Before long a man had hurried into the courtyard. Serena waited for a moment, perhaps to make sure it was the person she was expecting, then stepped out from her hiding place and pulled him in under the darkness of the colonnade.

"And you were . . . ?" Ruso prompted.

"I moved a bit to try and see them. I didn't go any closer."

He let Valens run through the whole story without interruption. How he had drawn the knife, how just at that moment he was startled to hear the door of the baths shut, and someone passed behind him and out into the courtyard carrying a lantern. "And that's when I thought, *This is insane.* I put the knife back and I walked away."

"Did you recognize who it was with the lantern?"

"At first I thought it must be one of the priests. Then he coughed and I heard the keys jingling on his belt and I realized it was Catus. I didn't think he'd seen me."

If Catus had been carrying the lantern behind him rather than in front—the only way not to night-blind himself—he might have been able to pick out a figure lurking by the pillar. And if he had come out of the door from the baths, the breeze might have wafted the perfumed oil toward him as he entered. It all made rather more sense than Ruso had been hoping. One thing, however, did not.

"Wait there." He stepped away from Valens and, making his way carefully backward, retreated along the colonnade. When he had counted off three columns he said, "Now go and stand by the wall and stay there." The shape he had been able to pick out only because he knew where it was now vanished completely into the blackness.

He returned to his friend, counting the columns again. As he reached the last one he said, "Where are you?" and the reply of "Here" startled him with its closeness.

"I still can't see you."

He jumped as he felt a hand on his shoulder and the voice said "Here" in his ear.

"Hm."

"What does that mean?"

"You said they were kissing. I'm wondering how you saw that in the dark."

"I didn't," Valens said softly. "I heard them. There was just me and them, and the sound of the water flowing out from the spring. And this frantic whispering. Breathing. Gasping. You'd be amazed how much noise—" He stopped. "I thought how easy it would be to take him. Just slip up behind him, clamp a hand over his mouth, and ram the blade in between the vertebrae. I was just seized by this utter, absolute blind fury. It was as if nothing else mattered. Except to make it stop."

Ruso held his breath.

Valens said, "You said you wanted the truth. This is it. If old Catus hadn't turned up, I would have killed them both."

22

WHOEVER IT WAS managed to open the bedroom door silently, but the rising sound of chatter from the bar gave their arrival away. A glow appeared around the edges of the curtain and a bright spot betrayed a small hole in it that Tilla hadn't noticed earlier. An intruder with a lamp seemed unlikely, but she reached under the pillow and slid out her knife anyway. She strained to hear the click of the latch being dropped, but the noise from downstairs faded with no other sound until the creak of a floorboard. She lifted the bedding, sat up, and planted her bare feet firmly on the floor. Softly, so as not to disturb Mara or Neena sleeping in the adjoining room, she asked, "Is that you?"

The light rose, the curtain shifted, and her husband's head appeared. "Who did you think it was?" His eyes widened as he caught the glint of the knife. She slipped it out of sight again and he sat beside her on the bed. He said, "You could have fastened the door."

"And have you knock and wake Mara?"

He leaned over and kissed her cheek. "Sorry. I didn't expect to be this late." He put the lamp on the trunk beside the bed and undressed, lowering his belt slowly onto the floor so the metal fittings and the strap ends didn't land with a clatter.

"All right?" he asked, the usual prelude to pinching out the lamp.

"All right."

The light died. As he slid under the covers beside her, she wound an arm and a leg around him and wriggled closer, enjoying the warmth of his body. "So. What happened?"

In place of a reply there was a grunt.

"Not good?"

"Not good."

She waited for him to explain, but instead he lay thinking, gently running his thumb across the curve of her shoulder blade. At least, she supposed he was thinking. As the movement of the thumb gradually ceased she began to wonder. It would be very annoying if he were drifting off to sleep after she had made an effort to stay awake for him. She shifted a little farther away to make him less comfortable.

"This is a very strange town," she told him. "Neena went shopping and she says there are lots of bars and places to buy souvenirs and jewelry but it is very hard to find anywhere to buy a cabbage."

Silence. Then, "What did she want a cabbage for?"

So he was listening. "You know what I mean. What happened with Valens?"

"Valens," he said, "has decided to leave town."

"What? Where is he going?"

"I'm not sure he knows."

"It must be better than hiding in a room all the time. He can send us a message when he gets there."

"True."

"It may be for the best. That local man was at the bar across the street until after dark, watching who went in and out of here. I think he got a bit drunk."

"Mm."

"If Valens has told you everything, he is safer somewhere else."

"Mm."

"Has he?"

"I said he could take Esico with him, so he's got someone who can speak to the locals. He'll send him back later."

She pulled herself up on one elbow. "Has Valens told you everything?"

He rolled away from her and lay on his back. "You know, I can remember my father saying that his friends' endearing quirks got more fixed and more annoying as they got older. At the time I thought it was just Pa getting more irritable. But I'm beginning to see what he meant."

"You have had an argument."

"He lied to me, Tilla. I'm his oldest friend, we came all this way, and he lied to me."

"So? Valens lies to everybody."

"Yes, but it never really mattered before."

Surely it had always mattered to Serena? But Valens had been charming and funny and handsome and a good doctor. It seemed that what his wife thought did not count. Now, though, when the truth mattered more than ever before, he had changed his story twice, and the first time only because he had been caught out. Tilla had to agree that it did not sound good. "So, what will happen?"

"If he doesn't come back to face trial, not only will he lose the boys but he'll leave them believing he murdered their mother."

She said very quietly, "Perhaps he did."

When he said, "Imagine growing up with that," she was not sure whether he had heard her or not.

Then he said, "I can't . . . I don't want to believe he did it. But between Valens and the local gossip, I'm not sure what's true and what isn't. I'm beginning to wonder if he knows the difference himself."

"So, if he has run away, do you want to carry on?"

"No," he said. "I want to do a bit of sightseeing, find out what Sulis Minerva does to her patients in that temple, and pretend none of this ever happened."

"And then what will you do?"

"I don't know," he said. "Oh, bugger."

"What?"

"I've just remembered. He's left your mirror behind in his room."

She said, "You can get it in the morning."

"In that place? Someone will have helped themselves."

Before she could stop him, he had slid out of the bed and into the darkness.

23

Faced with explaining to the doorkeeper at the Traveler's Repose that he had just dropped in at this strange hour to collect something from a friend, Ruso realized he probably should have bothered to get fully dressed after all. "I'm staying next door," he reminded the man, adding, "I was here last night."

The man let him pass with a warning to be quick and not disturb any of the other guests, and he helped himself to a lamp from the bracket before he slipped past the late drinkers and padded up the stairs in bare feet.

The latch was stiff, but just as Valens had said, the door was unlocked. Once in, he turned aside to find the lamp bracket. That was why he took his first step into the room without looking, and how he ended up stubbing his toe against something that caused him to swear and almost drop the lamp and lurch down toward his foot, and that was how the assailant who had been hiding behind the door failed to kill him. He felt the rush of air as something swept past, missing him by a fraction of an inch, and stumbled sideways.

He was still sprawled against the wall, weaponless, when the man came at him again, arm raised. Ruso flung the lamp at his face and dived, rolling across the floor and hearing the man yell out in pain.

By the time Ruso was back on his feet, his attacker was out of the door. Ruso hurled himself across the room and raced down the corridor in pursuit. He was almost in grabbing range of the dark cloak when the man swung around. The club in his hand smacked into Ruso's left shoulder. His upper arm exploded in pain, and he went sprawling again.

This time he did not bother to get up. He lay on the bare boards clutching his arm, vaguely aware of feet thundering down the stairs and a lot of shouting. Then someone was standing over him for the second time that day and asking if he was all right.

"Someone just tried to kill me."

"I'm very sorry, sir. We tried to grab him but he got away."

Ruso looked up to see the gray-bearded form of Kunaris leaning over him. "He was waiting in the room."

"Are you badly hurt, sir? Shall we call a doctor?"

"I *am* a doctor," Ruso confessed, flexing the arm gingerly and deciding nothing was broken. "I'll see to it." He grabbed the banister rail with his good arm and hauled himself to his feet. "Did you see who it was?"

The landlord shook his head. "I'll talk to the staff, sir, but I doubt anyone got a good look at him under that hood. I don't know how he got in."

"Probably over the gate and in the back door," Ruso suggested. "The same way my friend got out."

"Are you sure there's nothing we can do for you?"

"I just want to get what I came for and go to bed."

The pain in Ruso's arm was easing slightly as he borrowed another lamp, went into the room, and retrieved Tilla's mirror.

Standing in the doorway, he crouched down and righted the heavy chamber pot he had walked into earlier. Someone at the inn had finally taken the trouble to empty and return it, but instead of bothering to put it back in the corner they had just shoved it back through the open door. And in doing so, they had just saved his life.

24

As usual, Mara woke with the cockerels. Since nobody wanted to play, and Neena had left her safely in her parents' bed while going down to fetch breakfast, she busied herself by trying to burrow under Tilla and then, when Tilla pushed her away, by lifting her father's eyelids as if she wanted to show him what he was missing. Hearing his groan of protest, Tilla sat up and lifted her away from him. They had talked long into the night after the attack, and what with that and waking every time he rolled onto his left arm, he needed the rest. None of that would make any difference to Mara, of course. Babies were relentless.

He was awake and dressed by the time Neena came back. She brought bowls of porridge sweetened with honey, and a message to say the landlord was asking after his health and would like a word with him as soon as possible.

Tilla said, "Perhaps he has found the hooded man." Her husband was flexing his sore arm with a look of serious concentration. "The bruising is coming out now," she told him. "Do you want some more salve on it?"

He shook his head. "I've been thinking. Why didn't he come at me again when he had me cornered?"

Tilla tied a cloth around Mara's neck. "Perhaps he could not see you," she said. "Perhaps he was blinded by the lamp."

"Or he realized that I wasn't the man he wanted." He stepped across to the window and peered through the distortions and bubbles in the thick green glass, then opened it to get a better view. "The old boy's not there this morning."

"Maybe he was just an old man who likes to sit and drink beer."

"Or he's already done his job and sent someone to get rid of Valens."

"I have tried to think how Valens could leave a worse mess behind him," she said, grabbing the spoon that Mara was waving in the air and steering the porridge back in the right direction. "But I can't. Have you decided what to do?"

But all her husband would tell her was that he was going out. His last words as he left were "If Graybeard wants to know where I am, tell him I'm alive and well and I'll see him later."

There was no gray-bearded landlord in sight when Tilla set off for the oil shop, and the old man had not returned to the bar. Perhaps her husband had been right: He had done his job. The trouble was, when you knew there was a secret, everyone looked like a spy.

She forgot all about spies when she heard what Virana had to say.

"Because I can't," Tilla insisted, glad there was no one else in the oil shop so early in the morning. In a town that was sacred to local and Roman alike, there would be many people who understood their tongue. "I can't, not now I've met her. She didn't look anything like I was expecting. She looks . . . she does not look like a woman who chases after men. And she is a priestess."

"I know," Virana said, not looking up from the thin golden stream that was flowing between the lip of the oil jug and the mouth of the glass flask she was holding steady on the counter. "That is how clever she is. Even Serena thought she was all right to start with."

"Well, I still can't put a curse on her. Not until I know for certain that she deserves it."

"But I thought of some good things to say in bed last night! How about: *Make her bones turn to dust and her bowels to water and her blood to slime and*—oh, whoops." Virana redirected the stream of oil back into the flask. "We could say, *Make her never sleep by day nor night.* Do you know how to write it backwards? It is more powerful that way."

"No. Curses are not things to play with."

"How about cursing her limbs and her eyes? We could make all her hair fall out. I bet it's dyed anyway."

"No."

"Well, I don't see what harm it would do." Virana twisted the stopper into the flask and indicated the pool on the counter. "Want some? It's really expensive."

Tilla dabbed some of the spilled oil onto her wrists and decided she had been wise not to tell Virana about the attack on her husband in the rented room the night before. Virana would only be more enthusiastic about the cursing.

Virana paddled a forefinger in the pool and anointed her wrists and inner elbows and the skin behind her ears before wiping up. "My husband likes sandalwood," she explained, clearly still enjoying being able to use the word *husband* even to someone who knew him by name.

Just as Tilla said, "I have to go. I'm meeting Neena with Mara at the baths," a figure briefly blocked the light in the doorway.

"Oh, look!" exclaimed Virana, as if the visitor was a surprise. "Here is the scribe now!"

Tilla found herself face-to-face with a little stranger with inky fingers and a crooked foot. He was clutching a satchel very much like the one Albanus had carried in the days when he was an army clerk.

"I asked him to drop by," said Virana brightly, speaking in Latin, "because you said you wanted some writing done."

Tilla's glare failed to silence her.

"Her friend was murdered," Virana explained to the man, "and she wants to put a curse on the person who did it, and I know you did one for that girl with the frizzy hair when she lost her bracelet and then that slave found it in the drain, so we thought you would be the best person to ask. How much would it cost?"

But already the little man was backing out into the bright morning, explaining that vengeance for murder was beyond his powers. He did not know the right words. They needed to talk to a priest.

"You see?" Tilla hissed, wishing she had never agreed to Virana's suggestion in the first place. Watching the scribe hobble away, she said, "I hope he doesn't talk to anybody."

Virana wrinkled her nose. "They aren't all as stuffy as that one."
She leaned backward and shouted up the stairs, "I have to go and
do a delivery!"

A woman's voice called back, "Another one?"

Virana rolled her eyes and muttered, "Old Misery." Then, louder:
"It is the sandalwood for that rude one with the warts!"

Tilla heard the clump of footsteps coming down the stairs, and
the woman whose rumpled green skirts were gradually appearing
said, "Make sure you come straight back."

"I will!" Virana tucked an aromatic hand around Tilla's arm.
"Shall we go together? It is on your way."

It did not take long to make the delivery to a slave at the door of
the rude one with the warts. As soon as they were outside on the
pavement, Virana said, "Good. That's done. You did bring some
money, didn't you?"

"Why? You are going straight back to the shop."

"I will. As soon as we've finished." She tugged at the arm. "Come
on. I can find us a better scribe."

"No. You must go and work for the Old Misery, and I must go
to the baths."

There were links between Mara and her birth mother that would
never be broken, and that pout was one of them. Finally Virana said,
"Oh, all right, then. Will I see you later?"

"I will come to the shop," Tilla said, hoping her promise might
persuade Virana to stay there.

They were about to head in different directions when a male
voice called, "Ladies?"

A short, wide man draped in priestly white came limping along
the pavement, leaning on his stick. Politeness demanded that he
voice the question, "Are you the ladies from the oil shop?" even
though his nose must have answered it already.

"I am a visitor," Tilla told him, since Virana seemed to be struck
unusually dumb. "My friend works at the shop."

"The ladies who wanted to discuss a delicate matter with a scribe
just now?"

Holy goddess! It had hardly been the space of a dozen breaths,
and this man knew already! Tilla drew herself up to her full height.
"The words we spoke were private."

The man introduced himself as Dorios, chief priest, chief magistrate, and head of the Association of Sulis Minerva. He promised her that the scribe had consulted one person only—himself.

Whatever the Association of Sulis Minerva was, it did not sound good. *Chief magistrate* sounded even worse.

"Perhaps you would join me in the temple courtyard?"

The look in his eye said there was no "perhaps" about it. Virana whispered, "Don't tell my husband about this!" as the priest led them slowly beneath the arch and across the sunlit paving to the stone steps of the temple, where even at that hour the air was heavy with incense and the scent of the late roses on the altar. The stallholders were already selling food and souvenirs, and over in a corner of the courtyard an old woman was throwing crumbs to a flock of squabbling pigeons.

They seated themselves on the steps, the priest with an "Ouf!" as if some air needed to be let out on the way down. Tilla was careful to place herself in between him and Virana, although it would not do much good. She would not be able to catch Virana's words before they reached the ears of the chief magistrate.

"Now," he said, turning to Tilla. "Perhaps you could describe the problem."

"Her friend was murdered," put in Virana, craning around Tilla to speak.

"I am sorry to hear it."

Tilla explained, "Someone said I ought to put a curse on the killer while I am here."

"It was me who—" Virana began, and then, "Ow!" as Tilla's foot pressed on her toes.

"We do not know who did it," Tilla added.

"I do," put in Virana. "I could tell the goddess her name."

"My friend *thinks* she knows," said Tilla, increasing the pressure on Virana's foot. "But she might be wrong."

Virana said, "Oh!" and then, "Yes. We were going to put *whether man or woman, slave or free.* That's what they usually write when they don't know, isn't it?"

The priest tapped his forefinger thoughtfully on the top of his walking stick. "I have to say," he said, "this is very unusual." He went on to tell them, as if they might not know, that murder was a very serious matter. Not a matter for lighthearted accusations. After this, he bent forward as far as he could manage and looked each of them in the eye in turn, perhaps checking for signs of lightheartedness. "What was the name of your friend?"

"It is a private affair," Tilla told him, shuddering at the thought that news of this meeting might get back to her husband. "It happened a long way north of here, among my own people, but I hear Sulis Minerva is very powerful. I just need to know the proper way to do it. I will write it myself."

"She really can write," Virana assured him. "She can read too. She hardly ever gets stuck."

"It is not just a matter of writing."

Tilla said, "Can you suggest someone here who will help us?"

The man sighed. "Really, ladies, I would recommend not doing it at all. Curses are a desperate measure."

Virana said, "But people use them for lost property."

"Ah, yes, the visitors like to bring their private troubles to the goddess while they are here. But murder . . ."

Virana again: "Is the goddess not powerful enough?"

The priest's eyes widened. "The goddess is all-powerful! You see in front of you her eternal miracle with the spring, and everyone will tell you about the many healings that take place here. Just ask the staff up at the temple."

Tilla, who had only ever wanted to know what Gleva was up to and had no intention of dabbling with foreign curses and half-Roman gods, gathered up her skirts. "You are right, sir." She seized Virana by the hand. "I thank you very much for your kind warning. I have changed my mind. Virana, this is a dangerous path and we are not going to follow it."

"But—"

"We have been given good advice. We will stay out of this and not anger the goddess."

As they walked back through the arch, Tilla said, "Are you quite sure Gleva put a curse on Serena?"

"Everyone knows."

"If one person tells a lie and ten people hear it and pass it on, does it make it true?"

Virana looked baffled.

Tilla tried again. "Who told you?"

"Someone in the shop. I can't remember. I don't know why you're cross. I only tried to help."

"I know," she said. "And I thank you. But we need people to trust us so that we can get justice for Valens and the boys. Now that man, who has a lot of powerful friends, thinks we are crazy and dangerous."

But no matter what the priest thought of them, it was possible that Virana was right: that Gleva really had put a curse on Serena, and the priest knew it. They were being warned off because Serena was dead, and the last thing the officials here wanted was any further involvement of the goddess's name in the murky business of an untimely death.

25

M ARA KICKED HER legs in the warm water and smacked the surface with her palms. Her laughter blended with the cries and splashes echoing around the hall from the other bathers. As usual, she was delighted to be free of clothes. Neena too seemed untroubled to be standing waist-deep in water in a public place wearing nothing more than the braid that held her hair in a knot. Only Tilla, sitting on the steps with her feet submerged, was uncomfortable at the thought of shedding her towel, even though this was the women's session. Logic told her the male attendants around the Great Bath had seen it all before, especially that wizened old physician over there prodding a woman's shoulder, but somehow she felt awkward about showing it to them again. Even though the longer she clung to her towel, the sillier she felt.

If Virana's information was right, then Gleva might turn up for her daily bathing session at any moment. On the other hand, nothing would be normal in Pertinax's house these days, and if Gleva was keen to please, then she might be hanging around there, waiting for chances to look helpful.

Mara thrashed her arms and legs about and her dark head vanished in a cloud of spray. Tilla bit back, "Oh, be careful!" because reason told her Neena had a hand underneath. Sure enough, Mara emerged blinking and dripping and looking faintly surprised. Neena pointed her to Tilla and encouraged her to wave. "Very good!" Tilla called. "Good swimming!" even if it did make her own heart race. What was it about watching your child try new things that made you see all the ways the adventure might go horribly wrong? Did all the mothers here live with the same secret dread, never voiced for fear some malicious god might be listening? Perhaps not. Most of them seemed to be enjoying themselves.

She watched as a couple of women entered alongside a girl of perhaps twelve or thirteen who had a twisted leg. The girl made her way across to a pillar, propped her crutches against it, and untied her towel. The woman in the plainer tunic, who must be the servant, stepped forward and offered an arm for support. The girl ignored it. The other woman tried to intervene but the girl flapped an impatient hand at them both. Turning her back on them, she lowered herself awkwardly onto the steps and shuffled down into the water on her bottom.

Whatever fears you had, Tilla decided, it was probably as well not to annoy your child by voicing them. Instead she would toss some coins into the spring later on and ask Sulis Minerva for her protection.

A tall, athletic-looking young woman with black hair and dark skin sauntered into the hall next. Beside her was a girl whose blond curls and generous breasts bounced in time with her step. Each woman had a towel, but neither had chosen to wrap herself in it. The women stepped lightly over the stones in delicate strappy sandals that would have been useless for real walking. This was how Tilla had imagined Gleva to look before she had met her.

Moments later the real Gleva entered the hall. People who had paid no attention to the glamorous naked women stopped what they were doing to watch the tall, powerfully built figure stride along the paving. Gleva was simply dressed in a long pale green tunic belted at the waist with green-and-gold braid. The splendid red hair tumbled in a wild cascade down her back. Tilla wondered what the Romans made of the resemblance to the long-gone and famously red-haired Queen Boudica. Gleva certainly looked like someone who should not be approached lightly. Especially by someone who now felt very overexposed in nothing but a skimpy towel.

Gleva took a towel from one of the attendants and gave him a nod of thanks. He made a respectful bow in return. Tilla realized she was staring and turned her attention to a group of children who were splashing each other. Their shrieks and their guardians' cries of "Stop it!" echoed around the hall. The two naked women had chosen a place on the far side of the bath and sat half-submerged on the steps. Gleva strode past them without a glance and settled herself on a stone bench in an alcove. Perhaps it was the wrong time of the moon for her to go in the water. Although Tilla could not help feeling that whenever Gleva went in, everyone else would find an excuse to get out.

She took a firm grip on the wretched towel and muttered a quick prayer to the goddess for inspiration.

The answer came almost straightaway. A young girl with a deep wicker basket hooked over one arm hurried up to Gleva and looked as if she was saying sorry for being late. The girl put the basket on the bench and scuttled off through a side door, returning with a folding stool that she snapped open and invited Gleva to sit on. She laid the towel around Gleva's shoulders and began to comb through her hair.

Tilla waved to Mara, who wasn't looking, and set off around the pool.

"Excuse me?" She addressed the customer rather than the slave. "We met yesterday, at the house of Centurion Pertinax."

Gleva could have made more effort to make "I remember" sound friendly.

"Tilla." Tilla held out her hand and tried not to imagine the powerful fingers that gripped her own wrapped around a sacrificial knife. Stretching the truth a little, she said, "I was a friend of Serena."

"The wife of her husband's friend," said Gleva.

"Yes." Was that a correction or just an attempt at clarity? Seeking a safer subject, Tilla explained that her own hair had been ruined by the salt air on a long sea voyage, and now it was going frizzy in the steamy bathhouse. Gleva did not take the chance to say politely that it looked fine, so Tilla continued with "I could not help noticing yours. It is very beautiful." She could not help noticing also that there were fine lines around the priestess's mouth, and a weariness about her eyes when she glanced sideways to check Tilla's unkempt curls. Well, it must be tiring making other people nervous all the time.

To Tilla's relief the slave said, "You've got lovely hair yourself, miss! I've got some rosemary oil with lavender in my basket that would be just the thing for you. If you don't mind waiting, I can do you next."

Gleva looked about as pleased as a cornered rat, but the slave had her by the hair and Tilla had the perfect excuse to fetch a stool and sit beside her for a chat.

The priestess's hair was full of tangles and took a long time to comb through. By the time it was done, Tilla was regretting ever starting this.

Getting to speak to Gleva had been easier than she had feared. Getting information from her was not. Switching to the local tongue in the hope of a little more privacy, Tilla tried to soften her by saying how shocked and saddened they were to hear that Serena had died. She said nothing of the attack on her husband the night before, and if Gleva knew of it, she chose not to mention it. Or indeed anything else.

The slave separated out a section of red hair, divided it into three and began to pass one strand swiftly over another to form it into a tight plait.

"Aquae Sulis is a long way from where my people live on the northern border," Tilla continued, wondering if the woman was naturally quiet or just rude, "but we wanted to come and pay our respects."

The hairdresser pinned the first plait roughly into place and began to form a second. At last Gleva spoke again. Since she was tethered to the slave by her own hair, the words "Serena is a very sad loss" were spoken straight ahead to the pool and Tilla could see her face only from the side. Perhaps that was what made it sound as though she did not mean what she was saying.

Tilla shifted position on the stool, pulled the towel tighter, and rubbed her fist into the small of her back to catch a trickle of sweat. She wished she had taken the time to go and get dressed before rushing across. She glanced back over the water and was reassured to see Mara's head beside Neena's. "We are very sorry for Officer

Pertinax's troubles," she said, returning her attention to this difficult woman. "It was my husband who saved his life after the landslide last year." *Saved his life*, she thought, sounded better than *cut his leg off*. "Perhaps you know about that?"

Gleva's "Yes" could mean *Yes* or it could mean *No, and I don't want to hear about it.*

"I am glad to see Serena's boys doing so well."

"As well as can be expected," Gleva told the pool.

"I hear you are helping to look after them," Tilla said. "That is very kind of you."

"Someone has to do it," said Gleva. "Their mother is dead and their grandfather is the only one who truly cares for them."

Tilla bit back the words *You know nothing about it!* "Their father is very fond of them also."

"That is not what Publius says."

For a moment Tilla wondered who this Publius was and why he had any right to speak about Valens's family affairs. Then it dawned on her that even Pertinax must have a first name. Publius. Publius something-or-other Pertinax. The man who struck terror into the hearts of trained killers on the parade ground must once have been a child. It was almost as hard to imagine as this woman from a Southern tribe having the right to use his name as if she were part of the family.

The hairdresser reached for her needle and began to stitch the two plaits together at the nape of Gleva's neck with a length of russet wool in a very Roman fashion. Was Gleva taming her wild hair as part of her plan to lure Pertinax? While it was being done, she sat like a statue, her mouth shut as if she had spoken the last word on the subject of Valens and his children.

Tilla said, "I have known the boys since they were babies, and although Valens can be very annoying, he has never once beaten his wife or been unkind to his children. I have seen how the boys love and respect him. I am sure Serena would want us all to do the best for them that we possibly can."

The hairdresser passed between them. Gleva waited until she had moved out of the way and then said, "It is a shame you are not part of the family. If you were, you would be able to offer help and advice."

Tilla restrained an urge to grab Gleva's remaining loose hair and yank her off the stool. The slave tidied the hair into a roll and removed the temptation.

"All done, mistress," the slave murmured, holding out a mirror. Gleva, now looking more like a Roman wife than a local priestess, approved the front and sides of her hair, patted the back, and paid.

As the hairdresser stashed the money in the purse at her belt, Tilla murmured, "The boys are asking to see their father."

"Then it is a pity he did what he did," Gleva told her.

"But he—"

"Listen to me, woman from the North who calls herself Tilla. I understand that your man is a friend of the husband, and I have seen how loyal the soldiers are to their friends, but this is a family matter."

"But you are not—"

"There is nothing useful you can do here. When you have paid your respects to Serena, you and your man should go home to the border and allow her family to mourn in peace."

Before Tilla could think of an answer, Gleva turned and strode away. Tilla was left sitting on a stool wrapped in a skimpy towel and feeling hot and angry.

Several slaves paused to bow to Gleva as she passed.

Because Gleva was a priestess.

With that thought, Tilla was not hot and angry anymore. Invisible fingers began to slide icicles over her skin.

What if she had read things all wrong? What if Gleva had every reason to be cold? What if, in fact, she had been surprisingly polite?

What if Gleva knew, because her comrade the chief priest had stopped her on the way here to tell her, that Tilla and Virana had planned to put a curse on a woman who had murdered Tilla's friend? And what if she was not fooled by the it-happened-a-long-way-away story? The only woman with a reason to murder Serena was Gleva herself. And now she might put a curse on Tilla and Virana too.

Maybe they should have gone ahead with it and got in first.

26

R USO HAD INTENDED to challenge Pertinax about the attack the night before, but to his frustration the centurion was not at home and the elderly houseboy who opened the door would not say where he had gone. Albanus, who hurried out from the children's room at the sound of Ruso's voice, did not know. He peered at Ruso and said, "Are you all right, sir?"

"No, I'm not. When you see him, tell him I want to talk to him. It's important."

Albanus's "Oh, dear!" could have been sympathy for Ruso but was more likely alarm at the prospect of giving an unwanted message to Pertinax.

It was followed by a reassuring "Don't worry, sirs. I'll do it" from the houseboy, which might have prompted some interesting reflection on the relative status of slave and free in the centurion's household if Ruso had not been more interested in knowing, urgently, who had sent the assassin to the Traveler's Repose.

Unable to confront Pertinax, he went back to the Mercury to talk to the landlord, only to find Kunaris was out. The room upstairs was empty too. According to the chambermaid, Tilla and the others had gone to the baths.

The only person who was where he was expected to be was the old man sitting at the bar table across the road, watching Ruso over his beer. Ruso considered tackling him and then decided not to bother. He would only get entangled in argument and denial, and besides, his bruised arm was aching. The man he needed to find was Pertinax.

He would try Virana. As Valens had pointed out, she was always full of hot gossip, even if much of it wasn't true. If she didn't know where Pertinax was . . . well, this was a small town, and there couldn't be very many men in it with only one leg.

He was passing the entrance to the temple courtyard when a voice called "Sir!" and he turned to see a temple slave hurrying toward him, clutching a bundle of firewood. He recognized the man he had asked about the abandoned sandal—and the missing Terentius— the day before.

The man stopped and bowed.

"Yes?"

"Sir, do I have the honor of addressing Doctor Ruso?"

This was indeed a small town: Evidently word had already got around. Bracing himself for the sort of middle-of-the-street consultation that people seemed to think doctors went looking for, he said, "That's me." But instead of offering an ailment, the man said, "Sir, a message from Chief Priest Dorios. He invites you to speak with him."

Glancing at the firewood, Ruso guessed that the man had paused on an errand to somewhere else, which suggested that his own description must have been circulated to all the temple staff. If that was so, then Dorios must be very keen indeed to talk to him. Since it seemed nobody else was, he said, "Show me where he is."

"Doctor!" exclaimed the chief priest in exactly the same tone as he had exclaimed "Ruso!" the previous day, except that then he had been full of welcome. Today he was overflowing with concern and apology, and looking wearier than before. "Come with me."

Dorios limped across the courtyard, changing course to avoid a meandering family who were too busy cramming their mouths with honey cake to look where they were going. Nearby, a small boy was hanging on to his mother's skirts and wailing that he wanted cake for breakfast like that girl over there. The mother, who was ignoring him, was carrying a painted model of Sulis Minerva that made the goddess look like a frog.

Ushering Ruso to a quiet corner of the courtyard, the priest sank onto the bench and propped his stick against the wall before inquiring after Ruso's arm.

"Nothing's broken," Ruso assured him, pulling up the shoulder of his tunic to show a spectacular display of purple and red of which he was secretly rather proud. Dorios reacted with a pleasing amount of horror and dismay, and—glancing around and clearly hoping no one else had noticed—assured him that nothing like this had ever happened in the town before.

"You've just had a murder," Ruso pointed out.

The priest cleared his throat. "Ah. Yes. But that was very different, Doctor. That was a personal matter. An attack by a stranger on a guest in his own room! I can't begin to say how sorry we are."

Despite this, he had already begun to say how sorry he was several times, and again Ruso said, "Thank you."

"The landlord came straight to me this morning. I'd like to assure you that we're doing all we can to catch the culprit."

"Thank you," repeated Ruso, finding himself reluctant to mention his suspicion that Pertinax was behind the attack.

"I hear you threw a lamp at him. Well done, sir. Well done. A lesser man would never have thought of it."

"I didn't have anything else," Ruso pointed out. "And I should explain that it wasn't my room." There was no need to keep Valens's presence secret anymore. Nor his own purpose in visiting the town. It was hardly fair to leave the locals believing that some random attacker was prowling the inns and assaulting innocent visitors.

When he had explained, the priest said, "So the bereaved husband was hiding in the Traveler's Repose all along! I had no idea."

"He thought his presence there was a secret," Ruso explained. "But apparently it wasn't."

The priest shook his head. "This is very worrying. That particular landlord is usually very discreet. That's one of the reasons we chose to invite the governor to stay at the Mercury."

At least, Ruso reflected, he was no longer dreading the arrival of the governor. Now that Valens had fled, his own skills as a defense lawyer would remain untried. "It might not be the staff at the inn who betrayed my friend," he admitted. "I think it might have been my arrival there that gave him away."

Dorios nodded. "I'm afraid, Doctor, that you may have fallen foul of our rather powerful group of veterans."

"Really? The veterans I've spoken to assure me they respect the law."

"Hm."

Ruso flexed his arm around the bruising and said nothing.

"It's a very sad business," Dorios continued. "Several of us have done our best to resolve it, but we don't seem to be getting anywhere. Centurion Pertinax is determined to prosecute his son-in-law no matter what anyone says to him."

Ruso wished he had confided in this man earlier. He should have realized that Dorios would have a fair grip on the situation. Someone who was both chief priest and chief magistrate would have plenty of sources of information. Reserves of tact too: Dorios had been too polite to mention the disappearance of Ruso's imaginary investor friend, who had melted away in the night.

"The attacker may have bruising or burns on his face, or singed hair or eyebrows," Ruso pointed out. "You could check with anyone who might have been asked to treat him."

Dorios agreed to try but warned that the man might have left town. "Which reminds me . . ." He paused to glare at a slave who had come to remove the dead torch from a nearby bracket. The slave gave a hasty bow and hurried off to work somewhere else.

"Young Terentius," the priest continued. "We've been looking for him ourselves since the night of the murder. We even let it be known—discreetly, of course—that there would be a reward for useful information. To be honest, when I first heard that you were asking for him, I wondered if word had leaked out and you had come here to try and win the reward."

"No. I had no idea." So the slave he had met on his first day here had reported his curiosity about Terentius. That explained the chief priest's eagerness to meet him. The guided tour of the bathhouse had just been an excuse to look him over.

"Can I assume," Dorios continued, "that you had no letter to deliver to Terentius?"

"I made it up," Ruso confessed, relieved to be able to tell the truth at last. "And the investor friend too, I'm afraid. I was trying to be discreet."

"And we do appreciate it, believe me. Although the presence of another investor would have been very welcome." Dorios raised one plump arm to indicate the courtyard in front of them, which was already busier than when Ruso had arrived. "As we discussed: the most important monument in the province. A symbol of peace. But our goddess can only do her work in this place if our visitors choose to come here."

A choice the visitors might already be reconsidering after so many deaths on one night. Any association of the goddess's waters with a murder would deter all but a few ghoulish types who wanted to gawp at the scene of the crime.

"Apart from the family," Ruso said, "how many people know what really happened to Serena?"

Dorios counted them off on his fingers. "Myself; Memor, our haruspex; and the man you met yesterday—Latinus."

The pink-headed man who had looked out of the window and advised Ruso not to bathe in the sacred spring.

"It was Latinus who found the body."

Ruso said, "It must have been hard to keep it quiet."

"It was before dawn when he found her. We closed the court-yard straightaway. Catus harnessed up our own service vehicle himself and took her home while a ceremony of purification was held at the spring." Dorios cleared his throat. "It was all very distressing."

At last, the chance to ask a straight question. "Was there any sign of how she got there? Any blood, anything disturbed or damaged?"

"Nothing at all. A complete mystery." He lowered his voice. "Almost as if the goddess herself . . ."

A divine stabbing was not a possibility Ruso wanted to consider. "I assume you checked that there was nothing else unexpected in the pool?"

"Of course." A flicker of irritation crossed the priest's face. "The pool was drained straighaway to clear the contamination."

"Sorry. I had to ask."

"We told anyone who asked that the drainage was for regular maintenance—it has to be done to clear the silt—and we told everyone that the lady had been found on the temple steps. Of course, it hasn't stopped people spreading all kinds of ill-founded rumors."

"My wife was told that Valens lit the fire and Serena died in it."

"People will believe any kind of nonsense, I'm afraid."

Ruso said, "I haven't told anyone about last night's attack."

Dorios placed a slightly clammy hand over his. "Thank you, Doctor. I can see you understand the difficulty we're in—"

"I can't promise that nobody in the Repose has talked. Whoever it was made a bit of a disturbance in the bar when he ran out."

"Disgraceful," Dorios observed. "We can't have this sort of thing going on. That's why I'm hoping you might be able to help us."

"Help you?"

"We'll provide a couple of guards for your security, of course."

Ruso blinked. "What am I helping you with?"

"With Officer Pertinax."

To Ruso's relief the man removed his hand.

"Is it correct, Doctor, that you've known Pertinax for some years?"

"He was a senior centurion. I was just a medic."

"Even so. You stand a better chance than any of the rest of us."

Ruso said, "To do what?"

"To do what you came here to do. We think it's very unlikely that your friend is guilty of murder. Someone has to persuade the centurion to accept the latest evidence and withdraw his wild accusations."

"I haven't had much luck doing that so far."

"Ah." The priest smiled and leaned back against the stone wall. "That's because we haven't told you about the ring."

27

R USO ACCOMPANIED THE priest across to the sacred spring, where Dorios wished a hearty rather than a friendly "Good morning!" to a couple dallying in an alcove. The girl looked undernourished and her makeup was smudged. The customer groping her was old enough to be her grandfather.

"Really!" Dorios muttered as he unlocked the side door of the bath suite. "People do all sorts of things on holiday that they would never consider doing in public at home."

The girl was still writhing against her customer. The shape of the man's hand was roaming about inside her skimpy tunic. Dorios glanced out across the courtyard. Ruso barely caught the subtle twitch of the walking stick that pointed out the offending couple. Two muscular temple slaves with shaven heads emerged from the shade of the colonnade and strode toward them.

"Once you let standards fall," Dorios observed, "you end up attracting the wrong sort of visitors entirely." Without waiting to see the outcome, he led Ruso into the screened-off changing hall and locked the door behind them. "Follow me, please, sir. We don't want to disturb the ladies any more than we can help."

As they entered the steamy bathing hall, Ruso spotted Tilla sitting on the side of the baths, clutching a towel around herself. She was watching Neena and Mara splashing about. He thought of Serena, who must have bathed here regularly. He wanted to say, *Jump in. Enjoy yourself. Make the most of being alive.* Instead he followed the priest across to a side exit that led into a service area. Shutting out the sound of running water and the echoing voices of the morning bathers, Dorios said, "Just down here, now."

The corridor widened to a long storage area lit from above by barred windows empty of glass. Behind a battle-scarred wooden sawhorse Ruso could make out racks crammed with chisels and hammers and plastering tools and masons' equipment. Below them, an untidy collection of shovels and sledgehammers was propped against the wall. Despite the flow of fresh air, many of the tools bore witness to the constant battle with rust in the damp atmosphere.

"The maintenance stores," Dorios explained. "Terentius used to work here with Catus."

Beyond the racks of tools, piles of items that might be useful one day lay under a coating of dust and spiders' webs. Ruso was willing to bet that Catus knew exactly what was there and would be outraged if anyone dared to move it.

"And this is where our bathhouse manager works." Dorios rapped on the door of what appeared to be a shed built against one wall of the stores. "Latinus? A visitor for you."

The door was opened by the pink-headed man.

"Our guest needs to see the ring, Latinus," said Dorios. "He's kindly agreed to help us with our centurion problem, so if you could give him every assistance . . ."

He paused only to wish Ruso well and assure him that any difficulties should be referred straight to himself. "If you're quite sure you don't need one or two of our men, sir . . ."

Not liking the idea of being followed at every turn, Ruso repeated that he didn't need a bodyguard. Reflecting that it was just as well the bath manager was a thin man, he crammed himself up against the very splendid desk in order to shut the door. Latinus forced open a reluctant folding chair for him and slid aside a clutter of writing tablets. Then he reached two fingers into his purse and drew out a silver ring, which he placed on the worn surface of the desk. "This is it, sir."

It was heavier than Ruso had expected. He turned it this way and that, watching the light from the high window catch some sort of engraving in the orange gemstone.

"It's a panther," said Latinus. "Carved into a cornelian."

"And it definitely belonged to Terentius?"

"Yes, sir. I recognized it straightaway, and it's been identified by his landlord as well."

"And the slave was caught trying to sell it?"

"To a visitor. He must have been afraid a local person would recognize it. Fortunately, the visitor was sharp enough to query where a humble bathhouse cleaner had found something so valuable."

As expected, the man had broken down under questioning, but instead of confessing to theft, he had insisted that Terentius had given him the ring on the night of the fire in exchange for help with escaping.

"I'd like to talk to the slave."

Latinus squeezed his way past the desk to have the man summoned. In his absence Ruso slid the ring down to the joint on his third finger, slipped it off again, and pondered how desperate a man would have to be to part with something so valuable.

With the manager back in his seat, Ruso said, "What do you think actually happened on the night of the murder, Latinus?"

The man leaned his bony elbows on the desk. "Most of us, sir, think Terentius attacked the lady and fled. Chief Engineer Catus doesn't agree, of course. He was very fond of Terentius."

"The family all believe it was the husband."

"Yes."

Ruso shifted on the stool. He was beginning to feel sticky: The damp heat of the bath penetrated even in here. "Did Terentius have keys to this place?"

"If he didn't, he knew where they were kept."

Latinus's confirmation that nobody stayed in the baths overnight reinforced Ruso's suspicion that Terentius had been planning a private party somewhere in there with Serena. If it had ever begun, it had been abruptly ended by the news of the fire at the Little Eagle, where they had been seen together. Then something must have happened, the couple had fallen out, and he had killed her and fled town.

Ruso was aware that he was scratching his ear with one forefinger, a gesture his wife insisted meant he was uncertain. The exact nature of the "something" that had happened to change Terentius's attitude to Serena was puzzling. Could she have kissed the man with the passion Valens had described and then rejected him? Did women do that sort of thing? Setting the question aside to ask Tilla later, he said, "There's been no news of him since?"

"We thought he might send someone to collect his things, sir. But they're all still here."

Ruso glanced around. "Here?"

"Outside in the store. Would you like to have a look through? Perhaps you'll notice something we missed."

Back out in the storage area, Latinus reached up to a high shelf and slid a key out from beneath a faintly moldy pair of leather working gloves. "Just here, sir." He knelt and unlocked a wooden chest that had been shoved into a gap between a bulbous oil amphora and some bags of sand. "You won't mind if I stay while you look, sir?"

"Be my guest."

Latinus found a linen rag to wipe away the dust and Ruso cleared a space on the shelf above the chest.

Ruso lifted out a pile of three unremarkable tunics, shook each one flat, refolded it, and placed it up on the shelf. Below them was a toga that had evidently been a nourishing home for a colony of moths. He slid a scroll out of its container, scanned a few lines of the sort of poetry that appealed to amorous young men, and rolled it back up. He spent some time pondering the note tablets, which, as Latinus explained, contained diagrams and numbers and drawings of some improvement that Terentius had been convinced would mean less time lost to business while the spring was being drained and dredged of silt.

"Was he right?"

Latinus gave a sad smile. "Catus was doubtful, sir. But we'll never know."

Ruso was reminded of his own early belief that he would one day surpass his mentor and uncle, Theo, and find a cure for the winter fever that had snatched away his mother. Now he had learned to resign himself to smaller victories. But Terentius would still have been young enough to believe that if he applied enough hard work and determination, he could shape the world to his liking. It was just unfortunate that Terentius's liking had involved somebody else's wife.

Ruso put the cork stopper from a missing jar up on the shelf. It had a slice cut into it, with a copper coin stuck in the gap. Perhaps a reminder of a good party.

Latinus cleared his throat. "Is there anything in particular you're hoping to find, sir?"

Ruso, who didn't want to admit that he had no idea what he was looking for, pretended not to hear. His bruised arm ached as he carried on emptying the trunk and stacking the contents of the trunk on the shelf. A boxwood comb with a couple of short brown hairs caught between the teeth. A broken leather shoelace held together with a reef knot. Various well-worn items of underwear. Two odd socks. A clasp knife with one half of the bone handle missing. In the bottom left-hand corner, a leather bag that chinked when he lifted it. He tipped the money into his palm and slid it back and forth across the calluses formed by a summer of haymaking and harvesting that seemed a hundred years ago. The coins were a mix of silver denarii and copper: probably somewhere near a month's wages. He tipped the money back into the bag, and that went on the shelf too. He was just sniffing a bottle of bath oil—nothing special: Virana had not favored Serena's lover with the latest thing fresh off the boat—when the door from the bathing hall opened and a horribly familiar smell wafted in, followed by a small man who walked with a stoop.

Latinus greeted him with "Have you just walked through the bathing hall?"

"They said you wanted me, master." The man's voice was reedy and he shuffled uncomfortably from one foot to the other.

"You're supposed to use the other entrance."

"I never got that part of the message, master."

Latinus huffed in exasperation and indicated Ruso, who got to his feet and fought the urge to step away from the stink. He had once been compelled to scrub out a sewer. It was a smell you never forgot, and one which was surprisingly hard to wash off.

"This man will ask you some questions, Justus," Latinus told the slave. "Tell him the truth, and don't try to be clever. I'll be listening."

It seemed that, in the midst of all the confusion over the fire, Terentius had come to the slave demanding to know where he could get a boat.

"Why you?"

"I used to work at the wharf, sir."

"And when he came to find you, you were . . . where?"

"Out in the courtyard, sir. Taking some buckets to help with the fire."

"Carry on," said Ruso, keen for the smell to walk away as soon as possible, and wishing the unfortunate man would stop shuffling from foot to foot. The movement must surely be wafting the air about.

"So I took him up there and I found him a nice little skiff and the oars." Justus reached up a grimy hand to scratch his scalp. "It's finding the oars that's the tricky part, sir. Any fool can steal a boat."

"Theft is nothing to be proud of," put in the manager.

"No, master. Then he gave me his ring like he promised and I came away and that's the last I heard of it till morning."

Ruso said, "He didn't say where he was going?"

"There was only one way he could go, sir." The slave paused.

Ruso's "Where?" sounded more irritable than he had intended.

"Downstream, sir. He'd never have made it up against the flow."

Ruso had hoped for more. "Anywhere in particular?"

"He'd have had to change to something bigger by the time he got to Abona, sir. A little skiff like that, he'd be all right on this part of the river, but lower down he'd be Neptune's breakfast."

Ruso said, "How did he seem?"

"How did he seem, sir?" The man risked a glance up at Ruso as if he didn't understand the question.

"Was he flustered? Frightened? Calm? What was he wearing? Was there anything odd about him?"

"There was, sir."

"What was it?"

"He was asking for a boat in the middle of the night, sir."

As an outside door that Ruso had not noticed before banged shut behind the slave, the manager observed, "Not the brightest star in the sky, I'm afraid. No wonder he got caught."

"Has anyone made inquiries at Abona?"

"Nothing turned up, sir."

Ruso crouched down again by the trunk and brought out a thin rectangle of wood on which someone had sketched a few lines in

ink. Whoever it was had captured a likeness of Serena so remarkable that the loss hit him afresh. Finally he managed to say, "Do
you know where he got this?"

"It would be one of the street artists that sets up stall in the temple
courtyard, sir. A lot of the visitors like a souvenir. A painting of
yourself beside a famous landmark. One of them could identify the
style if you're interested."

"No." The sketch was just a slice of wood with soot and glue on
it. It went up on the shelf.

"If there's anything I can do to help, sir . . ."

"No, thanks." He stacked everything back in the trunk. It was
a random collection of items that could have come from the room
of any number of young men. If there had been any clue amongst
them to the whereabouts of Terentius, someone else would already
have found it. On the other hand, no one would willingly have
left that much money behind. It all fitted with the story of a
sudden flight. It wouldn't convince Pertinax, but it was a comfort
to Ruso. Whatever Valens might have felt like doing to Serena
and her lover, he hadn't done it.

Ruso closed the lid and got to his feet. "Thank you," he said.
"You've been a great help."

Before Latinus could reply, the door from the main hall crashed
open. A buxom woman clad in what appeared to be a bedsheet clattered toward them on wooden bathing sandals, complaining that
her clothes had been stolen.

Ruso left to the sound of Latinus assuring her that it must be
some unfortunate confusion and he would order his staff to search
for the clothes immediately.

Making his way back through the main hall toward the exit, he
saw that Tilla had moved to the other side of the pool and was
having her hair done. She still wasn't dressed. He walked out without
her knowing he was there, and reflected how privileged he was to
know exactly what treasures were hidden under that towel.

28

TERENTIUS'S LODGINGS WERE not far from the oil shop where Virana worked. The front held a shop selling lamps and inkpots and little terra-cotta models of shrines and gods and anything else that could be made quickly from a mold and sold for several times what it had cost to create. Ruso knocked on the insignificant door beside it.

Despite assuring himself that he was in no danger from the previous night's attacker, he still glanced both ways down the street and assessed the capabilities of the man strolling toward him. That bundle of fresh torches could be hiding a weapon.

If it was, the weapon wasn't meant for him. The man passed by and carried on up the street. Ruso was about to walk away when he heard the clack of the latch and the door creaked open.

An elderly woman peered up at him. "You're not the doctor."

"No," agreed Ruso, who had found that it was never wise to be a doctor unless he was intending to act like one.

"If you're here about the room, it's been taken."

When he explained that he was in town looking for Terentius, she warmed immediately. "Come in and meet the master. He'll want to see you." The woman shuffled down the corridor, moving from one handhold to another and observing, "Sorry, my dear. I'm not very fast these days."

She led him into a room filled with the sort of clutter that people amass around themselves when mobility is a struggle. Among the jumble of side tables and cups and medicine bottles was a wicker chair piled with blankets. Somewhere in the middle of the blankets—it was hard to tell where the man ended and the bedding began—was a wizened figure with a few strands of white hair combed across a mottled pate. The sight of Ruso occasioned a "Ha!" followed by a puzzled, "He's not the doctor."

The woman grasped the side of the wicker chair and leaned forward to shout, "He's come about Terentius!"

The man cupped a blue-veined hand over one ear. "What's that?"

"Terentius!"

The man frowned. "Tell him he's not here." Then, apparently not trusting her to relay the message, he turned to Ruso. "You're too late. He's gone away."

"He knows!" the woman shouted. "He's a friend. He wants to find him."

"No, we can't find him," the man agreed. Then to Ruso, "We can't find him. Do you know where he's gone?"

"No!" Ruso shook his head and gave an exaggerated shrug.

"Well, what are you here for, then?" the man demanded.

"He's asking if we know where he is!"

"I just said we can't find him!" The man turned back to Ruso. "He's a good boy, Terentius. Used to do jobs around the house, ran errands. We're not as lively as we used to be, you know. She's slowed down and I've stopped altogether. Still, I can see and she can hear. Between us, we're nearly a whole person."

Ruso grinned. Had he been their doctor, these were the sort of patients who would have cheered the heart.

"You're supposed to tell me I'm marvelous for my age," prompted the old man.

Ruso crouched beside the chair and shouted, "What is your age, sir?"

"Too old to remember!" The man's cackle of laughter at his own joke ended in a violent fit of coughing.

Ruso waited for it to pass while the woman grumbled that the silly old fool shouldn't be telling jokes at his age. "Stop making yourself cough!" she yelled. "You'll kill yourself!"

The man flapped a dismissive hand at her. "Agh, what does it matter? All my friends are dead anyway." The hand waved toward a couch strewn with cushions and bandages and a tabby cat Ruso had only just noticed. "Clear that off and sit down, boy."

It was a long time since Ruso had been called "boy." Before disturbing the cat he shouted, "Can you tell me about Terentius, sir? Anywhere he might have gone?"

"Terentius. Nice to see a youngster who loves his job. Always bringing bits of things home to mend, he was."

Golden boy in charge of the bath plug. Everyone except Valens seemed to like Terentius. Ruso shifted a couple of cushions and the cat glowered at him before leaping onto the back of the couch. He sat down in a warm nest of cat hairs.

The man squinted at Ruso. "Soldier, are you?"

"I served with the Twentieth in Deva."

The man tapped his chest. "Centurion with the Third Cohort. Served against the Druids in Mona, marched east to put down Boudica's rabble, helped to take the North and then marched back down again with nothing to show for it. I've seen sights you'll never see, boy, and never want to."

Ruso nodded his respect. Conversation was hard enough without adding unnecessary words. A rough attempt at mathematics suggested the man must be about eighty: a truly remarkable age and perhaps a testimony to the healing properties of Sulis Minerva's water.

"He would have made a good soldier, Terentius, but they wouldn't let him in." The old man pointed at the left side of his head. "Deaf in one ear, see? I used to say to him, I said, 'Two grown men and we've only got one ear between us!'" The cackle was gentler this time. "He was doing well for himself till he met that girl. Married, see? I said to him, 'You be careful. I've seen it before. It don't do to shear another man's sheep.' But he didn't listen, and now look what's happened. Who's going to mend things for us now?"

The couch gave an alarming crack as Ruso shifted his weight forward. The cat shot across the floor in front of him and vanished under the old man's chair. "Did anyone ask you about a ring?"

"What?" The hand rose to cup the ear again.

"Did anyone—"

"Scarpered when the husband turned up. And very wise too. Nasty business. Went off in a boat, they said. Must have been desperate: He was never one for boats. All that water and he still couldn't swim. What's it like in the North these days, then? How's the emperor's wall going? Still changing the plans every new moon?"

Ruso shouted that the Twentieth Legion were set to complete their allotted sections of wall before the Sixth this season, which pleased the old man enormously. When Ruso finally got across that the latest plan was to build the forts along the line of the wall instead of siting them behind it, the man was even happier. "I always said they should have done that in the first place. I told young Terentius that, didn't I?"

The old woman sighed. "I expect so."

Oblivious, the man carried on. "That boy had promise, see? He was doing well for himself here. The lads put him in charge of the new baths. At his age! That's how it was back in my day: If you had the ability, you were given the chance."

Ruso said, "Did anyone ask you about—"

"I never held with all this nonsense about it being his fault when it went wrong. How's the lad supposed to know what's under the ground? I told them, 'When you get to my age, you know every building project goes wrong somewhere or other.' I said, 'Give him a chance to make good.' But who listens to an old man? They were still arguing when that feller runs in shouting, '*Fire!*' I heard that all right. '*Fire!*' "

Ruso yelled, "You were in the veterans' meeting?"

"What?"

Ruso repeated the question.

The old man grinned. "They come and fetch me for all the meetings. There's nobody more veteran than me. And I know a good lad when I see one. Who knows how far he could have risen?"

"That boy did love his work," the old woman confirmed. "You couldn't cross his room for all the plans unrolled on the floor. And the lamp oil he went through!"

Ruso said, "Would you mind if I take a look at the room?"

The old woman leaned over the chair. "He wants to see the room!"

"Look as hard as you like; he's not there," the old man informed him. "Got a retired pay clerk from the Batavians in there now. Pays his rent but never offers to lend a hand." He pointed to the old woman and confided in a loud whisper, "I'm thinking of selling her and buying myself a younger one. One who does what she's told. A nice blond with big—" He cupped his hands around invisible breasts.

"Ha!" retorted the woman, reaching across to straighten his blanket. "Nobody else would put up with a stinky old bugger like you." She turned to Ruso. "You won't touch anything in there, will you?"

"I won't even go inside," he promised, but she shuffled down the corridor in front of him just to make sure. On the way, he ascertained that the last time either of these two had seen Terentius was on the morning before the fire, which moved him no further forward.

The woman paused in a doorway and leaned against it for support while he stood beside her.

Ruso surveyed a good-sized square room with fresh limewash on the walls, another man's boots under the bed, and nothing remarkable about it whatsoever.

"Terentius mended the shutters and painted the walls," put in the woman.

"Did he leave anything behind?"

"We kept his things safe for him, but that silly old fool in there needs the rent. The man from the baths came and collected it all."

"Catus? Or the manager, Latinus?"

"Very glum-faced, he was. Well, he'd just come from his niece's funeral, poor man. At least he wasn't spouting those terrible lies about Terentius. Our boy wouldn't hurt a fly. It was that husband that did it. I hope they catch him and finish him off."

Ruso said, "The plans were on scrolls?"

"Plans? Oh, yes. Right across the floor. A boot on each end to hold them open, so you could fall over those too. I don't know what use they'll be now. That other gloomy one was down here straight after the fire, standing by the spring with his daft hat on, telling everyone the goddess didn't want anyone building there. After they'd all gone, him in there said, 'Well we've had a fire and four people dead and the man in charge has run off. You don't need a white robe and a willy on your head to see the signs weren't good.' "

There had been no scrolls of plans in the possessions Ruso had examined.

She hauled herself upright from the wall and began to lead him back. Outside the door of her master's cluttered den, she paused. "That ring they brought round: That was his all right. His father gave it to him before he died. That's how we know he's run off."

"I'm sorry."

"If you find him, tell him the silly old fool in there misses him, and so do I."

"I will," he promised. But the more he learned, the more reasons it seemed Terentius had to stay firmly unfound.

29

Y OU'VE DONE SOMETHING with your hair," he said, pleased
  with himself for spotting it straight away. "And you smell
very, ah . . ."

"Sandalwood, rosemary, and lavender," Tilla told him, flinging
her bag down on the bed. Neena carried the sleeping Mara across
into the other room and closed the door behind her. "What do you
think? Truly."

He sniffed. "It's a bit strong," he admitted.

"Not the smell, the hair." She twirled around so he could see
the elaborate cap of blond plaits from all angles.

"Very nice," he said, because *I liked it better before* and *Why does it
have to be so complicated?* and *It looks as if your head has shrunk* would
not go down well. "Was it, ah . . ."

"Very expensive," she confirmed, patting the plaits. "It is the style
all the ladies are wearing in Rome."

"Are they?" He tried to remember. Then he tried to think what
the empress's hair had looked like on her visit to Britannia, but all
he could recall was being told that the empress's hair had originally
been grown by somebody else.

"I don't remember anyone looking like this," Tilla admitted. "She asked if I wanted the Sulis Minerva hairstyle with the wavy sides, but I thought it would be like telling everyone I was a visitor."

He was spared the need to comment by Neena, who emerged at that moment, confirmed that Mara was sleeping off her morning swim, and said that she would go out to fetch some lunch. "Something cheap," he told her. "So not from downstairs."

"But not something horrible," Tilla put in. "Ask around about a good snack shop." When she was gone, Tilla went across to the window. "That old man is back."

"I know," he told her. "Perhaps we were wrong about him."

Tilla eased the window open. "Perhaps he is spying for somebody else."

He said, "Everyone must know Valens is gone by now."

"I hope he is looking after Esico."

"Valens? Perhaps he'll decide to take him on."

"Esico would be safer with us," she said. "I am sure we will find something he is good at sooner or later."

There was more to be gained by holding back *I told you so* than by saying it. Esico's presence was a constant reminder of the folly of buying a slave you had no use for, just because your wife felt sorry for a fellow Briton.

"He doesn't wander off very much, really," she continued. "If he had been here he might have saved you last night."

"I managed without him," he pointed out.

"He was very brave defending us from the debt collectors in Rome, and he was very good with my cousin's mule when it was lame. It is not his fault we have no farm for him to work on, and no horses."

"Well, I definitely don't want him in the surgery," he said. "It's discouraging for the patients when the assistant turns the color of old parchment and rushes out to vomit."

"Abdominal surgery was not a good place to start," she said. "Perhaps you should give him another try when he comes back."

"I did," he told her. "He's reasonably competent with anything that doesn't involve blood, but he's not really interested."

"He does not have to be interested. He is a slave. He has to do as he is told."

"I prefer my patients to get the impression that we all care whether they get better or not." He moved across to join her by the window. Pertinax's spy was sipping beer through his straggly gray moustache.

She said, "Will you cheer up if I tell you I think this hair is very silly, and I only had it done so I could talk to Gleva?"

"You had to have your hair done to talk to Gleva?"

"And I found out she is a horrible woman, even if she is sensational in bed."

He said, "I was only speculating."

"Anyway," she continued, ignoring him, "I think Virana is right. Gleva put a curse on Serena. She acts as if she is one of the family already. I think she is the one pushing Pertinax to blame Valens for the murder."

"Just because she's a horrible woman, or for some other reason?"

She said, "If you really do not like the hair, I can pull all the pins out. Neena will have to help me unstitch it."

"The hair's fine," he assured her, knowing better than to admit that he didn't much like it after he had already said it was very nice. That was only storing up trouble for the future. "Tell me about Gleva."

"Virana says if Gleva marries Pertinax and they have a son . . ." Tilla went on to explain a possibility that sounded remarkably like the tales of long-dead empresses maneuvering their own offspring into power above older stepchildren.

"Virana told you this?"

"She says Albanus told her it is what stepmothers do in Rome."

Ruso had often wondered what two such different people as the native farm girl and the ex-legionary son of a Greek teacher found to talk about. It seemed Albanus entertained his young wife on long winter evenings with tales of ancient scandals. When he said, "It's entirely possible," his own wife looked relieved that he had not mocked her.

"It might have been Gleva who ordered the attack last night."

He said, "Perhaps it was Gleva who carried it out. She seems to be responsible for everything else."

She glanced at him. "Are you teasing me?"

"Just a little."

"Well, listen to this. Gleva really has been using a love potion. The hairdresser told me. She could be in lots of trouble."

"This hairdresser doesn't sound very discreet."

"She did not tell me it was Gleva," Tilla explained. "Not right away. I told her my man had lost interest and I wanted something to encourage him."

"Thank you." He could imagine that little morsel being passed on to the girl's next clients as the gossip of the day. It was just as well he wasn't looking for work here as a medic: It was always bad for business when you were seen to seek cures from other people. Even worse when your wife told people it was for a problem with your marital equipment.

"I told her you have lost interest in me because there are lots of other girls here," she added.

"That's better," he said, and then remembered Virana's *He is married to somebody else and so am I* and wondered how long it would be before the two rumors met and bred.

"And she said I ought to be very careful, because you can get into trouble for using that sort of thing."

"On your own husband?"

"I did not tell her that to start with. First of all I just said it was for *my man.*"

"Oh, good. That should fool everyone."

The eagerness of her "Do you think so?" took him by surprise.

He said, "So how did this discussion about my performance get around to Pertinax and the wild redheaded priestess?"

"I thought, *I do not want to make things even worse than they are now by starting a new scandal.*"

"Absolutely not."

"So when she said I could be in trouble, I told her the man was my husband."

"Right."

"And she said she had heard that I need a mixture of linseed with honey and pepper, or boiled turnip root and rocket and leek juice with frankincense, and . . . I think you can do something with cuckoopint. But I have forgotten what."

"Poison me, probably."

"And I said 'Does it work?' and she looked across at where Gleva was talking to somebody and she said, 'Well I hear it works for other people.' So now we know."

"I see," he said. "But what we don't know is whether Gleva really is full of evil intentions or simply an unfriendly woman who's set out to seduce a man with influence. Anyway, while you were at the baths. I found out—"

He was interrupted by a rap on the door that was too loud to be Neena. A voice called, "Visitor for you, sir!" It was swiftly followed by the sound of an uneven and unwelcome gait. Gleva's man with influence was clumping toward them along the landing.

30

THE QUIET CONTROL with which Pertinax shut the bedroom door was more unnerving than if he had slammed it. He had arrived without any henchmen, but Ruso guessed they must be downstairs. "I told you," he said, his glare fixed on Ruso, "to stop pestering my household."

Ruso pulled up the shoulder of his tunic and turned so Pertinax could see the spectacular purple bruising, which had now developed an impressive black patch in the middle. "Any comment?"

"I heard. Nothing to do with me."

"Valens should have been in that room."

"I told you. Not me."

"So if it wasn't you—"

"I'll tell you if I hear anything," Pertinax told him. "My advice is: Keep out of things that don't concern you. And get your woman under control."

Tilla was standing in full view, but the centurion was following the protocol of complaining to her commanding officer.

"I talked with Gleva at the baths this morning," she announced. "Perhaps you would like to get *her* under control. She speaks as if she is one of your family."

Still Pertinax behaved as though she were not in the room. "If you've got something to say," he told Ruso, "you say it to me."

"I just have."

But Pertinax had not finished. "It's a weak man who hides behind his wife."

"And it is a weak woman," declared Tilla, "who sends a man to make an argument for her."

Pertinax's denial that he had ordered the attack had taken Ruso by surprise: The old man had never been one to shirk responsibility. He needed to try a different approach, and Tilla's defense of her wounded dignity was not helping. Placing a hand on his wife's arm, he took a step forward to stand between them. "I've got something else to say too."

The old man's retort of "If she'll let you" was undermined by him losing his balance and having to grab the end of the bed for support.

Ruso leaned down to drag the trunk out from beside the bed. "Take a seat."

The centurion let go of the bedpost and lifted his chin. "I'm not feeble."

"I'm sorry we can't offer better hospitality. Can we fetch you a drink?"

Pertinax eyed him for a moment, then sat stiffly on the trunk. "Say what you've got to say."

Ruso placed himself on the end of the bed so he was still between Tilla and their visitor. He could tell from the way the man cupped one hand around the stump of his amputated leg that it was causing him pain. "There's a truth about what happened to your daughter that needs to be found, sir, and we won't find it by arguing with each other."

"The governor will determine the truth in court."

"He may well do, sir," Ruso conceded. "I believe Valens may have been capable of murdering your daughter and her lover."

He felt the bed shift beneath him as Tilla registered her surprise. Meanwhile it was not anger that Ruso read on the old man's face, nor sorrow. It was relief. And it was curiosity. And then it was gone.

"Valens felt more than the outrage of a cheated husband, sir. I know you don't agree, but I think he was genuinely fond of your daughter. That's why he was so upset when she wrote and asked for a divorce. Then, when he came to your house to see her, she told him about Terentius. There was an argument, and afterwards he followed her down to the temple court and he saw her and Terentius there together."

An elbow dug into his side, accompanied by the murmur of "Husband, are you mad?"

"And when a man sees a beloved wife in the arms of another man, who knows what goes through his mind?"

Pertinax grunted.

"I can see why you believe he was the killer, sir." Ruso paused to let that settle before he began again. "And I think at the time he felt strongly enough to do it. But I've found evidence that suggests he can't possibly be guilty." He was aware of Tilla sitting very still beside him as he left another pause, hopefully long enough to spark Pertinax's curiosity without being so long that it annoyed him. "When Valens saw them alone together," he said, "Serena and Terentius were in the temple courtyard. Catus saw him there, holding a knife. If he was going to attack, that's the time he would have done it. Straight after Catus had gone. But there's another witness who saw Serena and Terentius later on, over at the burning inn. Valens was already at the Traveler's Repose when news came of the fire, and after that he was helping with the injured, so there was no time when he could have attacked Serena. Whatever he felt when he saw them together, sir, he didn't act on it."

"You're wasting your time," Pertinax told him. "They've already tried this nonsense about the witness with me. I told them: I was at the fire. I know what it was like. Madness. I couldn't have told you who else was there, and neither could anybody else."

Ruso swallowed. It hadn't occurred to him that his news might have already reached Pertinax and been dismissed. Still, at least the old man was considering the practicalities of how the murder had been committed. Ruso allowed himself to hope.

"Besides, it doesn't prove a thing," Pertinax said. "Valens could have found my girl later."

"There's also the evidence of the ring," said Ruso, now proceeding with caution. "Have you been told about that?"

Pertinax's grunt gave no clue as to whether he had or not. Ruso was conscious of Tilla sitting very still beside him as he said, "Terentius left town in a tearing hurry that night. He wasn't much of a sailor but he gave a valuable ring to a slave in return for help with stealing a boat in the dark. I'd say that's more than a man trying to dodge an angry husband. That's a desperate man trying to avoid the consequences of murder."

"Or a man who knows what happened," retorted Pertinax, "and is too ashamed to admit he abandoned my girl in the middle of the night." His voice trailed off, then he gathered his thoughts again. "You'll have to try harder than that. If you're wanting me to withdraw the prosecution, you're wasting your time. I suppose that pompous little squirt of a priest put you up to this."

"Sir—"

"And don't you get up on your hind legs again about my grandsons. If it wasn't for them, I'd have tracked their father down and run him through weeks ago. But I won't have them growing up thinking there was any doubt. I want everything done properly. I want his lawyer to have a say in court. I want him tried and found guilty in public. And I'm getting no help from the idiots here." His voice turned to mockery. " 'Beyond our jurisdiction, sir.' 'It won't bring her back, you know.' 'Don't upset yourself, Centurion.' 'Don't upset yourself,' my arse! Did you know they offered me money toward the tomb?"

"I didn't know that, sir."

"I know a bribe when I see one. I said, you're not dealing with some wet-behind-the-ears recruit here. You're dealing with the chief centurion and the camp prefect of the Twentieth Valeria Victrix. My lads died so that you lot could have your hot baths and your fancy oils and your processions, and I'm going to the governor."

No wonder the chief priest had left it to Ruso to present the fresh evidence to Pertinax. Doubtless the trial of a Roman citizen for murder really was way beyond the authority of the local magistrates, but he could understand Pertinax's fury when these pampered officials had tried to buy the family's silence. He thought of the desperate struggles Terentius's ancient landlord had survived. Of the brief but bloody rebellion in the North that followed Hadrian's accession. He had treated many of the casualties himself, and even after the nightmares had faded, he could still be caught unawares by echoes of voices that had fallen silent long before their time.

Pertinax glanced at him. "I suppose you came running down here thinking you'd save your pal from a mad father out for revenge."

"Pretty much, sir," Ruso admitted. He felt as though he had shrunk while the old man was speaking.

"I'll take revenge if I have to. But first I'm asking for justice." Pertinax sat back and surveyed them both. "So. You said yourself he was capable of murder. Where is he?"

"I don't know, sir," Ruso confessed. "He was next door in the Traveler's Repose when I got here, but he left last night."

Pertinax's voice rose to something like its usual volume. "I knew all along where he *was*. I'm asking what you've done with him since."

Ruso blinked. "You admit that you knew?"

"Course I did. Only needed a bit longer with him being too scared to come out, and we'd have made it to the trial. But you had to interfere, and somebody else found out where he was hiding. Whoever had a go at you was trying to finish him off. Where is he?"

"He wouldn't tell me where he was going, sir," said Ruso, trying to adjust his thinking to this new revelation. No wonder Pertinax had been so confident that a trial would take place. "So you can tell your man to leave us alone now."

Pertinax frowned. "What man?"

Tilla said, "The spy sitting at the table across the road."

Pertinax lumbered to his feet and peered out of the window.

Ruso joined him. His attention was caught by a couple of figures meandering toward the river with what looked like a black sheep between them, and a boy trailing along behind. From the way each man was holding on to a horn, it looked as though the sheep was doing the steering. Ruso's experience of sheep rearing with his in-laws had been brief, but even he could see this was not a normal way of going about things.

The spy looked up from his beer to follow the uneven progress of men and animal. "The old boy at the table," Ruso said. "With the moustache. He's been watching the door here off and on since yesterday evening."

"Not on my orders," said Pertinax. "Never seen him before in my life. If I'd sent someone, you wouldn't know he was there."

Tilla said, "Then who is he? How did you know where Valens was? Who attacked my husband?" but Pertinax was already leaving.

Ruso followed him out onto the landing. "Sir, about the business with my wife and—"

"That woman of yours is a troublemaker. Always has been."

"She's concerned that Gleva—"

"None of your business."

"Sir, if Gleva's giving you medicine—"

"Don't be ridiculous. Do I look like a man who needs medicine?"

"You look tired."

"Are you trying to sell me something?"

"No, sir."

"I've got people looking for Valens. If I can't find him in time, there'll be no trial. That should please you."

"The presumption of guilt doesn't please me," Ruso told him. "I'm still looking for Terentius. And Valens might come back."

Pertinax snorted. "I offered him a chance to have his say in court. This is his answer." He lurched toward the door. "Not what I'd planned, but at least this way we can keep the details quiet. All the boys need to know is that he ran off and left them. I'll find him myself, and when I do, I'll deal out justice for my girl." He paused at the top of the stairs and turned to face Ruso. "Are you going to help?"

Ruso took a deep breath. "No, sir," he said, cursing Valens for making him feel like a traitor whatever he did. "I'm sorry for you, but I'm not."

The sound of Pertinax's uneven gait faded away down the stairs. Ruso sat on the bed and bent forward, massaging the back of his neck with both hands. "That didn't go quite the way I'd intended."

Tilla said, "If it was not him who sent that man last night, who was it?"

"I don't know."

"This story about the ring—why did you not tell me?"

"I was going to," he told her, "after we'd finished discussing your hair."

From the next room they could hear Mara making the first experimental calls that announced she was awake. There would be louder protests if nobody responded. He suspected Tilla was relieved to have an excuse to leave.

Alone, he stared at the flattened surface of the bedside rug and wondered if he had been right about anything at all. Nothing had turned out the way he had expected. Until last night he had refused to believe that Valens was capable of murder. But then Valens himself had admitted that he could, and would, have done it if he had not been interrupted. Given enough provocation, Ruso supposed any man would be as capable of killing off the battlefield as on it. Valens's knife did not match the wound he had described, but as the sole medically experienced examiner of the body, Valens could have lied to suit himself.

There were witnesses who'd seen him helping to treat the injured, but at some point he must have gone back to his lodgings at the Repose. Pertinax was right: If Terentius and Serena had separated after they were seen, she could have been wandering alone and unprotected during all the milling about after the fire. Valens had denied attacking her, but Valens had lied before. Now he had fled, and although Ruso could never share Pertinax's view of him, he was beginning to understand it. He could see why the old centurion might have sent an assassin last night.

The trouble was, he hadn't. So who had tried to kill Valens?

And then there was this business of Terentius and the boat. It was hard to see what would induce a man who couldn't swim to risk his life on the river in the dark. But perhaps Ruso had been too eager to interpret his dangerous flight as a sign of guilt. Terentius had stepped into someone else's marriage. He had taken on a major building project that his mentor had refused to touch. He was not a man who was averse to taking risks.

The door to the annex opened and a small head appeared at just above floor level. "Here she is!" announced Tilla brightly.

He leaned down and patted the rug. "Come to Pa," he invited, glad to have something simpler to think about.

"Pa!" Mara set off at an enthusiastic crawl, only to come to a sudden and apparently puzzling halt as she knelt on her own tunic. Tilla bent down and lifted her up by her hands, and the rest of the distance was covered in a sort of floating dance as Mara raised each knee in succession while her mother carried her across the floor.

"Clever girl," he told her.

Tilla lifted her higher and handed her over. "Hold her up."

He lowered her onto his knee, winced at the sudden feeling of cold, and lifted her off again. "She's wet."

"I know," said Tilla, deftly untying the soggy cloths and reaching under the bed. "Let's show your Pa how you sit on the pot like a big girl!"

The big girl seemed less interested in showing Pa anything than in staring at her mother's hair.

Tilla patted the tangle of braids. "I don't think she likes it, either."

"It's fine," said Ruso, hoping his wife would soon dismantle it of her own accord.

From inside the cupboard where the cloths were stored, Tilla said, "Did you really think you could make Pertinax change his mind?"

"I thought—" He stopped. "I should have known better." For a mad moment he had hoped that, by conceding the possibility of Valens's guilt, he might engage Pertinax in a joint search for the truth. It had looked—briefly—as though he might succeed. Instead, he had handed over a gift to the prosecution: *Even the best friend of the accused says he is capable of murder!*

On reflection, the only time Pertinax had ever been known to change his mind was halfway up a landslide when he was too weak to argue. Now Ruso had been given a sharp reminder that Serena's father was far less of a blustering old fool than he looked.

Cloth in hand, Tilla leaned sideways against the window to gaze along the street. "Neena is here with the lunch."

"At last."

She turned away from the window and laid the cloth on the bed to fold it. "There is something very wrong in that man's house," she said. "I am worried about those little boys."

"I know," he agreed. "But he's right: It's none of our business."

"Then we must find somebody whose business it is," she said.

31

IT WAS FOOLISH to feel responsible for a married woman who was soon to become a mother for the second time, but Tilla could not push away the thought that if she did not go across to the oil shop as she had promised, then Virana would find some excuse to desert her post and turn up at the Mercury, and sooner or later surely the Old Misery's patience would run out.

The old man glanced up from his beer as she stepped out into the street, and for a moment their eyes met. She looked away, feeling her cheeks flush, and reminded herself that there was no way the nosy old drunk could know that they had mistaken him for a spy.

Still, whatever his reasons, he was definitely watching her. Rather than walk past and give him a better view, she turned right and set off down the narrow street toward the river. She would take the long way around to the oil shop, following the path that led past the stable and along by the riverside vegetable plots.

Ahead of her she was surprised to see the men who had been walking on either side of the black ewe. A meandering line of trampled plants led to where they were now standing in the middle of a lettuce patch while the ewe lay at their feet, its head raised as it gazed around with mild interest at the view. Surely livestock should be chased out of vegetable plots, not allowed to lie in them and mangle the crop? It was such an odd sight that Tilla paused to watch. The ewe stretched out its neck and took a mouthful of lettuce.

She was wondering what the gardener would make of it when she heard footsteps behind her and a gruff voice told her "Move along please, miss" on the grounds that this was private business. She murmured an apology and walked on, wondering what sort of private business they could possibly be carrying out. It must be some sort of ceremony, but it seemed an odd time of year to be doing it. Normal people would either ask the gods to bless their planting before they put the seeds in or give thanks after they had taken off the harvest. Normal people would not let a sheep squash the lettuce before the family had a chance to pick and eat it.

Dismissing yet another strange Roman custom from her mind, she made her way toward the oil shop, pondering the far more important problem of how to approach the only person who could help her to keep the boys safe.

If only Valens had waited, the way forward would have been much simpler than her husband seemed to think. At least, as long as he had survived the mysterious assassin. The safest place for the boys would be with their father. If she could have found some way to persuade Albanus to take them out of Pertinax's house, Valens could have collected them, and the remains of the shattered little family could all have fled together. Of course, there would have been a fuss about Valens's return to military service after his absence without leave, but Valens was good at charming his way out of awkward places. Even if his charm had failed, he could have changed his name, gone to some other part of the empire and started again. People did these things. She had more or less done it herself. Once a slave with a name the Romans could not pronounce: now Tilla, respectable wife of a former legionary medical officer.

Turning left into the street that led to the oil shop, she pushed aside the thought that Valens might have begun his fresh start already and left his boys behind.

If only he had waited, he could have taken them with him. No doubt he would have had to knock Albanus on the head and tie him up, so it would look as though the tutor had been overpowered trying to defend the boys, but Albanus would forgive him. Valens was an old comrade, and old comrades stuck together like bull's glue. Which was why she had been amazed to hear her husband say, in front of Serena's father, that Valens was capable of murder.

Whatever complicated plan he'd had in mind at the time, it had gone wrong. Then he had tried to warn Pertinax about Gleva, but he had failed there too: It was plain that the old man had no idea what she was really like and would not hear a word spoken against her.

Now, with their father gone, the boys would have to stay with their grandfather, under the same roof as Gleva. Albanus would have to be prepared to whisk them away at the first sign of danger, and then . . . She was not sure what would happen then. Some family would have to take them in and hide them from Pertinax, and the chances of persuading her husband that they should be that family were very slim indeed.

Still, it was no use worrying about that now. Needing a safe home for the boys was a long way further down the road, and much could change before they got there. Perhaps Valens would reappear. Perhaps Pertinax would change his mind. Or die of old age. Or perhaps Gleva would tire of him and curse him too, and he would die of something else. None of these things was under Tilla's control. For now, all she could do was warn Albanus.

Two local girls were busy choosing sponges from the basketful on display by the shop entrance, squeezing them tight in their fists and then watching them expand. Tilla stepped into the scented gloom and leaned across the counter. That way, no one could hear her ask whether Virana had warned her husband yet that Gleva might be a danger to the boys.

Virana had not, but she would do it as soon as he came home. "I will tell him you said so."

"That won't help," Tilla told her. "Tell him my husband said so."

"Did he?"

"I have already spoken to him about it."

"That's all right, then," said Virana, and carried on wiping the counter.

Tilla envied the girl her lack of concern. She tried to reassure herself that, yes, it really was all right. She had indeed spoken to her husband about it. That had not gone well, but only because she had explained it badly. Or perhaps he had not been listening. If he had understood properly, he would surely never have said that the safety of Valens's family was none of their business. And in any case, he could not feel very strongly about staying out of it, because when she had said, *We must find someone whose business it is*, he had not objected. How could he? Everyone wanted what was best for the boys. And it was plain that what was best for them was to protect them from Gleva. So when a familiar voice greeted Virana from the doorway and Virana cried, "Husband!" and then, "See? You can tell him yourself!" Tilla knew she must take a deep breath, muster all the persuasion she could manage, and explain to Albanus that they needed to make a plan.

32

RUSO WAS STRETCHED out on a couch having his back trampled by a small elephant when a slave in the red-trimmed tunic of the temple staff appeared at eye level and explained that his master would like a word. Ruso held up the hand on the end of the arm that didn't hurt, and the masseur made a final attempt to crush his kidneys before pausing.

A summons to the chief priest was the perfect excuse to abandon the couch before the masseur had finished testing his resolve not to howl in pain. Easing himself upright, he answered the man's "How was that for you, sir?" with "Remarkable!"

Remarkable was turning out to be a useful word in Aquae Sulis.

He followed the slave into the main bathing hall, padding barefoot along paving that was slick with other bathers' wet footprints. The slave led him past a scribe and a snack vendor and a wizened doctor with a queue of patients to the corner of the pool opposite the entrance. He looked down at a pale round head and a bony brown one bobbing on the rippling surface, like buoys marking the positions of submerged dangers on the steps beneath. The slave bowed to the heads and murmured, "Doctor Ruso, master," before stepping back to stand in the corner—just out of earshot, but close enough to deter eavesdroppers.

The round head belonged to Dorios. Ruso recognized the bony one from the parade on his first night in Aquae Sulis. The deep eye sockets and sunken cheeks could have been the model for one of those artistic reminders of death that were supposed to encourage dinner guests to enjoy themselves while they could. Although Ruso's first wife, once obliged to dine above a mosaic of a skeleton serving drinks, had insisted that the sight of it gave her terrible indigestion.

Somehow it was no surprise to learn that this present apparition in the pool was Lucius Marcius Memor, the town haruspex, interpreter of signs from the gods.

Memor's voice was a disappointment, though. Ruso had been expecting something deep and sonorous, but the greeting and the expression of sympathy about the prior night's attack were delivered with the blurred consonants of a man whose false teeth were not well attached. As he spoke, Ruso caught a glimpse of gold wire and wondered why whoever had replaced the central incisors hadn't chosen a better match with the yellow teeth on either side.

The two men shuffled in opposite directions along the steps, making more space between them for Ruso to sit in the corner. From where, he noted as he tossed his towel aside and stepped into the warm water, he could not see both of their faces at once.

"Do submerge yourself as far as possible, Doctor," Dorios urged. "The water will be marvelous for that arm."

It would also hide the bruising from the curious stares of the other visitors. Wondering how many of his fellow bathers knew that a guest had been assaulted the night before, Ruso slid down to the priests' level and lifted his chin well clear of the water. He might be sitting in it, but he wasn't going to drink it.

When he was settled, Dorios explained to his companion that "the doctor has agreed to help us with this sad business of the lost wife." As if Serena had been mislaid and might be found at any moment in a cupboard or tucked away under the bed. Turning to Ruso, he added, "I hear you had a visit from the centurion. I hope he wasn't violent."

Ruso looked from one to the other of them. "You're spying on me?"

Dorios smiled. "No. This is a small town. People notice things."

There was a thunderous splash from farther up the pool as someone jumped in. One of the attendants shouted a reprimand and they all rose to ride the ensuing wave before Ruso said, "Pertinax and I had a discussion. I've told him about the evidence that Terentius left town, and he knows that Valens has gone too."

"I hope he apologized for that dreadful business last night."

"He says the attack was nothing to do with him." Ruso wiped a drop off the end of his nose. "If you want to know what he plans to do, you'll have to ask him." However misguided Pertinax might be, Ruso was not going to inform on him to a pair of civilians he barely knew.

Memor's lips were closed, but his jaw moved as if he was waggling his false teeth up and down.

Dorios said, "Might we be able to hope that—"

"I wouldn't rely too heavily on that slave's testimony if I were you. I went up to the wharf before I came here, and nobody seems to know anything about a missing boat."

Dorios's eyes widened. "Who did you ask?"

"A man and a woman who smelled of fish."

The two priests looked at each other. "I'm afraid that's our fault," Dorios explained. "We warned the locals not to say anything unnecessary about that night to any visitors. It seems they were listening after all."

Memor said, "I take it there's been no news."

"None," Dorios confirmed. To Ruso he said, "We alerted the port, put the word out around the local area, informed Londinium and Isca, and sent letters to several towns with a detailed description, but so far . . ." Pale, dimpled shoulders rose out of the water and sank away again.

Ruso said, "Did you tell them you're looking for him in connection with a murder?"

"We told them he left town owing money. We thought that would have the added advantage of making people reluctant to take him in."

"Perhaps just as well," Ruso observed, "since I don't think any of us can actually prove that he was the murderer."

Memor gave a particularly energetic waggle of his teeth before addressing Dorios. "I thought you said our friend was here to defend the husband?"

"I've been trying to think what a lawyer would say," said Ruso, who had been mulling over Pertinax's arguments just now in an attempt to take his mind off the efforts of the small elephant. "Given the failure of the veterans' building project, I think he would say Terentius had other reasons to leave."

Memor sniffed. "A failure that was entirely predictable."

"Really?" Ruso said. "I got the impression most of the veterans were very confident." Apart from Catus, who had refused to help.

Dorios said, "My colleague here saw very early on that the omens were not good for enclosing a second spring."

"I certainly did," Memor agreed. "But I'm sorry to say that the investors failed to consult as widely as they should have before starting the work."

Ruso supposed this was priest-speak for *I told you so*. Or, rather, *I could have told you if you'd bothered to ask*, which was even more irritating. "You must have been in demand lately," he observed, unable to resist. "What with Serena being found in the pool."

"Please!" Dorios's head swiveled back and forth as he reassured himself that no other bathers were within earshot. "The matter is dealt with."

"That was not an omen," the haruspex corrected Ruso. "That was an appalling human act of sacrilege."

"And the spring has been fully restored to purity," Dorios added. "The appropriate steps were taken immediately."

"The veterans' project," said the haruspex, who was clearly still annoyed about it, "was flawed from the start. The goddess denied any blessing to such an exclusive development."

"Sulis Minerva freely offers her healing waters to all," put in Dorios, as if he were quoting from a speech to visitors. "The veterans were trying to claim that spring for themselves and their friends. Not only divisive, but deeply offensive to some of our more traditionally minded locals. I advised young Terentius against taking it on, but he was dazzled by the prospect of fame."

Ruso tried to gather his thoughts. It was not easy when he was having to bob up and down like a cork to avoid getting water in his nose and mouth. He said, "I've come a long way for this, and I'm grateful for your help, but I don't seem to be a lot further forward. What do you suggest I try next?"

Again the priests exchanged a glance.

"Many of us feel the same way," Dorios told him. "A sad business for the family and very frustrating for everyone. But now we think it's time to turn our attention to the future. The governor should arrive tomorrow. He's bringing a new deputy engineer from Londinium. The new man will help Catus oversee the building of the eastern baths. Memor here has read the signs, and they're very good."

"I have," the haruspex agreed. "All the signs from the sacrifices suggest that if we honor the goddess, she will relent and grant her blessings to the town once more. We will be able to put this terrible business behind us and move forward, just as Rome intended when the shrine was built."

If they were waiting for Ruso to agree that he too would abandon the search for Serena's murderer, they would be disappointed. On the other hand, he needed their cooperation. "Do you think Pertinax will agree to move forward?" he asked. "What if either Terentius or Valens turns up?"

Dorios sighed. "If a trial would bring the young lady back, believe me, both the Sulis Minerva Association and my fellow magistrates would give their full support."

"But as things are," Ruso said, "would you rather there wasn't a trial of anyone?"

"That is our considered position," the chief priest agreed. "That's why we were hoping you could persuade the centurion to see sense."

"He's not a man open to persuasion."

"But you should know it would be in the best interests of your friend not to stand trial too."

Ruso frowned. "I thought you were confident Terentius was guilty?"

The two priests exchanged a glance. Memor had stopped chomping. Dorios said, "You might want to consider exactly what the witness who saw them at the fire has to say."

"The woman at the snack bar? But I thought—"

"You might not want her full testimony made public."

"Why not?"

"Nothing we can do will bring back the dead, Doctor. But we can do our best for the living. You of all men should know that."

Ruso said, "Are you saying she's not reliable?"

"She is entirely reliable, as far as we know. You should speak to her."

"I have." It seemed he had not probed deep enough.

The priest gave as much of a bow as he could manage without putting his face under water. "Doctor. You brought your family a great distance to help your friend. Out of respect for the deceased young lady and acknowledgment of your great inconvenience, the Sulis Minerva Association will be pleased to pay for your passage home."

Ruso looked from one to the other of them again. "You're asking me to leave?"

"Not at all," the priest assured him.

"The next ship north will leave Abona in four or five days, weather permitting," announced the haruspex. Ruso assumed this prediction had come from the port authorities rather than the gods.

"In the meantime," put in the priest, "we hope you'll make the most of your stay. We're merely asking that you and your wife help us to recover, rather than dwelling on past events and causing further distress. Does that seem reasonable to you?"

"Entirely," Ruso agreed, admiring the man's fond assumption that he could answer on Tilla's behalf. "I don't think it will go down well with Valens's boys in years to come, though."

"It must be very distressing for the children," agreed Dorios.

"We have the greatest sympathy for the bereaved family," put in the haruspex.

"We do," Dorios said. "Which is why we don't want any more tragedies. We desperately need the favor and protection of Sulis Minerva. It's my responsibility to order things in a way that will please her."

"I see that," Ruso conceded. "But those boys are being denied the love and protection of their father."

The silence that followed was filled with the sound of the water lapping against the steps and the echoing voices of the afternoon bathers. Finally, Dorios said, "This is a little awkward." He looked at Memor, who was chomping so furiously that the teeth would surely break away from their moorings at any moment. "We had hoped not to have to raise this."

Raise what? There was more? Ruso wondered if Virana's garbled account of her relationship with him was about to come full circle.

Although what a minor family scandal had to do with a couple of priests was beyond him.

"It's only fair to warn him," the haruspex pointed out.

"My friend is right," Dorios said. "If word were to get out, then it's quite possible that it would reach the ear of someone who would make a powerful enemy."

Ruso said, "Really?"

"Of course, nobody would want to make trouble for the wife of an honorable veteran like yourself, or for her young friend."

He sensed that they were enjoying his confusion. "If you want to threaten me," he said, "you'll have to be more specific."

Dorios looked hurt. "We've no intention of threatening anyone. This is a friendly, welcoming town and we're delighted to have you here. But for your own sakes we don't want it widely known that your wife has been making inquiries about illegal activities."

"Illegal activities?"

"We'd rather not make a fuss."

Ruso stifled a groan. He had thought there might be gossip after Tilla's conversation about love potions with the hairdresser, but he hadn't expected it to reach the chief priest. Or to be taken so seriously. He lifted his chin and took a deep breath of steamy air. "My wife has already told me all about it," he said. "I've explained to her that it wasn't a wise thing to discuss with a stranger, but she did it purely in the interests of justice for our murdered friend."

"Doubtless she had the best of motives," the haruspex observed, managing to pronounce the word *doubtless* as if it denoted a thin crust over a pit of uncertainty. "But if the news of her intentions were to reach the ears of the potential victim, there could be serious consequences."

Ruso was about to say, *But the only potential victim was me*, when Dorios said, "Rest assured, the scribe has been sworn to silence and we are the only two other people who know. But scandal has a habit of escaping and spreading."

The scribe? Why would you need a scribe for a love potion? Was there some other possible scandal that Tilla had not told him about?

"So"—the chief priest placed a wet pink hand on Ruso's shoulder—"I hope we understand each other now."

"I think we're nearly there," Ruso agreed, looking from one to the other of them. "How's the search going with the black ewe?"

"Black ewe?" The haruspex frowned.

At that moment another wave washed across from the center of the pool and Dorios's words were lost in the splutter of a man who had opened his mouth at just the wrong moment. When he had stopped coughing, the haruspex said, "Well?"

For the first time Dorios looked disconcerted. "I'm afraid I don't know . . ."

"A black ewe. This afternoon. Walking through the streets with two men and a boy following it."

Dorios said, "Probably on the way to the butcher."

"They were walking past the Mercury," Ruso told him. "There's no butcher nearby." In truth he had not thought to check, but if there was nowhere to buy a cabbage among the souvenir shops, there was probably nowhere to buy a lamb chop, either, and the only other animals he could recall in the street were a couple of ponies on their way to the stable. "The men were temple slaves dressed in off-duty clothes, but they were out there in daylight, so I assumed they were doing it with your knowledge."

"I expect they were preparing a beast for sacrifice. I shall make inquiries."

"Was it Terentius they were hunting for, or some other unquiet spirit that the visitors haven't been told about?"

"What?" The haruspex turned to his companion. "You didn't tell me about this!"

Ruso said, "Plenty of people will have seen what was going on, even if they didn't know what it meant."

The haruspex said, "I should have been consulted!"

"But if neither of you knows," Ruso continued, "it doesn't matter. I'll ask around until I find somebody who can tell me."

The chief priest shifted closer to Ruso. The haruspex did the same, chomping as he leaned forward to listen.

Dorios said, "This is confidential."

"So it would seem," muttered the haruspex.

"As you know," Dorios continued, ignoring him, "we have failed to find any trace of Terentius either here or anywhere else. Some of the magistrates have decided—"

"What do the magistrates know of these things?" the haruspex demanded. "None of them has any training at all! The signs should have been read beforehand!"

Dorios glared at his erstwhile ally, who muttered, "Ridiculous!" before adding "Go on. We may as well hear the worst."

"The magistrates have decided," Dorios repeated, "that just in case Terentius drowned before reaching Abona, we should seek out where his unfortunate spirit might be and put it to rest." He paused briefly to allow this to sink in.

The haruspex said, "And?"

"The ewe led our men to a site by the river. It's being sacrificed in private at this moment. The full ceremonies will be carried out later."

Ruso said, "So you'll be needing me to keep that quiet?"

"We would rather you didn't spread rumors that would cause further panic and distress amongst the visitors."

Rumors that would associate the town not only with accidental death and murder but with unquiet ghosts and dubious magic practices. "Just as I'd rather you didn't spread gossip about my wife," Ruso said. He looked from one head to the other. "I think we all understand each other now?"

"Perfectly." Dorios's smile was unconvincing.

"Good." Ruso leaned forward between them and propelled himself into the middle of the pool, leaving them to ride his bow wave. He was going to have to have firm words with Tilla. Meanwhile, he shut the world out by taking a deep breath and plunging beneath the surface of the sacred water. But instead of offering peace and healing, the warmth closing over his head felt cloying and sour.

33

LEAVING THE BATHS, Ruso strode past the souvenir sellers and the drink stalls and didn't wait to see the eager smile die on the face of a disappointed pimp. He only stopped when he reached the table at the bar opposite the entrance to the Mercury. He was in the mood to deal with things: He might as well deal with this too.

The whiskery old drunk carried on staring into his half-empty beer, apparently oblivious to the newcomer standing in front of his table. Ruso was about to remove the cup when a bony hand shot out and grabbed his wrist. "Thief!" declared the man in British.

"Spy!" retorted Ruso in the same tongue.

The man looked up in surprise and moved the beer farther away with his free hand before releasing Ruso's wrist.

Still in British, Ruso said, "Is my wife in?"

"How would I know?"

"Because you're watching the door of the Mercury. Who's paying you?"

The man shook his shaggy head, sending a delicate shower of dandruff onto the table and into the beer. "Nobody. I'm just visiting. Lodging upstairs. I come down here for a quiet drink."

"I don't believe you."

The leer said the man knew full well there was no way to get the truth out of him without causing a disturbance.

Ruso stepped away, wiping his wrist on his tunic as if to erase the memory of the grip. He was halfway across the street when the man called, "She went that way!"

He turned to see the bony hand pointing toward the vegetable plots and the river, and nodded his thanks, but no sooner had he taken a couple of paces than the man called out again, "And then she came back."

Feeling foolish, Ruso turned on his heel without replying and strode back into the Mercury. By the time he had found out for himself that his wife was indeed there, alone in their room, demurely spinning a section of fleece like a good Roman wife, he was in an even worse mood than when he had set out from the baths.

"Tell me," he said, reaching out to still the twirl of the spindle, "what the chief priest knows about you that I don't."

Tilla put the wool down beside her on the bed and laid the spindle on top. "And greetings to you too, husband."

"Illegal activities," he prompted. "Involving a scribe."

The words "I did not do anything" were less than reassuring.

"So what was the thing you didn't do that the scribe has been sworn not to mention?"

"I did not put a curse on Gleva."

"You didn't put a curse on Gleva," he repeated. Tilla had never had any problem with cursing people before. It was not clear why not cursing them should require the help of a scribe.

"I did not even want to put a curse on her," Tilla said, as if this might help.

"Oh. Good."

"I wanted to find out if she had put one on Serena."

He slumped down on the bed. "And?"

Tilla gave a small shrug. "I think we asked the wrong scribe."

We. So Virana was involved too. That explained the mention of the "young friend." "So the only people definitely known to have been making inquiries about cursing an enemy are . . . ?"

"People do it all the time here!" Tilla insisted. "Even just for things that have got lost and stolen. You pay the scribe to write the curse and then you throw it in the spring and ask the goddess for justice. Virana knows somebody who did it and got her bracelet back."

"So, what made your particular curse such a problem that the chief priest is still talking about it?"

Tilla cleared her throat. "I expect they are nervous about speaking of murder since Serena died."

"You asked someone else to help you put a curse on Gleva for murder?"

"No!"

"No?"

"Not exactly. We never said her name. And I told the priest it had happened a long way away in the North."

"Really? I can't think why that didn't reassure him."

"And I never did it! He advised us not to and I said thank you. I told him he was very wise and I am not going to do it."

He was not sure whether "I am not going to do it" meant she had still been contemplating it up to this moment, or whether his wife was mixing up her Latin tenses, as she sometimes did when she was agitated. He chose not to ask, on the grounds that the answer might only annoy him further. "The problem is," he explained, mustering as much patience as he could manage, "that the man who happens to be in charge of two of the most powerful groups in the town is threatening to tell people that you've been going around slandering Sulis Minerva's priestess. Even if it doesn't come to anything legal, insulting Pertinax's woman is another way to upset Pertinax, and he's the only other person apart from us who wants to see justice."

"But I was only—"

"Is there anything else you haven't told me?"

She reached up to finger the pale wisps of hair that had escaped from the plaits.

"Tilla, I want to help Valens's boys just as much as you do. If you don't like the way I'm doing it, say so. Don't go around undermining me."

She picked up the abandoned spindle and wound the loose thread around the spool. "I saw Albanus this afternoon," she said. "I told him to be careful because Gleva might want to hurt the boys, and he should look out for trouble."

He closed his eyes and took in a slow breath, not pleased to be proved right. "Did you say this to anyone else?"

"Of course not. And he said he will talk to you."

"Good." At least Albanus had some sense. "Does Virana know she has to keep this to herself?"

"Albanus said he will tell her."

Ruso silently thanked the gods for that long-gone day when Albanus, a man of education and good sense, had been assigned to be his clerk. Then he glanced at his wife, who was looking crest-fallen, and felt guilty for hounding her. At least, he felt guilty until she said, "And what have you found out that will help the boys, husband?"

The question seemed designed to probe his own failure. He had learned nothing that would help Valens's boys. In fact he had taken a step backward; just how far back would only be determined when he had a chance to find out what the problem was with the witness who could place Serena at the fire. He said, "Did you go down to the river this afternoon?"

"Yes."

"Then the drunk over the road is still watching us even though he denies being a spy."

"You asked him if he was a spy?" She sounded incredulous.

"I wasn't thinking," he admitted. "And I've also found out that, whatever they tell you, the locals aren't looking for Terentius anymore, if they ever were. Well, not in any real way."

She said, "Is there another way?"

"They're going to make one last plea to the gods before they give up and move on to build a new suite of baths and a brighter future, for the sake of the majority who haven't had any relatives murdered. Apparently our only part in it is to shut up and accept a free passage home."

Tilla said, "Ah," as if he had just explained something.

He glanced sideways at her. "I told them I wasn't interested. You haven't agreed to anything, have you?"

"The black ewe," she said, not answering his question. "So that is what they were doing."

He blinked. He had seen desperate relatives try the ancient method of searching for an unquiet spirit after the terrible earthquake in Antioch. He always assumed that the custom was confined to the East and that a Briton would neither recognize nor understand it, but he should have guessed. Tilla had an unhealthy fascination with anything that combined the religious, the optimistic, and the slightly mad. The last thing he wanted to do was encourage her. Fortunately he had the perfect excuse. He said, "I promised not to talk about it."

"Do not worry!" The hands she placed either side of his face smelled of lanolin. "In a place like this I am sure I can find somebody to tell me all about this searching for the dead."

He had used more or less those same words—*I'll find somebody who can tell me*—earlier this afternoon, and he had meant them as a threat. Now Tilla seemed to be using them in all innocence, not wanting him to break his vow of silence. "They want the search kept secret," he said. "The whole business is nonsense, obviously, but the fact that they've resorted to it proves they genuinely don't know where he's gone."

"I will say nothing," she promised, adding, "The ewe ended up down by the river, sitting in a lettuce patch."

So that, he supposed, was where Terentius's spirit was believed to be lingering. He said, "How old were the lettuces?"

She frowned. "Full-grown. Some gone to seed."

"Which means . . . how long?"

"Husband, you are the son of a farmer, and you make medicines from plants yourself, and yet you do not know this?"

He reminded her that his father had not been a farmer: He had been a man who owned a farm, which was not the same thing at all. Then she told him the lettuces she had seen must have been growing for at least one and a half moons. He was proud of his instant deduction that "Terentius only disappeared three weeks ago, so he can't be buried underneath them, can he?"

"I suppose not."

At least they had agreed on something.

"We need to be careful of the Sulis Minerva people," he told her. "That includes the bath manager and all the temple staff. They're desperate to keep all the bad news away from the tourists. We've only been given such a long rein until now because they were hoping we'd manage to calm Pertinax down and get him to give up the idea of a trial."

Tilla's snort of derision summed up his own feelings on the likelihood of that happening.

He explained about the bad blood between the officials and the veterans. "There were rival schemes to build new baths," he told her. "Pertinax rammed through an agreement for the veterans' scheme, but it ran into all sorts of problems on site. From what I can gather, the investors decided to cut off the funding until they saw some progress, and the builders walked away. Then the fire at the Little Eagle took what there was of the site with it, and that seems to have finished the whole thing off."

"Do you think the fire was started on purpose?"

"I don't know."

"Whoever started it," she said, "deserves to be haunted by the spirits of those poor men who were burned in their beds."

"Precisely," he said, admiring the seamless way his wife had moved from suspicion to outrage. "If someone did start it, they'll be desperate not to be found out." Suddenly he saw the obvious next step. "Maybe it was Terentius."

"Why would he do that?"

"To get himself out of a failed project," he said, thinking aloud. "I think quite a few of the veterans had put money into it. If it was ruined by accident, he would avoid the disgrace. When the flames got out of control and he realized there were casualties, he panicked and ran."

"Serena would never be part of anything like that."

"No," he agreed. "Especially since her father was one of the investors. But if she'd found out, Terentius would have to keep her quiet."

Tilla picked up her spindle. "That is all very complicated," she said, teasing out some fresh strands of fleece.

"That doesn't mean it's wrong."

"So"—Tilla set the spindle twirling and played out more wool— "this Terentius was bad at his job, he lit a fire that killed people, then he murdered Serena and ran away."

Put that baldly, it did not sound likely.

"How will we catch him?"

"I don't know," he admitted. "But we won't get any help from the priests."

"You think they will try to stop us?"

"They're definitely watching us," he told her. "Sometimes it's the old man across the road, sometimes it must be somebody else."

Tilla stilled the spindle in mid-twirl. "Perhaps it was you they meant to attack all along."

Ruso, who had been considering the same thing, said, "I've told them we're as lost as they are, which is pretty much true."

"And if we start to be not so lost?"

"Things could get difficult," he said, running his fingertips lightly over his bruised arm. "How far would you go to defend the honor of your goddess?"

Tilla lifted her chin. "If she is a powerful goddess, she will defend herself."

The fleeting thought that perhaps Sulis Minerva had already defended herself by sending the mysterious assassin told him that he had been spending too much time listening to his wife.

"Neena will be back soon with Mara," she announced, winding up the spun wool and securing the shortened strand around the spindle. "Then we can go downstairs for dinner. Perhaps the food will help us think."

"I've got to go out first."

"Where?"

"I need to talk to a young woman in a bar." Seeing his wife's expression he added, "Why don't we all go and eat over there? They need the business."

34

"YOU ARE RIGHT," Tilla murmured to her husband, glancing down the rutted street to where a bedraggled woman was hanging out washing and shouting at several unkempt children to clear off or she would set the dog on them. "This is not a place where strangers will want to come and eat."

The welcome at the bar was warm enough, though. The cheerful young woman greeted Tilla's husband like an old friend and seemed to find nothing unusual about Tilla's hairstyle, which was a relief. The place itself was well-kept and brightly painted. Tilla supposed there was little anyone could do about the lingering smell of burning, or about the lack of other customers. But there was further disappointment to come: They were no longer serving food. "Not until we get into the new place."

He said, "New place?"

The smile grew even broader. "We're moving! We're taking over a bar by the temple."

A wiry, gray-headed man approached from the kitchen with two small children in his wake. This must be the veteran her husband had spoken of. Much older than his wife, as they often were. Mara, catching sight of the children, scrambled to stand on Neena's lap for a better view. Tilla commented on it in British to Neena: The baby was not so shy now.

Ruso was saying, "I hear you're moving."

"I'll believe it when it's all signed and sealed," the man said. "Not before."

"Oh, you!" The woman gave him an affectionate rub on the shoulder. "It will be all right, Gnaeus." She turned to Tilla's husband. "Didn't I tell you he'd think of something?"

The man called Gnaeus said, "I didn't think of this."

"He'll be fine once we're there," the woman assured them. "We'd move tomorrow, only it's the Sulis Minerva festival and we don't want to miss it."

"*You* don't want to miss it," put in the husband.

The woman turned to Tilla and said in British, "You'll enjoy it." She switched back into Latin for "Once they've done all that business at the temple, there'll be free food, and proper music, and dancing by torchlight in the courtyard."

Tilla saw Ruso exchange a glance with Gnaeus. "You do not have to join in with the dancing," she told him. "Neena and Virana and I will dance while you and Albanus look after the baby."

From the way he looked at her, anyone would think she had suggested eating his grandmother. The young woman looked amused. "What can I get you to drink?"

Tilla and Neena both chose beer. Mara was given some milk, but, to Tilla's embarrassment, instead of drinking it, she decided to spray it out of her mouth and all over the table. For a moment even Mara looked amazed at what she had done. Then she saw that the watching children thought it was very funny, and her face lit up into a broad grin.

Looking back on it, Tilla saw that this was the moment when she should have asked Neena to take the baby out. But they had come here as a family and, besides, her husband was trying to hold a serious conversation with the bar owners about the night of the fire, and getting Mara out would have meant asking him to move. So she wrestled the spouted cup out of Mara's protesting grasp before she could do it again, and wiped up the mess. Meanwhile, seeing the baby was in need of distraction, Neena took out an apple she had bought from a stall earlier and cut it into slices.

"I wouldn't have noticed her," the young woman was saying, "I mean, there was lots of shouting going on. But she was different, you know? She wasn't shouting about the fire. It was like she was pleading with him."

"What did she say?"

"Something about not going back there. 'Don't confront him'—I think that's what she said."

Mara had grabbed a slice of apple in each small hand and was now waving them in the air, squealing with delight at the mirth this caused the owners' children.

" 'Don't confront him'?" asked Ruso, ignoring the excitement going on beside him. "Are you sure?"

" 'Don't confront him. Not now.' I thought it was a funny thing to say. I mean, the Little Eagle's ablaze, people are screaming, there are men tearing another building down with their bare hands, and that Terentius is off to pick a fight with somebody."

Tilla missed the next part and probably her husband did too, because Mara flung both chunks of apple at the table and one landed in his wine.

He spun round, slapping at his wet arm. "What was that?"

"I'll take her out, mistress!" whispered Neena, grabbing the bag of spare baby cloths and getting to her feet with a protesting Mara tucked under one arm.

The young woman hurried off to fetch a cloth while Gnaeus scolded his children, who both denied leading the baby on and solemnly agreed that it wasn't funny.

"Go outside and play," ordered their mother. "It's a lovely day. You shouldn't be in here at all."

When peace was restored and the wine refilled, Tilla asked, "How did the fire start?"

Gnaeus said, "Nobody knows."

"Fires start all the time," put in his wife. "And I know you shouldn't speak ill of the dead but it's no surprise people got burnt in their beds. It was badly managed, that place. The landlord was drunk half the time himself. Not in a fit state to look after guests."

Tilla frowned. "People must have ideas about how it happened."

"If they do," the wife told her, "they should keep them to themselves."

Ruso said, "Who's taking on this place, Gnaeus?"

The man looked at his wife. "It's confidential, sir," he said. "That was a condition of the deal. How's the beer, miss? Can I get either of you another drink?"

"We've still got some olives," the wife declared, and went to fetch them.

With both owners briefly out of the way Tilla looked at the wet patch on her husband's tunic and could not resist giggling. Ruso scowled.

"It was a very good shot," she said.

"Sometimes, wife," he growled, "I wonder what we're raising."

"A baby," she told him. She kept her voice bright, but a chill had rippled over her. He had always wanted a boy. What if Mara was a disappointment to him? What if he suggested handing her back to Virana?

On the way back to the Mercury, rejoined by Neena and a baby who was now fractious because she was hungry, Tilla decided to distract him. Stepping closer to him on the pavement, she said, "What the woman overheard at the fire does not sound good for Valens."

"It was never sounding good," Ruso told her. "We know Catus will testify that Valens was carrying a dagger, and Valens himself said that Serena was stabbed. Now we've got a witness to Serena begging Terentius not to go and confront somebody. No wonder the chief priest was so eager for me to talk to her."

"You think she is lying? She seemed nice."

"I don't know. I know they were desperate to move."

She said, "So, who is taking over their bar?"

"Presumably," he said, "somebody who doesn't want the trial to take place."

"But this new story will only encourage Pertinax to ask for a trial."

"It's not aimed at Pertinax," he said. "It's aimed at us. They're saying there's no point in trying to save Valens's reputation, so we might as well give up and go away. You know the only person I think we can trust in this place?"

She said, "Albanus?"

"Apart from Albanus."

"Virana."

"Try again."

She reached up to push a pin back into her hair. "I know you want me to say Pertinax," she said, "but you might be wrong."

35

THEIR SECOND ATTEMPT at dinner—in the bar of the Mercury—was more successful. To Ruso's relief, Mara had calmed down, and he felt ashamed of his earlier exasperation. A grown man really should be able to rise above the immaturity of an eleven-month-old baby.

As if to rebuke him, their daughter was now behaving delightfully, beaming in response to the admiring glances from the two elderly ladies on the next table, attracting the usual questions about how old she was and the she's-just-like-her-father remarks that he and Tilla had learned to accept with a smile.

One day they would have to decide what to tell Mara about her past, but that day was a long way off. Tonight he could sit proudly beside his beautiful ex-slave wife with her unusually formal hairstyle, accompanied by his much-admired adopted daughter, and by Neena, who was much better at looking after the household than Tilla had ever been. Tonight the pork-and-bean stew was both plentiful and good, and the pain in his arm had eased.

He wondered where Valens was now and decided it was best not to know. Nor was the absence of young Esico a major concern: The lad was old enough to look after himself, and if he didn't come

back . . . well, either Valens would be looking after him or he had
found a place for himself back amongst his own people.

Under the table, he slipped a hand onto Tilla's knee. She said,
"Is everything all right, husband?"

"It is," he assured her. At that moment everything was as all right
as it was ever likely to be while they were in Aquae Sulis.

Tilla turned away and resumed her conversation with Neena, and
he withdrew the hand. He had spoken the truth: Everything was
all right. As long as you didn't think too hard. As long as you didn't
imagine the skeleton watching you silently from the floor. Because
even though the meal was good and the wine was better and you
and your loved ones were in good health and enjoying a well-cooked
dinner and had nothing to complain about, it was impossible to
forget that just across town there were two little boys who had now
lost both mother and father.

Ruso's thoughts drifted back to that afternoon's watery meeting
with the chief priest and the haruspex. Recalling his own stubborn
insistence that he must track down Serena's killer for the sake of
the boys, he began to feel uneasy.

He didn't trust Dorios. In their desperation to avert a trial, the
priest or one of his cronies might well have bribed Gnaeus's young
wife to lie about what Serena had said at the fire. Certainly the
timing and the secrecy of the deal that had helped the couple escape
from their failing bar were very suspicious. Then there was that
business of the stolen boat. Either the slave or the pair at the wharf
had lied about it. And if Pertinax hadn't ordered the nighttime
ambush in the Traveler's Repose, who had?

It was equally hard to warm to Memor, the haruspex, but Ruso
supposed that if you were paid to speak for the gods, and people
ignored your warnings, it was more or less your job to say *I told you
so* when things went wrong. How else would you persuade anyone
to listen next time?

But whatever he and Tilla did now, it was inevitable that the boys
would end up living with their grandfather. Even if Tilla did have
a low opinion of the grandfather's new girlfriend. And if that was
the case, quarreling with Dorios and Memor was a waste of time.
Unappealing as they might be, the two men were just doing their
best to defend their goddess and their town from further scandal.

Ruso took a long draft of wine and rolled it slowly around his tongue before swallowing. For once, Valens had done the most sensible thing possible. Knowing that he would be convicted whether or not he turned up for trial, he had chosen not to stay and fight. Now it was time for his friends to step aside, accept the inevitable, and take advantage of a free passage home.

He was about to announce this decision to Tilla when he felt her knee pressing against his own and heard a murmur of "Husband!" He looked up to see her jabbing a dripping spoon toward something behind him. The gray-bearded landlord was standing by his shoulder, and Ruso, who had just finished his bowl of stew, decided it was time to go and listen to another apology.

36

K UNARIS LED RUSO through a connecting door and into
the privacy of a back room at the Repose. Then he shut out
the clatter and hiss of the kitchen and motioned Ruso to the only
stool. He perched himself on a strongbox, leaning back against a
rack of keys and wooden tags that jingled and swayed behind him.
"How's the arm, sir?"

Ruso flexed and extended it, then turned it to display the bruising,
allowing the landlord to make suitably shocked noises before he
said, "It's much better now, thanks."

The expected apology followed. It seemed that new rules had
been introduced for the staff of the Traveler's Repose, involving the
locking of doors and the questioning of strangers seen on the stairs.
"We've never had anything like that happen before, sir," the man
added. "But we've never had a guest like your friend before, either."

When Ruso did not respond he continued, "I was in two minds
about letting him stay here, to be honest, sir, but I felt sorry for
him."

"I see," said Ruso, who was not going to thank him for charging
Valens a lot of money for a gloomy hole that stank of urine.

"The truth is, sir, I'm in a bit of an awkward situation here."

"Really?"

The keys swayed again as the landlord leaned forward. "I was hoping you and I might be able to help each other out."

First the chief priest, now the landlord. Ruso tried to look like a man ready to do a good business deal. Since he could not remember a single occasion on which he had done a good business deal, it wasn't easy.

"The centurion tells me that you want to prove your friend is innocent of murder. Is that right?"

No. Not anymore. Valens was gone: What good would it do? "Yes."

"Good."

Ruso waited.

"You may have realized I'm a local man, sir. It's not a Roman name, Kunaris. I'm a full citizen of Rome and you might think I'm well established in the town, but it's always a bit . . . well, perhaps your wife could explain it better than I can."

Ruso did not need his wife to explain it. "You never feel fully accepted by either side," he said. "You always feel people are expecting you to prove your loyalty."

"That's exactly it, sir. The last thing I want is to get caught in the middle of this business between the temple people and the veterans. So I was thinking, if there's something I can do to help you . . ."

"In return for . . . ?"

"Quite a few people would be interested to hear that your friend was hiding here, sir. But I'd rather those people weren't told."

Ruso rubbed his chin. "The centurion already knew."

"I'm not thinking of him, sir."

"Is that because Pertinax doesn't worry you, or"—this was going to sound like a line from a comedy, but he couldn't think of another way to phrase it—"you knew already that he knew?"

"The centurion's a very well-informed man, sir."

It was a neat dodge around the question, but it gave Ruso his answer. "You could have warned Valens that his father-in-law knew where he was hiding."

The landlord shifted slightly, and all the keys behind him swayed in unison. "The slave who sold that information to the centurion has been given a good beating, sir. He won't do it again."

There was no way of knowing whether the disloyal slave had ever existed or whether the landlord had betrayed Valens himself. Either way, since he was being paid handsomely for the room, things must have been working out very nicely for both him and Pertinax until Valens ran away.

"So," said Ruso, "who mustn't find out that Valens was here?"

"The Sulis Minerva Association, sir. If Chief Priest Dorios hears I had some information and I didn't pass it on to him, things could get very awkward. Especially if he works out that the centurion knew and he didn't."

Ruso caught himself scratching one ear again. He was beginning to lose his way in the labyrinth of who was supposed to say what to whom.

"I was hoping to catch you earlier for a quiet word about all this, sir, but you'd gone out."

"Pity," Ruso said. "While I was out, Dorios spoke to me about the attack. And I mentioned that Valens had been staying here."

Kunaris said, "Ah."

"How awkward can he make things?"

"Very, sir." The man gestured around him. "Dorios owns the Repose. And the Mercury. He pays my wages."

It was Ruso's turn to say, "Ah." Then: "Does he own any other places like this?"

The man shot him a sharp glance, as if wondering why it mattered how many visitor attractions the priest owned when there were more serious things to discuss, then proceeded to mutter to himself and count on his fingers. The more fingers he tapped, the more likely it seemed to Ruso that Dorios had been in a position to offer the veteran Gnaeus and his young wife the move they were desperate to make. In exchange, perhaps, for giving Ruso the sort of false evidence that would encourage him to shut up and go away.

This whole business was like blundering around in a snowstorm. There were no clear landmarks. He had no idea whether he was making progress or stumbling back to where he'd started.

"Three inns, three bars at the last count," Kunaris concluded. "Sir, about Chief Priest Dorios knowing your friend was here . . . See, the wife never wanted your friend back here in the first place. She's been on at me all day, and——"

"A collection of bars seems like an odd investment for a priest."

"He's a businessman, sir," Kunaris explained. "Plenty of the priests are. People like me and the wife get paid to run them."

"And the priests have fallen out with the veterans."

"Yes, sir. A lot of the veterans own businesses too. There's fierce competition. Meanwhile people like me and the wife just do our best to make a living, and—"

"So, where do the magistrates fit into all this?"

"Both sides, sir. Most of the magistrates are either in the Sulis Minerva Association or the Veterans' Association. Sir, I wouldn't ask, but—"

"That must make for some interesting town council meetings."

But the landlord had had enough of being sidetracked. "Sir, would you mind telling me what you said to the chief priest about your friend being here?"

Feeling he had made the man suffer enough—for now—Ruso wrapped both hands around the back of his neck and bent forward, trying to remember the exact conversation. When there were so many different versions of the truth, it seemed important to be as accurate as possible himself. "I told him the attack might have been intended for my friend, who'd been using that room," he said. "I don't think I ever said that you knew who Valens was."

The landlord did not look encouraged. "But I *did* know who he was, sir," he pointed out. "He'd stayed here before, on the night of the fire."

"And," said Ruso, hearing the sound of argument from the kitchen and suddenly feeling sorry for the wife trapped in the middle of all this, "I think I told him that Pertinax had managed to find Valens by putting me under surveillance. I didn't say you told him anything."

"Ah." The keys swayed as the landlord leaned back. "Thank you, sir. I'll tell the wife. That might calm her down a bit."

Ruso nodded. "So, what can *you* do to help *me*?"

The man reached down to pick up a wooden key tag that had slipped off the rack. "I don't know who killed your friend's wife," he said, "but I don't think it was your friend."

"I've got that far already," Ruso told him. *And then begun to wonder if I was wrong.*

"Like I said, he was staying here the night it happened. He took a room that afternoon and went straight out. We didn't see him again till after dark. Sat in the corner with a jug of a nice Rhodian, staring at the table like it had just insulted his mother. He wasn't causing any bother, so we left him to it."

That must have been after the argument with Serena. Perhaps, if Valens was to be believed, after he had left her and Terentius kissing under the temple portico. "Did he have any weapons?"

"If he did, they were hidden. We don't search them unless they look like trouble."

Ruso said, "He didn't look—disheveled in any way?"

"He didn't look happy."

"Go on."

"Then someone came in shouting about a fire, and he stood up and asked if there was anyone hurt, and did they need a doctor."

"How much had he had to drink?"

Kunaris wrinkled his nose. "There was still half a jug left. And a whole jug of water. He was gone quite a while: My doorkeeper let him back in round about the start of third watch. My man says he stayed in his room. I was the one who woke him up not long after dawn so they could tell him his wife was dead, sir. He looked stunned."

"And you'd testify to all of that if need be?" Not that it was much help: Ruso had already seen how easy it was to slip in and out of the Traveler's Repose. In any case, the landlord was looking hesitant.

"What I hope you'll understand, sir, is that a man in my position, especially a local man with no powerful friends . . . I can't afford to upset people."

"Are you saying you wouldn't testify?"

"Oh, no, sir. If I was asked, I'd swear to what I just told you."

"Good."

"But when your friend came back in the middle of the night, my doorman saw blood on his clothes."

One step forward, another one back. Ruso tried to suppress a sigh and failed. "He's quite sure?"

"My man asked him if he was all right, and he said the blood was from a patient. If anybody asked, sir, we'd have to say that too."

Ruso let out a breath long enough to contain a silent prayer that Valens would never be heard of again, because if he were tried, there seemed less and less that anyone could do to defend him. He thanked the landlord for his information and got up to leave.

"I was thinking you might be able to find the patient, sir. Or somebody who saw him."

"Yes," said Ruso. But even if he did, some of the blood on Valens's clothes could still have belonged to Serena.

"Glad to have been of help, sir." Kunaris got to his feet and all the keys swayed and settled back into their starting positions, leaving one tag still swinging as Ruso paused with his hand on the latch.

"Can you just tell me one more thing?"

"Sir?"

"Who started the fire at the Little Eagle?"

"I don't know."

"Take a guess," Ruso suggested. "I won't quote you."

The landlord cleared his throat. "I don't want to speak ill of my own people, sir, but there are one or two old-fashioned types who don't approve of building over the springs."

The local man who had invited Ruso to share his pool had seemed cynical rather than angry. "They disapprove strongly enough to burn down a building with people asleep inside it?"

"That part might have been an accident, sir. They could have been aiming for the builders' toolshed. I heard the timbers for the crane were stacked beside it."

"You don't think the ill feeling between the temple people and the veterans had anything to do with it?"

"Oh, no, sir. They do all their arguing in the magistrates' meetings."

"I see."

"These are decent Roman citizens we're talking about, sir."

"Of course." It wasn't much, but for the first time today Ruso, who had spent most of his life among decent Roman citizens, felt like laughing.

37

Ruso's decent Roman citizen family were no longer sitting in the bar when he returned from the landlord's office. One of the elderly women who had been admiring Mara called out to tell him they had gone upstairs. Her sister put a hand on her arm. "Are you sure, dear? I thought the young lady went out."

"At this hour?" demanded her sister.

"I'm sure I saw her go past, dear. You weren't paying attention."

"Me? I haven't closed my eyes once since breakfast. You're the one who keeps dropping off to sleep."

Ruso thanked them and left them to bicker. He went upstairs to discover that, indeed, only two of his family were in the room. Predictably, those two were Neena and Mara. According to Neena, Tilla had gone for a walk.

"By herself?"

"She said to tell you she was going to see how the lettuces are doing, master." Neena's tone was carefully neutral, as if this message made no sense to her and it wasn't her fault if it made no sense to him, either.

Unfortunately it made far too much sense. "It's dark out there!"

Without asking, Neena stepped across to the door and unhooked his cloak.

"Thanks." He swung it around his shoulders, bent to kiss Mara on the forehead, and clattered back down the stairs.

The click of hobnails on stone marched down the street with him, but died abruptly as he passed the stable and the paving gave way to mud. He stopped, squinting at some sort of movement caught in the dim glow of a lantern out in the middle of the vegetable patch. He could hear the soft murmur of voices and see shapes, but the figures all seemed to be draped in heavy clothing and it was impossible to make out the sex from this distance. One of them had arms raised in prayer. None of them moved in any way that reminded him of his wife.

Something shifted in front of the lantern, blocking it from his view. Then the light died altogether and he was left with only the moon.

If Tilla was out there somewhere, the last thing he wanted to do was to betray her presence to anyone else. He stepped cautiously back until his outstretched fingers felt the rough timber of the stable wall. A faint whiff of incense and roast mutton mingled with sewage drifted past him and was gone. He pressed himself up against the wall. With luck, as far as any watcher was concerned, his own shape would blend in with it. Thus hidden, he began to survey the scene again. He could make out the line of the river parapet on the far side of the patch now, and the swell of the hills across the valley, black against the moonlit sky. He stared at a couple of suspicious shapes, but they soon transformed themselves from hunched, silent watchers into harmless bushes.

Out in the vegetable patch, the shrouded figures had finished whatever they were doing. They were heading straight toward him. He held his breath, not daring to move.

If his wife was out there somewhere, he had no idea where.

The soft padding of footfalls on mud grew closer and then three figures were tramping past him, heads down, silent. Two of them moving fast, the third, heavier, limping behind them. All intent on getting back into the town.

There was no sign of Tilla.

If she wasn't out there, where was she? Gods above, what was the matter with her? Was it not enough that one woman had been killed after going out alone in the dark?

"What do you think?" The words were softly spoken and followed by "Did you see anything?"

He sidestepped along the wall toward a shrub that was standing up and reshaping itself into his wife. "What the hell are you doing out here?"

"You were busy."

"But—"

"I thought if they find that Terentius, one of us must be here to listen. Is a spirit summoned not bound to tell the truth?"

"If they—" He stopped. Perhaps he should have been more forthcoming about this ceremony. He should have seized the chance to set her straight. To explain the difference between literal and figurative. Ritual and reality. For Tilla, the gap between the world that could be seen and the world that could not was never very wide. Evidently she had thought there was a real chance that Terentius might be out there amongst the vegetables. That they would dig up his body. Or that he would pop up out of the ground. Or float down from the sky. Or perhaps just return as a disembodied voice to chat to the curious and the gullible.

He slipped his hand around hers, feeling her cool fingers tighten around his own. Holding on across the vast gap between their ways of thinking. He said, "Let's get back indoors before they see us."

"I didn't see anything," she said, disappointed. "It was too dark."

"I shouldn't worry. He didn't come."

"How do you know?"

"Because if he had," he said, "they'd all have yelled in fright and run away."

38

Ruso rolled onto his left side, swore at the pain in his arm, rolled the other way, and then seized the end of the pillow and pulled it over his head. These days, the sound of someone pounding on a street door was no longer the signal to crawl out of bed and grope for his clothes in the dark. Whoever was making a commotion down there, it wasn't a worried relative come to summon him to a patient. In a moment his mind would float back to wherever it had been, drifting around the islands of his dreams.

The moment was longer coming than he had hoped. Whoever was responsible for answering the door was taking their time. He could hear the indistinct sounds of men shouting despite the pillow clamped to his ear. Probably a drunken gang of off-duty soldiers, arriving late and finding themselves locked out of the bar across the road.

He clutched the pillow tighter, but it didn't block out the angry voices. Now he was annoyed with both sides: the idiots causing the fuss and whoever should be dealing with them and wasn't. This wasn't what a man hoped for in such expensive lodgings.

He restrained an impulse to reach out for Tilla. If he did not disturb her, there was a chance she might not wake. He would tell her about the noise in the morning and she would say, "Really? I heard nothing," and he would say, "You slept through it all," and be secretly proud of not waking her to keep him company.

There was a new sound in the darkness now. Louder. He lifted the pillow, alarmed. The drunks had somehow got into the Mercury. Footsteps were thundering up the stairs. A woman's voice was calling after them. The straggle-haired wife who had not wanted Valens to hide in the Repose. He was glad he had secured the latch on the bedroom door. Then it struck him that he couldn't hear the voice of the landlord and that he should probably go out there and help the wife, and just as all this came to him the door crashed back against the wall and someone was in the room.

"Get out!" he yelled, flinging himself across the bed to shield his wife.

Pertinax was there, in the dark of the bedroom, shouting something about the boys, and Ruso was slapping at an empty bed, calling, "Tilla! Tilla, where are you?" and in the next room Mara was crying.

Ruso felt a body crash into his own. He rolled onto the floor, but his attacker's weight followed and held him down. Hands were closing around his throat. He felt Pertinax's spittle on his face as the old centurion roared, "Give me my boys!"

The knee in the groin wasn't dignified, but it worked. In the old days Pertinax would have been too fast, but these were not the old days. By the time Kunaris appeared with a lamp and several burly slaves in creased night tunics, Pertinax was curled up on the floor, moaning in pain. Ruso was standing guard in front of Mara's room, clutching the only object he had been able to find that might serve for a weapon: a hobnailed sandal. The light revealed Serena's uncle Catus over by the bed, convulsed with coughing, and clutching the cupboard for support.

From behind the door, Ruso could hear Neena trying to shush Mara's frightened crying. "Tilla?" he shouted.

No reply.

With his face against the door now: "Neena, do you know where Tilla is?"

If there was an answer, it was lost beneath Pertinax's groan of "Lying bitch has taken my boys!"

"*What?*" was all Ruso could manage. Then, in British: "Neena, answer me. Is Tilla with you?"

The reply he was dreading came in the same tongue. "No, master."

"Do you know where she is?"

Neena did not. She too had thought the mistress was asleep in bed.

"My boys!" Pertinax was still writhing on the floor. "What's he . . . done with . . . my boys?"

The landlord's wife appeared in the doorway beside her husband, clutching another lamp. Ruso said, "I can't find Tilla. Have you seen her?"

The landlord said, "I'm going to have to ask you all to leave, sirs."

"My wife's missing!"

From the floor: "My boys have been stolen!"

Kunaris turned to Ruso. "You too, sir. We can't have the other guests disturbed like this. I'm sorry."

"I'm the victim here," Ruso pointed out. "Again. I was asleep in bed. These men broke in."

Ignoring him, the landlord beckoned over his shoulder. Four more slaves moved forward and lined up on either side of their master. One of them lit the lamp in the bracket on the wall, illuminating a row of broad shoulders and grim faces.

Kunaris had not taken his eyes off Ruso. "It always seems to be you that's attracting the trouble, sir."

"Where's my wife?" Ignoring the landlord's pleas to keep quiet, he yelled, "Tilla? Tilla, can you hear me?"

"You'd be wise not to make a scene, sir. I think the other guests have suffered enough."

As if on cue, a man with just-out-of-bed hair shambled up behind him in the doorway and demanded to know what was going on. Without moving, Kunaris assured him it was all under control.

"No it isn't," Ruso said. "My wife's gone missing."

Kunaris put a hand on the guest's shoulder and assured him once more that it was all being dealt with. The man looked from one to the other of them, caught sight of the row of slaves, and blundered away into the dark, muttering to himself.

The room that had seemed spacious was crammed with people now. Catus regaining his breath over in the corner. Ruso clutching a shoe as if it might protect his daughter and her minder next door. Gray-bearded Kunaris standing with his henchmen blocking the exit. Pertinax still doubled over, swearing, clawing his way up to sit on the bed.

No Tilla.

Outside, Ruso could hear the landlord's wife fussing about, apologizing to more grumbling guests, offering to light them back to their rooms and promising them that it was all over.

A muffled female voice called out, "Is it him? That one with the two wives and one baby?"

"It's all right dear." It was the voice of one of Mara's elderly admirers. "No need to get up. The landlord is dealing with him."

"I told you there would be trouble!"

Pertinax had recovered enough to converse now. Addressing Kunaris, he said, "That murdering bastard you were sheltering has kidnapped my boys." He jerked his thumb toward Ruso. "And his wife's in on it."

Ruso said, "No, sir," and wished he could say the words with greater conviction. Helping Valens to steal the boys would have been an act of insanity. On the other hand, if Tilla wasn't with Valens, where the hell was she?

"I'm sorry about your boys, sir," Kunaris replied evenly. "But they're not here."

Pertinax turned to Catus. "Call out the veterans. Tell them to meet at the house."

Catus stumbled toward the door. The slaves parted to let him through, but one of them followed him down the corridor.

Pertinax turned his glare on the landlord. "I'll be searching every room in the place. You can come with me or you can get out of my way."

Kunaris's head rose. "This is the last time I'm asking nicely, sir. Your grandsons aren't here. My men will escort you into the street."

The slaves glanced at him, as if they were not used to hearing their master bargaining before throwing a customer out.

"Neena?" Ruso called through the door. "Pack all our things and wrap up the baby. We're leaving."

Was that gratitude in the landlord's glance? Whatever it was, it was swiftly gone. Ruso did not envy him trying to defend his other guests from Pertinax, but wherever Tilla was, she was plainly not there, and he could not help her if he were caught in the cross fire between the leader of the veterans and a landlord in the pay of the chief priest. He put the shoe down, stepped past the old centurion, and pulled an empty bag out from under the bed. Then he opened the cupboard, dragged out the contents and began to ram them into the bag.

"Coward," hissed Pertinax.

"I don't know where your boys are, sir."

"And you don't know where your wife is, either?"

He did not. But he could think of one person who might.

39

RUSO HAD EXPECTED to have to rouse the sleeping residents of the oil shop and explain himself. Instead the bolts rattled within moments of his knock. As a riot of perfumes assaulted his nostrils, a familiar voice said, "Have they found them, husband?"

"I don't know."

Virana gasped. "Doctor! What are you doing here? Where is Albanus?"

"Isn't he here?" For a moment he had a horrible fear that Tilla had persuaded Albanus to join in some crazy scheme to get the twins out of Pertinax's house.

"The centurion came for him," Virana explained. "He's very upset. The boys have gone missing. He's gone to wait at the house in case they come back."

"I can't find Tilla," he said, feeling helpless. "I woke up and she wasn't there."

"Why have you got all those bags?"

"This is all I could manage: I couldn't carry the trunk. Do you know where she is?"

But Virana did not. Only when he asked to come in did she lift the lamp higher and exclaim, "Oh! My baby!" Mara was in Neena's arms, peering out from beneath a shawl with a mild interest that suggested this sort of escapade happened every night in the Petreius household.

"We've been thrown out of the Mercury," Ruso explained. "We've got nowhere else to go."

"But where is—"

"I don't know."

"What did you do?"

"Pertinax came looking for trouble. Can we come in?"

Virana glanced behind her, then reached for one of the bags and confided in a loud whisper, "We must creep like mice. The landlady is already very cross."

They tiptoed in, Ruso trying not to crash into any furniture or knock over jars of expensive oil as he hauled the luggage through the shop and up the stairs. He avoided the third step on Virana's warning that it creaked.

Finally up in the modest attic room that Virana and Albanus called home, he lowered the bags and boxes gently to the floor and uncurled his stiff fingers from the handles. Then he leaned close to Virana to murmur, "Did Albanus say anything about the boys earlier? About getting them out of the house?"

"He was very worried about it," Virana told him. "But he said if you said it was all right he would try and help."

"Of course it wasn't all right!"

She looked puzzled. "But Tilla said she had asked you and you said it was a good idea."

"Tilla said *what?*"

Virana shrank away, putting a finger to her lips and turning to glance at the door. "Sh!"

He forced himself to lower his voice. "Tilla told Albanus that I said it was a good idea to steal the boys?"

Virana frowned. "Something like that. I think."

"Oh, holy gods." Ruso sank down onto the narrow bed. "Do you know where they've gone?"

"Albanus has gone to the centurion's house," she said, misunderstanding the question. "I don't know where Tilla went. Or where the boys are."

He would almost have preferred it if Albanus had gone with Tilla. At least one of them would have had some sense.

"But you think she's with the boys?"

She pulled forward a strand of hair and began to chew it. "I don't know. I thought it was all right. I thought you said—"

"Think, Virana! What did she say, exactly?"

A faint crunching sound came from Virana's mouth: the sound of teeth grinding hair. Then: "Do you know where I can borrow a spade?"

"What?"

"That is what she said: 'Do you know where I can borrow a spade?'"

40

AT FIRST IT was exciting. She was trembling at the thought of what she might find. It would be gruesome, of course, especially after a whole month. But the thought that she might learn the truth at last—or at least part of it—helped her push her fears aside. She squatted beside the crushed plants in the moonlight and shoved her hands into the cold earth she had loosened with the spade. Small roots and stones dragged at her fingers. Grit rammed itself in under her nails, and once she felt something smooth and yielding that might be a worm. She pushed that thought aside too.

From somewhere beyond the black line of the wall, she could hear the faint slap and gurgle of the river, risen to greet the moon.

Soon there was a pale row of wilting lettuce plants laid out alongside the plot. She had been careful to take a good clump of soil around each ball of roots. With luck, they would go back into their bed only slightly the worse for their latest adventure. Many were already ruined anyway: some crushed by the weight of the ewe and others half eaten. Tilla had never before considered whether sheep liked lettuce. Perhaps, since none had been completely eaten, the ewe hadn't been sure herself.

Strange how, even at a sacred moment like this, it was difficult to keep her mind on the important things. Perhaps because the important things were hard to face.

Now the surface was clear of plants, she wiped her hands on each other and then on the rough linen of her overtunic. When they were as clean as she could manage, she raised them to the skies and spoke a soft prayer to Sulis Minerva and to the native goddess of the earth and god of the harvest and then one to Christos as well, because Christos had more cheerful things to say about the next world than any of the other gods seemed to offer. Lowering her hands to her sides, she bowed her head as a sign of respect. Finally she took a deep breath, lifted the spade from where it stood to attention in the ground beside her, and placed it against the soft earth. One foot on the top of the ironshod wooden blade, as her father had taught her. She was glad of boots with proper soles. She could never have managed this in those silly little sandals that those women wore at the baths.

Keep your mind on what you are doing.

Stab down. Lean on the handle. Push with your foot. Slice through the soil, ease back to loosen it. She was glad there was no turf: It made the job a lot easier. Lift. Turn. Twist the spade. Drop. Work across the plot in a line. Don't put your spoil too near the edge. Things she could remember her father saying as they dug out the vegetable patch at home.

Stab, lean, push, ease back, lift. Turn. Twist and let the soil drop. Don't think about what you might find. Lean, push. Ease back, lift, turn. Twist.

Easy. Someone had worked this plot well. The soil was soft and it smelled good. It also smelled of the wine the men had poured out at their ceremony earlier in the night. Was that a whiff of roast mutton? She hoped they had burned all of the meat, or eaten it, and not buried any of it here. Digging into buried mutton would be horrible. But of course they wouldn't have buried it, because something else would come along and smell it and dig it up. A fox, or a dog, or a badger—or a woman in the secret hours of the night, digging for a body by the light of a cold moon.

In the woods somewhere on the far side of the river, a tawny owl hooted.

It was just a bird, calling as it must do every night. There was no reason to think Sulis Minerva had sent it to spy on her across the water. No need to be gripped by a sudden feeling that someone was watching. No need to look round and see who it was.

She looked anyway, one gritty hand resting on the spade.

The world of black and silver looming around her was a shock. She had been so fixed on what she was doing, staring at one little patch of ground, that she had forgotten about the sharp lines and deep shadows of the buildings. About the rows of silent vegetables standing to attention all around her.

Don't look. If there is anything to be afraid of here, it will be in front of you. In this spot that those men found but did not dare to test. She was not sure she wanted to test it, either, but who else was there? Her husband was the one who had told her the men were searching for an unquiet spirit, but he thought the whole thing was nonsense. He had been very pleased with himself when he dismissed the idea of Terentius being buried here. Seeing his satisfaction, she had not liked to point out that the lettuces growing in the plot could have sprouted and grown somewhere else and been moved here to mature after it had become a secret burial place.

She had been amazed when the searchers had made no real effort to find out whether they had the right spot. Her husband had been right: They did not really want to find Terentius. They just wanted to deal with their own fear of his ghost. So they had come here and made an offering and said prayers, but they had shied away from doing the one thing that might solve the mystery of where he had gone. That, it seemed, was up to her. And if she was not to be caught, she must work quickly.

She pushed the spade in again, alert for any change in smell or feel beneath her that would tell her to stop and . . . and what? If there was something—someone—down there, she was not going to lean into the shadowy hole and scoop the earth out with her hands. She would have to scrape a little more earth back with the iron edge of the blade, peer in carefully, and then drop the spade and run.

Lean, push down, ease back. Digging holes kept you warm, but it was harder work than she remembered. So much earth for such little progress. Lift. Turn. Twist, hear the soft patter of more earth landing onto the heap. Digging was noisier than she remembered too.

Now she thought about it, she had never worked alone like this. There had always been a couple of brothers around, or one of her parents, and they would take turns. And besides, digging was never a job to hurry. Slow and steady. The only people that dug in a hurry were soldiers, but then, soldiers under command were always more like ants than people. Lean. Push. Ease back . . .

Stop. Listen. Some sort of commotion back in the street. Men shouting and banging on doors.

She crouched down, lowering the spade to the ground in case the gang spilled down the street and saw her in the moonlight. A woman out alone at this hour would be easy prey.

The noise faded. She began work again, glad of the brief rest, but this time she tired more quickly, and the hole was only . . . Giving herself another excuse for a rest, she lowered the spade to test it. About two feet deep.

Perhaps she should stop soon. How deep could anyone have buried Terentius here without anybody noticing? They must have done it at night when no one was looking, and surely they too would have been in a hurry, and now she thought about it, who might "they" have been? Not Valens, who had been helping the fire victims and would not have had time. Gleva? What reason could she have for killing or burying Terentius? Who else? Serena, before she plunged a knife into her own heart and threw herself into the eternal waters? That made no sense. Why go to all the bother of hiding her lover's body if she wasn't going to be alive to be accused of his murder?

A chill passed through her despite the warmth of the work. What if her husband was right, and this was all nonsense? She could be digging here until the sun rose and just getting herself into more and more trouble. Besides, the night was passing and she must allow time to fill in the hole and put the plants back and find some way to fetch them water.

She looked up at the sky. "What shall I do?"

As if in reply, a small cloud began to drift slowly across the moon. The distant owl hooted again.

"But what does it *mean*?" she whispered, and jumped as another owl replied to the first, much closer.

Glancing wildly around her, she made a grab for the spade. She no longer cared what the signs meant. She just wanted to get out of this place and back to a warm bed, safely tucked in beside her sleeping husband.

41

Ruso STEPPED UP to balance on the narrow wall in the moonlight, aware of the wide river shimmering behind him. "Tilla!" he called softly, staring out across the gray mosaic of the silent vegetable plots. "Tilla, I'm not angry!" Although that might change when he found her. Hopefully very soon. "I just want to know you're safe!"

A sudden movement caught his eye, but it was too low and too fleet for a human being. Probably a fox. Which meant no human was likely to be out there. But he jumped down from the wall and began to trace the paths between the beds anyway, because he could not think of anywhere else his wife might want to wield a spade. And because he wanted her to be there. The idea that she was somewhere with Valens and the boys was unthinkable.

He followed every path he could find, surveying the plots on either side of him in case something terrible had happened to her out there. Some of the paths were clear and well tended. On the others, brambles and long grass and nettles tangled against his legs and he had to force his way through. He wished he had a stick.

He passed what he thought might be the plot where the ewe had lain down. The earth looked uneven and the plants askew, but there was no sign of whatever ceremony the priests had carried out after dark.

"Tilla?"

Over in the dark woods beyond the river, an owl replied. If he were Tilla he would probably have asked it for help. Since it would do no harm, and there was nobody to overhear, he muttered, "Where is she?" But of course the creature didn't answer. It was an owl.

"Where the hell are you?" he whispered, gazing around him. "What have you done? Why didn't you tell me?" Rubbing the nettle stings on his shins, he tried to reason. Was he such a monster that she was afraid to confide in him? He didn't think so. A monster would not be wandering around out here, looking for his wife, would he? Giving up what was left of a very bad night's sleep to be attacked by weeds and thoroughly worried.

Finally he abandoned the vegetable plots and made his way back down the street past the Mercury, now dark and silent once more. The only sign of life at the Traveler's Repose was a late torch still guttering in the bracket over the door. He supposed Pertinax had taken the search elsewhere. Ruso was almost certain Kunaris wouldn't have agreed to hide the boys in either of the inns, even if Valens had been crazy enough to ask.

Almost certain. The landlord was just as entangled in the complications of this affair as the rest of them, and evidently not above deceiving his employer if there was a decent amount of cash on offer.

Ruso was still wondering where to try next when he heard, to his surprise, the approach of marching boots. Surely a place the size of Aquae Sulis didn't have a night patrol?

No, it did not. What it had was a grizzled bunch of retired soldiers who surrounded him and demanded to know who he was, what he was doing out at that hour, and whether he had seen anyone with two small boys. "Or just two small boys," added one with more initiative than the others.

Both sides left the encounter disappointed: The search party had no more seen Tilla than Ruso had seen Valens or the children, although the soldiers seemed less keen to help once they found out who he was looking for.

As the tramp of boots faded away, Ruso was left wondering where else, in the name of all the gods, a woman would use a spade in the middle of the night in a place like Aquae Sulis.

The spring? Surely she couldn't be planning to hang over the side and try to scoop out knives and curses?

When he got to the courtyard, the only signs of activity were the drifting steam and the constant sound of the overflow trickling into the drain. Still, he crouched by the edge of the pool for a long time, peering at the surface of the water through the railings. Finally reassured that there was nothing—and nobody—floating in there, he got back to his feet, shaking the stiffness out of each leg.

Where now? She could have gone back to the Mercury and been let in—surely Kunaris would not throw a lone woman onto the street?—but to find out, he would have to knock on the door.

This time the doorkeeper at the Mercury was awake. Perhaps they all were. The slave who called to him through two inches of studded oak told him the doctor's wife had gone out hours ago and the doctor wasn't there either, and no, she hadn't said where she was going, and why didn't he clear off? Which was at least a definite answer, even though it wasn't the one Ruso wanted.

Now where? He could go back to the oil shop, but that would mean potentially disturbing Albanus's angry landlady yet again. Besides, nobody needed him there. Mara and Neena would be safe with Virana. He turned his footsteps toward the only place he could think of where he knew the household would be awake.

"Have they found the boys?" was his first question when the door was answered.

"What are you doing here?"

He said, "I'm looking for my wife."

"Your wife is not here."

The door began to close in his face, but Gleva wasn't fast enough, and nobody came forward to help her.

42

RUSO CLOSED THE door more gently than he had opened it, and found himself surrounded by half a dozen somber faces: a combination, he supposed, of Pertinax's staff and that of Catus. Most of the light by which he saw them was coming from a couple of triple-wicked lamps illuminating the painted shrine of the household gods, as if divine help might be drawn to the shrine like a sailor to a lighthouse. The air was thick with the smell of incense.

It was Pertinax's houseboy, looking much older than he had just a day ago, who spoke first. "Is there any news, sir?"

"If you had troubled to answer the door," put in Gleva, lifting her tousled nighttime hair with both hands and letting it fall down her back, "you would know."

The priestess was wasting her time. A man who had survived decades of being roared at by Pertinax knew exactly how to arrange his wrinkled face into an expression that registered nothing at all. Not resentment, not fear, and certainly not impertinence. Nor, in fact, any sign of having heard a word this native pretender had said to him now that Pertinax was not there to demand deference to her.

"Your master came to the Mercury," Ruso told him, "but we couldn't help."

The cook, her eyes already swollen with crying, began to sob. Beside her, a little maid stood wringing her thin hands and looking at him as if in the hope that he would come up with something more reassuring. He wondered how much of the staff's grief was fear for the boys, and how much was terror of what Pertinax might do to the household that had failed to protect them.

He was about to ask where Albanus was when the man appeared, almost at a run, wiping his mouth with a cloth. He stopped when he saw Ruso. "Sir?"

"Where's Tilla?"

Albanus's face, already pale, fell even further. "Sir?"

Ruso said, "My wife's missing. Do you know where she went?"

Albanus buried his face in his hands and groaned.

"She's helped to steal them," Gleva declared. When nobody spoke up to support her, she said, "What is the matter with you all? It's obvious."

Ruso said, "Not to me." He needed to talk to Albanus alone, but first there were questions to be asked here. He looked around at the assembled household. "Did anyone see the boys go?"

Silence.

"Anyone know anything at all?"

Silence.

"Who was the last person to see them?"

"It was their grandfather, sir," put in Albanus. "He went in to say good night."

"And who found out they were missing?"

"Pertinax again, sir. He got up in the middle of the night for the pot and went in to look at them."

"Doesn't anyone sleep with them?"

The cook raised a nervous hand. "Mistress Serena often stayed in there with them, sir. After she'd gone, Mistress Gleva offered, but they didn't want her."

So. Had it not been for an old man's need to pee, the boys would not have been missed until daybreak. "Somebody needs to wait by the door," Ruso told them. "The rest of you should probably try and get some sleep. You'll need to be alert when your masters get back."

Gleva said, "Who are you to give orders?" but the houseboy took up position on a stool by the door and the cook and the little maid scuttled away into the darkness. Gleva lit a lamp from the shrine before walking out with "I shall tell the masters about this!"

The sound of her sandals slapping against her heels faded away into some distant part of the house. Albanus spat into the cloth and gave his mouth and chin another vigorous wipe. Ruso said, "Are you all right?"

"Quite all right, yes, sir. Sorry, sir."

Ruso indicated the cloth. "Was that because you're worried or because you're ill?"

Albanus swallowed. "I'm feeling much better now, sir. Sorry. I was just thinking about what might happen."

"Well, don't," Ruso told him. "Your losing your dinner doesn't help anybody. Go and get a drink of water and then take me somewhere we can talk."

"Yes, sir." Albanus hunted for a clean patch of cloth and dabbed at the front of his tunic. "I'm very glad you're here, sir. We'll go to the boys' room. I need to show you something."

The boys' room was on the far side of the courtyard garden, at the back of the house: a large white-walled space with two low desks, a bed wide enough for both boys, and a set of shelves that held a jumble of wooden toys and clothes and small boots and board games. Ruso closed the door before asking softly, "Did my wife tell you I'd approved some mad scheme to rescue the boys?"

Albanus's hand went to his mouth. "Sir, you can't possibly think I—"

"Yes or no?"

"She said she thought they were in danger, sir, but—"

"Did you go along with it?"

"No, sir!"

Ruso felt himself relax.

"I said I would have to talk to you about it, sir."

Ruso put a hand on his shoulder. "Thank you. I'm sorry. There's been a misunderstanding." It was probably best not to mention the name of Virana. Albanus was suffering enough already without being told that it was his own wife who had caused the confusion. "What was she suggesting, exactly?"

Albanus indicated the empty room. "Nothing like this, sir. She just wanted me to look out for trouble." He swallowed. "I didn't expect the trouble to come like this."

Ruso sighed. "Sit down, Albanus. Tell me exactly what's been going on."

Albanus helped himself to one undersized stool from beneath a desk and perched on it with his knees up under his chin. Ruso eyed the other one with some trepidation. "It's all right, sir," Albanus told him. "The centurion had them made by a legionary carpenter. You could sit an elephant on it."

Ruso lowered himself onto the seat and felt a surge of sadness at the thought of the small boy who should be sitting here—swiftly followed by shame at the realization that, had the child actually been here, he would not have known which twin it was. He rested his elbows on his knees and said, "Talk to me."

Instead of speaking, Albanus retrieved a slate from the nearest desk and handed it across.

Ruso turned the surface toward the light and read, in an awkward scrawl, the words,

THE BOYS ARE WITH ME. I HAD NO HELP FROM THE STAFF. VALENS.

"It was under the bed, sir."

Ruso read it again, very slowly, not sure what to say. He knew he should be relieved. But this . . . "This is very odd." He glanced at the window.

"It doesn't open, sir."

There were six glass panes high up on the outside wall to let in the light, but no way of moving them aside to allow the passage of air. The door they had used opened onto the walkway around the courtyard garden. The only other way out was via an adjoining bedroom that had belonged to the boys' mother. This also opened onto the courtyard. "Is there another way into the house?"

"No, sir. The back of the house joins the neighbor's up the hill. I suppose Doctor Valens could have come in over the roof, but he'd have needed a ladder and there's no sign of one anywhere."

Ruso returned his attention to the note.

"Do you think it's his writing, sir?"

He squinted at it. "It could be," he conceded. But slate was not the easiest medium to write on, and evidently something clumsy had been used to scratch the lettering. "It looks as if somebody wrote it with their eyes shut," he said.

"Or in the dark," Albanus said.

"Or in the dark."

"But you couldn't swear that it's his writing, sir?"

"Not really," Ruso admitted. "I can't imagine the boys would have gone willingly with anyone else, though."

Albanus's sigh did not convey the relief Ruso would have expected.

"It must be him," Ruso explained.

"Oh, it must be him who's taken them, sir," Albanus agreed. "But it's hard to see how he did it without help. And if someone on the staff had helped him, they might be very keen to absolve themselves from responsibility."

"So they asked him to write this?"

Albanus swallowed. "Or they wrote it themselves, sir."

Ruso was not sure whether to be impressed by such subtlety of thought in the middle of the night, or amazed by the complex depths into which Albanus's anxiety had plunged him. He examined the slate again, seeking some clear evidence of Valens's hand. But even if he had found some, how could anyone prove that this was not a fine imitation by a clerk who had worked alongside Doctor Valens in the hospital at Deva? "How many of the staff can write?"

Albanus's face was glum. "Just me, sir."

"What about Gleva?"

"I believe not, sir. She asked me to read a very simple note to her the other day."

Ruso held out the slate and looked him straight in the eye. "Did you write this, Albanus?"

There was no hesitation. "No, sir."

"Then what's the problem? Either you did it or he did it, and since you didn't, and the boys certainly didn't, and nobody else would have, it must be genuine."

Albanus still looked blank.

"Well, if you're the only one who can write, and it wasn't you, who else would they have gone with?"

"Nobody, sir. Thank you. I'm so sorry to trouble you with this when you're looking for your wife."

"One thing at a time," Ruso suggested, hoping simultaneously that Tilla was safely with Valens and the boys and that she wasn't. "At least we can be sure the boys are with someone who'll look after them."

Albanus, however, was still not happy. "The message was under the bed, sir. I could have hidden it there earlier and it wouldn't be found until the room was searched."

"But you just said you didn't."

"No, sir, I didn't."

"Then why are you desperate to implicate yourself?"

"I'm not, sir. I'm just trying to imagine how Centurion Pertinax will see things when he comes back."

Ruso shook his head, understanding now how Albanus had worked himself up into such a state that he had vomited. "If we're going to speculate," he said, "then let's speculate about something useful. How did Valens do it without anyone seeing?"

Albanus looked at him with the same level of desperation as the little maid in the entrance hall. "I don't know, sir. I wasn't here."

Ruso shifted off the stool and crouched on the floor. Then he lay down and rolled under the bed, squeezing himself up against the wall. "Can you see me?"

"No, sir."

Ruso rolled back out, stood up, and brushed at his tunic, but there did not seem to be much dust. "He must have come in here when the room was empty, and hidden. Then they all crept out when everyone was asleep. He probably told them they were going on an adventure."

The tone of Albanus's "Yes, sir" was wary.

"I'm not saying you hid him!"

"No, sir. He might have come in when I took the boys out for a walk, but I swear I had no idea."

"I know you didn't," said Ruso. Albanus's panic was sending his thoughts scurrying in circles. Valens, on the other hand, seemed to have had a plan all along—a plan he hadn't been willing to confide to his best friend. "Tilla can write," he mused, realizing a potential complication. "But she was with me at dinner. She came to bed with me. She couldn't possibly have sneaked in here after dark." Yet she too had vanished in the middle of the night. Had she made some arrangement with Valens? Had she known where he was all along?

He said, "Did you know Tilla asked Virana about borrowing a spade?"

It was a moment before Albanus looked up. "I'm sorry, sir, what did you say?"

"A spade," Ruso repeated.

"Yes. That's what I thought you said, sir. My wife didn't say anything about a spade. Why would she want one?"

"I thought I knew," Ruso told him. "But she wasn't where I expected to find her, and I don't know where else to look."

43

T HE HOUSEBOY WAS slumped on the stool beside the front door at a perilous angle. When Ruso greeted him he jerked awake and almost toppled onto the tiled floor. "Bedding," Ruso announced, dragging the straw mattress and the blanket that Albanus had found for him across the hallway. "Put it behind the door when I've gone and you can sleep and guard the door at the same time."

The houseboy scratched at his thin hair and blinked as he drifted back into consciousness, then hauled himself to his feet. "I'm all right, sir, thank you. I was just resting my eyes."

"Then at least put the bedding around the stool so you don't break something when you fall."

The man mumbled his consent.

"Before I go, can you just run over exactly what the security arrangements are here?"

The houseboy would have been within his rights to refuse to speak, but fortunately he had more sense than that. In answer to Ruso's question, he agreed that although the main door was locked at sunset, it was usually open in the daytime to allow the daylight and fresh air in. The twins couldn't reach the latch on the gate to the road, and the family relied on seeing any visitors coming up the steps. Yes, the boys had been out for an afternoon walk with Albanus as usual. The female staff? "In the kitchen all afternoon, sir. All the shopping is done in the morning." The master? "In his study, sir." Master Catus? "Out at work, sir. He's been very busy since he lost his assistant." Gleva had been out too. The houseboy did not know where and to judge by his tone, neither did he care. Ruso noted that she was no longer referred to as "Mistress Gleva" in her absence.

"So with everyone busy it might have been possible for somebody to slip into the house?"

The houseboy bristled. "Not without me noticing, sir. I was tidying up the plants around the terrace all afternoon."

While Ruso was wondering how to get him to admit he might have sat on the bench and rested his eyes in the sunshine, the houseboy said, "There was some native who tried to get in, but I saw him off."

"Native?"

"Tall, gangling thing he was. Not very old. Not very bright, either. Came wandering in, trying to sell onions. Kept saying 'I speak to cook' but he didn't understand a word of Latin."

"Did he speak to the cook?"

"No he did not, sir. He was lucky I saw him off before the master caught him."

"He was," Ruso agreed, because he doubted Esico would have stood up to much questioning by Pertinax. Once his suspicions were aroused, Pertinax might have had the house and garden searched, and Valens, who must have slipped in during the distraction, would have been found.

"One last question," Ruso said. "Do you know where Gleva was on the night Serena died?"

"I don't, sir. Not here. I'll ask the cook if she knows in the morning." The man stifled a yawn. "We don't know much about what Gleva does, to be honest."

"No matter." Ruso found himself yawning in return. "I was trying to place everyone. But we've all got more pressing things to worry about now."

"The masters have called out the veterans to search for the children, sir. Perhaps they'll find your wife too."

"Perhaps they will." He was grateful for the man's concern, but he doubted that any lone woman would allow herself to be found by a bunch of unfamiliar soldiers tramping the streets at night.

The houseboy unlocked the door. A gust of cold damp air swept in. "It's raining, sir. Quite heavily."

"Oh, perfect." As if tonight had not been difficult enough already.

"Would you like to wait inside till it eases off, sir?"

If he sat down, he would not want to get up again. So he bade the man good night, pulled his cloak up over his head, and strode out into the wet, raising one hand to acknowledge the houseboy's "Good luck, sir."

As he picked his way down the front steps with cold water spattering his face and seeping into his sandals, two things struck him. The first was that if the attack at the inn really had been aimed at him rather than Valens, it was not very sensible to be wandering about the streets at night on his own, armed only with a folding dinner knife. The second was that the only way the veterans would find Tilla was if she wasn't in a fit state to run away. Neither thought was of any comfort at all, and he realized he was getting as nervous as Albanus. It wouldn't do.

He fumbled for the gate latch, then took a deep breath and counted to three before lifting it and slipping out onto the street.

44

THE DOORKEEPER AT the Mercury was not pleased to be disturbed yet again. No, the doctor's wife still wasn't there. No, there hadn't been any sign of her. Ruso ignored the man's suggestions about where he could take himself, but he had few better ideas of his own. He was running out of places to try. Should he go back to the vegetable patch? Or the temple courtyard? At least it would be dry under the colonnade. But why would Tilla linger in a place where another woman had been murdered?

Finally he found himself standing under the dripping eaves of the oil shop, inhaling the rich aromas from within and wondering whether setting his mind at rest about Tilla was worth the risk of having Albanus and Virana evicted by an irate landlady. On balance, he decided it wasn't. If his wife was there, she was safe, whether or not he knew about it.

There couldn't be much of the night left. Since he had nowhere to sleep, he might as well keep looking. And since he had no plan, he began to splash his way up and down the streets of Aquae Sulis, pausing to call "Tilla?" over the gurgle of the water in the gutters, and to wait for a response that never came.

He was in an unfamiliar area between Pertinax's house and the
temple when the approaching tramp of boots reminded him that
he was not the only one on a search—although how the veterans
expected to run across any fugitives when they were making that
much noise and carrying torches was a mystery to him. Then he
heard the sound of fists hammering on doors and realized the four
men weren't expecting to stumble across Valens. They had turned
themselves into an unofficial night watch. They were conducting a
dawn raid on the pretext of alerting the occupants of Aquae Sulis
to the presence of a child snatcher who broke into people's houses
in the night. A child snatcher who was working with a native
woman accomplice.

When the doors of bemused and alarmed residents had closed
again, he approached the men in the street. They turned out to
be a different group from the veterans he had met before, so he
introduced himself before they could seize him and demand to
know what he was doing, wandering around in the rain at this
hour.

No, they had not seen any sign of a lone woman. "Quite tall,"
he persisted, realizing he had no idea what she might be wearing
and neither could he remember the color of her woolen wrap. "Slim,
curly fair hair; it might be done up tight in . . ." He was aware of
gesticulating vaguely toward his head, as if that might help. "Whatever those twist things are called."

"Plaits," the leader said, glancing at his comrades.

"That's the one," said one of the others.

"You've found her?"

"Not yet," said the leader. "You'd better come with us."

It sounded more like an order than a welcome. He followed them
under the shelter of a porch. "She isn't with Valens and the boys,"
he said, hoping it was true.

"No? What's she doing out in this, then?"

"She couldn't sleep." It was a better answer than *I think she went
to try and dig up a body*, but not much.

The leader's "Hm" suggested that he was not impressed. "She
got any friends she might have gone to?"

"It's possible she's gone to the bath-oil shop since I checked,"
Ruso explained, "but I don't want to give our friends more trouble
with their landlady at this hour."

The leader exchanged another glance with his men, one of whom said, "Worth going back there, boss?"

Ruso looked from one to the other of them in the torchlight. "You've been there already?"

They ignored his question, leaving him to speculate on the effect of yet another nocturnal interruption on Albanus's long-suffering landlady. "The boys definitely aren't there," he insisted. "That's where their tutor lives. Pertinax has already been there himself."

There was a pause while the veterans decided whether to believe him.

"I've just come from Pertinax's house," he continued. "I should have explained. I've known him for years. We served together. The staff can vouch for me."

"Then why does he think your wife's stolen his grandsons?" There was an understandable hint of *aha!* about the tone.

"Because she happened to go missing at the same time. Look, if you can't help, I'll move on." Although where he should go, he still had no idea.

"Nah, you don't want to go wandering off in the dark."

It was not exactly an arrest, but not far off. For all these men knew, he could be an accomplice in the kidnapping of the boys.

Conversely, for all Ruso knew, he could now be sharing the shelter of the porch with the man who had attacked him at the Traveler's Repose. Pertinax had denied any involvement, but what if one of his cronies had decided to silence Valens without telling the old man?

"Pertinax's daughter was a friend," he told them, glancing around the group but seeing no signs of a damaged face or singed hair in the shifting light. "We want justice for her, the same as you do. You might be able to help."

"We're helping already, mate," the leader pointed out. "We're looking for the bastard who did it."

Loitering in the background as more households were persuaded to open the door to wet visitors in the dark, Ruso noticed that the veterans were now warning of "a man who's taken two boys, and he might have a blond woman with him."

The search was, of course, organized rather than random. Even in his agitation, Pertinax was a professional. After years of occupying the troublesome island of Britannia—or, rather, the half of it they had managed to conquer and retain—one thing Rome's men knew how to do was conduct an efficient door-to-door search. They also knew how to time the completion of their allotted duties with the opening of the nearest bakery. To his surprise, the leader offered Ruso a share. He supposed it helped to preserve the illusion that they were all on the same side while conveniently encouraging him to stay where they could keep an eye on him.

Seated under the porch of a locked wineshop and nibbling at a chunk of bread that was almost too hot to hold, Ruso was struck by how much he missed the companionship of the legion. He supposed that was why the veterans continued to keep each other's company. Many of these men must have spent twenty-five years under orders, and while the priests seemed to view the Veterans' Association as a threat, its members probably saw it as a safe haven in an unfamiliar civilian world. *I've seen sights you'll never see, boy, and never want to.* Easier to be with people who didn't need you to explain.

"Tell me something," said Ruso, breaking off a hot flake of crust. "That fire at the Little Eagle—was that really an accident?"

"Bloody convenient one," observed the leader. "Not for the lads who died, of course."

"So who do you think . . . ?"

The man snorted. "Put it this way: If it was up to me, I'd lock up the whole of the Sulis Minerva Association till they hand over the one that did it."

Perhaps encouraged by this frankness, someone else put in, "I reckon it was that Terentius. Did it himself. What a waste of time he turned out to be."

"Or some drunk," offered a third voice.

They were warming to their theme now. "Or the natives."

"Maybe a drunk native. There's always one or two hanging around there."

"Anyhow," put in the leader, "it's got nothing to do with the centurion's daughter. Or the missing kids."

But his companions were too busy enjoying the speculation to be silenced. "It could have just been an accident," suggested someone.

"My money's on Terentius," repeated his accuser. "Couldn't swallow what he'd bitten off with them new baths and wanted out."

"But after it all went tits up, that was him in the clear, right? The fire finished it. The builders had nothing to come back to and nobody else would have taken it on. He didn't have to run."

"What would you do if you'd lit a fire that killed people?"

"I'd sit tight and keep my mouth shut."

"It was that lot from the temple," the leader insisted. "Didn't want to share the trade. Obvious."

Ruso said, "Is it?"

"Course. As long as I've been here, the priests have been talking about expanding the old baths. Always some reason why it couldn't start just yet."

"That's religion for you," said one of the others. "All talk and no action."

"I hear that's what they say about you too," observed one of his comrades.

"You want to ask your wife, mate."

"Hah! You wish."

"Anyway," continued the leader, undeterred, "then Pertinax came along and said it was a bloody disgrace. The legions built the whole lot in the first place and now we're only allowed in for half the day. So he stuck a few hornets up a few arses and in no time it's all happening. The magistrates vote it through, the plans are all put together, and a bunch of old tentmates turn up to do the job."

"It was never going to work, though," put in the man who favored Terentius as culprit. "Old Catus had more sense than his brother right from the start."

"Catus had to say that. He works for the temple lot. He was frightened of losing his job."

"That haruspex was against it."

The soldier snorted. "Old Willy-hat is best mates with the chief priest. What did you expect him to say?"

"Whatever the gods tell him," came the unexpectedly pious reply. "It's asking for trouble, arguing with the gods. See what's happened."

There was a brief silence and several of the men turned their attention to the bread. Then somebody said, "I still reckon it was the natives. The one that hangs round there looks like some sort of druid. And he's the brother of the boss's woman."

"Her with the hair?"

"Her who says she's a priestess. And hardly a virgin, right?"

"Not if the boss can help it."

"The boss can't help anything where she's concerned, mate. I tell you, she's put a spell on him."

"What would she want to burn down the Little Eagle for?"

"It's obvious, mate. Sabotage. The natives never wanted to give us that spring. Or the big one, either. Look at the way she flings herself around at the processions. It's not respectful, is it?"

"That's how they do things. The natives."

"I tell you, it's her. She's got powers."

"Well, you'd better hope she can't hear you with her powers," said the leader, heaving himself up from the borrowed bench with a grunt. "Time to get back to the house and report in."

45

COLD. COLD AND stiff. There was something foul in her mouth and her wrists hurt and her shoulders screamed with pain as she tried to move. She remembered where she was, and was suddenly wide-awake and on the alert and—what was that noise, cutting through the drumming of the rain on the roof? Something scuttling? Something nearby? Something *on her*?

Tilla shuddered and curled herself into a ball on the cold mud floor, scrabbling with her feet to pull her skirts down so she could tuck her legs underneath the protection of the wool, but it was not easy with hands and feet bound behind her.

There must be something I can do. She had tried kicking out earlier, when they first left her alone here. Her feet collided with what seemed to be an empty wooden box, which made a satisfying boom. But the hammering on the door that followed was only her captors telling her to shut up or they would tie her to a post. Did she want to be tied to a post?

No, she did not. And besides, there was nobody around to hear. As far as she could tell, this was some sort of old shed out on the edge of town.

She curled her tongue back and pushed it forward, trying again to shove the foul ball of cloth out of her mouth, but it was too big and they had tied the gag tight to hold it in. She stopped, afraid she would make herself vomit and choke.

After all the shifting about, she paused to listen, but there was nothing moving around her now. *Keep moving,* she told herself. *Mice are frightened of movement.*

Rats are bolder.

There are no rats in here. I would have heard them before.

She would have liked to draw on the courage of her ancestors, but with the gag around her mouth she could sing the words of the old songs only in her head, and it was hard not to be distracted.

My arms hurt. My shoulders hurt. The back of my head aches where they hit me. My ankles hurt. I want to be sick.

Don't think about feeling sick.

That's what I told my husband on the ship. I should have been kinder to him.

Don't think about feeling sick. Think about—

I need to pee.

Don't think about that, either.

But I really, really do need to— Was that a cockerel?

There it was again. She opened one eye and could make out dim shapes around and above her. The angles of crates, the bulges of sacks. Long, tilting stems that must be amphorae propped against a wall. The light was coming, and with it whatever the day would bring. Compared with the urge to pee, none of it seemed very important.

A lot of painful wriggling told her it was not easy to get up from the floor with hands and feet tied. The nearest crate shifted away as she pushed her shoulder against it, scraping across the floor and knocking something else over with a crash. She did not bother to stop and listen. She was desperate now. The crate seemed to have wedged against something and she leaned on it, gradually edging her ankles under herself until at last she was kneeling on top of her outstretched feet. It was as she leaned forward so she could put the soles of her feet on the floor—gritting her teeth against the pain— that she realized. She must have been too stunned last night to think of it. Her captors, who seemed never to have done this sort of thing before, had not thought of it, either. Her hands, tied behind her back, could now reach the knot in the cord around her ankles. Clumsily, with prickles running through her fingers as the movement brought the feeling back, she began to pick at the knot.

Later, finally able to take a few wobbly steps, she tottered across to the door and dragged the gag down off her mouth by hooking the edge of the fabric over the latch. Then she spat out the horrible soggy cloth.

By the time the rain had stopped and it was light outside, she was sitting on a box and sawing at the binding around her wrists with a shard of broken pot. That was when they came for her.

46

I F THE CLERK to the town magistrates was hoping to spend a quiet morning preparing for the arrival of the governor, he was to be disappointed. He had made the serious error of turning up to open the office, only to find three men already waiting outside. Pertinax heaved himself up from a damp bench overlooking the street. Ruso stepped away from the wall he had been lolling against and tried to pretend he wasn't racing the third man—who smelled of the stable—to be first in the queue.

"No business today, gentlemen, sorry." The clerk strode past the jostling trio and rattled the heavy iron key back and forth inside the lock until it found the right place. "Holiday for the Feast of Sulis Minerva and the governor's visit."

Pertinax put a heavy hand on the doorframe. "Holidays can wait."

"I've had two horses stolen!" declared the ostler.

Pertinax said, "I've come to liaise about the kidnapped children."

"And I can't find my wife," said Ruso, feeling upstaged.

"Two bay mares, one with a white blaze."

"She's the one who's taken my boys."

The clerk twisted the key and pretended not to have heard any of them.

Pertinax said, "I want to know what's being done."

"Valuable animals. Vanished overnight."

"She'll have taken them too," said Pertinax. "What's being done about it?"

Finally acknowledging them, the clerk looked down his nose at the centurion with the air of a man who was used to being told what to do, but not necessarily by people who knew what they were talking about. "The office is closed today, sir," he said. "The other magistrates have already been notified about the children, and any news will be sent to you. There have been several complaints about householders being woken during the night. The chief magistrate wants it known that any unofficial disturbance of residents will be frowned upon."

"That's it?" demanded Pertinax. "Tell him the veterans are getting ready to do more house searches."

The clerk looked alarmed at the suggestion. "But if the boys have been taken on horses, they won't be in the town, will they?"

Ruso had to admire the man's courage, if not his intelligence.

Pertinax's voice was dangerously quiet. "Are you arguing with me?"

The gulping movement in the clerk's throat betrayed his sudden awareness that he had made a mistake. "Sir, I'm sorry, but there's nobody here who can help you today. The other magistrates are all preparing for the festival. The governor will be here at any moment and the sacrifice will be made as soon as he gives the word. I've only come to collect the guest list for the official dinner."

"I would like," Pertinax repeated softly, "in a spirit of cooperation, to make an official report to my fellow members of the council of magistrates of Aquae Sulis that the two Roman citizens who were abducted from their home last night have still not been found, and that I, with the help of the Veterans' Association, will be doing whatever it takes to find them."

The clerk took a deep breath. "Yes, sir," he said, pushing open the door. "Please follow me and I'll take down the details and deliver your message to the chief magistrate."

Pertinax paused in the doorway to say to the ostler, "Send messages out with all the riders and vehicles leaving town, and report to me if they're found. There's a reward."

Ruso stepped forward, but Pertinax shut the door in his face.

"And me!" Ruso shouted. There was no response. "My wife could be in danger!"

The ostler said, "She's in danger all right if she's stolen my horses."

"Of course she hasn't stolen your horses! She's my wife!" As if that made it impossible. As if marriage had wiped away the skills and the memory of a woman brought up as the daughter of a horse breeder.

The ostler muttered that this was a waste of time and walked off. Ruso slumped down in the dry patch that Pertinax had left on the bench. He watched as a cat skirted a large puddle in the empty marketplace. Moments later he caught himself yawning, and forced himself to sit up straight. He wriggled his toes inside the damp chill of his sandals. This was not the time to fall asleep. What sort of man fell asleep when his wife had gone missing?

Things seemed to be ominously quiet inside the council office. Then he heard a roar of "Because he's a murderer!" and felt reassured that the clerk must still be capable of arguing.

A slave walked past with a basket of bread balanced on his head, and Ruso wondered whether his wife was hungry and whether he ought to go and check on his daughter.

Someone was entering the marketplace from the far corner. A woman. Three women.

"Tilla!" Ruso leapt off the bench.

"Husband!" She tried to move toward him, but the women on either side of her held her back. They had tied her arms.

He ran to her, seizing her face between his hands and looking into her eyes. "I've been looking all night! Are you all right?"

"They locked me in a shed," she told him.

There was mud on her chin, a graze on her cheek, and a bruise under one eye. The smart hairstyle was a straggled mess. He stepped back. "This is my wife. Let her go."

"This is thief!" declared one of the women. She had a weather-beaten face and an accent he couldn't place. Something Eastern.

"We have catch her!" declared the other one, obviously a relative. "We catch her stealing, doing damage, go to magistrate."

"Don't be ridiculous!" Tilla had not, as far as he was aware, stolen anything for a very long time. She certainly—well, probably—wouldn't have got out of bed in the middle of the night to do it. "You're making a mistake," he told them. "Let her go."

"Go to magistrate," insisted the woman, dragging Tilla forward in the direction of the council office. "You pay for stealing."

"There's nobody there," Ruso told them. "You're wasting your time. It's all shut for the holiday."

At that moment he heard the door open behind him. The clerk, evidently chastened by the encounter with Pertinax, called, "Sir, would you like to report your wife missing now?"

"There!" declared one of the women in triumph. "See? Magistrate!"

"This is thief!" cried the one who did not seem to know any other Latin.

The clerk evidently thought Ruso had not heard the invitation, and came closer. "Sir, if you'd like to report your wife—"

Ruso said, "She's not missing now."

"That's her!" cried Pertinax from the doorway.

The clerk looked at the trio of women and then back at Ruso.

"She'd been kidnapped," Ruso explained.

"This is thief!"

"Don't move!" ordered Pertinax, lurching toward them. Pushing Ruso aside and thrusting his face into Tilla's, he demanded, "Where are my boys?"

Tilla stared at him blankly.

"Where's he taken them?"

The women spoke rapidly to each other in their own tongue while Ruso hauled Pertinax aside. "Let me deal with this."

"This is thief!"

"Let her go," Ruso insisted, "and we'll sort this out."

"Thief!"

"What's she supposed to have stolen?"

"Vegetable, sir," said the one with more Latin, addressing Pertinax. "Lettuce. Carrot. Onion. Every week, something. And now we catch her in the night."

"*Vegetables*?" said Pertinax.

The ruined hairstyle flopped again as Tilla nodded a confession. Pertinax's voice was suddenly weary. "Let her go, you two."

"You've got the wrong person," Ruso insisted, relieved.

"We take her to magistrate. Magistrate decide."

Pertinax's "Let her go!" was loud enough to be heard on the other side of town. The two women leapt away from Tilla as if she were on fire.

Ruso stepped behind her, reaching for the little folding knife strapped to his belt. She flinched as he began to saw through the frayed rope around her swollen wrists. He murmured, "Are you sure you're all right?"

The ruined hairstyle flopped about again as she nodded.

Ruso held out the length of grimy rope and one of the women snatched it as if Tilla had tried to steal that too. Then he put his arm around his wife's shoulders and led her to the bench. The others crowded round as he sat beside her and said, "What happened?"

Tilla, busy rubbing her wrists, had barely drawn breath to reply when one of the women cried, "Magistrate!"

"Let her speak!" snapped Ruso, but the woman cried "Magistrate!" again, and pointed.

The council clerk was sprinting away down a side street with a scroll in one hand and a set of keys dangling from the other. Ruso lowered his head into his hands. "Tilla, Valens's boys have been taken. Do you know anything about it?"

"No! Who has taken them?"

"Valens, we think."

Pertinax remained silent.

Ruso said, "What's all this about vegetables?"

"This is thief!"

Unusually, it seemed Tilla had nothing to say in her own defense.

"She only came here two days ago," Ruso pointed out. "If you've been losing vegetables for weeks, it can't be my wife."

The women spoke to each other again in their own language.

"There is damage. Dead plants. All dig up. All flat. She is there in night with spade."

"There's damage to my wife too," he pointed out. "I won't sue you for kidnap and assault if you agree not to sue for anything that happened last night."

The woman with the Latin thought about that for a moment, then said, "We let her go." Her sister asked a question in their own tongue but, instead of replying, the first woman seized her by the elbow and hurried her away. As the sound of their argument faded, Pertinax said, "About that business at the inn last night . . ."

"Forget it," Ruso told him. "In your position, I'd have done the same."

He was aware of Tilla swaying beside him on the bench. "Let's get you back to, uh . . ." He stopped. Back to where, exactly?

"They call it the Mercury," she reminded him. "You look very tired, husband."

"We aren't in the Mercury anymore," he told her. "Neena's taken Mara over to the oil shop."

Pertinax said something and seemed to be expecting an answer.

Ruso yawned. Tilla was right: He was, indeed, very tired. He ran over what he thought Pertinax had said in his mind, trying to work out what he had managed to mishear as *I'll tell Gleva to get a room ready.*

"Sir?"

Pertinax said, "I'll tell Gleva to get a room ready."

47

TILLA STOOD IN the tub and poured another jug of warm water very slowly over her head. On Gleva's orders the little maid, looking puffy-eyed, had stayed to help her disentangle the strands of wool from her hair, but after that, Tilla had sent her away. It was sad enough to be offered Serena's bed in the room where she had slept next door to her boys, and Serena's comb, and Serena's old blue dress with the gold edging to change into: She did not want to be a burden on staff who were now mourning the loss of the children as well as their mother. "It's so quiet without the boys, miss!" the maid had explained, looking as though she was about to burst into tears again. "After we lost the mistress, they kept us all going with their chatter and running about. I keep wondering what's happening to them now."

Tilla had tried to explain that Valens had only stolen the boys because he was fond of them and that he was bound to be keeping them safe. The maid had sniffed and said, "Yes, miss," but showed no sign of believing Valens would care for his boys. Why would he if he had already murdered their mother?

What a mess.

Tilla bent down and refilled the jug. The sun was streaming in through the window and making bright shapes across the floor and up the wall. The weight of the heavy jug strained her bruised wrist, but she forced herself to lift it one-handed and pour slowly, letting the water trickle down over her scalp and using her free hand to dangle the loose strands of hair under the cleansing stream.

The wet hair was veiling her eyes when someone came into the room without knocking and announced, "It's me."

This was the moment she had been dreading. Her husband had barely spoken to her on the way there. Should she say sorry now, or wait for him to say what he had to say first? That might be better. It was hard to know where to start with someone who had every right to be angry with you, especially when you couldn't see his face.

"You look very appealing for a vegetable thief."

Perhaps he did not know how to start, either. She wiped the water out of her eyes and groped for the towel. She was not sure why, but she wanted to have all her clothes on before the argument started.

"Feeling better?"

"Much better." Perhaps it wasn't starting yet. She wrapped the towel around herself and stepped out of the tub.

"Gleva's gone out to the baths," he told her. "Albanus has gone home, and Pertinax and Catus are in a meeting with some veterans."

"I must go and fetch Mara." She should have said that earlier: as soon as she was freed. If she were a proper mother, her child would have been the first thing on her mind. But then, if she were a proper mother, she would not have abandoned her family and gone out disturbing the spirits of the dead with a spade in the middle of the night.

"I'll go across and fetch them both in a moment," he said. "Pertinax says we can all stay here for a while."

"Really?" She pulled Serena's blue dress over her head. "Why?"

"Maybe as an apology for getting us thrown out of the Mercury," he said. "With the added advantage that he's got us where he can keep an eye on us."

The sound of gruff voices and footsteps swelled outside and then faded. The centurion's meeting had finished. Tilla reached for the golden-yellow belt that matched the edging on the dress. She supposed the men were all going back out to carry on the hunt for Valens and the children.

He said, "Do you want me to go and find that spade and return it while I'm out?"

He was lying on the bed now, staring at the painted ceiling, sandaled feet dangling clear of the covers. He probably didn't know it was Serena's bed. He certainly wouldn't have recognized the clothes: Most evenings, if Tilla asked him what she herself had worn that day, he would have had to guess.

"It belongs to Virana's neighbor," she told him, wondering whether he really would leave it at that or whether he was waiting for her to explain. "The one in the pastry shop."

"Right."

One of them had to begin. Since he had mentioned the spade, she said, "I thought it would help if I went to look. I thought he might be buried there."

"Terentius?"

She nodded. "They did all that thing to find him but then nobody looked to see if they were right."

"So you decided to go and dig."

"I knew you would think it was silly, so I thought I would do it and not tell you."

"Hm." Then: "In the list of—" He stopped, searching for a word. "In the list of interesting and peculiar things you've done since I've known you, wife, that has to be the most interesting and peculiar of all."

"I thought you would be cross," she said.

"Yes," he said. "So did I."

She said, "So you will not ask to give Mara back?"

"What?" He rolled over and stared at her. "Back to Virana? Why would I do that?"

"Because I do interesting and peculiar things and I am not always there to look after her."

He thought about that for a moment. "Were there mice in the shed?"

She nodded. "And rats, I think."

He grinned. "That's all right, then."

"It was horrible."

"Good."

She gave her hair a quick rub and then draped the towel around her shoulders before sitting next to him on the bed. "I wish I had not done it."

"Well, at least it's satisfied you that he isn't there." When she did not reply, he said, "Hasn't it?"

She let go of the edge of the towel she had been twisting tight between her fingers, and smoothed it out. "What if his spirit really is there," she said, "and I have disturbed it?"

He sat up, pushed the wet hair aside, and put his mouth close to her ear. "He isn't there," he said very slowly, sounding the edges of each word. "He never was."

"How do you know? Those lettuces could have been transplanted. I should have told you."

He swung his feet down from the bed. "Terentius isn't there, wife. You looked and didn't find him. And the reason you didn't find him is that he's alive and well somewhere else, keeping clear of all the people who want to talk to him."

"So it really was him who killed Serena?"

There was a longer pause than she had expected. Then he said, "I'm going to go and fetch the others and pick up the luggage. If I can find the spade, I'll take it back. Then, if you like, we can go out and watch the parade."

After he had gone she reached for Serena's comb and began to tease out the ends of her hair. There had been no argument. She should have been relieved, but instead she felt confused.

48

THE VEGETABLE PLOTS did not look at all sinister in daylight. To Ruso's relief the borrowed spade was still lying in the mud of the lettuce bed. There was no sign of the outraged gardeners; just a couple of slaves hoeing weeds from a plot over by the wall. He guessed most of the town would have taken time off to watch the governor's arrival.

The streets were busy as he went to return the spade to its owner. Next door, Virana was sitting behind the counter of the empty oil shop with her feet propped on a stool. She greeted him with "You're back! Did you find Tilla? Albanus is asleep upstairs and Neena's taken Mara out for a walk. It's just me stuck here, and nobody tells me what's going on. I don't know why we're open. There's no customers."

He confirmed that his wife had turned up safe and well after being looked after by some local women.

"Why was she out in the middle of the night? Did you hear that rain?"

"She's over at Pertinax's house," he said, not elaborating. "Valens is—"

"What did she want a spade for?"

"To do some digging," he told her, unable to think of a plausible lie and hurrying on to explain that Valens and the boys were still missing, possibly on horseback, and Pertinax and Catus and the veterans were still looking for them. No, he still did not know who had killed poor Serena or where Terentius had gone.

"So," Virana said, shifting her weight on the chair and tugging her rumpled tunic down over her belly, "we don't know anything we didn't know before."

"I'm moving everything over to Pertinax's house," he told her, not wanting to admit that she was right.

Virana seemed less surprised by the news of the move than he had expected. "I should think that old man ought to be nice to you," she said. "You did cut his leg off for him."

"If only everyone saw things that way."

"Well, they should," she told him. "I always tell people you are a nice man underneath."

He said, "Can you tell Neena where we've moved to?"

"What's happened to that other one? The tall one."

"Esico?"

"That's him."

"I don't know," he admitted. "He does tend to wander."

Virana reached out to dip one finger in a jar of oil and sniff it. "You should give him a good beating," she suggested, dabbing the oil behind her ears.

"You think that would encourage him to stay?"

"Probably not," she conceded. "You can go up and talk to my husband if you like. The Old Misery's gone to watch the parade, so I can let in anybody I want. I'm only staying because she gets the neighbors to tell her if I close the shop. She was really horrible about being woken up last night. You'd think she'd want to help, wouldn't you?"

"Not everyone is like you, Virana," he told her. "When Albanus wakes up, tell him I'll see him later."

The Mercury was not as he remembered it. Instead of the front being wide open in welcome, two burly doormen were standing outside a row of closed shutters with their arms folded and glaring straight through anyone who dared to approach. When this didn't frighten Ruso away, the nearest one announced, "Private party for the governor."

"I left a trunk here."

"All luggage has been cleared. Governor's guests only."

He was on the verge of arguing when he heard a familiar voice cry, "Master!"

Esico sprinted across the road, flung himself at Ruso's feet, and cried again, in Latin, "Master! Forgive!"

Before Ruso could reply, they were both seized and manhandled away from the Mercury's entrance.

It was over as quickly as it began. The doormen stepped back to resume their stations as if nothing had happened, leaving Ruso standing in the middle of the street and Esico sprawled on the stones. Glancing around to see who had witnessed his humiliation, Ruso saw that the old man was back in his usual seat outside the bar, not only watching, but now raising a hand to beckon him over. There were two cups beside his jug of beer now instead of one, but no sign of a companion.

"Did you come for a big wooden box?" the man asked in British.

"Yes."

"It was in the front this morning, then Beardy came out and told his boys to take it through into the yard."

"Thank you." Ruso reached for his purse. There were some benefits to having nosy neighbors.

Light of a couple of coppers, he turned back to Esico, who was now hovering anxiously as if he thought Ruso might be about to run away from him. "Master—"

"Come and help me shift some luggage," Ruso told him. "You can tell me what you've done and I'll decide what to do about it."

The trunk was indeed in the backyard of the Mercury, to which Ruso gained access by sending an unusually willing Esico scrambling over the gate to let him in. When they were safely in the back lane and he had checked that the lock on the trunk was intact, he said, "Right. Talk."

Esico dropped to his knees on the gravel. Ruso told him in British not to be annoying and reached for one handle of the trunk. "Take the other end of this. You can talk and walk at the same time."

Esico dusted off his knees and heaved up the other end of the trunk. "In my own tongue, master?"

"In your own tongue," Ruso confirmed. "This is important. Do you know where Valens took them?"

"No, master. He didn't tell me."

"Do you know anything that would help me find out?"

"No, master. He said it was best for me not to know too much." He stopped. "Esico, you smell of horses."

"Yes, master!" The lad seemed to be unaccountably proud of it.

"When did you last see Valens?"

"Yesterday morning early, master." So before either the horses or the boys had gone missing.

"Where?"

Esico raised one long arm in the direction of the river. "We slept in the woods, master. I didn't like it much. It's cold at night and you wake up itchy."

Nor for the first time, Ruso wondered what sort of a warrior Esico had been.

"Doctor Valens sent me to buy food, but after that there was no work for me to do."

"That's never bothered you before."

"Doctor Valens said I could come back to you."

"So, where have you been since yesterday morning?"

"I went for a walk, master."

"This going for walks has got to stop. I've spoken to you about it before."

"Yes, master. I am sorry, master."

"Well, you're here now. Get on with it."

"I thought I might walk back to my own people. But then I was tired and hungry and all by myself in the woods, and I thought, *It is a long way and it is raining, and I am a fool.*"

Ruso did not argue.

"I thought, *My master and mistress have been good to me, and this is no way to repay them.* So I turned around to come back and prayed to the gods for some way to make amends, and this morning the gods answered my prayer and they sent—"

"Two bay mares, one with a white blaze?" Ruso suggested.

The weight of the trunk jolted in his hand as Esico turned to stare at him. "Did you have a vision, master?"

"Not exactly."

"I found them loose on the Abona road," Esico continued, "saddled, but with no riders. So I rode back into town to sound the alarm and the owner of the stables said they were stolen and he gave me this in thanks, master." Esico delved into a fold of his tunic. "So I am giving it to you." He reached across and placed something on the trunk.

To Ruso's amazement he saw a silver denarius. "Oh, holy gods." He snatched up the small coin, hoping no one had seen it. It would have paid a legionary for a day, and hired a slave for longer.

"It is yours, master. Because I ran away."

He wanted to say *No it isn't*. Largely because it wasn't rightfully Esico's, either. "They must have been good horses."

Esico grinned. "The best."

Ruso tried to gather his thoughts while dealing with the awkward task of shoving the denarius one-handed into his purse. Only when he had finished did he say, "Is any of that story true, Esico?"

"Oh, yes, master! It is all truth, I will swear to it!"

"Please don't," Ruso told him. "We've had enough vengeance of the gods as it is. When I asked 'Do you know where Valens took them' just now, you were supposed to say 'Took who?' But you didn't. You already knew I was talking about the boys. You helped him take them. You were the visitor who went to their house pretending to sell onions."

"I did not understand the question, master."

"But we've already agreed that if you don't understand something, you'll say so."

"I am sorry, master."

"Stop saying sorry. It's annoying. So again: Is any of that story true?"

There was a pause. Then, "I did buy food. And it was very cold and itchy in the woods."

Ruso sighed. "Virana says I should give you a good beating for running away."

"Yes, master."

They had reached the gate that led to Pertinax's house. Lowering his end of the trunk to the ground and gesturing to Esico to do the same, he said, "Before we go in there, I want to know what really happened."

Instead of answering, Esico turned to face the wall and appeared to be trying to retract his head into his body like a turtle.

"What's the matter?"

"This is not a good place to stand, master. Someone might remember me."

Ruso pushed open the gate, and Esico shuffled sideways as they carried the trunk inside and set it down at the foot of the steps. The little maid ran down to greet them. Her face fell when she heard there was still no news, but she managed to remember her duties enough to offer to help with the luggage.

"Don't worry," Ruso assured her. "I just need a chat with Esico here, then he's going to carry it up all those steps by himself."

The maid retreated, but before Ruso could extract the truth from his slave, they were interrupted by a knock on the gate. Esico shot an alarmed look at Ruso and plunged into the shrubbery that grew against the inside of the wall. Ruso opened the gate and found himself staring into a face that was familiar and yet totally out of place.

Not only had Ruso never seen the old man anywhere other than the bar opposite the Mercury before, he had never seen him standing up. He was unexpectedly tall. And he had come, he said, to ask for his son.

Wondering if the word had a different meaning in the South, Ruso said, "Your what?"

"My son," the man repeated. "My boy." And then, in case Ruso was having trouble with the language, "*Filius.*"

So. Pertinax had lied when he said he'd never seen this man before in his life. The man had family connections at Pertinax's house. He had been spying on them after all.

Ruso stepped aside to let him go up to the house, but the man seemed reluctant to pass.

"Where is my son?"

Ruso pointed at the steps. "You'll have to ask up there."

"My son is here! I saw him!"

Ruso began to explain that he had only just arrived himself, but the man interrupted him with "I know you are here, boy!"

A brief silence, then a rustling from the shrubbery. One of the bushes was thrashing about as if a large and clumsy animal had got itself stuck in there. Moments later Esico's head appeared above the leaves.

"My son!" cried the man, holding out one bony hand as if to introduce him to Ruso. "See? Esico!"

Ruso looked from one to the other, realizing at last why the old man had looked familiar. And understanding why there had been two cups on the table beside the beer jug earlier. But not understanding at all why nobody had told him any of this before.

"I think I'd better fetch my wife," he said.

49

Ruso paced across to the far wall, spun on his heel, and paced back. The smallness of the room annoyed him. The sight of his wife sitting on the bed annoyed him. The fact that he was annoyed annoyed him, because until now he had remained calm in the face of intolerable behavior. He had put up with ingratitude, treachery, willfulness, disobedience, stubborn ignorance, and mockery. He had told himself that his tolerance was patient strength. He had pictured himself as a modern-day Atlas, bearing the weight of the heavens upon his shoulders, but now he was beginning to wonder. Maybe he wasn't as heroic as he liked to imagine. Maybe he had been shirking his responsibilities.

Ever since he had first arrived in this wretched province, he now saw, he had allowed himself to be surrounded by natives who did whatever they wanted at his expense. Every attempt to escape—to Gaul, to Rome—had ended with a return to Britannia. Well, it was time to change. He was the head of the household. He would assert some authority.

"We're going," he repeated. "And Esico isn't coming with us."

"But—"

"We can go to the celebrations tonight if you want. Dance if you have to. But we're leaving on the first boat in the morning."

"It is not the leaving I mind," she said. "It is—"

"Tilla, I've had enough!"

She did not reply. Not even to point out that he was shouting and that everyone in the house must be able to hear. He lowered his voice and said, "Well?"

"Well," she said, "you have had enough. So we will leave on the first boat in the morning."

"Exactly," he said. "Which is why it's not worth unpacking anything."

"No."

"I've made my decision."

"Yes."

He paced to the end of the room and turned. "Aren't you going to say something?"

"No."

He waited, but that was it.

That was *it*? "There's no need to sulk."

The wide gray-blue eyes looked into his own, just as they had on that day when he had first met her, a slave at the point of death. She said, "What would you like me to say, husband?"

For some reason that request was more annoying than anything that had gone before. And that was what led him to grasp the air above his head and let out a roar of exasperation.

In the silence that followed, he began to suspect that his wife, sitting very still on the bed as if trying not to be noticed, secretly thought he had gone mad. And that she might be right. To his surprise, nobody knocked on the door. Then he remembered that this was Pertinax's house. They were used to shouting.

Tilla reached for her spinning and silently put it away in a cloth bag. He pulled his tunic straight, cleared his throat, and said, "You have to understand, wife. There's nothing more we can do here. Valens has taken his boys to Abona and sailed off on some ship to the-gods-know-where, Pertinax can fight his own battles with the chief priest, and nobody's going to help us find the man who killed Serena. The only thing that's likely to happen if we stay is that I'm going to be accused of harboring a horse thief."

"It was very brave," Tilla murmured, "to take two of the best mares and all their tack."

"So Esico seemed to think," Ruso told her. "Men have been executed for less. And as soon as word gets around—which it will—the landlord at the Mercury will remember seeing Esico with Valens. And somebody will work out that the same slave who helpfully brought back the stolen horses was probably the one who stole them in the first place so that Valens could make a quick getaway."

Tilla said, "Oh."

"At last we've found something he can do. And now we know what it is, the sooner we get rid of him, the better."

Tilla said, "That old man does not want him back."

"Of course he does. He's been hanging around here for days, plucking up the courage to ask."

"If he wanted him back," she said, "he would be offering you money, not asking for it."

"He's not getting any money. I told him. We bought his son in good faith from a legitimate dealer. If he wants compensation, he'll have to go after the people who stole the boy in the first place."

Tilla said, "He sold the boy himself, husband. To pay a debt."

"What?"

"Esico told me while you were talking to the father. Why do you think he did not say 'There is my father' when he first saw him? Who do you think taught him how to steal horses? Why did he make up a story about his father being thrown out of the tribe so we would not send him home?"

Ruso sank down onto the bed and pondered this new information. "It's no good," he told her eventually. "I can't solve everyone's problems. All I want is to live in peace and help a few patients. If Esico needs help, he can go and ask Sulis Minerva for a miracle. Frankly, he can go where he likes as long as I'm not responsible for him anymore. He can't stay with us."

"Anywhere but with us," Tilla agreed sadly. "Do you want me to tell him?"

"No." He got to his feet. "It's my job. I'll do it."

He was already rehearsing what to say when he heard a commotion over in the entrance hall. Gleva was shouting for the staff to come right away. He got there just as Pertinax lurched out of his study with a rare smile on his face, stood in the middle of the hall, and announced, "Good news, everyone! They've got him! Our boys are on the way home!"

50

TILLA HAD HOPED that an evening of food and music and dancing might cheer them all up, but since the news that Valens had been captured, even the sun had lost heart and left early. The sky had turned iron gray and a cold wind was whipping across the open space of the courtyard. Slaves were hurrying to dismantle a cluster of flapping stalls set out beside the temple steps, and lugging tables laden with wares in under the shelter of the portico. People were squinting up at the clouds and telling each other there was going to be a storm. Those who had set out in the sunshine to watch the parade tightened their flimsy wraps around their shoulders and glanced enviously at others who had thought to bring cloaks and blankets. Nobody seemed to be leaving, though. Tilla supposed that most people would rather stay out in the cold and be entertained than go back to chilly boardinghouse rooms shared with strangers.

"Not a good start," observed a local man with a faded ginger moustache who was gazing at the sky. "Looks like the gods are planning to piss on the new governor."

"When you're a god, Brecc," someone retorted, "you can piss on the new governor yourself. Till then, you'd best keep your mouth shut."

Tilla followed her husband across the courtyard to the shelter of
the portico. They had chosen to spend the evening here rather than
wait at Pertinax's house for the children to be returned, but neither
of them seemed to be looking forward to the evening's events. The
look of betrayal in Esico's eyes still haunted her, even though she
could see why her husband felt the lad had to go. As he had pointed
out, Esico was old enough to live independently of his father. But
with a treacherous parent and a tribe who knew him as the son of
the horse thief, where would he go? Not every slave was better off
in freedom. Surely they had some lingering duty to him?

Even the sight of Virana carrying Mara across to join them and
calling, "She likes me now, see?" failed to lift Tilla's spirits, although
Mara did her best by beaming and reaching out for her parents.
Neena, following close behind, looked relieved as Virana handed
Mara over to be hoisted onto the safety of her father's shoulders. He
and Albanus stepped aside to talk, both looking very serious, while
Virana was keen to share the latest news. "The boys are found. Did
you hear?"

Tilla said, "How did you know?"

"Everyone knows. Poor Doctor Valens, he'll be very disappointed. I hope the centurion doesn't hurt him too badly. Oh,
look, they're opening up the bathhouse early! I was hoping they
would." Virana grabbed her husband's arm. "Quick, let's go across.
We can warm up in the hall while they do all the temple stuff out
here."

Albanus said, "Wife, they will be expecting you to help set up
the pastry stall."

"In a minute," Virana told him, and turned to Tilla. "I said I'd
help next door sell pastries. She's much nicer than the Old Misery.
I'll go and find her in a moment."

They joined the general drift toward the sacred spring and
the bathhouse, but everyone else had the same idea, and progress
was slow. They were still outside when there was a clatter of
hooves from the direction of the archway. A ripple of expectation
ran through the courtyard as the rider pulled his mount to a halt
and caused it to rear up, which made a fine spectacle for the crowd.
Mara, who could see everything from her high perch, cried out
and smacked her father on the head in her excitement.

"Aulus Platorius Nepos, governor of the province of Britannia, is approaching!" the man shouted. "He is now crossing the Londinium Road bridge!"

The crowd cheered. Tilla felt a splash of cold on her cheek and wiped away a raindrop just as another voice cried, "More good news, friends!"

Everyone turned to see Chief Priest Dorios swathed in a gleaming white toga standing at the top of the temple steps. "The child thief has been caught!"

The cheering was mixed with jeers and threats against the child thief. Dorios raised a hand and waited for silence before he added, "And the missing children are being returned!" That brought the greatest cheer of them all, followed by a loud buzz of excited conversation. In spite of the weather, this year's Feast of Sulis Minerva was off to a splendid start.

People hurried forward to talk to the priest as he descended the steps. Tilla felt more raindrops and her husband swung their daughter down to shelter her in the crook of his arm.

Tilla tugged Mara's wrap up over her head. The crowd trying to push its way into the bathing hall was barely moving. They gave up and returned to the shelter of the colonnade. Tilla said, "What do you think is happening to Valens?" But of course her husband knew no more than she did.

Virana, though, was much better informed. "The centurion sent Gnaeus to Abona in the night with a message," she announced. To her husband she said, "You know, the one who used to be a dispatch rider. He owns the bar behind the temple with the fishes on the wall."

"Used to own," put in Tilla, irritated that the girl seemed to know so much more than they did themselves.

Virana paused. "Really? They've sold it at last? Where are they going?"

"Somewhere on this side of town," said Tilla, wishing she had not set Virana off on a side path. "What happened in Abona?"

Albanus said, "Wife, the pastry stall—"

"I'm doing my best," Virana told him. "She'll be in the bathhouse, and it's not my fault we can't get in." Turning to Tilla, she said, "I suppose Gnaeus just told everybody in Abona to look for a man with twins. It's hard to hide two boys that look the same, isn't it? I suppose you could dress one as a girl or carry one on board in a sack or something, but I don't suppose there was time to do that."

Albanus, no doubt used to filtering out the little scraps of news that flowed past in his wife's torrent of words, suggested, "Valens was caught getting on a ship?"

"That's what I heard," Virana agreed. "It's a shame for him, isn't it? After all that trouble he must have gone to. But if the boys are back, then at least you still have a job teaching them, so the Old Misery might throw us out for making too much noise but she won't be able to say we can't pay the—oh, there's the fire-eaters!"

"Wife, you need to—"

"Two parades in one week: Isn't it good? I expect they want to perform before the rain puts them out. You can see it coming down now. Look."

Albanus took her by the arm. "Wife, the pastry stall."

As he hurried her away through the water dripping off the colonnade roof Tilla heard her own husband murmur, "I'm hoping Mara takes after her father. Whoever he is."

"Virana has a good heart," Tilla reminded him. "And she is just what Albanus needs."

She never found out what he thought of this because there was something new happening out in the courtyard. People who had scattered to take shelter from the rain were surging back into the open, yelling, "Stop him!" and "Mind the children!" and "Child stealer!"

Ruso startled her with a yell of "Leave him alone!" so loud that Mara was crying in fright as he bundled her into Tilla's arms. "Wait there."

Ahead of them, a gang of temple slaves had appeared from somewhere and were piling into the crowd, clubs and staves raised above their heads.

Tilla handed the baby to her minder. "Neena will keep you safe, little one," she promised, kissing Mara on the head. Then, dodging the crush by the altar, she sprinted across the wet flagstones to the temple steps.

Even standing halfway up to the temple, it was very hard to see what was happening through the rain. Below her was a mass of heads and shoulders and flailing arms and clubs rising and falling:

people screaming and trying to escape and others trying to shove their way into the fight, yelling "Child stealer!"

Her husband's bloodied face appeared by the high altar and then vanished again in the confusion. "Leave them alone!" she screamed, as if it would do any good. And then: "They are his own boys! He is not a child stealer!" And when that had no effect: "Holy Sulis, save them!"

And then as she watched, helpless, something out there changed: Some of the temple slaves and men who looked like old soldiers seemed to have rallied and were trying to form a protective wall, and inside it her husband and Valens were racing up the temple steps toward her, each carrying one of the boys. Her husband had blood dripping from somewhere under his wet hair. Valens's eye looked swollen. Both were yelling one word over and over again: "Sanctuary!"

She ran forward to help, but someone pushed her out of the way.

"Great Sulis, help them!" she cried again, but the goddess's plinth in the temple was empty, and as the men approached the sanctuary the great doors were closing to keep them out.

Tilla ran up the steps and flung her shoulder against the massive expanse of studded bronze. She pushed with all her strength, but the door was still moving, forcing her back. Then someone seized her by the hair and dragged her across the temple entrance and she was tumbling down the cold steps, banging her head and her elbows and then being grabbed again and hauled to her feet.

By the time she had gathered her wits, the great doors had clamped shut. Five or six disheveled and blood-spattered temple slaves were lined up in front of the entrance, several smacking their clubs into their palms as if they were daring anyone to come up the steps for a beating.

She tugged at the plaid sleeve of a woman beside her and asked in British, "The men with the boys: Where did they go?"

"Threw the staff out and shut themselves in the temple," said the woman. She leaned forward to spit on the ground, narrowly missing Tilla's boots. "Scum. Both of 'em." She raised her voice to shout, "They've got the kids in there! Break the door down, you cowards!"

Tilla said, "But they are his own children!"

"People like that don't deserve to have children."

One of the temple staff stepped forward and yelled at the crowd to stand back. He was greeted with a cacophony of jeering and demands to save the boys and bring the men out here for the crowd to deal with.

When he cried, "They are his own children!" a shoe flew toward him and hit the door inches from his head. A hail of footwear followed. Then there were voices from somewhere else: a wild blast on a trumpet and a steady *thud-thud-thud* that Tilla remembered from the awfulness of the troubles in the North: the beating of drawn swords on shields. The terrible music that signaled the advance of men who showed no mercy.

Behind and below her, the crowd began to scatter. There was a shriek as someone slipped and tumbled off the side of the steps in their haste to get away.

"Romans!" complained the woman Tilla had spoken to. "Pathetic. Always defend their own. They ought to break the doors down." But she too joined the retreat.

Tilla stepped forward, trying to find out what was happening, but the guards threatened to turn her over to the soldiers. Rubbing the bump on her head and each sore elbow in turn, she slipped away to find her frightened baby. She would have to leave her husband, Valens, and the boys inside the temple, under the protection of— she was not sure who, really. The spirit of Sulis Minerva, whose statue was still somewhere on the parade? Or the temple slaves, who had heeded Valens's plea for sanctuary? Or the governor's guard? Or perhaps just a few inches of bronze-plated wood that would have to be opened sometime. She could not imagine what would happen when they were.

51

GIVEN THE GODS' lively reputations for seduction, betrayal, and murder, Ruso had never understood why honoring them involved such a lot of tedious recitation and meandering around. Today, though, he was glad of it. The longer the procession took to circle the courtyard, the longer the voices droned on in the rain, the longer the sacrificial innards took to burn, and the more verses there were to the hymns being chanted by the choir out on the porch, the better. Perhaps the chief priest and the governor were conspiring to bore the Britons into docility.

The chairs and bedsteads he and Valens had piled against the inside of the temple doors were still there, but nobody was trying to invade. The rioters had gone into retreat at the sound of the governor's troops. There had been a pause while Dorios and the other officials stood outside to debate whether the ceremony could proceed with the goddess locked out of her own temple. In the end they had agreed that, since Sulis Minerva was able to survey proceedings from the top of the steps, it was safe to go ahead and sacrifice the ram as planned.

Meanwhile, Ruso tried not to drip his own blood on the pure-white temple blankets as he made up one of the beds supplied for the goddess's patients while Valens coaxed his frightened children out of their wet clothes.

Once the children were in bed, Valens clambered across the heap of furniture, peered out through the gap between the doors, and observed that the priests were having trouble getting the altar fire lit. "They've left the big statue out there to protect us, boys," he said. "I'm looking out past Sulis Minerva's armpit."

The goddess's presence seemed to offer little cheer to the pale and frightened children. Ruso was even less impressed. Doubtless the difficulty of lighting the fire would be blamed not on the rain but on the sacrilege of the two men who had barricaded the goddess out of her own home. Still, they were safe in there for a while. Nothing would be allowed to interrupt the ceremony, because if that happened the priests might have to go back to the start and begin again. It was hard to imagine anyone except Valens and himself wanting that.

Eventually the boys stopped crying and dropped off to sleep, cuddled together under the watchful gaze of one of the temple treasures: a painted stone maiden whose skimpy clothes served no apparent purpose at all.

If ever anyone needed divine assistance, Ruso decided, it was Valens's children. They had lost their mother, heard their father accused of killing her, been spirited away from home on horseback in the middle of the night—"I told them it was an adventure," Valens explained—seen their father arrested, and been in the middle of a melee in which he was almost murdered by an angry mob. Now they were trapped in the richly painted gloom of a temple with no windows, and Valens was adamant that none of them would leave until he got justice.

Meanwhile their father's friend was sitting on the marble floor beneath a plaque commemorating the miraculous healing of one Bodukus of the Cornovii. He was holding a blood-soaked cloth to his forehead and was drifting into a sentimental and sleepy reverie about the innocent pleasures of making hay and tending sheep on Tilla's family farm when he heard Valens's voice.

"Uh?"

"How's the head?"

"Could be worse."

Valens removed a lamp from one of the brackets beside the treasure display and knelt beside him. "Let me see."

Ruso lifted the cloth for a moment and got a close view of the swollen purple lids that had now met over his friend's left eye.

Valens handed him the lamp, squinted at Ruso's injury, and poked it with a forefinger before declaring it to be only superficial. "They can't throw you out of a temple if you claim sanctuary, can they?"

"Can't they?"

"No, I'm sure of it. That would be outrageous."

As outrageous as horse theft or invading the house of a goddess and locking her outside in the rain.

"You need a few stitches," Valens told him, "but I doubt there's anything here to do them with."

Ruso clamped the cloth back against his head. "I don't want it stitched by a one-eyed man in the dark anyway."

"In case you feel like asking," Valens told him, "my eye is throbbing, and it feels like a watermelon. But I'm not complaining." He got to his feet and wandered back to the treasure table. "For a goddess of healing, she hasn't got anything here that's very useful." He picked up a bronze ring, slid it onto one finger, then removed it and put it down again. There was a little ivory carving with two lumps that might represent breasts in need of the goddess's assistance, and a clay model of a foot. "Although these might come in handy." He held up a bronze ceremonial sword and a brightly painted round shield that would barely have protected a ten-year-old.

"If you get in any more fights," Ruso told him, "you're on your own."

From somewhere outside came the wail of a horn. The choir burst into a new hymn. The ceremony was grinding its way forward. Sooner or later there would be angry men outside again, shouting demands through the door.

"Cheer up, Ruso," announced Valens, bringing a pewter jug over. "Somebody's given the goddess some wine. I can at least clean you up."

"Marvelous."

"Even though you don't sound very grateful."

They were already in so much trouble that there was no point in telling Valens to leave the wine alone. "I thought they were going to kill us," Ruso said. "What the hell were you doing, running into the temple courtyard with all those people there?"

Valens glanced at the boys. "By the time I worked out how to spring the lock on the carriage door, we were back in town. I thought the best chance of escape was to hide in the crowd." He folded a cloth into a pad and poured some wine onto it. "I didn't know we were famous." He dabbed Ruso's injured head with the damp cloth. "Nothing's quite gone to plan lately."

"At least your career in horse theft seems to have been a—ow!"

"I think the bleeding's stopped now. I had no idea those horses were stolen. I sent your lad straight back with them when I found out."

"Where did you think they came from?"

"I don't know. He said he could get them for me."

Ruso said, "By magic?"

"I assumed he had local contacts."

"He does. His father is a horse thief."

Valens paused with the cloth in midair. "You didn't tell me that."

"I didn't—ow!—I didn't know."

Valens put his head on one side to survey his work. "That'll have to do. You don't look quite as frightening as you did."

Ruso grunted something that Valens could interpret as thanks if he wanted to.

Valens dragged an ornately carved folding chair off the barricade and set it up next to Ruso, facing toward the shapes that were his children, asleep under the blood-spattered blanket. Ruso pondered the effort required to heave himself up and fetch another chair, and decided he could doze just as well where he was. "Throw me a pillow, will you?"

Valens obliged. "I'm not leaving them, you know."

"I know."

Ruso lay back and closed his eyes. Moments later he heard the creak of the chair as Valens got up. That was good. Better to keep one man on watch. Meanwhile, this was the place where patients were supposed to be sent helpful dreams. Perhaps while Ruso caught up with the lost sleep from last night, Sulis Minerva would tell him who had killed Serena.

He hardly seemed to have dropped off when he heard the voice. "Bodukus," it said.

Bodukus? A native name. Bodukus. It sounded familiar.

"Of the Cornovii," continued the voice, "had a painful shoulder for a year. Sulis Minerva prescribed daily bathing in the waters and a plaster of barley meal and bear's fat and—"

"Shut up. I'm trying to sleep."

"These things are fascinating," said Valens, unabashed. "He'd had this bad shoulder for a year and the goddess cured it in a month."

"Hmph."

"Of course, it doesn't say whether he'd seen a mortal doctor first."

"Or whether he'd done what he was told to do when he did," Ruso grunted.

Valens stepped over Ruso and carried on exploring the walls, holding up the lamp to illuminate the plaques and painted inscriptions in between the pillars. "Lots of infertility," he remarked. "Tilla might be—sorry, is that a sore point?"

"No," Ruso lied.

"Oh, this one's interesting!"

"Tell me in the morning."

"Some chap's cure for blindness was withdrawn until he brought the offering he had promised. So first he can't see, then he can, and then he can't, and then—"

"I really don't care," Ruso told him.

"I think this Sulis Minerva might be my new favorite goddess."

When Ruso did not reply, he said, "D'you think there are sacred snakes in here?"

"No."

"It's all right, the boys aren't listening. They're sound asleep."

Ruso sighed and hauled himself back up to a sitting position. It was clear that Valens was too agitated to stop talking, and no amount of complaining would help. Sleep would have to wait a little longer.

After remarking on a daughter who was cured of dropsy when her mother bathed in the local waters ("How does that work, with someone else taking the cure?"), Valens wandered back to the treasure table, picked up a small bottle, and shook it. "I think these might be somebody's gallstones. They're quite splendid. Want a look?"

"No."

Valens put the bottle down and helped himself to a pair of decorated silver cups. He blew into them, then wiped them both out with a fistful of his tunic before pouring wine into each one. He took a sniff at a second jug and wrinkled his nose.

Ruso said, "No good?"

"Water from the spring."

The statement was terse, and Ruso wished he hadn't asked. He looked at the glittering cup in his friend's hand, reminded himself that it wasn't sensible to drink unwatered wine on an empty stomach, and took it anyway. Valens raised his matching silverware in salutation. "To Sulis Minerva, and sanctuary," he said.

"Sulis Minerva, and sanctuary."

They both tipped their heads back.

Valens jerked forward as he tried to control the choking, while the wine seemed to be stripping several layers off the inside of Ruso's mouth.

Recovering, Valens gasped, "No wonder she didn't want it."

"She can drink the rest herself." Ruso handed back the cup.

Valens poured the rejected wine back into the jug, shook out the remaining drops, and wiped the cups clean with his tunic. Then he helped himself to a pillow from somewhere in the corner and finally settled down in the chair.

Ruso leaned against the wall and glanced up into the gloom that hid the temple ceiling. He wondered when Valens would realize that he was going to be alone in this sanctuary with his boys before long, because Ruso didn't have to stay here, and he wasn't going to. He closed his eyes.

His gentle drift into oblivion was interrupted by "If the boys had been hurt out there, it would have been my fault."

"They weren't."

One of the boys muttered something. The bed creaked.

"Ruso?"

"Mm?"

"I need to know something."

"I'm trying to sleep."

"This is important. I need to know before they come for us."

Ruso stifled a yawn. "Go on, then."

"Do you believe I did it?"

"Did you?"

"No."

Ruso heard himself say, "Then we'll fight Pertinax in court."

"I suppose it's the only way now."

"Mm."

Valens said, "What have you found that we can use?"

Ruso took a slow breath in and wondered how to break the news that he had found nothing conclusive at all. He said, "We'll ask the governor for time to track down Terentius."

"That might take months. I can't keep the boys in here forever."

"The boys aren't in need of sanctuary," Ruso pointed out. "You are."

Instead of easing off, the rain had grown heavier; he could hear it drumming on the roof tiles now. He continued, "Everything's a lot more complicated when you have children."

Valens said, "They are when you haven't got a wife."

Outside, the choir burst into song again.

Valens said, "They'll go to Pertinax, won't they?"

"You know he'll look after them."

"So. After all this bloody time and effort, we're back where we started."

"No." Ruso bowed his head and tried to massage the stiffness out of his shoulders. "When we started, you could just walk out of the inn. This time you're trapped."

52

TO TILLA'S SURPRISE the priests who were gathered around the altar in the rain showed no sign of wanting to hurry, although the slaves who had the job of holding the covers up over their heads might have thought differently. Beside them, Gleva stood tall with no shelter of any kind. Her head was crowned with a garland of wilting white flowers and the rain had plastered long ripples of red hair flat against her dripping green garments. Still she raised her bare arms to the skies as if she had not noticed the weather. Tilla might even have admired the woman had she not known so much about her.

While many of the crowd had retreated to the warm bathhouse, the hardy and the devoted, whose clothes mostly suggested they were keen to be Romans, were standing under the shelter of the colonnade to watch. The governor and some of his followers—including a glum-faced woman who must be his wife—had been installed under a rain shelter close to the altar and were probably hoping some of the warmth from the flames would blow in their direction. Tilla shivered alongside the common people, wishing the priests would get on with it, yet at the same time hoping they wouldn't. As long as the golden goddess stood out on the temple porch, the fugitives behind the closed doors were safe. Once the priests wanted to put her back in her rightful place, who knew what would happen?

Tilla was prepared to wait, but Mara had had enough, and although the whining and wriggling could be pacified, there was no taming the smell.

Tilla glanced at Neena, who wrinkled her nose and said, "Shall I take her away, mistress?"

Tilla hesitated. She knew almost no one here, and she had seen how quickly the crowds could turn nasty. She peered out through the rain at the golden statue in front of the temple doors, and murmured a quiet prayer for Sulis Minerva to keep the priests busy and her man and his friends safe while she was not there to watch.

On the way into the bathhouse she remembered Esico, all alone somewhere on his first wet evening of freedom, and promised herself she would pray for him too. Not until this present trouble was over, though. For now, the men and boys in the temple needed the goddess's full attention.

Mara shrank against her as they entered the torchlit hubbub of the changing hall. "The latrines," Tilla urged Neena, pointing across the hall. She caught sight of Virana serving behind a food stall and raised a hand in greeting. Virana grinned and waved a pastry in reply. Tilla and Neena edged their way toward the latrines, trying not to bump into anyone's beer or tread on small children. They were surrounded by people all trying to shout over each other in the echoing hall, many of them speaking the local tongue. To Tilla's surprise, not all the talk was of the men in the temple. She caught snatches of conversation about children and neighbors, about the price of cows, about the effect of the damp on bad knees, about how all child snatchers ought to be nailed up, and about what a bad sign it was to see the gods raining on the new governor.

"Sulis isn't pleased with him."

"And they couldn't get that fire lit."

"Things have never been right since they interfered with the other spring."

"It's all because of that doctor who murdered—ow! Watch where you're going!"

But Tilla was out of reach and did not bother to apologize.

The two elderly ladies who had admired Mara over yesterday's dinner in the Mercury were crammed onto a bench by the latrine door, each clutching an untouched pastry and gazing about them as if they were wondering where all these people had come from and how they could escape.

Tilla bent down and greeted them in Latin. Seeing their alarm, she leaned closer and explained, "My husband and I met you in the Mercury!"

The nearer of the two clutched her pastry against her chest as if Tilla might have come to snatch it. The other one leaned across and shouted above the hubbub, "My poor sister and I didn't get a wink of sleep last night!" as if this were somehow Tilla's fault.

Baffled, she shouted that she hoped they would be feeling better soon.

She should have guessed that the latrines would be full. Men and women were seated side by side all along both rows, five or six people were standing in the middle waiting to take the first place that came free, and there was already another baby laid out on the floor having his cloths changed.

"Try the cold room," suggested a motherly-looking woman in the queue.

She was right: There were far fewer people in the chillier room. It was just bad luck that one of them recognized Tilla.

"Aren't you the one who was helping the child stealers?"

"No."

"Funny. You look just like her."

"They are not child stealers," she explained, allowing Neena to lift Mara from her arms. "One of them is the father of the boys."

"That priest said that they were child stealers," insisted the woman, who was standing in front of a torch at such an angle that her hair looked as though it were on fire. Tilla was sorry that it wasn't.

"We all heard him say it!" chimed in someone else.

"Well, they aren't," Tilla told them. "The priests wouldn't leave the children shut in there with them if they were."

"I knew there was something not right about those two," put in another voice from behind the woman. "You could tell from looking at them."

Tilla tried to object but nobody was listening. She flinched as a restraining hand was laid on her arm, then realized it was Neena. "Come away, mistress," the slave urged. "Mara needs you."

"One of them was that doctor. The one who murdered his wife."

"No! Really? The man who murdered his wife is a doctor?"

"My cousin met him, you know. On the night of the fire. Pretending to help people. And all the time—"

"The priests left two little boys in there with a wife killer?"

"Somebody ought to do something."

"They'll bring bad luck on all of us."

"They ought to break the doors down!"

They were enjoying this. Tilla was weary and exasperated. She wanted to walk away. But if you did not correct people, how would the truth ever be known? She squared her shoulders and lifted her chin. "Doctor Valens did not murder his wife!"

Everyone in the cold room stopped talking and turned to look at her. The woman who deserved to have her hair set alight raised her eyebrows. The little smile said she had wanted an argument, and Tilla had fallen for it.

Too late, she remembered that a mother should never get into a fight with her baby looking on. Not unless she was confident of winning. "Doctor Valens has every right to take his own children wherever he wants," she said. "And the man with him is my husband. He is a good man. They are only hiding in there because stupid people chased them."

The woman said softly, "Are you calling us stupid?"

She said, "What would you call a person who refuses to hear the truth?"

"A Northerner!" shouted someone. The laughter that followed was not kind.

The woman stepped closer. "You want to watch yourself, coming here, insulting people." A fleck of spittle landed on Tilla's cheek.

Remember to breathe.

"And she has steal vegetable!" cried a voice from somewhere.

The woman smiled. "A thief too, eh?"

They were all closing in around her now, pushing her toward the edge of the cold plunge. Tilla looked around for Neena and Mara, but she could not see them anywhere.

The woman put her face up so close that Tilla could not only smell the wine-laden breath but feel it on her neck. "I reckon," the woman said, "that some people ought to mind their own business and go back where they came from."

"Perhaps they should," Tilla agreed, determined not to be the first to look away, because if she did, she was lost.

"Perhaps we'll have to help you."

The stone rim of the cold plunge was pressing into the backs of her calves. There was nowhere left to retreat to. In a moment someone would give her a push and she would topple in. But if she could get a good grip, she would take the woman with her, and then it would be one-on-one.

"Ladies!" cried a voice from the doorway. A couple of people turned to glance at the skinny little Roman standing there, clutching a tray, and the slave with the baby who had slipped into the room behind him. "The dancing is about to start. But first, who would like to try our special festival apple pastries? Flavored with real cinnamon!"

"We're busy," growled the woman.

"Freshly baked this afternoon, spiced with cinnamon all the way from India, the land of tribes where people live to be two hundred years old! Just one each, ladies, please. Absolutely free for the festival. Try one and tell me they aren't the best apple pastries you've ever eaten."

The woman with the wine-laden breath continued to glare at Tilla, then muttered, "Next time!" before turning smartly on her heel to join her friends snatching up the pastries from Albanus's tray. Tilla felt Neena dragging her away, and this time she did not resist.

53

SOMEONE'S COMING," RUSO said, squinting out through the gap between the doors.

Valens swung round to face him, ceremonial sword in hand. "Who is it?"

"Sh!" Ruso, who had only caught a glimpse of movement beyond the divine armpit, pressed his ear against the door.

From outside came ". . . and don't let him give you any nonsense about omens."

Ruso recognized the voice. The speaker must be at the top of the steps, and he sounded out of breath.

"I'm not having him shifting the blame," the man continued. "If that wood had been stored properly, in the dry, we'd have had no trouble."

"Dorios," Ruso whispered to Valens. "High priest."

"You men," continued the voice, "wait outside until I give the order. And remember, the children are not to be hurt."

Footsteps. The door vibrated against Ruso's ear. Dorios meant business.

Valens put down the sword and shield and stepped forward to haul on the handle. The door slowly swung open. It let in a gust of cool damp air and the strains of native musicians playing the pipes, and it revealed the broad silhouette of the chief priest. The four slaves who had been holding a dripping canopy above his head stayed outside with Sulis Minerva. To either side of her, not quite out of sight, stood more temple slaves carrying clubs.

Pausing on the threshold, Dorios called out, "Doctor Valens!" as though he were summoning the dead. He was visibly startled when Valens appeared from behind the door, dipped down onto one knee, and declared, "Sir! My boys and I can't thank you enough."

Dorios stepped inside, looking down at him with an expression that suggested he hadn't expected this. Then he gazed around the orderly temple with its display of gleaming treasure, at Ruso, standing unarmed in a bloodstained tunic, and at the bed where two identical small boys sat wrapped in a temple blanket and blinking at the sudden intrusion of the last rays of daylight.

Ruso hoped he and Valens had put everything back more or less where they found it. With luck those dents on the back of the door had always been there, and the scratches on the polished chair would not show in the dim interior of the temple.

"You were an answer to prayer, sir!" Keeping at a distance that the priest could not possibly interpret as a threat, Valens rose to his feet. "When I saw the steps open up in front of us and your men holding the crowd back, it was as if the goddess herself had offered her protection." He shook his head, as if he could still hardly believe what had happened. "You and your men saved all of our lives." He turned to his boys. "Say 'Thank you, Master High Priest,' boys."

The boys' chorus of thanks would have done credit to the choir.

The priest took in Valens's black eye and the blood on Ruso's tunic and managed, "I hope the children weren't injured?"

"Saved by the arm of the goddess, sir," Valens assured him, stepping across to stand behind his boys. "What sort of offering do you think I should make as thanks for sanctuary? Do you think an actual ox would be acceptable, or would the value in money be better?"

Faced with this surprisingly generous choice, the priest appeared lost for words. Out on the temple porch, someone sneezed.

Ruso realized he was holding his breath.

"I think," Dorios said, "the monetary value would be preferable."

Valens was profoundly grateful and eager to pay up. So it was fortunate the chief priest did not know that most of Valens's savings would be back in the strong room of the Second Augusta over in Isca—a place from which a man who was currently absent without leave could not possibly retrieve them. Nor did he know that Valens's best friend had spent most of his own money bringing his household to Aquae Sulis and had little spare to lend. Certainly not the value of an ox, whatever that might be.

"I suppose a testimonial plaque wouldn't really be the thing, would it?" Valens was asking, glancing around the walls. "I shouldn't think the people out there will want a reminder once they find out I was with my own children."

Dorios, the man who had stirred up the crowd in the first place by announcing Valens as a child thief, grunted.

"The veterans must regret calling him a child thief now," put in Ruso, seeing a way for Dorios to save face.

"Outrageous," Dorios agreed. "Causing a disturbance in the middle of the night, telling the whole town someone was stealing children. I've already complained in the strongest possible terms. If I'd been told they were your own boys, we'd never have supported any move to bring them back. Frankly, I think the veterans owe you an apology."

Ruso had to admire the way the man had neatly distanced himself from all the blame. Valens, meanwhile, was apologizing for the disturbance and asking if the priest could recommend a safe place for him and the boys to spend the night. "We'll be gone in the morning," he promised. "I'll carry on with my original plan to take them to Isca."

If Dorios understood the game Valens was playing, he pretended not to. After giving the matter some thought, he suggested that as there were no supplicants sleeping in the temple that night, and as he himself had to hurry away and entertain the governor, perhaps Valens and the children would like to remain here? "We have beds, as you see. My people can fetch you some food."

Valens professed himself delighted with the brilliance of this solution. Ruso, meanwhile, found himself torn between admiration and anxiety. Anyone who could manipulate people as neatly as Valens just had could lie about anything. Including whether or not he had murdered his wife.

"And will your friend be staying too?"

"No, thanks," said Ruso. "I need to get back to my family."

And some sanity. Even Tilla was straightforward compared to this.

54

NOW THAT THE rain had stopped, the crowd seemed to have forgotten the child thief altogether. The people clustered under the torchlit porticos appeared to be enjoying the beer and the music. Others had formed a big unwieldy circle that enclosed the temple and the altar and were doing a cheerful and splashy dance through the puddles. In the near darkness nobody paid any attention to the man following the priest out of the temple and hurrying down the steps.

Waiting at the foot of the steps for a chance to pass through the circle of dancers, Ruso caught sight of a bald-headed veteran prancing about with a cluster of children as if he had always been a Briton underneath the armor. He felt a faint stirring of envy.

When the dance finally broke up, he bent to pick up an abandoned straw hat and pushed it back into some sort of shape. Thus disguised, he went in search of Tilla.

The chances of her listening to "Wait there!" had been slim, and even if she had waited, he could hardly expect her to be standing there still. Skirting the edge of the crowds under the portico, he went to search for Virana, who might know where Tilla had gone. He needed to find his family. He had no idea what to do after that.

What had Valens said? *Come on, man. You've done this sort of thing before. You know what to do much better than I do.*

But Ruso had been trying to think what to do ever since they had arrived in Aquae Sulis. He was tired and he was disillusioned. His injured head hurt, and none of his efforts so far appeared to have done Valens the least bit of good. If it weren't for the children, he would have given up before now.

It was strange how many diametrically opposed actions could be justified by insisting you were taking them for the sake of two small boys.

"Whoops. Sorry!"

He staggered sideways. The hat fell off. As he regained his balance, the laughing woman who had collided with him grabbed the hat, jammed it onto her own head, and danced off arm-in-arm with her friends, all of whom seemed to be holding each other up.

He was making his way across to the bathhouse when the last voice he wanted to hear growled in his left ear, "Was it you who put the priest up to that, then?"

Ruso stopped. "Up to what?"

"You're wasting your time," Pertinax told him. "I'll get my boys back anyway when your pal's convicted."

"Good," said Ruso, stepping away from the nearest group of partygoers lest anyone should recognize him as the friend of the child stealer.

"You can tell him that from me: I'm putting the request for trial in tomorrow."

"You can tell him yourself," Ruso said. "I'm not your messenger."

When had he stopped calling Pertinax "sir"?

If Pertinax was offended by the lack of respect, he made a good job of hiding it. "They won't let him stay up there in that temple tomorrow, you know. They'll throw him out. They want the doors open for the visitors."

"I'm looking for Tilla," Ruso told him. "Have you seen her?"

"These priests can't be trusted. I know what they're like. And if you think I'm falling for a deal like that, you're more of a fool than I thought."

"I doubt that's possible," Ruso told him. "And I don't know anything about a deal." He put one foot onto the base of a pillar and pulled himself up to see beyond Pertinax and over the heads of the crowd. "Have you seen Tilla?"

"So it wasn't you who put him up to it, then?"

Ruso's gaze followed a gleam of blond hair in the lamplight. The woman turned. She was a stranger. He sighed and stepped down. "Put who up to what?"

So Pertinax explained the deal he had just rejected. And exactly as Ruso had said in the first place, it had nothing to do with him.

55

TILLA WAS ONE of a row of three women and a baby behind a stall in the main bathing hall. All of them looked pink-faced and sticky in the heat from the pool, and the table in front of them had only a couple of unsold pastries and four empty trays left on it. Which was just as well, because although Ruso found it very gratifying that all three women leapt to their feet when they saw him, Virana's pregnant bulge caught the loose top of the table. The remaining pastries and the trays all slid onto the floor at his feet, and then nobody was paying him any attention at all.

When the mess had been cleared up, he assured them that Valens and the boys were fine and so was he. He did not need stitches. Neither did he need beer or a reconstructed and slightly dusty apple pastry. Just in case anyone was about to ask, he added that he didn't need to dance, either. What he wanted was to go somewhere quiet and think.

Virana looked at Tilla and sighed. "My husband is just the same. I tell him, 'You will enjoy yourself once you try it,' but he won't try."

He said, "You stay and dance with Virana if you want."

Tilla shook her head. "I want to look after you."

He restrained an urge to wrap his arms around her and rest his weary head on her shoulder.

Shortly afterward, sitting rigid on the trunk of Terentius's things in the maintenance stores while Tilla stood over him and seemed to be gouging out the cut on his head with her fingernails, he was feeling less grateful for being looked after.

"It must be clean now," he insisted, trying not to sound like a man talking through clenched teeth. "Valens has done it once already."

"I think so," she agreed.

At the sight of her draping the cloth over the side of the bowl, the worst of the pain from the vinegar began to ebb. His clenched muscles began to relax at last.

She said, "It needs stitches."

The muscles tightened again until he remembered his case was safely over at Pertinax's house. "I shouldn't worry," he assured her. "Valens says it's only superficial."

"Wait there."

"But the kit is—"

Too late. He heard the rise of voices outside as she opened the door, and then it faded and he was left staring at a row of chisels hung on the wall above a stack of spades and sledgehammers.

She returned in triumph, holding up a needle case. "From that doctor in the baths."

He tried telling her that the cut was not deep, that the light was no good, that head wounds always bled a lot—"I know that," she told him—but to no avail.

"Ready?"

He fought down the words *No! Get off me!* "Yes."

"I cannot do this if you do not sit still."

"I am sitting still."

"So, what did Pertinax say to you?"

It was the continuation of a conversation they had started before the vinegar began to eat its way into his skull. "He said the chief priest met him on the temple steps," he said. "Dorios actually offered to hand over the boys to him if—ow!"

"What is the matter?"

"Nothing. I just didn't know you were going to start."

She said, "You tell me I must talk to the patient and take their mind off it."

"You have to give a warning first. You can't just jab people out of nowhere."

"It was not out of nowhere," she pointed out. "I said, 'Are you ready?' and you said yes."

"But then you asked me about—ow! Do you have to stitch it? I'm sure a bandage would do."

"You cannot see it," she reminded him. "I can. Try to think about something else. The chief priest offered to hand over the boys to Pertinax if what?"

Ruso attempted to concentrate on the proposed deal that had outraged the old centurion. "Dorios offered to get the boys out of the temple and hand them over to Pertinax if Pertinax agreed not to insist on a trial—ow!"

"You are a terrible patient."

He said, "Nobody else has ever complained."

"Then somebody else can treat you next time," she told him. "Last stitch going in now. How can the priest—"

"Watch the needle, wife! Never mind the priest."

The hand in his peripheral vision stopped moving. She said, "How can anyone take the boys away from Valens? He is their father. Is it not against your law?"

"I doubt Dorios cares. He's got Valens trapped, and he's clearly desperate to avoid a trial."

She said, "But you heard him give his word to keep Valens and the boys safe."

"He did."

"Perhaps this Dorios is in league with Gleva."

Given the stark way that priest and priestess ignored each other during the ceremonies, it was hard to imagine. But then, it was hard to imagine Gleva and Pertinax together too. It was hard for a man with a needle being pushed through his skin to imagine anything.

Tilla said, "Perhaps Pertinax told Gleva that Valens was hiding in the Repose, and she told the priest, and he sent that man to attack him."

Ruso tried to follow this and gave up. All he could manage was "There's got to be something extra Dorios thinks will come out at a trial that he doesn't want people to know."

"What can a lawyer find out that you have not already found yourself?"

"I don't know. We're going to have to go over everything again."

"Yes," she said, and then: "Finished!"

"Thank the gods for that."

"Did you notice how I took your thoughts somewhere else?"

"I noticed how your mind wasn't on what you were doing."

A small pair of shears appeared, very close to his head. "Next time," she said as she squeezed the blades together to snip the ends of the thread, "you can do it yourself and see how that goes."

56

RUSO WOULD WILLINGLY have sat recuperating in the relative peace and cool of the maintenance stores all evening, but no sooner had his wife put the needle away than they heard a female voice outside declare, "In here!" and the door burst open.

It revealed a young man who had dealt with the perpetual toga problem (there was always too much of a toga if you planned to use both hands for something else) by gallantly draping one half of it around the shoulders of a female in clothes that were unsuitable for an outdoor party. Ruso recognized her as the girl who had been writhing under the caresses of the old man by the sacred spring.

The girl eyed the man and woman sitting in the pool of lamplight. "Have you two finished?"

Tilla wiped the shears on the wine-soaked cloth and picked up the bowl. "We have."

"Watch your step," Ruso murmured to the youth on the way out. He gestured toward his stitches. "Look what that one did to me."

He left Tilla in the care of Virana and Neena, who were dutifully waiting for her where the pastry stall had been. All three women were keen to head out into the courtyard to join in the dancing. When he said, "What about Mara?" and then explained that he was too busy to look after her, he was told that Albanus would do it. "It will give him a good excuse not to dance," Tilla added.

"And good practice," put in Virana. When Tilla asked Ruso where he was going, he said, "To ask some questions."

Out in the courtyard the figures of Gnaeus and his wife whirled past him, Gnaeus dancing like a bear and clearly enjoying himself despite his earlier misgivings.

Dorios was not hard to find, because the first slave whom Ruso asked told him the chief priest was with the governor, and the governor was not hard to find, because the official party had all trooped up the temple steps to watch from a safe distance as the happy people of Aquae Sulis celebrated Roman rule by dancing around the courtyard. The governor was in the middle of the group. The torches held aloft by his guards illuminated a bald head that gleamed only marginally less than his polished breastplate. He was chatting to a less shiny companion on his right, while on his left, the glum wife was gazing out from within a warm woolen wrap. What was visible of her face showed no emotion at all. There was no sign of Gleva in her role as native priestess, but Ruso could just make out Dorios beyond the governor and to the left. So not in his immediate circle, then. Disappointing for the priest, but good news for anyone wanting to speak to him.

Up on the podium, out of the glare of the torches, four temple slaves still stood guard outside Sulis Minerva's closed doors. Ruso wondered how Valens was getting on in his ornate prison. He pushed his hair back so the stitches were clearly visible, and set off up the damp steps. He took it slowly, with his gaze fixed on Dorios. He was almost certain the priest had identified him before one of the governor's guards stepped sideways to block his progress.

"Urgent message for the chief priest," Ruso told the guard. As expected, the words had no effect whatsoever. He craned past the man's shoulder to try and catch Dorios's attention. "It's about something we discussed earlier."

"Not now," said the guard.

"Ah, well, never mind," said Ruso. "When would be a good time to talk to him?"

"Not now."

"Perhaps you could give him the message?"

"No."

Another guard stepped across to stare through him.

Ruso shrugged. "Fair enough." He glanced back in the direction of the priest, then turned to head back down the steps to where three small children had formed a breakaway dance and were twirling around with their arms wide and their eyes shut, shrieking with delight as their balance began to fail and they staggered sideways.

By the time he reached ground level, Dorios had arrived, leaning on his stick and smelling of something expensive. "What is it? I'm supposed to be with the governor!"

"Sorry about that," said Ruso, reaching to grab one of the children and sit her down before she fell and cracked her head on the steps, and steadying the others before they did the same.

"Actually, Doctor," Dorios murmured as Ruso led him toward the back of the courtyard in search of a quiet place to talk. "I do need a brief word with you. But I can't stop. I'm hosting the governor's dinner."

"This won't take long," Ruso promised, steering him away from an alcove that he now saw held a courting couple. The dancers had abandoned their circuit of the temple and several of the torches on the back wall of the colonnade had died. They retreated into the shadows, from where they could see anyone who might be approaching to listen in.

"You don't want a trial," Ruso began.

"The Sulis Minerva Association has never been opposed to a trial in principle," said Dorios, "but—"

"But you are opposed to Pertinax prosecuting Valens."

"I'm opposed to one man being executed for another man's crimes."

"You really think Valens is innocent?"

Dorios said, "Don't you?"

"Of course," said Ruso, feeling his toes curl involuntarily inside his sandals.

"One has only to see him with those boys to know he should be left to bring them up in peace. Which is why I suggest you don't trouble yourself with any more investigations, Doctor. I think it's safe to say that by the time the sun rises tomorrow, your friend will be elsewhere and your defense won't be needed."

"You're going to get him out?"

"It was a mistake to allow him to be brought back. I see that now. The veterans' claim that he was a child snatcher was unacceptable. If that's going to be the standard of the centurion's conduct in the trial, I think it's better for all of us that it doesn't happen."

"I've had a bang on the head," Ruso told him, "so excuse me if I'm a little slow, but . . . you're prepared to let an accused man escape because you like the look of him and you don't want a fuss?"

"If you put it that way, yes."

Ruso fingered the line of stitches. "Maybe when my head clears, that will make sense."

"I'm sure it will," the priest agreed. "Of course, if you mention this conversation anywhere else, I shall deny every word."

"As it is," Ruso said, "someone tried to kill Valens in his room at the Repose. How do I know the attack wasn't ordered by you, trying to avoid a trial? How do I know that you won't just order your guards to get rid of him during the night and then tell me he's run away?"

He was aware of Dorios shifting position against the wall. "That bang on the head certainly is affecting you, Doctor. Your friend and the children can be released to you if you like. Just as long as he goes away. It's time this wretched business was over."

"Why?"

"Why not? I thought it was what you came all this way to achieve."

Ruso said, "What will you do with Pertinax?"

"I'll deal with Pertinax."

Ruso gazed at the back of the temple, silhouetted by the rising moon. "There's just something not quite right about it."

Dorios sighed. "Doctor, please try to understand. Aquae Sulis is not just a town with a shrine. We are a beacon of hope to light a troubled province. On an island with a history of war, we are a symbol of peace. We show that *this is how it can be*."

Ruso said, "I see," but the priest was not finished.

"Not only the province, but her people." He was clutching Ruso's wrist now. "Sulis Minerva can heal even when the best of doctors cannot. She offers consolation when the light of hope has burned dim. I won't allow that comfort to be snatched away."

"You really think all of that would be destroyed by one murder trial?"

"Yes."

Ruso loosened the man's grip on his wrist. "It's no good. I still don't see it."

"Trust me, Doctor. I've served at the temple here for a long time. I know what our visitors expect. Our goddess doesn't want them to see a trial."

And that, of course, was the problem. Dorios was prepared to do a deal with anyone in order to avert a trial. His current offer to release Valens and the boys into Ruso's custody seemed generous enough, but he had made a totally different proposition to Pertinax earlier this evening. He was prepared to snatch the boys away from their father and hand them over to Pertinax, breaking all promises of sanctuary in exchange for the withdrawal of the murder charge.

"You'd better go and take the governor to his dinner," Ruso told him. As soon as the governor's party had cleared the steps, he must find some way of warning Valens that the goddess might be offering him and the boys a safe haven, but her chief servant definitely wasn't.

"We can provide your friend with safe passage to Abona," said Dorios, sounding desperate. "You and your family can go with him if you want. Then you can pick up a ship going north."

"I don't understand exactly what you're trying to hide here," Ruso said, beginning to move back toward the light, "but the more you try and hide it, the more I think a trial would be a very good idea."

"No! You must believe me, Doctor . . . the damage it would do . . . and you yourself a healer!"

"I'll think about it," Ruso promised, not sure the man was entirely in his right mind and not wanting to put Valens at any further risk. If the temple slaves were ordered to turn nasty, a ceremonial sword and an ancient shield would do almost nothing to protect him.

"There are things I can't tell you."

"Never mind," Ruso said. "Go and have your dinner and you can not tell them to me again tomorrow."

The hand grabbed his wrist again. "I need you to promise—"

"It's been a long day," Ruso told him. "I don't think I can make any promises tonight."

"But you must! Your friend is in danger! If this doesn't stop, I don't know what they'll do!"

Ruso leaned back against the wall. "Who?"

"Everybody!"

Ruso folded his arms and waited.

"I mean, everybody will suffer. The temple, the sacred spring—ruined!"

"Really?" said Ruso. "How?"

There was a long pause, then a whisper of "You must swear not to tell anyone."

Ruso said nothing.

"At least swear not to tell the centurion. There's no telling what damage his men might do if they knew."

Ruso decided it was better to hide behind silence than betray his confusion by opening his mouth.

He was aware of the fat little priest pressing up against him. A voice whispered in his ear, "It's the water."

57

"TILLA!" GLEVA'S VOICE cut across the music and the laughter and the sound of Tilla's own breathing as the dance spiraled away from the torchlit columns and back out into the courtyard. "Daughter of Lugh! Pertinax is asking for your husband!"

"My husband is busy!" Tilla shouted over her shoulder. Neena's hand tugged at her own and the dance swirled them both away. When the steps led her back round, she caught a fresh glimpse of Gleva standing under the light, pushing damp hair out of her eyes and looking annoyed. Well, she could look as annoyed as she liked. Tilla's feet carried her out across the courtyard with the others, friends and strangers alike, each following the dancer in front. Her husband was not under Pertinax's orders now. And he certainly wasn't obliged to come running at the request of a woman like Gleva, who for all Tilla knew might be trying to lure him into a trap. Anyway, what business did she have using the name Tilla's family had given her? How did she even know it? They were not old friends. They were not friends at all.

"She's still standing there!" Virana called over the wail of the pipes as the line of dancers wound its way back around the columns.

This time Gleva shouted, "Pertinax is ill!"

Tilla dragged her hand free of Virana's and waved an arm about her. "There are plenty of doctors here!"

"I told him, but he wants your husband!"

The dance took them again, but there was no pleasure in it anymore. Tilla knew her husband would be angry if he found out she had ignored a call to a patient. Even one that came from a woman like Gleva. Ducking out of the line, she made her way back to where the priestess was waiting and admitted, breathless, that she did not know where he had gone.

"What is the matter with Pertinax?"

"We are both supposed to be dining with the governor," Gleva told her, "but he can hardly stand up. I have looked for your husband already. And that tutor does not know where he is, either."

There was an answer to this, and it was not one Tilla liked. "I will come myself."

"You are not what the centurion asked for."

"Then find somebody else."

Gleva sighed. "I suppose we can see what he says."

The strange couple of the priestess and the old soldier had one thing in common: They were both very rude.

Albanus must have been watching, because he appeared out of the darkness with Mara asleep on his shoulder and said, "Your husband said I should look after you."

"She will be safe with me," Gleva told him. "You can look for the husband and send him over as soon as you find him."

Albanus, who found it difficult to refuse an order no matter where it came from, said, "You'll bring her back?"

"I am not a parcel," Tilla told them both. "Or a child."

As she and Tilla hurried along the dark street together, Gleva seemed too worried about Pertinax to care that she had just ruined everyone's evening. "I have never seen him like this," she confided.

"You have not known him long."

If Gleva noticed the barb, she pretended not to. She put a hand on Tilla's arm. "Mind the step on this corner." And then: "Pertinax asked for your husband because he does not trust the doctors from the temple. He has made enemies in this place."

Tilla hoped Albanus would find her husband quickly. What if this was not an illness but an attempt to harm Pertinax, just as someone had tried to attack Valens in the room at the inn? Her husband would never claim to be an expert on poisons, but he knew a great deal more than she did. "When did the centurion fall ill?"

"On the way back from town to get ready for the dinner. He felt faint and giddy and now he has pains in the stomach."

It did not sound good.

58

ALONE IN THE dark at the back of the portico, Ruso wondered what would happen if all these people who had come together to celebrate the Feast of Sulis Minerva knew what Dorios had just told him. No doubt the reputation of the shrine could be rebuilt, but it would be a struggle. People had long memories. What had happened here was the sort of gruesome tale that would be told around smoky fires in native houses for generations.

And all because a couple of well-intentioned slaves had used their initiative.

It was easy to see how it had happened. When customers were banging on the bathhouse door at way past the usual opening time and your boss had been called away to a meeting and left no instructions, what should you do? Leave the doors locked and dissatisfied customers grumbling outside until his return? Or, since everyone knew where the key was kept, go and fetch it from his office and open up?

The answer had seemed obvious. As answers often did when the people in search of them didn't have all the information. The slaves had no way of knowing that this was a morning like no other, nor that the meeting had just agreed to announce an immediate closure of the bathing halls for emergency repair work. When the slaves finally dragged the main doors open, a couple of the waiting women even took the trouble to thank them. Everyone was relieved to be able to relax in the pleasant surroundings of the baths after the terrible business of that fire the night before.

The thanks, more than anything, were what had struck fear into the heart of Chief Priest Dorios and the few other officials who knew the real reason for the closure. That was why they were doing their utmost to prevent a trial. And as soon as the truth about Serena's killing became public, every woman who had entered the great bath at Aquae Sulis on the morning after the fire would realize she had spent her leisure time wallowing in the very same hot water that had marinated a corpse through the long hours of the night.

As for anyone who had swallowed it . . . that didn't bear thinking about.

The healing waters of Aquae Sulis, the great symbol of Roman peace in Britannia, would gain a new and unwanted reputation. The officials who had allowed it to happen would be ruined.

Ruso had tried to assure Dorios that there must be some way around the problem. That both sides could be asked to swear not to mention the circumstances of the death in court. That the governor could be asked to hear some of the case in private. That if Pertinax understood what was at stake, he might be persuaded to . . . No, Ruso had to agree that any scheme involving the persuasion of Pertinax would never work. And Dorios was right: The quarrel over Valens's children was so bitter that whatever promises were made, there was no telling whether they would be kept in the heat of battle.

Dorios and the other keepers of the secret—the haruspex and the bath manager—believed they were fighting not only for their own livelihoods and reputations but for the honor of the goddess, the future of the town, the sense that peace was restored in the province, and the welfare of everyone here who depended upon the visitors for an income. With that kind of motive, Ruso was beginning to wonder just how far they would be prepared to go.

He headed back to where the dancers were still cavorting about in front of the temple, waited until Gnaeus appeared in the line, then ran out to grab him and explain what he wanted.

★ ★ ★

"Something very thin?" The scribe squinted up at his new customer in the dim light of his booth, and Ruso wondered how the man could see to write anything at all.

"Something very thin," Ruso repeated. "And I need something to write on it with. Quickly."

The man scratched his head. "It's an all-in-one price per sheet, sir. I do the writing, discount for the second side, curses extra because of the cost of the lead. No charge for writing backwards."

Ruso, who did not have time to argue, said, "I'll pay for the writing, then. But I'll do it myself."

"I don't supply pens, sir. I've only got two and I need both of them."

Ruso placed a hand upon the man's shoulder, slid his finger and thumb into position, and squeezed.

"Ow!" The scribe glanced around wildly for someone who might come and rescue him, but everyone was too busy dancing, drinking, and gossiping.

"I'm a customer," Ruso told him. "I'm the only one you've got, and I'm in a hurry."

If the slaves leaning against the temple pillars were surprised to see Ruso return, they hid it well. He thanked them for looking after Valens and agreed with them that it would be out of the question to open the doors without an order from the chief priest: He would not even consider asking.

The exchange of glances that followed his next question told him that nobody had told them what to do with a man who just wanted to chat to his friend through the closed doors. So, after warning him not to try anything, they stood back and let him approach.

There was no need to call out: A muffled voice from the other side said, "Is that you, Ruso?"

"It's me."

"What's happening out there?"

"Dancing."

"The boys heard the music. I thought they might ask to go and join in, but they're frightened of the crowd."

It was sad but hardly surprising. "All the officials have gone off to dine with the governor in the Mercury," Ruso told him. "They've left you four men out here to guard the door."

"Good."

It wasn't necessarily good, and Valens needed to be told that, but without alerting the guards themselves. Fortunately, even though the skies had cleared and the moon was up, the gloom under the temple porch was such that none of them noticed Ruso slipping a thin leaf of wood through the gap between the bronze-covered doors. Only when he had shoved it out of reach did it strike him that the doors were thick and it might not be long enough to emerge on the other side. Hoping the guards would not understand him, he said in Greek, "Read the note in the door."

Valens asked, "What note?" in the same tongue, and then, "Oh. Wait a moment . . ."

Ruso felt the doors shift and jolt, and then: "I knew that sword would come in handy for something."

Ruso leaned back against the doors, listening to the pipes wailing around the rhythm of the drums and gazing at the patterns of figures moving about in the moonlit courtyard. The Britons, he had to admit, knew how to throw a party. He was willing to bet that Pertinax's mad priestess would rather be out here than dining with the governor.

From behind the door there was another "Oh" and then: "You're absolutely sure about this?"

"Yes." He switched back into Latin. "How's the eye?"

"Bloody awful. How's the head?"

"Tilla stitched it."

"Tilla?" A pause, then: "This is turning into quite an evening."

"How are the boys?"

"Gone back to sleep. The temple slaves brought some food in." Then, back into Greek: "I suppose we'd better not eat the next lot."

"I don't think anyone would poison the boys."

"No. Of course they wouldn't." The words were confident, but the tone was not. Now that he knew how desperate Dorios and his pals were to cover up their unsavory little secret. Ruso was not sure, either. He had spared Valens the detail about the polluted water but made clear his suspicion that if it would avert a trial, either Valens or Pertinax might be silenced by morning.

He was reassured to hear the scrape of furniture being moved. Valens was replacing the barricade that would help to keep out any

potential assassins. He put his mouth to the gap between the doors
again. "Have you got everything you need in there?"

"We'll manage," Valens assured him. "I'll have a word with Sulis
Minerva. She's looking very lovely in here, back up on her pedestal."

Ruso turned and leaned back against the doors. From there he
could see the view that the goddess enjoyed when her temple doors
were open. It stretched way beyond the confines of her courtyard.
The moon was up above the eastern hills, and the river was a wide
streak of silver beyond the angular silhouettes of the buildings.

The words of the fishermen came back to him: *Neptune rises to
greet the goddess of the moon.*

"Did you say," he murmured to the door, "that there was no
moon on the night Serena died?"

"Did I? There wasn't, anyway. Just the stars."

Something didn't make sense. He said, "I've got to go."

"You aren't planning to dance, are you? You know it'll end
badly."

"I'll be back," he promised.

"Be careful, Ruso."

"Yes," he said. "You too."

On the way back down he was pleased to see that Gnaeus had
several veterans casually gathered around him at the foot of the steps,
clutching drinks. If Gnaeus had thought about it, he might have
wondered why Ruso had asked him to protect Valens from the same
temple guards who had saved him and the boys from the crowd
earlier that evening. Fortunately the continuing enmity between
veterans and temple meant that Gnaeus and his friends were unlikely
to trust anyone in a temple tunic.

If Ruso had any doubts himself, they had just been silenced as
he walked across the temple porch and glanced at one of the slave
guards leaning against a column in the moonlight. The odd shadow
down one side of the man's face was not a shadow but a burn. Valens
was being guarded by the mystery attacker from the Traveler's
Repose. And that man, it was now clear, worked for the chief priest.

"I've told my friend you're here to keep an eye on him," Ruso
murmured to Gnaeus as he passed.

"Don't you worry, sir," Gnaeus replied. "I brought him back here
for a fair trial. I'm going to see to it that he gets one."

59

IF TILLA HAD ever wondered about Pertinax's bedroom—which she had not—she would have imagined it just like this. Stark white walls, looming chest of drawers that smelled of beeswax polish, one pale little island of rug on the floorboards, and above it, crammed against the wall, a narrow bed that looked as if the owner had only put it there out of duty and would be just as happy sleeping on the floor. Tilla supposed Gleva slept somewhere else and was only summoned when required.

The figure under the striped covers opened his eyes as they approached. "What's *she* doing here?"

Gleva set the lamp on top of the chest. "You need a healer and I could not find the husband."

"Uh."

"You said not to bring one of those temple types. There are not many left to choose from."

Pertinax sighed and closed his eyes for a moment before dragging himself up the bed. Gleva tried to help him, but even so it was a struggle. By the time he was sitting with his back propped against the one pillow, his head hung forward and the broad shoulders were heaving with the effort.

It frightened Tilla to see him looking so old. She tried to remember what she needed to check, but after she accepted Gleva's invitation and perched awkwardly on the edge of the bed, she could not think beyond *I am sitting next to Centurion Pertinax!*

Don't alarm the patient, her husband would have said. *Stay calm. Ask questions. Give yourself time to think.*

"So," she began, as brightly as she could manage. And then, in desperation: "What is the matter with you?"

The head lifted. "You tell me."

She reached for his hand, turned it over, and ran her fingertips along the thick wrist in search of a pulse.

The pulse was rushing and it felt somehow wobbly. His breathing was quick and shallow, but he had no fever. She remembered some better questions, asking how long he had been feeling ill, how he would describe how he felt, whether or not it was getting worse . . .

"You are worse," Gleva told him before he had a chance to answer. "You are sure the priests or their men gave you nothing? Did nothing?"

"Nothing."

She glanced at Tilla. "He said he ate an apple pastry from a stall and drank wine at a bar he often goes to. And now he has pains in the stomach."

"Apple pastry from Albanus," mumbled the patient.

Tilla shook her head. "I ate from that stall too. It is not the pastry." Although, if it had been, all those women in the cold plunge room had eaten them too. It would have served them right.

"What is it, then?" said Pertinax. "Can't lie here. Me and her are supposed to be . . ." His voice trailed off, as if he was having trouble remembering where they were supposed to be. "The governor. Arse Face from the temple is having a dinner for him."

When Tilla did not reply, he said, "Well? What is it, then?"

Tilla thought of all the medical wisdom that was stored in her husband's luggage just across the courtyard. The scrolls might as well have been on the moon: She could barely read a word of Greek. "I don't know yet," she confessed. "I do not think you will be going to the dinner."

He sighed and looked up at Gleva. "Find me a proper doctor."

"I'll wake your brother to sit with you."

"Catus is sicker than me with that cough, or he'd have been at Arse Face's dinner. Let him sleep. I want a doctor. I'm dying."

Gleva reached for her cloak. "I'll go back and look for the husband." It would have been hard to tell which of the three of them was the most desperate to see a proper doctor, and quickly. But in the meantime Tilla was glad of a few moments alone with her patient. There was a question she needed to ask.

"Has Gleva given you anything?"

"No."

"No medicine? No drinks or special foods for strength?"

"Fresh air and exercise. Best medicine. Always tell the men."

This was not a time for polite silence. "I was told," she said, "that your daughter thought Gleva was giving you love potion."

Pertinax said, "Gleva?"

"I was told your daughter was very worried about you and Gleva."

"I'm ill."

Tilla was wondering if she dared search the room for medicines, when there was a faint tap on the open door behind her. The cook bowed to her master and in response to Tilla's question assured her that, no, nobody had given her anything to put in the master's food. No, the food and drink were never left anywhere where someone could tamper with them.

It seemed nobody could have poisoned Pertinax, and yet that was the only explanation Tilla could think of. She beckoned the cook out into the corridor, where she found the rest of the staff lined up to listen.

The houseboy shook his head sadly. "Forty-seven years, and I've never seen the master like this."

"I wouldn't put anything past that woman," hissed the cook. "Mistress Serena never trusted her."

The maid's thin hands were gripping a cleaning rag as if she were hoping to wring the truth out of it. "Will he die?"

"First the mistress," muttered the houseboy, "now the master."

"He's not dead yet," the cook pointed out.

Tilla looked around the group. "Does anyone know if he's been given anything unusual?"

Half a dozen blank and frightened faces stared back at her in the lamplight.

The maid had her lips pressed close together. The rag was twisted so tightly, it was dripping on the floor.

"And just when we'd got the boys back," sighed the cook.

Tilla placed a hand on the cook's arm. "Could you watch him for a moment? I have just thought of something."

"Me?"

"Send someone to fetch me if you need me." She snatched up the lamp from the bracket and beckoned to the maid. "I need you to come and help."

Moments later, in the privacy of Serena's old room, she demanded, "What do you know?"

She had guessed well. There was a wail of "I can't tell you, miss!"

"This is not a time for secrets!" Tilla hissed, holding the lamp close to the girl's face. "Your master is very ill. If you know something, you must speak."

The girl shrank away, shaking her head. "I swore not to tell."

Tilla stepped forward and lifted the girl's chin. "And I swear to you," she said, looking into the frightened eyes that blinked in the bright light, "that if you don't tell, and your master dies, I will make sure you get the blame."

60

NEPTUNE RISES TO greet the goddess of the moon.
    The musicians were still flinging wild tunes into the night air, but the crowd was changing now: Young children were being taken home to bed or settled in small huddles of blankets under the portico. The child snatcher tales had had their effect: As Ruso peered at a sleeping toddler to reassure himself it was not Mara, a shawled old woman hissed, "What are you looking at? Clear off!" from the shadows.

Dodging the dancers and gossipers and the altars now providing useful support for drunks, Ruso made his way across the courtyard and retrieved the straw hat from the head of a statue. With the alarming stitches thus hidden, he was just in time to catch the oyster stall. A man was lifting one of a row of barrels while a woman was tying a length of rope around a stack of wooden lids. She glanced up at his approach. "All gone, sir, sorry. We'll have a fresh lot up from the coast in a couple of days."

"It's not really oysters I wanted," Ruso told her. "I'm hoping you can give me some information."

The smile was tired, but it was there. "Right-oh, sir. How can we help?"

That, Ruso thought, was the difference between visiting an ordinary town and visiting one that depended on tourists for a living. "It's about the tide," he said. "In the river. I thought you might know."

"It's in." The man sounded less accommodating than his partner.

"Yes," Ruso agreed. "I'm told it follows the moon."

The man eyed Ruso's straw hat, gave the woman a what-have-you-got-me-into? look, and said, "Of course."

Ruso indicated the row of barrels. "Need some help?"

He was on his way back from loading a cart and less enlightened than he had hoped, because the oysterman had been down at the coast on the night of the fire, when he heard, "Master!"

It was Neena, carrying his sleeping daughter and looking more than a little weary. "I have been looking for you!"

For some reason Tilla had gone back to the centurion's house without taking Mara, and Virana had gone off to return trays to the bakery. Having totally ignored his suggestion that they all stay together for safety, Tilla had left Neena with a message for him to follow her to the centurion's house as soon as possible. It was more than a little annoying, but it was not Neena's fault. So, rather than argue, he sent Neena back there to put their daughter to bed and assure Tilla that there was no need to worry: His head was fine now and he would be back just as soon as he had finished what he was doing.

"And Albanus is looking for you as well, master."

Probably to warn him that Tilla had wandered off on her own. Sometimes people could be too helpful. "I'll try and find him before I come back," he promised, striding away in pursuit of the oysterman and the information that was proving much harder to get than he had imagined.

Apparently the timing of high and low water could indeed be calculated, but it was a tricky business, partly because it involved both the moon and the sun while daylight hours were getting shorter and night hours getting longer all the time, and partly because Ruso's lack of sleep was starting to catch up with him.

In the end it was the woman who told him what he wanted to know. "Oh, the tide was on the way out that evening," she said. "I remember because it was a lovely sunset and my little girl was watching the birds feeding down on the mud and she said how it looked all pink with the glow on it, and then a bit later she called down from her bed to say the sun had turned his chariot round and come back. Only it wasn't, was it? It was the Little Eagle."

"So the tide wouldn't be up again till late into the night," explained the oysterman, who, after his initial reluctance, now seemed determined not to let Ruso go until he had completed his education. "And the moon must have been waning, so she was late up too, see." Ruso did not see, but he did not care, either. He had found out what he needed to know. He thanked them both, dumped the second barrel in the cart, and sprinted back to the baths.

The bathhouse was less crowded than before, but a couple of stall-holders were still pouring drinks and little clusters of guests had gathered in the alcoves to chat. Others had decided to bathe by the fitful light of the surrounding torches, men and women keeping to the spirit of the emperor's ban on mixed bathing by not bothering to undress first. The slaves standing in attendance were doing nothing to stop them. Ruso was not surprised: Apparently the manager was dining with the governor. After the disaster with the water, he guessed that any use of initiative in the manager's absence had been strongly discouraged. However, the nearest man did provide the answer to his question: Justus, the malodorous little slave with the stoop, had gone to retrieve something dropped in the latrine.

By the time Ruso got there, the rescue was over. Someone was washing a purse and its contents in the water channel that ran down the middle of the room, and the slave was crouching downstream of him, rinsing a long pole with a hook on the end. Around them, an audience of glum-faced customers sat over the holes in the surrounding benches.

Ruso turned aside for a deep breath before approaching.

The slave dropped the pole in alarm.

"I think we need another chat," Ruso said. "In private."

The man looked around. "I can't desert my post, sir."

"Yes you can," urged a voice from one of the seats.

"Please do," put in another. "And take your stinky poking stick with you."

★ ★ ★

The girl and the lad with the toga were gone now; the maintenance stores were empty and silent. Glancing down into the darkness at the far end, Ruso decided that this was a good place to
frighten somebody. Just in case Justus wasn't frightened enough,
Ruso helped himself to a chisel from the rack, grabbed him, and
put it to his throat.

"Now tell me," he whispered, "where did you really get that
ring?"

"I told you, sir—"

He pressed the point of the chisel into the jugular notch. "The
tide was out. Terentius couldn't swim. He didn't like boats. He
would never have waited around to escape that way in the dark.
Where did you get it?"

The man was shaking now. "I found it, sir."

"Did they tell you I'm a doctor?" Ruso whispered. "I might not
kill you. I might just make you hurt in ways you wouldn't believe."
Then, louder: "Where did you get it?"

"It's true, sir, I swear! I found it!"

"Where?"

"I daren't tell, sir."

Ruso felt the chisel move as the man swallowed.

"I might end up there myself."

"Where?"

The man gulped. "In the drain, sir."

"You found Terentius's ring in the drain?" Ruso tried to keep
the disappointment out of his voice.

"Yes, sir. The main drain down from the bath."

Where the slave, he supposed, spent a great deal of time on official business. "So why couldn't you tell anyone?"

"I didn't want to get involved in anything!"

"But you kept the ring."

He swallowed. "I didn't know what to do with it, sir!"

"You could have handed it in."

"No, sir!"

Ruso tightened his grip. "Why not?"

The man swallowed. "Because I found it on Master Terentius's
body, sir. And I reckoned whoever put him there might kill me
too."

61

I MADE HIM vomit," Tilla said. "And he does seem a little better."

Ruso said, "Well done," and saw the relief on her face. He would have said *Well done* to almost anything, but she didn't need to know that. He knew how it felt to be facing a desperate patient you had no idea how to treat. He knew also that if he had come as soon as he got her message, he would have been able to reassure her. When you were lost, it was always good to have a companion. There would have been two of them who did not know what was in the mysterious greenish-brown pills the maid had described finding in a pot under Pertinax's bed the other day.

"You go and see to Mara," he told her. "I'll take over here."

When she had gone, he leaned back against the closed door, blew all the air out of his lungs, and then took a deep breath, trying to settle his mind on his patient. The business of Terentius's body—if indeed the slave was telling the truth—would have to wait. So would the danger to Valens: He had done everything he could about that for now. He must concentrate on the old man in the bed in front of him.

Gleva had run most of the way alongside Ruso after she had found him at the baths. Now she was bent over Pertinax. The red hair hung down over the pair of them like a damp veil, excluding everyone else. From beneath it she claimed to know nothing of any pills. A second voice from beneath it pointed out that he couldn't see the bloody doctor if she didn't get off.

Perched on the edge of the hard bed, Ruso ran through the usual questions. Pertinax was still breathing too fast but his pulse was not as wild as Tilla had described it. Finally they got to the point: "Sir, I need to know what's in those pills."

Pertinax closed his eyes as if he had not heard. Ruso was not surprised: According to Tilla, the old centurion had burst in while the maid was supposed to be cleaning the room and caught her with the pot in her hand. He had snatched it away, causing the lid to fall off and a shower of greenish-brown things about the size of peas to scatter in all directions. He had told the girl to keep her nose out and her mouth shut and ordered her out of the room before she had a chance to pick them up.

"This is the work of the other priests," said Gleva, repeating the accusations she had made to Ruso on the way. "Dorios has been looking for a chance to tame this man ever since he came here. I hear the priest and the haruspex talking. I think he has laid a curse on this house."

Ruso said, "I can't see how Dorios could persuade him to poison himself," just as Pertinax grunted something. He leaned closer. "Sir?"

"Not the priests."

"Sir, I need you to tell me about the pills. I'm fighting with one hand tied behind my back here. Have you taken any today?"

"Your woman said I'm getting better."

"His woman is not a medicus," put in Gleva. "You said so yourself."

Ruso turned to her. "I'll search in here. You do his study."

But the search produced nothing. It was as if the maid had seen the pills in a vision that was not granted to anyone else. Meanwhile, Pertinax drank a little water but refused to answer any more questions.

"I shall go and wake your brother and see what he can tell us," Gleva announced.

She turned to Ruso. "Catus has been asleep for hours. He is very tired after last night."

Their eyes met. Suddenly she said, "Blessed Sulis!" and ran from the room with Ruso in pursuit.

Their fears were unfounded. The old engineer rolled over and began to cough as Ruso shook his shoulder and Gleva shouted his name. When he had recovered he made it clear that he knew nothing of pills.

By now Pertinax was feeling sufficiently better to insist that everyone stop making a fuss. At least this had got him out of Arse Face's bloody dinner, and he would see the governor himself in the morning. "Did I tell you I served with him in Germania?"

Back in the bedroom that Pertinax had offered them—was it only last night? It seemed a month ago—Ruso said, "I think he's going to be all right." Then he wrapped his arms around his wife, whose breath smelled of beer, and put his tired head on her shoulder.

"At last," she said. "I am so glad you are safe."

He said nothing in reply, because if he spoke, it would be to say that he was going out again, and she would want to know why, and he would have to tell her. And she would ask what the slave's report of the body meant, and he would say he didn't know, but that it didn't look good for Valens. And then he would have to say it all over again to poor old Catus, who was still hoping his young apprentice was alive somewhere.

He would have to do all those things in a moment, but just for now he wanted to hide here in silence and pretend it was all over.

62

R USO COULD HEAR his own breath over the rush and gurgle of the water. He had known it would be bad, but this—the dark, the suffocating stench, the brick walls and roof closing in on him while warm muck flowed over his feet . . . His heart was hammering to be let out. He wanted to curl up and whimper like a dog.

Breathe slowly. Count each pace. The only thing holding him back from panic was the knowledge that he must hold the lamp steady, because if he dropped it everything would be much worse. He must keep going. One step. The next. Feeling the waste flow in and out of his sandals. Squelch around his toes.

Left.

Right.

Left.

Glancing ahead to make sure the tall form of Catus was still there, moving steadily along in front of him. Glad he was not the one walking into the blackness, probing ahead with a hook on the end of a wooden pole, hoping to find something in the water and hoping not to.

Gazing up at the square gap in the tunnel roof, glimpsing the rope that dangled down from the blackness and wanting to seize it and hang on. Knowing that it was madness to be down here when the river was swollen with rain and combining with the highest tide of the month to fill the outlet of the tunnel and raise the water levels; knowing also that if they did not find Terentius tonight, all sign of him might be washed away by morning.

He thought about Tilla, safely over at Pertinax's house with Mara and Neena. About Gleva, gone to the banquet more to please her lover than herself. About Valens and his boys, waiting in the temple. About Pertinax himself, recovering in his hard bed, with no idea that his brother and Ruso were down here searching for the body of Serena's lover. About Justus, the nervous little slave waiting at the tunnel entrance with orders to fetch help if they didn't come back. About all the priests and veterans and tourists and locals partying up in the courtyard and the baths. Most of them innocent of the truth of what was hidden down here. And one of them, surely, who was not.

"Ledge under the surface here on the right." The engineer's interruption of his thoughts came almost as a surprise. "Watch you don't slip."

Ruso wanted to say there was no need to tell him to be careful, but the man was right: It was hard to keep your mind clear down here. Hard not to let it follow your imagination down the tunnel to where the body of Terentius, or what was left of it, might be shifting with the rising tide.

He was sure the water was deeper now.

Watch you don't slip.

Ruso's head banged against the roof. He fell sideways. Clawed at the damp wall. Pushed himself back upright. One foot. Then the next.

The air was thick and the water was well over his knees now, beginning to soak up into his tunic. He felt the flow tugging him forward each time he lifted a foot. *Watch you don't—*

"Something here." Catus had stopped. Ahead of him there seemed to be a blank wall, but the water was flowing off away from it: The tunnel must turn to the right. The light caught the length of the pole: the glint of moving water. The shape of something lifting and straining against the hook. Fabric. Whatever it was under there had caught in the angle of the drain.

An explosion of noise and the item dropped back into the water as Catus convulsed into a coughing fit, collapsing sideways and using the wall to keep himself upright.

Ruso leaned forward and took the pole from his grasp. Pressing himself against the opposite wall, he squeezed past the struggling engineer, lifted the lamp as high as the roof allowed, and probed into the water. The hook caught on something substantial. He moved himself into a position that would block his companion's view before hauling up and back. Then he lowered the lamp and stared, trying to work out what he was looking at.

Catus had stopped coughing now. *Give him something to do before he sees and understands.* Ruso twisted round, handing over the lamp. "Hold that, sir." He wedged the pole behind him and bent down, groping in the water, keeping his face as high above the surface as he could. He swore. Then he fumbled about again, this time finding what he wanted and feeling a huge sense of relief as it came free.

"Is it him?"

Ruso leaned back against one wall to brace himself against the flow of the water before lifting each foot in turn, gradually maneuvering round to face the engineer. "We can get out now."

"Is it him?"

Ruso held out the slick black remains of a leather belt. At one end was a filthy metal buckle. He rinsed the buckle in the water and held it closer to the lamp. The pattern of a horse was clearer now.

Catus took the buckle.

"Is it . . . ?"

Catus nodded and slumped lower against the wall.

"I'm sorry."

"Oh, my boy," Catus groaned, staring at the rippling surface of the water. "Forgive me."

He jerked forward in another fit of coughing and Ruso grabbed the lamp before he could drop it. The water was halfway up Ruso's thighs now, silently pushing him away into the blackness beyond. He could feel the warm damp creeping up his back.

"We have to get out!" He snatched up the pole as it slid sideways and fell into the water. Then he edged past Catus, eager to begin the long walk back up the tunnel.

Catus tried to speak, but the cough seemed to rise up from the depths of his lungs. He held out his own lamp with a trembling hand, jabbing it in the direction they had just come.

"I know!" Ruso was short of breath and fighting the return of the panic. "We must get out!"

Catus shook his head. "You go."

"Now! Come on!" The effort of shouting left him gasping for air. He was reduced to grabbing the old man's arm. "The water's rising. We need air. Please."

If Catus did not move this time, Ruso thought he might weep.

But Catus was still facing the wrong way down the tunnel. "Oh, my poor boy!" he cried, pausing to catch his breath. "All this time I've been waiting for you to come back."

"Catus, please!"

"None of what went wrong over there was your fault. I should have spoken up for you. But I was a coward."

"Catus—"

"He told me if I set that fire it would help you. It would stop them building. It would set you free. Then, after you were gone, he burned all the plans."

"Grab hold of the stick. Follow me!"

"I should never have listened to him. He said—" Catus's cry was anguished. "He promised me the goddess would be pleased."

"Engineer, shift your miserable arse! There's work to do!"

But even Ruso's best imitation of Pertinax had no effect. All that happened was that Catus turned halfway round and said, "It was never meant to spread like it did. The toolshed was next to the kitchen. I didn't think about them storing oil."

The water was up to his waist now, and he was struggling to keep his feet. How could it be rising this fast? Ruso swung the pole, caught the hook on Catus's clothing, and pulled. "Move, or we're both going to die down here!"

"Don't be the fool I was, Doctor. Don't listen to him." Catus lifted the lamp to his lips and blew.

Ruso yelled, "*No!*" and hauled on the pole, but it came free and the old man was already out of reach, the pale shape of his head growing fainter in the light of the one remaining lamp as he drifted away into the dark.

"Come back!" Ruso shouted after him. "Don't listen to who?"

From farther down the tunnel came a faint cry of "He promised the goddess would heal me!"

As Catus's voice died away, Ruso felt a sudden rush of air and heard the slap of water on brick. He turned. There was a huge black wave churning down the tunnel toward him.

63

TILLA TWIRLED THE spindle and let it drop, teasing out the strands of fleece and not bothering to pull out a knot that fed itself down and tightened into the thread. She would regret that when she came to wind it into the skein, but at the moment it was hard to care. She needed to do something, and the something was not sitting around here, twiddling about with wool and waiting for news.

She hoped her husband was feeling as fine as he had claimed to be. He had looked weary, and she had caught him smearing rose oil on his forehead. On the way out he had promised her the remedy was already clearing his headache, but he would have said that anyway, because he did not want her to worry.

How many lies did people tell each other to stave off worry? Like *It's perfectly safe: I'm with the chief engineer. Catus wouldn't be going down there if it were dangerous.*

She wondered about going to check on Pertinax again, but he had been dozing last time she looked, and the little maid had instructions to call her if he woke. Mara was asleep over in the corner, lying on her back with both arms flung above her head. Neena was squinting over her efforts to patch a tunic neatly in the poor light, and Tilla was making a mess of good wool and telling herself that all of this would be over soon, and then they would be out of there. Worrying would not make the time pass faster. Nor would it change anything. She must think about the future.

She eyed the trunk that contained the box of useless medical scrolls. Perhaps she could try to learn Greek. Could it be any harder than Latin?

There were voices over in the entrance hall. She flung the spindle onto the bed and ran to see if the men were back. When she got there, there was nothing but a cold draft and the houseboy, bending to scowl into the lock and fiddling with the angle of the big iron key.

"Who was here?"

The old slave wiggled the key back and forth, ignoring her.

"Is there any news of my husband?"

The lock finally scraped into place. Straightening up, the houseboy eyed her, clearly trying to decide whether the visitor was any of her business. "Just a slave," he said, "asking for Master Catus."

"He is at the baths."

"That's what I said. I told him to go back and look harder."

"The slave came from the baths?"

"I told him it's no good asking me about sluices. Why would I know anything?"

"But Catus is already there! My husband went with him."

The houseboy shook his head. "Probably been at the beer."

Tilla was already halfway back to the bedroom, calling behind her, "You must open the door again! I'm going out."

Neena was already on her feet by the time Tilla arrived to snatch up her wrap from the end of the bed. "I am trusting you to look after Mara and the old centurion," said Tilla, flinging the wrap around her shoulders. "While I am gone, pray very hard for your master. Pray for us both!"

64

STAY BRACED: FEET on one wall, back rammed against the other. Fight it. Don't let it drag you down there. Don't think about the air dying in your lungs.

Air. The inspection hatches. *That square opening in the roof—how far back?* The force of the water . . . not so strong now. *Stay braced: Edge your way along the tunnel. Keep hold of the pole. Force your arm upward against the flow.*

Weak as a kitten.

Prod at the roof.

Solid. No way out.

This is how it ends. With no chance to say good-bye as your treacherous lungs betray you, sucking in warm black water in desperation.

Wait—yes! Nothing up above. The inspection hatch! The rope. There was a rope. *Find the rope—yes! Hold on. Push against the floor with the pole now . . . pull up . . .*

His head banged against the roof of the tunnel and he only just stopped himself gasping in a lungful of warm black water. So near— but the flow was too strong. One more try, then he would let himself

go. He longed to go now. Death was a welcome— *Pay attention!*
Feet down; brace against the sides of the tunnel; pray; haul up—

Dizzy. No strength left.

This was it.

Open mouth—draw in—

Air! Thick, steamy, precious—

Trembling, Ruso clung onto the slimy rope, straining to keep
his face above the surface.

Gulping in the heavy atmosphere of the shaft while the water
below still tugged at his body. Opening one eye: nothing. Opening
the other one, blinking to make sure they really were open. Nothing.
Just—

Nothing.

Only one thing to do now.

Hold on.

His sore arm ached. He could feel his pulse throbbing in the
wound on his scalp.

Hold on. The water will go down.

How long would that take, with him trapped in this suffocating
black hole? How long would the air last?

Don't think about that. For this moment:

Hold on.

His muscles were rivers of pain. His injured arm, pressed against
the hard brick of the shaft, felt as though it was being torn apart.

Hold on.

No! He had so nearly succumbed to the temptation for a quick
rest.

Hold on.

For this moment.

And the next moment.

And the next.

Hold on.

The warmth splashed over his face and into his mouth. He hauled
himself higher, trying to spit out the disgusting taste, clamping his
stiff hands one by one into new positions and hooking the rope
around one leg. He should have done this before; the current was
not pulling as strongly at his legs up here.

But his face was no clearer. It didn't make sense.

Yes it did. But not a sense he wanted. The water was rising to fill the shaft, and the shaft was not very high.

What was it Catus had told Tilla about the river flooding back up the drain and into the bath? Here, under the ground, how far below the bath level was he trapped? How far below ground?

"Help!"

It sounded feeble even to him. He peered upward, praying for some chink of light to appear, but there was nothing. He hauled himself up again. Even if he could float up, what would happen if the water rose to the top? There must be something substantial covering the opening. He could bang the pole on the— No, the pole had gone. He had no idea when. And now his head brushed against whatever was covering the top of the shaft. One hand to push against it: nothing. The stone slab was unyielding. He was only succeeding in pushing himself back down.

"Help me!"

No reply. Only the gentle sound of water lapping against brick.

Ruso rested his head against the rope and whispered, "Sulis Minerva, have mercy on me."

65

TILLA RACED ACROSS the terrace and down the steps in the moonlight. She fumbled with the latch on the tall gate and slammed it behind her, hearing the clatter as it bounced back instead of closing.

There were people on the road, making their way back to their beds after the celebrations. She could only make out one traveler going in the direction of the temple: a small figure who gave a hasty glance back over his shoulder when he heard her behind him, and broke into a run. Her cry of "Stop!" only seemed to frighten him more. Realizing her mistake, she picked up her skirts and sprinted after him, calling, "I know where Catus is!"

"Whoa there, girlie!" shouted a drunken fool from a group ahead of her. He staggered sideways into the middle of the road as she approached, holding his arms wide as if he were trying to halt a runaway horse.

There was no time to avoid him, but he had left himself wide-open to the punch, and stepping around his toppling form wasted almost no time at all. The messenger boy, who had paused to hear her news about Catus, now joined her in fleeing before the drunk could get up.

They did not stop until they reached the busier streets. For a moment they both stood panting in the middle of the road, hearing the music waft out over the courtyard wall as chattering partygoers wandered past them.

"Catus went to the baths," Tilla told him. "With my husband. About an hour ago. They were going to—" She bit back the words, *look for something.* "They had to check something in the drainage tunnel."

The boy frowned in puzzlement. "But he's not at the baths now, miss. They sent me to fetch him."

"You have checked in the tunnel?"

The dark eyes widened. "Miss, there's a full-moon tide and it's been raining."

"I know that!" she snapped. Then, because it was not the boy's fault, she said more gently, "Something went wrong, and they were going in together to sort it out. It's very important that we find them."

The boy looked relieved. "So Master Catus is already sorting everything out?"

"What is this business about sluices?"

The boy shook his head. "I don't know, miss. If Master Catus is there, he will—"

"But he's not there, is he? You just said you don't know where he is!"

He began to back away.

"Don't—" Tilla lunged for him, but he ducked out of her grasp and barged through a group of people in the courtyard entrance. She followed him, ignoring the shouts of protest, only to find herself back in amongst the musicians and a few late-night revelers gathered beneath the sputtering torches. Where was the boy?

Several knots of people had formed by the sacred spring and were peering down and pointing. Dreading what she might find, she ran across to join them. The boy was there, standing beside a slave in a bathhouse tunic. They were both leaning over the railings on the far side of the pool, but there was nothing terrible to see. Instead, the pool was almost empty. A tall opening had been revealed in the far wall, and the people gathered around were watching the water drain out of it.

She said, "What is happening?"

"It's all right," someone farther along the railing assured her. "The slave says they do this from time to time. It washes the silt out."

But surely not in the middle of a party? She hurried across to where the boy was standing with the bathhouse slave. "Engineer Catus left his house an hour ago to come here," she said. "He was with my husband. They said they were going to check something down in the tunnel."

The man glanced at the boy and then straightened up. "Not tonight, miss. It's a—"

"I know, a full-moon tide and it has been raining. But that is what they said."

He shook his head. "We have a rule here, miss. When somebody goes down, we leave another man at the top for safety. There's nobody at the top."

Tilla said, "This was urgent. Perhaps they did not bother. Someone needs to go down there and look for them."

The boy shrank closer to the man and said, "Is that why the entrance hatch . . . ?"

"Course not," the older man told him. "That was the same jokers as opened the spring sluice—"

Tilla said, "What sluice?"

"—and pulled the plug on the main bath," continued the man. "We've had a right fine time here this evening, miss. We've been looking for the boss to tell us whether to let it all drain and get the silt out now it's open, or close it back up. We don't do nothing without orders, see, and the manager's off having dinner with the governor and can't be interrupted. But it's a bit late now anyway."

Tilla stared at the center of the empty pool, where steaming water still bubbled up through the mud and flowed out through the opening. Vaguely aware of a familiar voice calling her name, she said, "All the water from this pool has gone down into the tunnel?"

"And half the bath, miss. Don't worry, he won't be down there."

"Then *where is he*?" she shrieked, finally losing her patience. She turned to the boy. "Show me how to get in there. I am going to find them."

That familiar voice again, calling her name. She turned, still impatient, to see Albanus elbowing his way past a group of partygoers to reach them. He was saying something about a centurion. "Did your husband find him?"

For a moment Tilla could not think what he was talking about. Then she remembered Pertinax's illness. "The centurion is feeling better," she assured Albanus. "But my husband and Serena's uncle went into the drainage tunnel and nobody has seen them since."

Albanus turned to the bath slaves. "Is this true?"

The man said, "Sir, there's nothing that would have sent the boss down there on a night like this."

"It was important," Tilla said.

The slave gave her the sort of look he might give a woman who expected him to risk his life for a lost earring.

The boy was wide-eyed. "What would happen," he said, "if Master Catus was in the tunnel with all that water?"

His companion stepped away from the railing. "Find Celer and Docilis," he said to the boy. "Tell them I want them by the first hatch right now. I'll fetch a rope and a hook."

Tilla said, "I will come!"

The slave turned back to address Albanus. "Keep the lady out of the way, will you please, sir?"

Both slaves hurried away into the bathhouse. Now, without the anger to cling to, Tilla began to tremble. What *would* happen if somebody was in the tunnel with all that water? She made to follow the slaves, but Albanus's grip on her arm was surprisingly strong. "We must leave them to do it," he insisted. "The doctor would never forgive me if I let anything happen to you."

"Then what are we going to do?"

"We are going to wait," he told her.

The sight of the black river water slapping at the wall below her made Tilla shudder. It was so close, it seemed to be reaching out for her. Albanus said this was where the tunnel came out, beyond the vegetable plots, but there was no sign of a tunnel now. The river had risen over the outlet. There was no escape here except by swimming.

But it was a big tunnel, Albanus had insisted. Such things were built high enough for slaves to walk down and clear them. So it must surely be possible to be swept out with the flow of the water and to swim to safety.

She raised her head and peered out at the shifting surface of the river in the moonlight. "Husband! Husband, can you hear me? Where are you? Blessed spirit of the river, bring him back to us!"

The river flowed on, silent and indifferent.

"Why does nobody fetch a boat?"

Albanus, also staring out into night, said, "He is a better swimmer than he is a sailor."

The words were kindly meant, but not a great comfort.

"He might have climbed out further downstream. He might be on his way back."

An owl hooted from the woods across the water as if it were mocking them.

"Husband!" Tilla cried. "Speak to us: Where are you?"

The owl's cry went unanswered. The wall was cold and damp under her hands. She leaned back and whispered a prayer to the moon goddess, who gazed back with her wide, bright, beautiful face. Perhaps she too was searching.

Perhaps she had already seen him. Lying pale and drowned out there on the riverbank.

"I think we should go back to the baths," Albanus said. "The staff might be looking for us."

It was kinder than saying, *He is not here.*

They picked their way along the mud paths between the vegetable patches, now slippery with the rain. Tilla remembered how she had taken fright out here on her own, even though in the end there were only two angry women to be afraid of. Perhaps that fear had been an omen: a warning that none of them had understood or heeded.

As they trudged back up the lane, the kitchen smells from the Mercury wafted toward them. Ahead, torches were blazing outside the door, picking out the angles of the armor on the guards stationed beneath and glinting on the puddles in the street. From somewhere inside there was a too-hearty gust of laughter: the sound of people determined to be jolly. Perhaps the governor had just told a joke.

"Mistress, is that you?"

The voice was so close it made her jump.

"It is me!" it said. "Esico!"

Earlier today she would have been pleased to see him. Now she barely managed to reply as he fell into step alongside her. She could smell the beer on him as he chattered in his native tongue about begging the master to take him back and making a new start.

"Not now, Esico."

"I will learn to speak Latin!" He stepped in front of them, walking backward as he pleaded. "I will work hard."

Tilla stopped in the middle of the lane. She had no energy to force her way past him. Ahead of them, a helmet moved under the torchlight as a guard outside the Mercury turned to watch. She said, "Your master is missing."

"I will never wander off again, I swear. Please, mistress—"

It was Albanus who stepped forward to put him in his place. Glaring up at the youth, who was a head taller than himself, he announced that the doctor had gone missing and was feared drowned, and if Esico had any respect he would not be pestering the mistress on this of all nights.

Esico said, "Eh?" and Albanus cried, "Oh, gods above!" in exasperation. "After all your master has done for you, and you never even bothered to learn Latin! He should have sold you months ago, you foolish boy!"

Tilla placed a hand on Albanus's arm. "It does us no good to argue."

"Well, I'm sorry," Albanus spluttered, "but really . . ."

"I know." So Tilla made the lad stand in the middle of the lane and listen while she explained, watching his eager face crumple as he understood, and then he said, "I fear he is gone, mistress."

Albanus, who had no idea what Esico had just said, muttered, "We should go," but nobody took any notice.

"We may be wrong," Tilla told Esico, feeling sorry for him now. Perhaps the gods had sent him as a gangling and annoying mercy: someone to lift her mind for a moment from her own fears. "He might be safe somewhere else."

"No, mistress. I heard his ghost."

"He might be quite safe and—what?"

"I was lying down to sleep in the stable because I had nowhere else to go, and I heard him, mistress. Calling from a long way away. 'Help me.' I got up and looked out but there was only the guards standing there and I thought it was a dream, or the beer, so I—"

"Did you go to the river?"

He looked stricken. "I never thought—"

"There you are, my boy!" The voice was not sober, and neither was it welcome.

Esico turned to face the figure shambling toward them. "You can piss off," he told his father. "You're no use."

"Wait!" Tilla turned to the old man. "My husband has gone missing. Have you seen him?"

But the old man had not. "Nothing but stuck-up guards and fancy types in daft clothes down here tonight."

"Esico thought he heard someone calling."

The man paused and scratched his head. "Hm."

Tilla stepped closer and stared up into the creased and whiskery face. "Did you hear something? Where did it come from? Did it come from the river?"

The old man frowned. "Nah." He stared back up the street and scratched his head again. "He can't be down in that cellar thing. I'd have seen him climb in."

"'Cellar thing'?"

He waved a hand toward the middle of the paved area outside the Mercury. "Over there. I reckon it's a bit damp. Well, it's a daft place to put—" But Tilla was already there, hauling at the ring set into the stone and screaming at the guards to come across and help her, and when they got a spear through the ring and heaved the stone aside there was water, and something was floating in it.

66

TILLA WAS NOT dressed for a smart dinner and Pertinax had only made it down there because some of his men had loaded him onto a borrowed mule, but still the sight of him, and his gruff "She's with me," worked like a magic spell to get her past the governor's guards.

The conversation on the dining room couches died as they entered. The pipe players faltered into silence. The big bald man on the central couch raised his eyebrows and looked at the chief priest lounging next to him as if waiting for an explanation. Everyone else stared at the sight before them: an old man dressed in full centurion's regalia, his breastplate glittering with awards for bravery. Below the metal-tipped straps that hung from his belt, he had one leg made of human flesh and one of wood. He limped forward, a crested helmet under one arm and Tilla on the other.

Gleva was the first to move. She leapt up from her wicker chair, dodging between the musicians and a lampstand. Taking the helmet and handing it to a servant, she seized his arm and whispered, "What are you doing here?"

"Pertinax?" said the governor. "I was told you were ill."

"I was, sir. Sorry I'm late. Here on urgent business."

Tilla felt the old man begin to sway and tightened her grip on his arm. She hoped he wasn't going to pass out. A slave who had slipped in beside them scuttled across the room and bent to whisper something into the ear of the pink-headed man she had seen giving orders at the bathhouse.

The governor said, "Can't it wait till morning?"

"No, sir," Pertinax told him. "It can't."

Over on another couch, the bathhouse manager was raising his hand as if hoping to be excused.

Moments later the musicians were gone, several bejeweled lady diners had been escorted out, and the staff had all followed, closing the doors behind them. The rest of the guests, including a couple of middle-aged men who must be the governor's advisers, were left to stare at Pertinax across a confusion of small tables and dirty crockery. If they had been enjoying the party before, they certainly weren't now.

One of the advisers glanced at Tilla and Gleva, then said something to the governor about "those women."

"They can stay," snapped the governor. "Pertinax, sit down. Have some wine before you collapse."

Pertinax sank into Gleva's empty chair and waved away the cup she offered. "Sir, I've just had news that my brother Catus is missing, believed dead."

There was a murmur of shock from around the room. The fat priest's eyes were wide. The way the glum-faced one had stopped chomping on his false teeth reminded Tilla of a nervous sheep that stopped chewing while it watched to see if you were dangerous. Next to him, the bathhouse manager was wriggling about on the couch as if he were trying to slide his body away while leaving his face in place.

"My condolences," said the governor. "So soon after the loss of your daughter."

"He went to inspect something in the drainage tunnel," Pertinax said. "Someone opened the sluices to empty the pools while he was down there."

The bathhouse manager had his hand in the air again. "Sir?"

"Speak."

"My staff are searching for him, sir. With your permission, I'd like to—"

"Go," the governor told him. As he scrambled down and scurried away, the governor said, "Catus is a good engineer and a good soldier. I remember him well from Germania."

"There was another man with him," said Pertinax. "One of my lads from the Twentieth." He placed a heavy hand on Tilla's arm. "This is his wife."

Tilla bowed her head.

"My man's been found, sir. In a bit of a state, but he managed to get out of an inspection hatch."

The governor said, "Good."

Tilla whispered, "I must go and see him!" because plainly her husband's *I'll be all right!* when they pulled him out of the water had been a wish rather than a truth. But Pertinax still had a grip on her arm.

The officials were talking all around them now: the two priests, the governor, and his advisers saying all the sorts of useless things people said as a tragedy unfolded. Telling each other how terrible it was, and wondering how it could have happened, and urging Pertinax not to give up hope. And underneath all the sympathy and the shock, she could sense each man's relief that he had not been snatched into the next world himself.

Then Pertinax was saying something about murder, and the chief priest was reminding him—not very gently—that not every death was a murder, and the governor said "Who would want to harm Catus?"

But now the chief priest was saying something she hadn't expected. "I'm very much afraid, sir, that this may not have been an accident."

"That's what I just said," Pertinax growled.

Instead of saying more, the chief priest was now telling everyone this would be better dealt with in the morning. The thing to do tonight was to concentrate on the search, and perhaps the governor—

He was interrupted by a knock on the door. The governor shouted, "Come!"

A strong smell of drains wafted in and a little slave appeared, wiping his hands on his grimy tunic. Ordered to speak, he said he had been sent by Master Latinus.

The governor scowled at him. "Is there news?"

The man hesitated, then said, "Sorry, sir."

"There is news, or there isn't?" demanded Pertinax.

The slave gulped. "Sirs, he said I was to tell you it was me that opened the sluices."

"You?" Pertinax made an effort to leap up but fell back.

"Yes, sir." The slave seemed transfixed by the sight of the glittering awards on the centurion's breastplate. "M–Master Catus told me to do it, sir."

"*Catus* told you?"

"Yes, sir. He said I was to count to a hundred and fifty after they went in and then open everything up."

For a moment there was silence in the dining room. Then the governor said, "Go and thank Latinus for sending you. Tell him to carry on the search. He's to send word the moment there's any news, and if there isn't, report to me first thing in the morning."

When the slave had gone the governor said, "I'm sorry, Centurion."

Memor said, "But what possible reason could Catus have—"

The chief priest cleared his throat. "We should deal with this in the morning, sir."

The governor turned to him. "If you know something, Dorios, I want to hear it now."

"Sir, I'd rather not—"

"Well, I'd rather you did."

Dorios swallowed. "I've been afraid of something like this, sir. Ever since we had a tragic fire at an inn that killed—"

"I know about the fire."

"I'm sorry to have to say this, sir," Dorios continued. "I'm sure it was never his intention to harm anyone. But Engineer Catus confessed to me some time ago that he was the one who set the fire. He did it to bring an end to his brother's failing building project."

Pertinax looked stunned.

Tilla took a deep breath. Catus had started that dreadful fire on purpose? And the priest had known?

Pertinax put his head in his hands. Gleva crouched beside him. "He is not well," she said, looking up. "He needs to be taken home."

For once, Pertinax did not argue. Instead he let out a long sigh. "My brother's health was failing," he said. "We both knew he didn't have long to live. But to take another man with him? Why would he do that?"

Dorios said, "Perhaps he was still trying to help you." He turned to the governor. "The man Catus took with him was trying to stop the centurion bringing a court case."

The governor raised his eyebrows but said nothing. Tilla was wondering whether she could slip away to find her man, when the silence was broken by another knock on the door.

67

A GHOSTLIKE FIGURE appeared in the doorway, swathed in a moth-eaten toga. A row of black stitches ran across one side of its pale forehead and its hair was still wet from a cleansing dip in the cold plunge.

Tilla rushed forward to welcome it. "Husband!"

The chief priest and the haruspex both cried, "Doctor?" and Gleva said, "Is Catus found?" but the apparition shook its damp head.

The governor frowned at it over the remains of the dinner, and turned to Pertinax. "This is the man who was in the tunnel with Catus?"

"That's him, sir."

"What's he doing here?"

It was one of the many questions Tilla wanted to ask. Why wasn't he safely recovering in bed? After they had hauled him out of the water, she had wanted to clutch his wet body tight against her own: to feel the precious breath swelling his lungs over and over again. *Promise me*, she had begged. *Promise me you will never do such a foolish thing again!* But he had pushed her away, repeating that Catus had drowned and she must go and tell Pertinax. Finally she had left him in the care of Esico and gone to break the bad news to the centurion, who had insisted on coming to tell the governor.

Now Pertinax gave the sigh of a weary man and said, "What are you doing here, Ruso?"

"I've come with some news." He turned to the governor. "Do you mind if I sit, sir? I don't feel at my best."

"You should be thanking Fortuna you're still alive." The governor gestured to a couch. "I take it this isn't going to be good news."

"No, sir."

Her husband clattered across the tiled floor in a borrowed pair of wooden bath sandals, and Tilla settled herself on the edge of the couch beside him. Gleva was watching him intently, all the time keeping one protective hand on Pertinax's shoulder. The chief priest reached for his wine and took a swig, and the glum one with the false teeth did the same.

The governor said, "Well?"

"As you know, sir, Centurion Pertinax's daughter Serena was murdered."

"We all know that."

"And her, ah—her friend Terentius was murdered too."

The glum one jerked his head up. "No, that's not—"

"Terentius ran away sir," the chief priest told the governor. "He stole a boat from the wharf on the night the young lady died. We're still looking for him."

"You don't need to look any more," her husband told them. "What's left of him was down in the tunnel with an iron pick in his skull. Catus identified the clothing before he and the body were swept away."

There was a murmur of horror. The chief priest frowned. "Then who stole the boat?"

The centurion turned to the governor. "It seems, sir," he said, "that the husband really did murder both of them."

"Not necessarily," Ruso said.

"The husband must have killed the wife and her lover," agreed the glum one, ignoring him. "And hid the lover's body to make everyone think he was guilty."

"There might be some other—"

"Stop!" The governor held up one hand. "I won't listen to speculation if there's a legal case pending. Doctor, is there a chance of saving the engineer, or not?"

"I doubt it, sir. But there are lots of men out looking for him anyway."

"In that case," the governor announced, surveying the room, "I suggest we call it a night and try and get some sleep." He gestured toward the doors. "Somebody tell the staff they can clear up. Centurion, I'll get my men to take you home. I hope there's better news very soon."

It was Pertinax who objected. "I've lost two of my family, sir. I'll stay to hear what the doctor's got to say."

The governor hesitated for a moment.

"It might change everything."

The governor sighed. "Very well. I suppose we could give the man a moment or two."

Ruso turned to Pertinax. "Sir, if you're not well, we could leave it till—"

"Stop fussing and get on with it," growled Pertinax.

Tilla looked at her husband and wondered what other secrets he had learned in the tunnel. Did he know what had happened to Serena? He must know something or he would never have said, *Not necessarily.* Now he was looking around the room, waiting for his audience to give him their full attention. She shuffled to get comfortable on the couch—which was not as soft as it looked—and prepared to feel very proud.

68

FROM HIS PERCH beside his wife on the edge of the dining couch, Ruso surveyed the remnants of the governor's dinner party. The great man himself, still reclining on the central couch as if expecting some after-dinner entertainment; his two cronies; the fat priest and the thin one; Pertinax, Gleva . . . all of them concentrating their attention on what he was about to say. Glancing sideways, he saw his own wife gazing at him in something alarmingly close to admiration, as if he were about to perform a miracle in front of them and make everything clear at last.

Except he wasn't.

He would not have been there at all, except that he needed to get Valens and the boys safely out of that temple as soon as possible. Gnaeus and the veterans stationed outside had promised to protect them if the temple guards stormed the doors, but many of the veterans would have been awake for most of the night searching for the missing boys. They wouldn't be at their best.

"Get on with it, man," urged the governor. "It's late."

Ruso squared his shoulders, took a deep breath, and addressed the most powerful man in the province. "I'm not very clear about some of this myself, sir."

He was conscious of his audience shifting uneasily.

"Well," demanded the governor, "do you want to tell us or don't you?"

He didn't, but since nobody else was going to, he had to try. He was aware of Tilla pressing her thigh against his own in what he supposed was encouragement.

"I came to Aquae Sulis to try and help my friend Valens, sir; he's the centurion's son-in-law—"

"I know who he is," the governor reminded him.

"Yes, sir. Valens told me he was falsely accused of murdering his wife."

"No doubt."

"I tried to find out where everybody was on the night the lady died, sir, but once the fire had broken out, nobody really knows. We know Valens quarreled with his wife earlier, and he admits he saw her with Terentius in the courtyard, but the arrival of Catus frightened him off and he says he didn't see them again after that. He himself was seen tending the injured, but he could have gone somewhere else before he went back to his room at the inn. The last sighting I can find of Serena and Terentius anywhere is over at the fire. They were having an argument, and she was begging him not to go back and confront somebody."

He paused, aware of his audience's confusion. They had been hoping for a revelation and instead they were getting a garbled version of a military intelligence report. He wondered about trying again and instead resorted to "So I can't prove that Valens is innocent, sir."

Pertinax gave a loud sigh.

"But he wasn't the only one who had a disagreement with Serena." He turned to where Gleva was still standing beside Pertinax's chair. "I've never asked where you were that night."

"She was with her own people!" said Pertinax.

"No I wasn't," put in Gleva, placing a hand over the centurion's own. "Not all the time." Turning to the governor, she said, "I was with my family, over in the western hills. Then we saw the fire in the sky and some of us came into town and stayed to help. And it is true that I was not a friend of Serena. She tried to keep me away from her father."

Ruso said, "There are rumors that you put a curse on her."

"Nonsense!" muttered Pertinax.

"I have put a curse on her killer," Gleva declared, lifting her head and eyeing each of the diners in turn. "The one who took human life in the presence of the goddess will suffer a terrible fate. Sulis will not be mocked."

"You're a strong woman," Ruso observed. "You could have killed Serena and then made Terentius disappear so he would get the blame."

"She couldn't have killed a man!" put in Pertinax.

Ignoring Tilla's "You think women are weak?" Ruso said, "Terentius was deaf in one ear. Gleva would have known how to approach him without being heard, and the wound was on that side of the head."

"Nonsense," said Pertinax again.

"Yes," said Ruso. "I agree." To Gleva he said, "I think you're fond of Pertinax. I don't think you'd harm his daughter."

"See?" Gleva pushed her hair out of her eyes and glared at the two priests. "I told you it was nothing to do with me."

Ruso was aware of a dramatic sigh from the direction of the governor, who said, "I hope you're not planning to go around having these sort of chats with everyone in the room."

"No, sir. Apart from Valens, there are only two other people who might have wanted to hurt Serena."

"Good."

"Terentius might have killed her out of jealousy if she'd decided to end their affair after her husband's visit."

The governor said, "And then murdered himself?"

"No, sir. That's why he's off the list now. Or Serena might have killed Terentius and then taken her own life for the sake of family honor."

There was a grunt of protest from Pertinax. Before the man could speak, Ruso continued, "But Serena would never willingly leave her boys. So then unless there's some random murderer in town, the only person who seems to have had a motive is Valens."

He could sense the disappointment. Even his wife eased her thigh away from his own. "Sir," put in Dorios, "this is getting us nowhere."

"I agree," said the governor.

Ruso said, "I haven't finished, sir."

"Well, hurry up and get somewhere. It's late and the centurion's ill."

"Yes, sir." *Get somewhere,* Ruso urged himself, trying to remember the sequence of reasoning that had seemed so clear when he was lying in the dry straw of the stable, savoring the luxury of breathing. "What if it wasn't about Serena but about Terentius? You see, sir, just before Catus was swept away, he confessed to me that he lit the fire."

"We know that," put in the governor.

Ruso blinked. He had expected a stunned pause.

What else did they know?

"He confessed to me a few days later," put in Dorios. "It was a misguided attempt to release his friends and family from a disastrous building project."

Ruso turned to the priest. "Why didn't you say so?"

"I told you everything that was relevant to the murder," Dorios said. "Catus was a good man who made a mistake. I may have been wrong, but I thought he deserved protection."

The renewed pressure of Tilla's thigh against Ruso's own felt more like a reproach than a reassurance. "Catus's guilt could be very relevant," he continued. "When I heard that Serena had been begging Terentius not to confront somebody, I thought at first that he was off to pick a fight with Valens. Or that it was all made up, anyway. But now I think it was true and that he was going to confront Catus. He'd seen Catus heading over there with a lantern. He must have guessed Catus had had something to do with the fire." He turned to Pertinax. "Catus was a fine engineer, sir, but he wasn't very good at deceit. When my wife talked to him, he lied about why he was there that night. He said he was checking the sandbags because of the high tide. But that makes no sense, because there wasn't a high tide at the time. He was lying to cover something up."

Pertinax said, "But Catus could have been carrying a lantern for any number of reasons. Terentius couldn't have known he was going to lie to your wife."

Ruso stared at the centurion for a moment. The man was absolutely right. He opened his mouth to reply, but nothing came out. How could Terentius possibly have guessed who had lit the fire? He glanced down at Tilla, but she offered no help.

He was rescued by Gleva. "Terentius knew who started the fire," said Gleva, "because my brother was over in the other spring taking a night dip and saw what happened, and told him."

"What?" Pertinax's head jerked round. "Why didn't you tell me?"

"What good would it have done?"

Pertinax did not answer.

Ruso thought about the native he had met lying naked in a pool of warm water, and decided he should show the gods more respect in future. Perhaps Sulis Minerva was helping him after all. "So," he said, mentally scrambling back onto the path, "Terentius knew who had sabotaged his project. Whatever he thought of Catus, he couldn't be expected to keep quiet about that. But the one thing practically everyone has in common in this town is that they don't want to upset the visitors. An accidental fire was bad enough, but to have it known that guests had died as a result of a local quarrel . . ."

"Disastrous," put in the governor. "So poor old Catus decided to shut him up. And the young woman must have got in the way."

"Impossible!" cried Pertinax. "His own niece! Never, sir. This man's misleading you to save his friend."

The governor turned to Ruso. "Well?"

Ruso looked around the room at all the eyes trained on him. Suddenly he felt nostalgic for the daily grind of the farm up on the distant border. Life had been so much simpler when he was chasing goats off the haystack and grumbling about the weather.

Tilla's warm thigh pressed firmly against his. He heard the urgency in her soft murmur of "Husband?"

"I was hoping," he said, "that if I went through all the facts here, somebody might have another idea." He surveyed them all. "No?" He turned back to Pertinax. "I'm sorry to cause you further grief, sir."

Pertinax addressed the governor. "He knows they can't win at trial, sir." Gleva's hand reached for his, but he pushed it aside. "They can't win, so he's sunk to blaming a man who can't defend himself. It won't work, sir. I won't be intimidated. I'll be lodging a formal accusation against my son-in-law first thing in the morning."

69

IT WAS AS well that the rain had stopped because there were plenty of people hanging about in the street outside the Mercury. The governor's guards. Some of Pertinax's veterans, ready to take him home on the mule. A couple of temple slaves, waiting to escort the priests to their homes by torchlight. Esico, still contrite and doing his best to be helpful. "I tried to get a mule for you too, master, but—"

"Please don't," Ruso told him, although he was glad that there were two people who were still prepared to speak to him.

The other one was Tilla, who was trying to steer him in the direction of Pertinax's house, asking if he could walk that far in wooden sandals and in the same breath telling him he needed to lie down. "You are very tired."

He said, "I thought he would abandon the trial."

"Never mind that now. Nobody could have done more to help Valens. We have all had a very difficult evening. Now, those sandals—"

"I want to talk to the priest," he said, glancing past her and catching sight of the wide form vanishing around the corner.

"Do it tomorrow."

"It's important."

"What?" She leaned closer and hissed, "Look at yourself, husband! You look like a man who has escaped from his keepers!"

He had embarrassed her and upset Pertinax, and he hoped he wasn't soon going to be even more sorry for it than he was already. "I won't be a moment," he promised, pushing away her guiding arm and forcing his tired limbs into action once more, clacking along the street in pursuit of the priests.

Memor must have gone in a different direction. Ruso caught up with the chief priest and his escorting slave at the entrance to the temple courtyard. "Dorios? I need a quiet word."

"Not tonight." The priest turned in under the archway and kept walking.

"It's not to do with the death," Ruso insisted, pausing to pull off the noisy sandals and setting out barefoot across the paving. It struck him that the courtyard was unusually silent. With the pool emptied, there was no trickle of sacred water overflowing from the spring and cascading down toward the river. He could just about make out some figures seated at the base of the temple steps: hopefully, Gnaeus and his little group of veteran protectors, still there to make sure the temple guards did not burst through the doors and tear Valens away from his supposed sanctuary.

"I need to consult you urgently in your capacity as priest of Sulis Minerva," he persisted, following the torch and hoping Dorios wouldn't call the guards down to get rid of him.

Dorios paused, the uncertain torchlight flickering over his scowl. "I shall be here in the morning, Doctor."

"It's about something in the temple. Something that—at least, I think it happened. I've never seen anything quite . . . well, I'm not really a religious man. But I've been thinking about it since, and I think it might be important. I won't keep you long."

Dorios sighed. "Very well, then."

Moments later the two men were seated under the darkness of the portico just as they had been when Dorios finally confessed about the polluted water.

"This is a bit embarrassing, to be honest," Ruso confessed. "I'm not a great one for the gods. Absolute respect, obviously, but we tend not to bother each other, if you see what I mean."

"Of course."

"And it might be nothing. But if it was real, I need your advice on what to do."

"Tell me exactly what happened."

"Well," Ruso began, leaning closer. In the dark he could sense rather than see the priest's stillness. "It was during the ceremony. We were in the temple, and there wasn't much light, and the boys were asleep, and there was just the sound of the choir singing outside. I was tired, and I think I must have drifted off. Of course, I'd had a bang on the head, which might explain what I saw. But not what I heard." He paused. "To be honest, I feel foolish telling anyone this."

"What did you see?"

"It's hard to describe. A shape, a sort of golden glow, like something standing over me. And I had the very strong sense that, whatever it was, it was wishing me well. I'm sorry. This probably sounds ridiculous."

"Not necessarily."

"Up to that point it could all just have been the bang on the head. But not the words. That's why I need your help."

"Words?"

"'The one who is seeking purity shall bring me a white cockerel.' Just that. Very clear and distinct, but if you asked me to describe the voice, I couldn't do it."

"Hm."

"What do you think?"

Dorios said slowly, "It has the pattern of truth about it."

"I was afraid you might say that." Ruso paused. "Why me?"

"The gods choose whom they will, Doctor."

"So should I bring the goddess a cockerel? Or am I just a messenger?"

"Are you seeking purity?"

Ruso frowned and then wished he hadn't, because it pulled on the stitches. "It wouldn't do any harm," he admitted. "But I'm wondering if the message was for somebody else."

When Dorios did not reply, he cleared his throat. "When I spoke in front of the governor, I was hoping one of you would convince me Catus hadn't done it."

"I see."

"But nobody did."

Dorios said, "It's all very distressing. Poor Catus must have been desperate."

"It's too late to give him the message now. He's already suffered the awful fate in Gleva's curse."

"Indeed."

"But perhaps I could still do something for Valens. Maybe that's why the goddess kept me safe in the tunnel."

"Hm."

"Should I have told all this to the haruspex?"

There was a shuffle of fabric as the priest shifted on the stone bench. "Leave it to me," he said. "I'll discuss it with him in the morning and get back to you."

But Ruso wanted more reassurance. "If Valens offers the cockerel, perhaps Sulis Minerva will save him from the trial and let him stay with his boys."

"Let me talk to Memor. We'll come up with a decision."

Ruso thanked him and got to his feet. "I tell you what," he said. "I'll bring a cockerel along in the morning and you can tell me what to do with it."

Dorios grunted as he hauled himself upright. "Our goddess is gracious to all who honor her," he said. "Come back tomorrow and we'll see what we can do."

70

IT WAS NOT quite dawn when something nudged Ruso out of sleep. He grunted a response and instantly a hand clamped over his mouth, startling him fully awake.

"Sh!" The hand was removed and he felt his wife's hair tickle his face as she breathed in his ear, "At the altar. Look."

He rolled over in the tangle of borrowed blankets and squinted out across the courtyard, breathing in the cold air. Then he shifted himself into a sitting position, moving slowly to ease the stiffness that had crept in from the stone floor of the portico.

Tilla murmured, "See him?"

He rubbed his eyes and tried again. She was right: There was someone moving beside the pale rectangle of the altar. But, try as he might, it was impossible to reconcile the figure out there in the uncertain light with the one he had been expecting.

Maybe, even now, he was wrong.

The figure circled the altar three times. Then he crouched, and there was a creak of wicker. Something white appeared. It flapped about and squawked, and he felt Tilla clutch his arm in excitement.

"It is him!" Tilla whispered.

"It's not."

"But he brought the cockerel."

Ruso shrugged off the extra blankets and peered over at the foot of the temple steps. He could just about make out a couple of standing figures: Gnaeus's men still keeping watch over Valens's place of safety. He hoped they weren't going to interrupt. There had been no way of getting a message to them without arousing the suspicion of the temple guards, lurking up there in front of Sulis Minerva's heavy doors.

The unknown figure seized the bird and pressed it down onto the ground in front of the altar. As he did so the glow of a lamp appeared from behind the temple. A second figure came lurching across the paving stones with an unmistakable gait.

Tilla whispered, "Dorios! You were right!"

The cockerel seemed to have stopped moving. The man who had brought it stepped back, leaving the white shape lying motionless on the ground.

"That was quick." Tilla sounded puzzled.

"Sh." He heard a clink as Dorios placed the lamp on the ground. There was some sort of activity he couldn't make out. Then the priest and the other man stepped apart, there was the glimmer of a flame and Ruso caught a whiff of incense and something less desirable.

Just as Ruso recognized the bent form of Justus the drain slave, there was a thud and a muffled female cry from behind him.

Dorios called, "Who's there?" and then, louder: "Guards!"

Ruso's cry of "Veterans, to me!" rang out over the clatter and scrape of the temple guards' boots descending the stone steps. He strode toward the altar. Behind him, Tilla whispered an apology. "I fell over the blankets."

"Doctor?" Dorios peered at him in the light of the brazier as the temple guards and Gnaeus's little band of veterans clustered around the altar. "There's no need for you to be here. Everything is under control."

Ruso glanced at the collapsed white shape of the bird. "Is it?"

"This slave caused the death of Catus. Now he has sacrificed the bird to purify himself."

The slave said, "I didn't—" but whatever else he might have said was silenced by a rapid motion that Ruso guessed was a jab from Dorios's walking stick.

"I came myself," the priest continued, "to see that the correct form was observed so that the goddess will accept his gift."

"But it is not dead!" declared Tilla. "See?"

As if to prove her right, the cockerel gave a squawk, scrambled to its feet, and flapped away from them.

"Catch it!" cried Dorios, but the slave was not fast enough. The cockerel was a fading white shape skittering across the courtyard. "You should have tied its legs, you fool!" shouted Dorios. Then, turning to the temple guards: "Don't just stand there! Help him!"

Ruso said, "What about Valens?" but Dorios was busy shouting at the guards to bring the bird straight back to the altar.

"What will Valens do?"

But the priest had not had time to think about Valens.

"Will the goddess accept two birds from different people?" Ruso persisted. "If she doesn't, what should he do?"

"Never mind about him," muttered Dorios, straining to see where the cockerel had got to. "I'm sure Catus was the killer anyway. You should have given the message from the goddess to Catus."

Tilla said, "It's flown up onto the portico roof."

The priest gave a wail of distress.

"A reluctant victim," put in Ruso, bending to pick up a lone white feather. "Not a good sign."

Dorios did not reply.

"I tell you what," Ruso suggested. "While they catch it, we could go and tell Valens what really happened to his wife."

Dorios said, "You tell him, Doctor. You know him better."

The cries of the cockerel chasers rang out from somewhere on the far side of the temple. The tone of exasperation suggested they might be gone for some time. Ruso stepped forward and took the priest by the arm. "I'm thinking," he said softly, "that if between us we can make a good case for Catus being guilty, we might still be able to avert a trial. That's what you want, isn't it? It's certainly what Valens wants."

"But—"

"Why don't we go up to the temple and talk about it?"

"Surely it would be better to wait and—"

But Tilla had seized the priest's other arm. His own guards had run off in pursuit of the cockerel, and the veterans were closing in around him.

71

Y OU'RE TAKING THEM outside?" Valens demanded as Tilla hurried his sleepy boys toward the great doors of the temple. "Who's out there?"

"My husband and the priest have things to say to you," Tilla told him. "But the boys do not need to hear them. We will sit on the steps and watch the sun bring the new day while you talk."

"Don't let them out of your sight."

"They will be safe with me," Tilla promised.

The temple doors thudded shut between Valens and the children he had fought so hard to retain. Inside, the lamps around Sulis Minerva's plinth had burned low but still there was enough light to glint on the golden features of the goddess as she stared out above the heads of the three mortals in her gloomy temple: a military doctor who was accused of murdering his wife, his weary and slightly battered friend, and a priest who was struggling to pull some folds of his shambolic toga up over his head without letting go of his walking stick.

"Perhaps," Ruso said, "we should all approach the goddess and ask for her help." He turned to the priest. "What do you think?"

Dorios's eyes were bulging like a frog's. The loose skin under his throat shook. He glanced back at the doors, which were firmly shut, and whispered, "I only ever tried to help you, Doctor."

Ruso glared at Valens, who was clearly more interested in knowing what was going on outside with his boys. Finally getting the message, Valens stepped up and took Dorios's other arm. They moved forward as a threesome across the polished marble floor and paused to bow at the foot of the statue. Ruso said, "Would our priest like to say a prayer?"

Dorios gulped, then muttered, "That won't be necessary."

"Then perhaps here, in the presence of the goddess, you could tell Valens who it was that caused the death of his wife."

For a moment there was silence. Then the priest wrenched himself free of their grasp and cried out, "Forgive me, goddess—it was Catus!"

"If it was Catus," put in Ruso, "why were you here to sacrifice a cockerel in search of purity?"

"I told you, the slave—"

"Are you saying, in front of the goddess, that you weren't willing to make the sacrifice?"

Dorios gazed up at the perfect, impassive golden features. "Sulis Minerva knows the truth. The gods will not be mocked!"

"The slave didn't come here to sacrifice the bird," Ruso said. "He was here to deliver it and soothe it for you so you could offer a willing victim."

Dorios was backing away from the statue now. He collided with the rumpled bed that the boys had just left, and it creaked as he collapsed down onto it. "It was the slave who opened the sluices and drowned the engineer."

"Yes," Ruso agreed, ignoring Valens's "What? Catus? What happened?" and stepping to one side so he could watch the priest without irreverently turning his back on the goddess. "On whose orders?"

Dorios was silent.

"It doesn't matter if you don't answer," Ruso assured him. "The governor's men will get the truth out of him: It'll only be a matter of time. But I expect Justus has been doing whatever you tell him to do ever since he was caught with Terentius's ring, because he's afraid that if he's not useful to you, he'll be silenced too."

Dorios jumped as Valens grasped his shoulders from behind and growled, "Who killed my wife?"

The priest wriggled, and Valens tightened his grip. He bent closer. "I'm waiting."

"It was all Catus's fault—ow! If the fool hadn't lit that fire, everything would have been— You're hurting me! Doctor, make him stop! This is a holy temple!"

"It is," Ruso agreed, glancing up at Sulis Minerva and hoping that Dorios really did believe in her power. "So in this sacred temple," he said, "just between us and the goddess, who suggested to Catus that he should light the fire?"

"It wasn't like that!"

"Wasn't it? The goddess is listening. Who promised him Sulis Minerva would heal him in return?"

"It was necessary!" Dorios cried. "Someone had to bring an end to that disastrous building project. It was a blight on the town."

"And when you found out that Terentius knew who'd done it . . ."

"I begged him not to make a fuss. Catus only did it to help him."

"And if Catus was exposed, he'd have implicated you too," continued Ruso mildly. "So. Now are you going to tell us, in front of the goddess, who killed Serena and Terentius? Or shall we just ask her to strike the killer down?"

For a moment Dorios was still. Then he wrenched himself out of Valens's grasp and ran for the statue. He tripped on his toga and skidded full-length on the marble floor, his hands grasping toward his unseeing goddess and his cries echoing around the shadowed corners of her temple. "Blessed goddess, holy Minerva, save me!"

Valens was on him before Ruso could intervene.

Dorios's voice rose to a scream. "Save me!"

"Why"—Valens punctuated his words by banging the priest's head on the floor— "did you kill my wife?"

"She was going to tell everyone! Ruin the town! I had to— Help! Save me, mistress! Save—" But Valens's hands had closed around Dorios's throat, and now the only sound was the feeble drumming of the priest's feet on the marble as he struggled for breath beneath the unrelenting gaze of his holy mistress.

72

THE MORNING SUN was doing his best to creep around the shutters of the bedroom window. Tilla could hear Valens's boys shouting to each other as they raced around the courtyard, then Albanus's voice as he shepherded them back to their room. The household was in mourning for Catus now as well as Serena, but their grandfather had declared that what the boys needed was to get back into their routine, and he was probably right.

There was not much space in the bed that had been Serena's. That suited Tilla nicely, because it was a good excuse to cuddle up close to the warmth of her man and feel the steady beat of his heart and the lift of his chest with every breath.

Neena had taken Mara out to play so they could catch up on their missed sleep, but Tilla was not sleepy now. She could tell from her husband's breathing that he was awake too. So at last there was a chance to ask her question.

"When you made that long speech at the governor's dinner," she said, "did you already know it was Dorios who killed them?"

"No," he said. "But Catus implied that he was behind the fire, and that gave him a motive."

"But why make a speech?"

"I was trying to put him off guard."

"That was clever."

His arm squeezed her tighter, as if he was pleased at the compliment. "There was no way to catch him unless he confessed. He had an answer for everything. Even when he turned up to sacrifice that cockerel, he found a way to blame the slave."

"So, did he tell the truth to the governor just now?"

"Not exactly. He says he's the loyal servant of the emperor and the goddess, everything that went wrong after the murders was Gleva's fault because she cursed him, and if I hadn't interfered, he would have had the whole scandal under control. He had to silence Terentius to save the honor of—oh, Catus, the town, Rome, the gods . . . I can't remember. The governor just let him go on and on until he'd run out of excuses."

"What did he say about Serena?"

"She went to him for help that night because she'd lost touch with Terentius in the dark. He didn't want to hurt her, but when he found out she knew who'd lit the fire, what else could he do?"

She stiffened. "*What else?*"

She felt, rather than heard, the long sigh before his "I know."

"I think," she said, "he killed her so that he could make up a story about Terentius doing it and running away. Perhaps Pertinax's lawyer will make him confess at the trial."

He shifted in her arms. "There won't be a trial," he told her. "Dorios was right about one thing: Aquae Sulis is too important to fail. The governor's done a deal with Pertinax. The lawyer's stood down, we'll be sworn to silence, and Dorios will be given a new job in Londinium."

Tilla jerked her head up from the pillow. "Surely not? People are dead, you could have drowned, and they have done a deal? I thought Pertinax wanted justice?"

He yawned. "It's not up to us, wife."

"Are you not angry?"

The murmur of Neena's voice drifted in from the courtyard, followed by their daughter's squeal of laughter. He said, "Being angry won't change anything."

"It is all wrong!"

Whatever he thought of that, he said nothing. Finally she settled back into the bed. "I wish I had never let Neena take Mara into that water."

"It was clean by then," he told her. "And the women who bathed in it when it wasn't will never know."

When he put it that way, she could see the sense of keeping quiet. She said, "So, the goddess has saved her honor and the honor of her shrine in spite of her priest."

"She had some help. I made up that business about the cockerel."

She said, "I know."

"I was afraid you might believe it."

"Not for a moment," she told him. "But I knew it would work. It was inspired."

"Thank you."

"My mother used to say," she said, realizing he had misunderstood, "that sometimes the things we think are our own thoughts and desires are put into our minds by the gods."

He said, "I'm sure that's exactly what Dorios has been telling himself for years."

Had he? If you looked at it like that, Mam's words were not as comforting as they had always seemed before. How could you tell if your ideas were your own or not? It was all faintly unsettling, and she did not want to think about it now. Or perhaps ever. Nor did she want to think about Dorios enjoying his new job in Londinium. So, instead of replying, she lay silent, feeling her breathing drift in and out of step with her man's until she was no longer aware of anything at all.

73

THE OLD CENTURION stumbled on the uneven hillside. Tilla saw her husband put out a hand to steady him, but Pertinax shook it off. "Still as proud as ever," she murmured, glad that he was recovered enough to manage the walk. Ahead of him, Valens was striding down toward the house with one boy on his shoulders and another holding his hand, and Gleva was walking up to meet them. "I know what you would say," Tilla said, turning away to address the little door set in the blank tomb. "I reminded him to be careful with your precious boys, but I don't think he was listening."

She settled herself on the rug and carried on speaking to the tomb as she reached across to pull Mara's socks up. "Your father is going to take Valens back to the fort at Isca after Catus's funeral," she said. "He will ask the legate to give him his job back and not punish him very badly for being absent. And Valens is leaving the boys here, just as you wanted, and they will be a big comfort to everybody."

She paused, wondering if the dead needed time to think about what they heard or whether you could just rattle on. It must be very annoying to be told lots of things all at once and have no chance to reply. But the breeze was getting up now, and there were gray clouds moving in across the western hills; so if she were to tell Serena everything, she would have to hurry.

"Virana has given birth to a boy," she said. "He is very small, but he is feeding well, and Albanus is beside himself with excitement. I expect you can imagine. So now all three of them are fathers, and none of them is really sure what he is doing, but they are all doing their best."

She stretched out and retrieved a sock from where Mara had thrown it onto the damp grass. "Our slave Esico has gone to work for the ostler in the town, because at last we have found something he is good at; and his father has gone away, because there is no money to be made from him."

The breeze tugged at her wrap. As if the fingers of Serena were tugging at her, wanting to make her listen to something. "The priest?" Tilla guessed. What should she say about the priest? Was it fair to leave Serena angry and disappointed that there had been no justice? "The truth has come out at last," she said, "and the priest said that he never meant for you to fall into the goddess's water, and fate has been very cruel to him."

After a moment's pause she said, "Yes. That is what I think too. And I have been thinking that perhaps when you knew you were dying, you threw yourself into that spring as revenge on him. And if you did, it was very clever of you. And if you didn't, it served him right anyway."

She waited a moment for Serena to enjoy that, but the dark clouds were closer now, and there was not much time to say the things that needed to be said.

"I think your Terentius must have been a good man," she said, "and I am sad for you both that there was nothing found of him to bury. But my husband was down there to say good-bye to him before the river took him away, and yesterday some nicer priests did the ceremony above the place where he was found. And now I have thought about it, he was right under the place where the black ewe said he was all the time, but my husband still says—" She stopped. There was no reason Serena should know how hard her husband found it to listen to the gods, and neither would she care. You had to be careful to talk *to* the dead rather than *at* them. You did not want to be like one of those people who visited the sick and left them feeling worse than before. What if the dead wished you would stop talking and go away? How would they tell you if they had had enough?

"Tilla!" The voice came from lower down the hill. Her husband was striding up toward her, waving an arm to indicate the clouds. "Don't hang around up there! It's going to rain!"

Tilla scrambled across on all fours and restrained Mara before she could grab the vase of flowers propped outside the little door. "We will be staying in your house for a while," she told Serena. "My husband does not want to go near any water for a long time, and anyway, he says he wants to make sure your pa is all right after all the pills he took. See, we were all wrong about Gleva and the love potion. My husband finally got it out of him yesterday. The silly man was worrying that he is too old and not as much of a man as Gleva needs, so he was buying special pills from some women who work the vegetable plots, and he took too many and poisoned himself." She could not resist a smile. "So now he is very embarrassed."

"Tilla!"

The breeze was ruffling Mara's hair. Tilla wished she had brought a hat for her. "We could have been better friends in life, you and I," she told Serena. "But this Roman-and-Briton business is not easy, even in a town like Aquae Sulis. In the years we knew each other, I wasted much time wishing your people would go back to where they came from."

"Tilla!"

She raised a hand to him and turned back to the tomb. "And I still do," she said. "But perhaps not quite so soon."

By the time he reached her, she was on her feet with the rug rolled up.

"Pertinax has just had a message from the governor," he told her. "There's been a horrible accident on the road to Londinium. Dorios is dead."

She stared at him in confusion. "Dead?"

"Miraculously, nobody else was hurt."

"So," she said, handing him the rug. "The gods have brought justice."

He grinned. "Pertinax didn't seem at all surprised."

"You think the governor arranged—"

"Pertinax and the governor go back a long way. Old soldiers stick together." He glanced around. "But I expect you're right: Fate will get the blame. Have you finished talking to Serena?"

Tilla took a last glance at the little house. "I think she has heard everything she would want to know now."

Her husband was holding out the palm of his hand to the sky. "Rain," he told Mara.

"Come, daughter," said Tilla, bending down and lifting Mara's hands high so she could raise her knees as if she were stepping through long grass. "It is time to go home."

Author's Note

Aquae Sulis is one of the most visited sites in Roman Britain, perhaps because it combines a lovely setting with spectacular remains and over 130 curse tablets deposited in the waters by past visitors.

From floor level down, the Great Bath is much the same today as it was when Ruso swam in it. The sacred spring still fills it with over two hundred thousand gallons of hot water every day, and it is possible—though not permitted to visitors—to walk through the original tunnels that still carry the wastewater away to the river. The river, incidentally, is no longer tidal, but the structures that control it were not built until many centuries after this story is set.

The moustachioed face on the temple pediment can still be seen, as can the tombstone of Memor the haruspex and the golden head of Sulis Minerva, although if she had a feast day, we don't know the date. The Mercury, the Traveler's Repose, and their competitors are my own invention, as is much of the street plan of Aquae Sulis, whose finer details are lost to us. While the struggle of Pertinax and his veterans to create a new shrine at one of the other hot springs in the town has left no trace, there is a small amount of evidence to suggest that one of their successors had better luck.

Testimonies to miraculous cures seem to have been a common feature on the walls of temples at healing shrines, but as none survives from Aquae Sulis, the ones that Ruso sees are inspired by finds elsewhere. Cursing also seems to have been a popular activity all over the empire, although, disappointingly, most of the requests so far found in Aquae Sulis relate to petty theft rather than anything that suggests a murder mystery. Still, much of what lies below the spring remains unexcavated, and who knows what might be hidden there?

Looking at the scale of the remains, it is easy to forget that the Roman development of the hot springs did not take place in the midst of peace and prosperity but during the decade that followed the insecurity and violence of the Boudican rebellion. Perhaps we are seeing a bold attempt at a new start: evidence of money being poured in from Rome to help a struggling young province get back on its feet.

It is still possible to bathe in the waters of Aquae Sulis. The ancient facilities are no longer suitable for use, but after a hard day's sightseeing, it's only a short walk to the modern spa, fed by another of Sulis Minerva's springs. At the time of writing, this is where to find out more: https://www.thermaebathspa.com/

FURTHER READING

Memento Mori is a work of fiction and therefore contains lies, inventions, and possibly mistakes, for which I am entirely responsible. Here are some sources of more reliable information:

Magic, Witchcraft, and Ghosts in the Greek and Roman Worlds: A Sourcebook by Daniel Ogden (New York: Oxford University Press, 2009).
Travel in the Ancient World by Lionel Casson (Baltimore: Johns Hopkins University Press, 1994).

Books on Roman Bath abound: The Roman Baths Museum produces an elegant guidebook and there is much to enjoy on their website: https://www.romanbaths.co.uk/. For more detail, any of the several books on Bath by Professor Barry Cunliffe will be helpful.

Readers interested in re-creating Roman hairstyles will enjoy the series of videos by Janet Stephens currently available on YouTube.

ACKNOWLEDGMENTS

Many thanks, as ever, go to Araminta Whitley and George Lucas for timely guidance and for taking care of the complicated stuff; to Lea Beresford, whose editing is both perceptive and tactful; to David Chesanow for sorting out the fine detail; and to the folks at Bloomsbury who do the many other mysterious things that turn words into books.

For comments on early drafts and for general encouragement, I'm grateful to the Barnstaple Library "WIP" Group, Bill Wahl, and Ernesto Spinelli. For checking the Latin translations at the front, my thanks go to Richard Sturch. Either Aidan James or Helen Robinson—none of us can remember—came up with the title. For everything else I am grateful, as ever, to Andy Downie.

Finally—my thanks go to all the readers who travel with Ruso and Tilla. The journey has only been possible because of you.

A Note on the Author

Ruth Downie is the author of the *New York Times* bestselling *Medicus*, as well as *Terra Incognita*, *Persona Non Grata*, *Caveat Emptor*, *Semper Fidelis*, *Tabula Rasa*, and *Vita Brevis*. She is married with two sons and lives in Devon, England.